The Foolish Things

By Rebekah Tyne McKamie

Settings Christian Publishing, LLC
Calhan, CO

Rebekah Tyne McKamie

Copyright © 2020 Rebekah Tyne McKamie

All rights reserved. No part of this publication may be reproduced, distributed, or transmitted in any form or by any means, including photocopying, recording, or other electronic or mechanical methods, without the prior written permission of the publisher, except in the case of brief quotations embodied in critical reviews and certain other noncommercial uses permitted by copyright law.

Print ISBN: 978-1-7348040-0-3
Digital ISBN: 978-1-734804-0-10

Any references to historical events, real people, or real places are used fictitiously. Names, characters, and places are products of the author's imagination.

Front cover photograph by Caleb McKamie
Book design by Settings Christian Publishing, LLC

Scripture taken from the New King James Version®. Copyright © 1982 by Thomas Nelson. Used by permission. All rights reserved.

Printed in the United States of America.

First printing edition 2020.

Settings Christian Publishing, LLC
Calhan, CO 80808

www.rebekahtynemckamie.com

The Foolish Things

__For Tiffany-__
In case no one has ever told you that you're an inspiration.
Psalms 20:4

and

__For Lesley Lynn -__
God doesn't always take us down the path we expect, and sometimes our journey is missing the people we always expected to be there. Still, I'm overwhelmed with gratitude for the parts we walked together. I love you, my beautiful friend (not like that, you know what I mean).
Philippians 1:3

For you see your calling, brethren, that not many wise according to the flesh, not many mighty, not many noble, are called. But God has chosen the foolish things of the world to put to shame the wise, and God has chosen the weak things of the world to put to shame the things which are mighty; and the base things of the world and the things which are despised God has chosen, and the things which are not, to bring to nothing the things that are, that no flesh should glory in His presence. But of Him you are in Christ Jesus, who became for us wisdom from God—and righteousness and sanctification and redemption—that, as it is written,

"He who glories, let him glory in the Lord."

I Corinthians 1:26–31

1

Sharon's Size

When something is small, people will affectionately refer to it as *pint-sized*. I suppose if one is accustomed to a gallon of ice cream, the pint-sized carton is minuscule. Just a pint of creamy vanilla or delectable chocolate ice cream would not do well to satisfy the cravings of more than a few birthday partygoers. Yet a pint is more than enough for lonely late-night sorrow-drownings and just enough for the clanging of two spoons when there is enough sorrow to share.

Pint-sized. I'm not sure where that saying originated. Sometimes a pint is plenty, or more than plenty. Our saying assumes the innocuous nature of anything pint-sized, so I naturally think of ice cream. But often a pint is enough to make one person tipsy, or to begin a long evening for another person, with a glass filled with something no one should consider cute or pint-sized at all.

Either way, when compared to a gallon, a pint does require a bit of overflowing before reaching its potential. But what if a gallon isn't the goal? That's certainly all the milk I'd like to carry in one container. But supposing a pint is at its full potential and everything else is gross overindulgence, what then would pint-sized mean? What would happen if the whole world was after only pints?

I suppose none of that matters. Because even if everyone spent their lives looking for something pint-sized, as in the original idiom, they'd be extremely disappointed to find only a cup, and devastated to find a meaningless tablespoon. Maybe here you'll see how foolish the teaspoon is.

A teaspoon. That's what they should use to define small. Anything smaller is merely considered a fraction of a teaspoon in this system of measurement. Sure, without that almost imperceptible measure of baking soda, the cake will not rise. But on its own, without some greater purpose, that same measurement in rain or in sand is meaningless.

In that spirit, let's measure joy, wonders, the handiwork of God in our lives—those events often referred to as *miracles*.

We all spend our lives searching for gallon-sized miracles. We seek impossible things like walking on water and the parting of seas. Some people keep breathing simply to someday see with their own eyes some miracle like that. Others are content with pint-sized miracles that work with the laws of nature but are obviously the hand of God—like a baby's first cry.

And then there are those who know they are unworthy, even of a teaspoon miracle. Something like. . .well, I'm getting ahead of myself. Because now we are going to meet Sharon Mehlmann. Her father's family had German and Hebrew roots and the like. He was born in the USA, but the DNA kept, as science goes. He's the one who taught her that gallon-sized miracles are nonexistent, and pint-sized miracles are earned through hard work and strong character. But that was a teaching he nearly nullified when the way he spoiled his three children could be measured in bathtubs and truckloads.

For now, know that Sharon was painfully average by many standards. Since she operated in the tangible, let's confess now that a pint—of ice cream—was often Sharon's dearest companion and worst enemy. The nose she received from her father was prominent, and the flat brown hair, like her mother's, simply didn't fit with the expanse of her hips. Although she was named after some biblical flower whose name encompasses many flowers, she was not the type of flower most men preferred. Therefore, besides a few boys in her teen years who were only after what they knew she'd give for the mere illusion of love, Sharon remained single, to say the absolute least.

To say more, Sharon was introverted. She had read every romance novel by many authors, pressing tissues to her nose and glasses back up against kind, light-brown eyes. She stretched her hated curves and five-and-a-half feet across a couch in a living room that never seated more than a handful of people. And that was only if her parents and siblings and her one close friend came to visit the one bedroom apartment.

To say the most, Sharon was sad—the kind of sad so flooded with hope that it was an easy mask. Even she believed it. You see, she knew just exactly how her prince charming would show up—what he looked like, what he'd wear, the timbre of his voice. In her fantasies, an amalgamation of all those novels, he would come along and fix it all—all the sad she pushed aside, all the mundane, and all the pain she still held onto from all the bullying. But besides those fantasies, Sharon clung to what was real—to pints of ice cream and the job teaching second graders at a school for deaf children. To the six years she still had in her twenties. To the only family and friends she had in the world.

Just as dust and decay cling to death.

But Sharon was not aware of her clinging. Even if she was, she wouldn't have been thinking about it in the place we'll meet her. Just then, she felt like a sausage stuffed into a keyhole, especially next to Sophie—her twenty-one-year-old sister—and Sophie's bridesmaids. Sophie was a fit college cheerleader, and the company she kept always resembled them. Don't slip into the stereotype just yet. Because if you assume that Sophie was some cruel, snobby soul who didn't appreciate her family and the relationship with her sister, you'd be wrong. About Sophie. You may now apply whatever stereotype you had in your mind to Sophie's bridesmaids and best friends. I'm not sure I'll find an occasion to tell you their names.

"It isn't quite the right size. But the bride will get the picture," the bridal store attendant commented in the dressing room while the other perfectly formed maids awaited the honorable, and plus-sized, Sharon.

When Sharon emerged, Sophie got her discerning look on her face and hipped her hands. Her perfect brown ponytail was pulled back from her slightly tanned skin. Her sparkling amber eyes examined all.

"Now this is the one you didn't have plus sizes in, right?" Sophie asked to the embarrassment of Sharon. The other girls had pulled twos and fours off the rack.

"Correct." The attendant held the back of Sharon's dress where the zipper couldn't comply.

"Well, my dress is pretty light and flowy, I'm not sure I like the satin anyway. Not for a beach wedding." Sophie analyzed, tearing her sister deeply with that word, "anyway." Promptly correcting it when she smiled with a, "Sharon, you seemed happier in the other one."

Sophie didn't really care what the other bridesmaids thought, and they could wear anything. Sharon was the "issue." They were just playing dress-up, rolling their eyes whenever Sharon felt like bright pink haggis.

"I did like the other one. But it isn't my wedding. I'll wear whatever you want me to, Sophie." Sharon assured her sister.

The other girls laughed, because of *course* it wasn't Sharon's wedding. Or maybe because of the tiny lisp Sharon developed before she got the hearing aids that restored most of her hearing at age five. But Sharon was used to all that. Used to ridicule. To being the biggest, ugliest thing in the room. I'm not saying it didn't hurt anymore. Of course not.

If it didn't hurt anymore, I wouldn't have been doing my job. Sure, she was used to me. But I didn't plan on going anywhere anytime soon. In her, I had a safe, long-term home.

Sharon was used to me even more than she was used to the warmth of her father's smile as he walked into the bridal store with her baby brother Sean. They were an irritation to me. They made her smile and suppressed me ever so slightly. But only a minor irritation. In those days, I was always there with her. Always clinging to her.

Sean, twenty-three then, looked around at the "hot" college cheerleaders in hot pink dresses. Then looked at Sharon the salami, hating their looks of disdain.

"This dress is awful, Sophie." He told his other sister.

"We know. There's one we like much better. I think we'll go with the other one. Sharon's stunning in it." Sophie had winked at her sister then. Their mother had smiled. Dad hugged Sharon deeply, just because. Just like he always did.

"Well, as much as she can be," a bridesmaid said just then. Just right. Just beautifully. And the others giggled.

"Brielle!" Sophie shouted. Well, I suppose you should learn one of their names. "Sharon is my sister."

That was all she said in defense, and Brielle apologized. But no matter, I made sure to play those words over and over and over in Sharon's head all night long, even after that pint of ice cream and gallons of self-doubt.

Most people want gallon miracles and settle for pints. But Sharon isn't most people; she knew her place. At that point, I figured it was likely she would spend her painfully average and meaningless life hoping for a teaspoon or two. But hope is so fickle, I assumed I could do away with that easily, too.

See, I'm in the business of working against. Blocking out the light and the hope and often, though not always, the truth. I'm good at it. Sometimes I'm all that stands between a gallon-sized miracle and destruction. God likes to choose the weak. But first, as the weak often think, He always has to get rid of me.

Am I the devil? What a question! Is a wrench a mechanic? No. But a mechanic *uses* a wrench to the point of need, and even stereotype. I'm not the devil. Merely a tool, to be used by whomever may have need, and the devil often does. And in Sharon's life, I got comfortable. The devil didn't need another tool. I was thriving. I was powerful. And then…

Well, I can't tell you yet. I have to make my case. So first, you have to hear about average Sharon Ruth Mehlmann and her teaspoon miracle. Afterward, you can decide who was evil and who was weak. It's my job to make you wonder. To make you less. To make you doubt yourself.

2

Lavender-Dawn's Eyes

"The wedding is far away on an island. So, in addition to our Spring Break, I'll be gone for another week, and you'll have a substitute teacher," Sharon told her class in January of that year, her students sitting before her cross-legged during circle time.

"What's an island?" One of her students asked in sign.

"It is a piece of land that is completely surrounded by water. My sister has always wanted a beach wedding, so we are all flying to the Virgin Islands where she'll get married," Sharon explained.

And that's when I told her *she* is like an island. Isolated and alone and she'll never have a wedding, so she'd better enjoy Sophie's. She tried to ignore me, but I think it stuck. All day, she considered that notion.

She was headed to the freezer for her chosen self-soothing agent after a long day on her feet when her best friend's ringtone echoed into the kitchen.

"If you're headed for the frozen cow pus, S.R., I'll have to object." This, with barely a hello from Sharon.

"You know me too well," Sharon grumbled, but smiled and put that ice cream right back.

"Bad day, huh?" Her friend adjusted something to make the sound quality better on her end. "I bet I can make it better."

"I bet you can't, but I'll bite." Sharon leaned against her kitchen counter.

Sharon's best friend has an unfortunate name, but at that time, I was rarely allowed in her life. See, just like Sharon's brother Sean, Lavender-Dawn Meadow George was a light. A beacon for Sharon.

With naturally purple eyes her too-young mother unfortunately noticed before filling out the birth certificate with just "Dawn."

"I got the time off!" L.D. exclaimed on the phone.

"For the wedding?"

"Of course! I was concerned because I've been at this job a year, but I don't have seniority quite yet. But they are letting me take it! We get to veg on a beach in the Virgin Islands, baby."

L.D. was a free spirit. Unattached to a man, but not regrettably so. She was a receptionist for a pediatric audiologist's office at that time. She loved the job, but in years before had moved from job to job with the wind. A habit learned from the kind of parenting that also named her Lavender-Dawn. A name she would only mumble, and only if someone official asked it. To anyone else, she was L.D.

I took that moment to tell Sharon the truth. *Nobody wants to see you on a beach, Sharon.*

Sharon laughed into the phone.

"What?" L.D. asked.

"The beach? Really?" Lisp and downtrodden mumble and all. "Says the size 6 *babe*."

"Come on S.R. Don't let those anorexic airheads decide what you can do with your amazing body." L.D. tried to call out Sharon's confidence. A futile attempt, as usual.

It was Sharon that gave Lavender-Dawn the nickname she's used since fourth grade. The two bonded that year when L.D. was the "new kid" whose single, free-spirited mom had just uprooted her and moved her across the country. Again. They bonded over names they hated. So, when Sharon suggested using initials for Lavender-Dawn's name, L.D. naturally called Sharon Ruth "S.R.". Something Sharon's father Samuel didn't like, since he gave Sharon that name. But he didn't complain after meeting L.D. herself. A girl that had practically been adopted into the family fold.

I certainly don't have anything against single moms like L.D.'s. In fact, I'm well acquainted with most of them. But most of them are only hindered by me, and don't actually lack the ability to do the best they can for their children. I say most. Because the year she met

Sharon at age nine, L.D.'s mother was twenty-three. Not simply having made a mistake that created her daughter (and not sure *which* mistake had). But proving herself a tepid mother daily. The first time L.D. stayed the night at Sharon's, it had been after she called her at midnight crying, because her mother hadn't come home yet.

She was nine. And her mother didn't return for three more nights after that. Sharon's family, to L.D., was salvation. She didn't mind Sharon's self-centered little sister or the little brother that bullied L.D. relentlessly. L.D. didn't even mind that her best friend was a buzz kill sometimes. To her, Sharon represented stability. L.D. had a place where she was loved, and because her mother noticed she had to buy less groceries and be around less, she never moved again. When the Mehlmann family came into L.D.'s life, I was no longer welcome in it, except in seasons here or there. Until then, at least. We've only just begun the retelling of this tale.

"L.D., an eating disorder isn't something to joke about." Sharon rolled her eyes, which L.D. heard in her voice. "And my body is not amazing."

"Well, that's your opinion. *My* opinion is true, so…"

L.D. had formed her opinion in high school when Sharon was going through a particularly dark phase and they'd gone to an art museum. The exhibit was controversial, and many people claimed that it condoned obesity. It was a room filled with paintings of overweight naked women. That day, both young women saw only beauty, and not even Sharon listened to me for an entire week. Since then, L.D. has known Sharon to harbor more beauty than even a paintbrush could realize. More poise. Just like all those stone-faced, rosy portrayals of women long ago. L.D. dreaded since that day that Sharon might consider losing weight. But she had peace in the possibility.

"L.D., I have to go over to my parents' for dinner and wedding stuff. Sophie has to get her invitations out. You're welcome to join us if you like." Sharon looked at the clock, changing out of her work clothes with L.D. now on speaker phone.

"Actually, I'd love to. But the roads are a little slick and traffic is slow-going. I just left visitation with my mom."

"Oh." Sharon had forgotten. "Um…how is she?"

She, of course, was incarcerated. Her original sentence was twenty years to life, but L.D.'s mother was only capable of bad behavior behind bars, and there was little chance she'd ever get out. Multiple drug and prostitution charges landed her in jail for months at a time while L.D. worked her way through high school. Finally, an armed robbery with yet another shady boyfriend turned into second degree murder. But despite the childhood she was given, and usually getting cussed out every week, L.D. continued to visit her mother and occupy the tiny apartment the two used to share.

"She's doing alright. She has color in her face, so I know she's at least *feeling* better than last week when she had the flu. And she hasn't been in solitary in a month." L.D. managed cheerily, of all things. "I praise God for any glimmer of improvement, you know that."

I suppose I did have some place in L.D.'s life. Just not much of a say. I rarely do once a person realizes that God is big enough to fill in the gaps of any shortcomings. That Jesus forgives and redeems. And if L.D. knows nothing else, she knows that.

It was L.D. that got the Mehlmann family attending church regularly. It was her that reminded Samuel to raise his family to fear the Lord. And since there isn't much to help my case when we consider the long, loose, ash-brown haired, glistening purple-eyed spirit of Lavender-Dawn, I guess I better mention that though the family came to Christ, it seemed too little too late for the Mehlmann children.

Sharon's little brother Sean wasn't an alcoholic, but he did drink for recreation with friends, and frequently. He loved his family. Excelled at his job as an EMT. His friends adored him. And women fell at his feet and into his bed with a mere curl of his lip if he was in the mood. He'd never been in love as far as his family knew, but he'd certainly made a lot of it. Usually with near strangers on weekends when I started to whisper in his ear. He'd tethered his soul to Christ years ago, but his spirit was rebellious. Grace was his only hope.

Sean thought he never would. At least, I had him well convinced. But he'd always hoped to rise to and dwell within his big sister's standards for good behavior. Indeed, Sharon always found his charm disgusting until she realized it extended to her too. Sean would never utter a negative word about his sister and kept his teasing outside what could offend her.

He was handsome, with statuesque features, dark curls, dark seductive eyes and a deep, smoky voice. Somehow, he resembled the average Sharon greatly, but neither he nor their baby sister Sophie managed to be average at all in that respect.

Sharon was thinking that exact thought, jealous beyond all reason, as she ended her phone call and arrived at her parents' house. There, Sean was teasing Sophie on the porch of the old house in the heart of downtown. Sophie still lived at home at the time, giving the world the illusion of traditional innocence. But Sean was teasing her over the video conversation she just ended with her fiancé Eric.

"Will you come over later tonight after I get off work?" Eric had asked.

Sean had caught "tonight" and "work." But he wasn't nearly as fluent in American Sign Language as Sophie or Sharon.

"I will try. I can't stay the night this time. Dad asks too many questions and I have to lie," Sophie had said in Sean's hearing and gaze. She always whispered as she signed. Eric liked to read her lips.

Eric laughed his deep, hollow laugh. He nodded, smiled.

"I love you, Sophie."

Sean knew those signs well, and smirked at his sister's happiness, shaking his head as Sophie replied.

"I love you too, Eric. Soon I can stay every night."

They ended the call, and as Sharon was approaching, Sean was making a joke about Sophie's wedding.

"You little *sinner*. The 'Virgin Islands.' Was that irony intentional, or…" Sean had Sophie giggling before fighting back.

"Oh, like you're complaining. I'm sure you'll find a dive on St. John suitable to your style, Sean. It's Spring Break week for a lot of students."

"I'd better, if I have to wear a bright pink bow tie and suspenders." Sean smiled when he finally saw Sharon approaching. "Hey, Beautiful!"

"Hey, guys. It's cold out here." Sharon pulled her winter coat tight around her body.

"Yeah…" Sean revealed his right hand, putting his glowing, smoking addiction to his lips to explain their presence outdoors.

"I stepped out for a call," Sophie explained, hugging her sister.

"A *booty* call," Sean mumbled.

Sophie giggled. "Eric got stuck at work. So, we'll have a couple less hands. L.D. gonna make it?"

"The Jesus Freak?" Sean, of course. His general feelings toward Sharon's best friend. He had a million or so of those nicknames for her. As loving and gentle as he was with Sharon, he was equally as cruel to L.D.

"Shut up, Sean." Sharon smiled. "And no, she most likely can't tonight. She was visiting her mom. But she can make it to the wedding! Found out today."

"Oh no!" Sophie frowned. "She asked me not to make her a bridesmaid because she didn't think she'd make it. Now she'll be there but not in the wedding. I really wanted her in pictures if she'd be there."

"She won't mind. She'll be happy to be there at all, Sophie. I'm sure she'll still be in pictures too," Sharon said. "And she said she'd come by when she gets back into town if we're still working."

"Oh good, I have a date when we're done here so I don't have to put up with her. What other guy spends his Friday night stuffing invitations for his little sister?"

"*My* amazing brother," Sophie complimented, hugging her big brother's arm.

"Well you say I'm amazing *now*. We'll see how you feel after Eric's bachelor party." Sean laughed.

"You can get him as trashed as you want, but no women, Sean. I mean it," Sophie warned.

Sean stomped out his cigarette and followed his sisters inside as he spoke. "Please, that guy only has eyes for you. Which is somewhat disconcerting, but since I'd have to kill him otherwise, it keeps my hands clean."

Sharon knew the truth in that. She had a boyfriend once in high school. He told her he loved her, so she gave him everything, and even got an STD out of the deal. And when that boyfriend told Sharon, to her face, that she was a fat, ugly, means to an end, Sean spent the night in juvie. Sharon hadn't had a boyfriend since. I kept her from that. And kept her feeling the way she felt thinking about how Eric only had eyes for Sophie.

It wasn't that she didn't want Sophie to have that happiness. Or for Sean to have that charm. She loved her siblings and their happiness was important to her. But approving of it didn't make it any easier for Sharon to watch. Sophie was only twenty-one. Getting married to a man that loved her like he loved his own soul. Sharon was twenty-four, and knew that she'd see thirty before she ever saw a coffee date with anyone but L.D. Then there was Sean. With the ability to take a dog of a woman and make her feel like a princess. Used that ability only for one night at a time, when Sharon knew he had the ability, and likely the desire, to apply it to one woman for a lifetime. Just like Eric did for Sophie. And Dad did for Mom.

It wasn't much to ask for. Sharon only wanted a husband and children—A life she'd seen people take for granted and despise. That's all Sharon wanted. A man to look at her the way Eric looked at Sophie. But Sophie was beautiful. And Sharon knew her place. Yet the jealousy and longing didn't seem to wane.

"My Rose of Sharon!" Dad said as Sharon walked in, wrapping his arms around his first-born child.

"Hey, Dad."

They are only nice to you because they have to be. Everyone knows it's true. Just stating a fact.

"How is your class this semester?" Mom was stirring the beef stew.

"They're great! I got a new little girl today and some of the other girls were making fun of her. The hearing loss is new… So, I had to deal with that, but other than that, the first week back went pretty well." Sharon balanced herself onto the barstool that barely supported her weight.

"How'd you deal with it? That's a tough one." Samuel, always wanting Sharon to learn something about who she was and how God sees her. He was likely my worst enemy when it came to her.

"I just put her at the table with the new girl they made fun of last semester and the girl that's nice to everybody. They are showing her the ropes, and I even saw their moms arranging play dates. Fast friends," Sharon explained, happy about how things turned out.

"Like you and L.D., right?" Dad kept on teaching.

"Maybe." *Except you were L.D.'s only option. That's the blessing. That a prettier girl wasn't put at that table with her in fourth grade.* "I mean, it's a little different. Oh, hey. Have you booked the flight for the wedding yet? L.D. can make it, and I bet she'd want to be on a plane with us."

"Can I book mine on a different *airline*, then?" Sean rolled his eyes. Endlessly annoyed by the girl who saw his lifestyle as an abomination and had told him in so many words.

"Stop that, Sean Joseph." His mom, of course. "We are L.D.'s only real family. At what point will you accept that? Sharon, we'll make sure she gets on our flight. Our gift to her, of course."

"Oh, Sharon!" Sophie was mindlessly signing, as she did when she had Eric on the mind. "We had a video call with the pastor we hired to marry us and found out he has a thick accent and Eric can't read his lips. He wanted me to ask you to interpret the wedding? A couple of the guests are deaf or hard of hearing anyway, so we really should have an interpreter. Since you'll be right next to us, Eric will know what to say for our vows and everything."

"Of course, Sophie!" Sharon said with enthusiasm. American Sign Language was her first language, and interpreting was nothing for Sharon. She was always involved. Always right next to all the joy, and sometimes she was a tool for others to experience it. But it simply wasn't for her to know on her own.

3

Sean's Predicament

"They'll fix it, Sophie," Sharon encouraged her sister, who hadn't been able to zip the dress at her first fitting. "I bet they ordered the wrong size."

"They kept saying they didn't." Sophie sighed through tears. "It fit so well when I bought it."

"But that was the sample, Soph. It was probably stretched out." L.D. said from the backseat. The three women were headed to the mall for L.D.'s wedding attire after Sophie's fitting.

She chose a pale blue, flowing bohemian dress, gladiator sandals, and large jewelry in natural tones that Sophie was sure would make all her bridesmaids jealous of L.D.'s beauty. So simple and basic, likely with flowing locks that would barely commune with a curling iron the day of the wedding. Such was L.D. Everything seemed effortless for her.

But when the women arrived at the Mehlmann home after the outing and L.D. spotted Sean's car in the driveway, not even her breath was effortless anymore. Increasingly in the past year or so, she knew that wherever Sean was, I was lurking just behind. That time, I started right in.

So much for feeling beautiful today.

But she didn't respond to me. Not ever. L.D. always appealed to Him.

"Lord, why do You always ask me to put up with Sean? It hurts."

"I don't want you to put up with him. I want you to love him."

"I do love him. That's why it hurts."

14

"You know what I've commanded you to do."

"I don't see how Your command is possible."

"You need only trust Me."

"I trust You. And You know I'll obey You. But I can't do this today."

"I should probably head home," she told the Mehlmann sisters aloud after her moment with God.

Sharon turned backward before exiting her car. "No! Mom wants you to stay for family dinner. Why would you need to go home? You even brought that tea."

Yeah, L.D. Why would you pass up a perfectly good opportunity to be picked apart flaw by flaw and have your value as a human being challenged?

"That's right. Sorry. Of course, I'll stay," she said aloud for the sake of Sharon. But in her heart, _"God, give me strength. I can't do this without You. I'll need my battle armor today, please."_

"'Now may the Lord direct your heart into the love of God and into the patience of Christ.'"

"Thessalonians. Thanks, Abba."

As they entered the house, L.D. heard Sean laughing with his parents. When they arrived in the kitchen where everyone usually convened, Sean hugged his sisters warmly.

At a glance—even a long, slow, careful one—he was noble. Ideal, even. Aesthetically agreeable, and always tending toward kindness. Had L.D. the luxury of only glancing, she might see him as the rest of humanity did. Just then, as Sophie whined and ranted about her dress and wedding details, Sean met her with compassion. Sean called Sharon beautiful and asked about her day and had been helping his mother with dinner preparations. He had likely saved a life or two that day at work. Maybe if she read about him in a magazine or something, he might have caused far different feelings. Why could she not simply admire him as a stranger or a celebrity? Instead, Sean made it difficult for L.D. to admire him at all, despite all those virtues and any commands she'd been given.

"Oh," he said in a glance her way, the smile disappearing. Disgust overtaking his tone.

"Hello, Sean," L.D. said as a cold professional. Clinging to her promise to be Christlike in love and patience. Failing. Wishing her heart was intact enough to be warmer.

Sean himself faltered a moment. Pushing past the way her cordiality softened him. And doing something she hated. "Hello, Lavender-Dawn Meadow George." Mocking her with her own name. The very core of who she was. There was no rebuttal for that. She could never win. She couldn't even be defended by Sharon and the family. He had, after all, only said her name.

At that moment, Eric, often as silent as his own perspective of the world, sneaked into the crowded kitchen with a wave before lifting Sophie from the ground with an embrace. The couple received a throat clear from Samuel after their quick hello kiss. Eric apologized in a sign to Samuel, who nodded before the couple began signing enthusiastically, Sophie as dramatic as ever about the dress fitting.

"Did you get to go shopping for your outfit, L.D.?" Lynn wondered.

"Yep. I was hoping for coral, but Sophie was pretty adamant about me not clashing with the bridesmaids for family pictures, so I went with a light blue." L.D. spoke to Lynn as she would to her own mother, if her mother were to care about her in the least.

"And you'll be in family pictures because…?" Sean launched another attack.

"Because Sophie asked. No other reason, Sean," L.D. explained timidly, not looking his way.

"I agree, the blue will look nice against the pink." Lynn had ignored Sean. Not sure how to approach his cruelty. "May I see the outfit?"

"It's already in my car. Did you want me to go grab it?" *Please say no. Please say no.*

"Yeah! You don't have to try it on, but I feel bad I had to work and couldn't go with you girls. I'd love to see it," Lynn begged.

"Okay." L.D. nodded, then headed back out to her car to grab her treasures.

As she walked off, Eric looked at Sean and asked Sophie something in sign. Something that made Sophie laugh hysterically.

"What?" Sean saw that the laughter was directed at him.

Sophie recovered from laughter to explain.

"Eric didn't see what you two were saying. He asked if you were flirting with L.D. Thinks you have a thing for her." Sophie giggled.

Sean scoffed. Looked at Eric. "Yes, I have a lot of 'things' for her. None of those things involve flirting."

Eric nodded with a smile. As if the words weren't necessary.

L.D. returned with a clear plastic garment bag and pulled it back for Lynn to see.

Lynn gasped. "That is lovely, L.D."

"Thanks. The hem is high-low. So, the back is longer than the front. It's hard to see that unless it's on." L.D. could still feel she was under the watch of Sean. Her suspicions were confirmed.

"Yikes, I hope you got a discount for that."

L.D. rolled her eyes as she replaced the plastic over the dress and began showing Lynn the shoes and accessories.

Sean hid it well. Even from himself at times. But years of realized urges with others had chipped away at his ability to pretend he wasn't imagining the flow of that dress against the ocean breeze and L.D.'s flawless curves. He couldn't wait to see her in it. Then again, he knew that when that day came, the usual would occur. His mind would set to racing and he would likely imagine that dress on the floor of his hotel room. Or his own bedroom. Maybe *their* bedroom. Or in the closet safely tucked away with all of her other clothes as she did nothing at all but sleep peacefully at his side. Or just laugh over coffee in his kitchen, wearing a wedding band and whatever else she wore for comfort. Her laugh was enchanting. Dreams he'd never attempt to accomplish, of course. So, she remained his unwitting torturer, and I lay my torment bare.

Sean. You are disgusting. She's perfect. It will never happen with her. Let it go.

But he couldn't let it go. He wouldn't say he had a "thing" for her. Or that he was attracted to her like he was to every other woman he encountered. She wasn't a conquest or a fleeting fantasy. She was something else. Something dangerous. She was standing in that kitchen, terrified of the next thing he'd say to push her away. But cautious and timid and vulnerable, she had power over every part of him and not the conviction to ever use it. Sean liked it that way. He loved that she hated him. It was safer. It gave her a chance at happiness and kept them all oblivious.

Better they all hate him than that Lavender-Dawn Meadow George ever look his way. And the closer she got to doing it, the more he had to hide.

"What do you think of the sandals, Sean?" Sharon made a half-attempt to engage his positivity.

"They look like something Jesus would wear. Were you going for 'ancient vintage'? Because you nailed it." *Not mean enough.* "Again… discount, right?"

All at once, L.D. lost her capacity to be cold and professional. She was too fiery for that. "Sandals similar to this would have been worn by Roman soldiers, who captured Jesus and tortured Him before hanging Him on a cross to die. Paul later used them when he gave an image for the armor of God. The shoes of peace? They reminded me of that."

"And yet you're wearing them. Are you now supportive of Roman soldiers killing Jesus?" Sean thought he'd caught her easily. Sadistically happy he finally got a rise out of her.

"I *am* part of the reason He died. It's fitting." L.D. cleared her throat.

Sean nearly perceived a sniffle as she hurried off to put her things back in her car.

"Why do you have to do that, Sean?" Sharon whispered fiercely.

"Why do you have to bring that stray cat around? We don't run a charity for abandoned animals and hippies."

L.D. had forgotten the shoe box and heard Sean's opinions as she re-entered the kitchen.

She sighed. "I have an early morning. I promised to help serve breakfast at the homeless shelter before church. I should just go."

"Let's all praise the bleeding-heart hippie for her service to humanity," Sean continued, faking slow applause.

But L.D. was already out the front door, planting a kiss to her hand, then atop a snow globe that belonged to her as she passed through the dining room. Her signature promise to return. Mindless by then.

"Why doesn't she just take that stupid thing home?" Sean commented.

Sophie punched him in the arm. Everyone knew why.

The infamous snow globe, with a sculpted representation of a dove with an olive branch, a rainbow in the backdrop. When she was ten, she learned at church the importance of the rainbow in the story of Noah's Ark. It wasn't just a sign. It was a promise that no matter how humanity messed things up, God would never resort to mass drowning again. The olive branch in the dove's mouth was proof that the ark would make landfall. Promises that a ten-year-old with a miserable home life needed to hear. That God would take care of her. Protect her. And that someday, she'd make landfall.

So, when she saw that snow globe on an outing with Sharon and Mr. Mehlmann to a Christian bookstore, it was the most beautiful thing she'd ever seen. On the base, a gold plate read, "God Keeps His Promises." L.D. didn't know her father, and she barely received basic necessities as a child, let alone random gifts. When Samuel saw L.D.'s eyes light up when she spotted that twenty-dollar snow globe, it was a gallon miracle to her that Samuel swept it right up and bought it for her.

As much as that meant to L.D., she never took that snow globe home with her. It had been displayed on a shelf in the Mehlmann dining room for nearly fifteen years. She made sure to admire it whenever she was there.

Lynn defended her where she could, "You know L.D.'s snow globe can stay here as long as she likes. And so can she."

Samuel took his son aside. "Son, you need to sort out whatever this is with L.D. and make it go away. She has done nothing to provoke this kind of behavior, and even if she had, that is not how a young man is to treat a young woman. I raised you better."

"I'm messing with her, Dad. She needs to lighten up." Sean shrugged, heartbroken over hurting L.D. again.

"She needs to change absolutely nothing. You're the problem here, Sean. Please tell me you see that."

But you'll never change enough to please her. Face it. This is the way things will always be.

•••

"And he just *assumed* I'm vegan. Just because of the way I dress. Sure, I think milk is weird, but why do I have to be a stereotype? Can't I just have my own opinions and live my life without people making assumptions? I don't assume things about people. Oh well, God loves him, too." L.D. snacked on frozen grapes while Sharon repeatedly dipped her spoon into a carton of ice cream.

"And this was one of the doctors?" Sharon clarified. "Is he single?"

"No, he had his wife and kids in the office the other day. He seems like the faithful type, so I don't have to worry about him coming after me. He was probably just making conversation. I really shouldn't complain." L.D. shrugged. "It wasn't about my name or my eyes, so that was new."

Sharon swallowed a spoonful. "I read this thing online that said girls with purple eyes are rare, and they don't have body hair and they don't menstruate. It's called—"

"Alexandria's Genesis. I get asked about that twice a year, usually by complete strangers. Because apparently, if you have purple eyes, you also live in an alternate universe where it's okay to ask about a stranger's body hair and menstrual cycle." L.D. wobbled her head to imply her confusion. "Doesn't exist. The only weirdness genetically that I'd have would be albinism, but I don't. I just have an interesting shade of blue eyes."

"They are totally purple, L.D." Sharon smiled.

"And I totally menstruate." L.D. giggled. "Wouldn't that be nice, though?"

"Yeah. For you. But I'd just be jealous." Sharon finally addressed the subject they were avoiding. "You know Sean doesn't mean anything by the things he says."

"Then why does he say them?" L.D. snapped. "I swear he keeps getting worse."

"I don't know. But it really upset us when you left. We love you. Please don't consider Sean's stupid opinion as how the rest of us feel about you," Sharon begged.

"I don't, S.R. I just wish I knew what I did that made him hate me so much. I mean *besides* the stupid childhood pranks I used to play on him. But I apologized for that. This isn't kid stuff. He genuinely seems to hate me." L.D. sighed. "Every time I'm about to see him, my amygdala gets all excited and wonders 'What will he come up with next?' He never disappoints."

"He's just being stupid. Don't let it get to you."

"I can't not let it get to me." L.D. didn't know why, but that was truth. Why she valued such a demeaning opinion was beyond her. "But can we not talk about Sean, please?"

"Did you see how mad Sophie was yesterday?" Sharon changed the subject as requested.

"I think she's, uh, in the family way," L.D. blurted. "That's why the dress wouldn't fit and why she's being all diva drama queen about everything."

"You mean pregnant? Dad would be livid." Sharon bit a lip. "He still thinks Sophie is a virgin. She lies when he asks because she knows he's really religious and doesn't want to disappoint him."

L.D. gasped at the gossip. She ignored that description of her father: "religious." Samuel loved the Lord and raised his children to do the same. Religion wasn't a part of that.

"I think if you have to lie, there is some issue with your relationship," Sharon surmised.

"Not necessarily. I think romance, by nature, requires some secrecy. Like you and me can tell your dad everything we do because we're friends. But I definitely don't care to know what Dad does with Mom. When someone's married, they don't broadcast their bedroom happenings, right?" L.D. half joked.

"They don't. But they *could* because there's no shame in their romance if they are married. But Sophie is, and should be, ashamed of herself," Sharon concluded.

She would, of course, never tell Sophie to be ashamed of anything. Sophie was beautiful, but never beautiful enough for the group she ran with in high school. With the way they made fun of Sharon, Sophie had to be sure never to come close to having weight issues. She would look in the mirror and I'd tell her that every bit of healthy flesh was too much. She was too fat. Samuel and Lynn were always involved and connected with their children, so they caught the anorexia early. After a short stint in rehab where she renewed her walk with Christ, Sophie felt like she had been rebirthed with a healthy new perspective.

Sharon was in college then, and for spending money she found a job as an interpreter for weekend services at a local Baptist church. It was a small church, with mostly black attendees, and only the one family had a deaf son—already out of college then. The services were lively and powerful. Sharon found a lot of joy in interpreting for that young man. So much joy that it was all she talked about. Sophie asked if she could attend a service, just to watch her sister sign. To experience a greater depth of life. After one service where she and Eric were the only people with their eyes mostly on Sharon, they were smitten. Sophie forced Sharon to teach her to sign.

Sophie was just shy of eighteen then, a senior in high school, and Eric was a twenty-three-year-old software engineer. Samuel Mehlmann didn't like the age gap or the language barrier at first. But when they met Eric and realized that Sophie had gone from starving herself to please friends that nit-picked every flaw to falling in love with a Christian man who had to lip-read her cheers, they knew it was about more than his physical handsomeness and a fat bank account. Sophie had a lot more heart than she let on. But her journey, too, was barely beginning.

At Sophie's final alteration appointment, three days before the flight to St. John, the zipper barely, and snugly, caught the white, gauzy, flowing dress around Sophie's tiny frame.

"I thought you let it out," Sophie accused.

"We did," The seamstress insisted. "Perhaps you gained weight."

To which Sophie responded by ignoring me completely. Defensively and crudely lashing out. Not wanting to go back to the place that took her to rock bottom.

"Excuse me? Daddy, tell this witch I am not fat."

"Sophie…" Samuel tried to keep the peace. Though also worried at what being "accused" of weight gain might do to Sophie.

"*Tell* her," Sophie insisted, almost hearing me say the opposite.

"I doubt my daughter has gained weight." Samuel caved and said calmly to the seamstress.

"I bet you say that about your other daughter, too," the woman mumbled.

Which crushed Sharon's spirit. Sharon hadn't eaten lunch in a week to make sure that very plus-size dress didn't need a shred of fabric added to it. Something else she wouldn't tell Sophie, who was going to school for nutrition.

"Whoa," L.D. said. Always the peacemaker. "Let's not get all escalate-y, here. Sophie, does the dress fit well enough for your wedding?"

"If I do a cleanse." Sophie eyed the seamstress viciously.

"Awesome sauce. And witch seamstress lady, insults to my bestie and the bride who has struggled with an eating disorder are worth the price of crap alterations, right?" L.D. continued.

"I will comp them, yes. My apologies." The seamstress said with bitter remorse.

"Good, then everyone's happy!" L.D. exclaimed. "But seriously, Soph. Take a preggo test. Pretty obvious."

Sophie gasped. "That's impossible." But Sophie was more honest to herself than that. Otherwise I'd have had a better foothold. A hand went to her mouth.

Mom's knowing panic was silent. Dad's gaze snapped to his youngest child.

"I was under the impression that you and Eric were abstinent." He was making a fool of himself, not them, and didn't care.

"Seriously, Dad? Eric is twenty-six. How long did you expect the guy to wait?" Sean said, having been present, but chatting with a stranger on his phone until then.

"It shouldn't matter. Eric is a respectable young man." Samuel sighed.

"We *were* abstinent," Sophie whined nasally but spoke firmly. "We still are. . .sometimes. . .but I swear to you, we tried. Dad, I'm marrying him in a week, okay? And I'm probably not pregnant. Eric and I have been sleeping together for years and for it to happen now would just be. . ."

"Classic," Sean jested.

"Years?!" Dad didn't miss a beat.

"Not in high school or anything!" Sophie clarified, wide-eyed. "I don't want you to think he crossed that line."

"Tell me you knew that, Samuel," Lynn said.

"It's really not a big deal, Dad. I've only been with *him*. And we'd been in love for a while before it happened." Sophie. Always right, whether right or wrong. "Maybe you should lecture *Sean*, instead."

"I'm not the one that's knocked up for my wedding. Sean needs no lectures for being as safe as possible," Sean defended in third person.

"Oh my God, Sean. I'm on the pill," Sophie argued, misrepresenting the Lord's name.

"Seems to be working out for you," L.D. said, sarcastically. Trying to ease the tension.

"Hey, at least she knows who her baby daddy is, bastard hippie," Sean lashed out, turning his self-defense into sibling defense.

"Enough!" Samuel Mehlmann yelled in the bridal shop. Embarrassed by his wayward children in front of an amused seamstress and a few other brides across the shop. Silencing them all. "Did I teach you kids nothing at all? And Lynn, do you just *accept* this? There are things you shouldn't toy with."

Samuel walked out. And I whispered to the most vulnerable woman in the room. Sharon. Always Sharon.

Don't worry. You'll never let him down like this. God knows no one will ever "cross a line" with you again.

4

Eric's Ears

The automatic airline seat assignments on a nearly full flight had placed Eric and Sophie across the aisle from one another. Sharon was in a quiet corner in the back of the plane with her father – both requiring two seats because of their size. Lynn was seated with Eric's parents, and they happily chatted about the wedding.

L.D. was grateful to have been gifted with a plane ticket and was excited to share a room with her best friend in paradise. So, it almost didn't faze her that she was seated on the wing between Eric, who was worried about the greenish looking Sophie, and Sean, who wasn't content or grateful about anything.

"Seriously, there's an entire empty row back there and they won't let me move to it?"

"If this plane crashes, they will identify casualties by seat numbers," L.D. explained the process. "You have a window seat, why are you complaining?" She crossed her arms, closing her eyes to attempt a nap, and trying to shut out the frustrated Sean.

"Because I can smell the hippie on you."

"Interesting. What does 'hippie' smell like exactly?" L.D. stayed strong. Eyes closed. Able to sway him from seeing how deeply his bullying cut her.

"Do you wash your hair with cow dung?"

"Nope." She sighed. "Shampoo."

"Hippie shampoo though, right?" He prodded viciously.

That's right. He hates every hair on your head.

"Yep. All-natural. No cancer-causing poison like in yours."

"Oh, the stuff that teams of genius scientific experts synthesized to actually *clean* my hair?"

"That's right, I suppose you don't care much about cancer, do you? I honestly don't know how you'd smell my shampoo past all the smoke you weave into your clothes."

"Not near enough. Nicotine withdrawals and getting seated next to *you*? This is really my day."

"You know, it's a federal offense to tamper with smoke detectors on planes. Maybe you should go try it and relieve us all of your boyish charm."

"I think maybe you should—"

"Sean, I would love to take a nap. Can you stop extruding your idiot upon the world for three hours and thirty-seven minutes please? Is that possible? We have a lot of traveling to do today." L.D. was angry over her loss of control, but happy for the silence.

She closed her eyes and Sean spotted Eric flexing his jaw and wincing in pain.

"You okay, Eric?" He called across the row.

You know, she's right Sean, you are an idiot sometimes.

He shook his head at himself, then reluctantly reached across L.D. to tap Eric's shoulder. Eric turned immediately, always concerned he missed something.

"Are you okay?" Sean pointed to Eric's jaw and enunciated. But just a little, because Sophie had scolded him before for *over-*enunciating. Reminding him that Eric could read lips better than most, provided you didn't mumble.

Eric hated to talk. He'd been teased for his voice. He preferred to sign, but due to the void of ASL outside the deaf community, he also spoke quite well if one listened. Sean listened well, knowing Eric hated to talk. The soon-to-be brothers shared profound mutual respect from the start. The seeds of lasting friendship.

"The pressure hurts my ears," Eric said. Muffled and nasal and hollow. But Sean just knew it as a voice he was glad Eric felt comfortable to use with him.

It astonished Sean enough to ask it.

"Oh, it can still do that? Or is it worse for you, or. . .?" Sophie hated it when Sean asked Eric questions about being deaf. But she was across the aisle with her eyes closed tight, so Sean appeased his medically-oriented intrigue and asked it.

Eric smiled. He relished the questions, especially from Sean. What he didn't like was being feared. Sean didn't fear him and could understand complex answers.

Except he didn't understand Eric's answer because of pressure in his own ears. Sighed, embarrassed. "I. . .can you say that again? It is really hard to hear on a plane."

Idiot. You idiot.

Eric laughed. Spoke louder, likely having been taught to do so. "I said my eustachian tubes and eardrums are just like yours. My hearing loss is because of damage to my auditory nerve in utero. We both have pressure problems."

"Oh." Sean laughed. "Interesting."

Eric smiled. Lit up a little. "So, you can't hear very well on a plane?"

Sean was glad he had gestured, probably signed, but he didn't speak the language. "Nobody can." Sean smiled, gesturing with his hands as he often did. "Levels the playing field."

Eric snorted laughter. Sean rolled his eyes, lowering his head. Eric laughing after he said something was only sometimes because he thought what Sean said was funny. Most often, Eric was laughing because Sean's gestures never meant what he said.

"What did I say?" Sean asked, exasperated.

"You sort of said you were embarrassed to pee." Eric used the same gestures as he spoke, then taught Sean as he spoke and signed again. "*Level. . .field. . .*or just *equal.*"

Sophie moaned, and Sean glanced at her. Eric looked in response. Said a common word with his voice. It sounded like "Zof." But Sophie reacted to it like anyone would to their name.

"I'm fine," she whispered and signed. But she wasn't. She'd been eyeing it, and at that moment grabbed the airsick bag and put it to use. When Eric about jumped up from his seat, Sophie waved him off with various adamant signs. She rose and headed to the lavatory.

"She alright?" L.D. opened her eyes, having been attempting to ignore Sean suddenly being civil with another human being, as he always was with everyone else. She signed fluently with Eric.

Eric told her that Sophie was fine. But L.D. smirked.

"Is she. . ." Then she just signed, *"pregnant."*

Eric laughed. Told L.D. that would make Samuel angry. And Sean understood that.

"Yeah, but *is* she though?" he prodded.

L.D. understood Eric's next sign that he was sworn to secrecy, and she didn't prod. Sean reached across L.D. to punch Eric's arm, and then finally crossed his arms and settled against the window to sleep. Sophie returned, and Eric spent the next few moments ensuring her comfort and well-being from across the aisle. Asking the flight attendant for water and the like. L.D. watched to be sure that Sean was asleep enough to both ward off cigarette cravings and leave her alone.

Eric tapped L.D.'s shoulder after she watched Sean close his eyes. He signed to her.

"You are disappointed in us."

"It is not my place to judge," L.D. encouraged.

Eric nodded. Laughed a little. Thought a moment, then made sure Sean was asleep before signing. *"There are walls language cannot break."*

L.D. giggled. "Are you pulling the deaf card as an excuse for sleeping with Sophie?"

Eric shook his head. Signed. *"I should have married her sooner. Her parents thought she was too young, but I take responsibility for what happened because we waited. What I meant was body language is much easier to understand than what someone is saying. Sophie says I listen better than most people, because I can't always tell what they're saying."*

"I agree." L.D. smiled.

"You like to learn. You sign well. You are gracious. I think you could learn to listen with your eyes. . .and your heart." Eric turned his own eyes to the sleeping man in the window seat.

L.D. glanced over at him before looking back at Eric in confusion, thinking she misunderstood. But Eric was winking before closing his eyes to sleep.

Despite some nasty airsickness from the bride, the wedding week went smoothly. The bachelor and bachelorette parties more joy than drinking. The rehearsal without a hitch. And Sophie met her husband on a beach at the end of an aisle of flower petals on the arm of her daddy. Sharon's jealousy raging as she interpreted their ceremony. But her joy just as full.

At the reception, Sharon and L.D. cooed at Eric and Sophie when he pulled her to a speaker on the floor, placed her hands on it and covered her ears. Sophie smiled brightly, watching everyone dance and have a wonderful time.

Eric signed something to Sophie, and she shook her head violently. But he convinced her in the next moment to ask the DJ for the microphone. When the song was over, she spoke into it.

"Here goes," L.D. sing-songed in her best friend's ear.

Sophie cleared her throat into the mic and spoke timidly. "Hi, everyone. Um, Eric wanted to say something, and he asked me to translate for you. . ." Eric signed something. "Exactly what he says, I have to tell you." Sophie nodded to him. "Okay, he says, 'Thank you for flying here to be with us today. I'm glad you're enjoying the music. I always imagined that Sophie's voice is like music, so this interruption probably isn't too painful.' " Sophie gave a teary-eyed giggle as all the guests cooed.

Eric continued signing, and Sophie interpreting. "He says, 'Marriage is a time when two families come together and make one big family. I thought this would be a good day to tell our new big family that it is bigger than you thought.' Eric, No." Sophie interjected in a whisper. Eric hummed adamantly for her to continue. She sighed. Continued. " 'Sophie and I are having a baby.' "

Sophie signed to Eric that the tent-full of devout Christian guests was expressing severe disappointment, which didn't require hearing to know. She continued. "He says, 'I would apologize, but we have already been forgiven, and committed our lives to one another. You may say what you want to me. But when Sophie puts down this microphone, please do not tell her you are disappointed. Tell her she will be a good mother. And tell her you are excited to be family and friends to a new baby that will join a big family.' "

After the shock, the crowd realized that there was no other righteousness to be done that could remedy it. And they all began congratulating the couple. I, for one, knew I'd be seeing a lot more of Sophie. But for that day, I stuck with Sharon and L.D. in their hotel room after the reception was over but the night wasn't yet.

"Here's me not saying I totally called this one," L.D. said it first. Teased. "Those crazy sinners."

They both heard Sean exit his hotel room into the hall, talking to one of the other groomsmen about a "date" he had at a bar with a girl he met on an app.

"I'm surprised *Sean* doesn't have ten kids by now," Sharon added. She took out her hearing aids and set them aside with a sigh. L.D. began signing as she spoke.

"I know! Seriously. Sophie's sin, though still not so great, makes sense. She and Eric are in love. But Sean just does whatever with whomever. I can't even imagine doing what he does. Exposing my body to all those unknown germs and toxins and diseases. Bleh!" L.D. shuddered.

"And he's an EMT too!" Sharon laughed. "You think he'd know better."

"Part of me thinks he does," L.D. analyzed. "I have this philosophy. . ."

L.D. had lots of philosophies. Most of them were derived from things of God, just like everything else about her. But if she couldn't find it in the Word, she considered it a personal philosophy, not wanting God to be ridiculed should it ever prove untrue. Most of them didn't though. And though Sharon rolled her eyes teasingly at L.D.'s familiar announcement because it would likely result in a long conversation, she was also eager to hear the wisdom she'd soon take straight to heart.

"What's your philosophy?" Sharon said in a sigh, putting in one of her hearing aids.

"Well, I think the worst thing about a person is also the best thing about a person." L.D. shrugged, waiting for a reaction.

Sharon laughed once, because she didn't even think she possessed a "best" thing. With my help, she'd never awaken to that knowledge.

L.D. rolled her eyes, still trying to make a point about Sean, but knowing she needed to clarify first.

"What do you hate about me, Sharon?"

"Nothing." Sharon sat up, turning her eyes into compassion. Defending her friend against me. L.D., loving that part of Sharon, smiled a little.

"You're telling me we've been best friends since we were nine and *nothing* about me drives you crazy?" L.D. insisted brightly.

Sharon bit her lip. "You're sort of a Jesus Freak. And you never take medical advice and you just *insist* on being different. But at the same time, you're just way too nice to everybody. Including your mother, who doesn't deserve it."

"Wow. Thought we were friends," L.D. teased.

"You know I love you, L.D. But you asked!"

"Well, tell me what you *love* about me."

"You're the kindest person I know. But you don't let people tell you who you're supposed to be. You're just an all-around good person and your faith inspires me." Sharon smiled, loving the sister God didn't give her by blood. Because she realized before the smile flowed across L.D.'s face that she just said she hated those very same things about her.

"See?" They both giggled. L.D. elaborated, "I think that can be applied to anyone."

"Good philosophy." Sharon nodded. "But what does that have to do with my sleazy brother?"

"Well, if it holds true, you should be able to turn around the worst thing about him to see that it's also the best. And we're saying that this promiscuity is the worst thing about him. I'm not buying. Because how can that be good?" L.D. wondered.

"He's popular. Charming. Women like him." Sharon smirked. "Except you, of course. Speaking of which, you hate him. Why are you analyzing him?"

"I don't know. Might be something Eric said to me on the plane. Maybe it just bothers me that Sean doesn't fit the philosophy." L.D. looked to the ground. "But if he does, that would mean he's either a world class loser and certain women love that sort of thing, *or* he's hiding his extremes. The best and the worst. And he's just floating in the middle, so no one suspects it. Because garden variety charm can't be someone's absolute best quality. That would make for a shallow, boring person. I just don't think he's either."

"I think you're wrong. Well, right about the philosophy. Wrong about Sean."

"How so?" L.D. asked.

"I think he has the biggest heart of anyone I know. So that'd be his best thing. And he's extremely, *extremely* protective of the people he loves. He's always been kind to me, even when it would have been easier for him to be cruel to me like everyone else is. And more than once, he's disregarded rules, laws even, to protect me."

Yes. Rub it in, Sharon. He's a light. We all know.

"You're not wrong, except. . ." L.D. shook her head. Forbidding the tears from her eyes.

Sharon thought a few seconds. Bit her lip, then opened up to L.D. Something that was as easy to her as breathing. "Except he's mean to you. I don't know. To me *that's* the worst thing about him. So maybe your philosophy needs more field testing."

"Maybe," L.D. pondered, standing suddenly. "I'm gonna go for a walk on the beach. You in?" She was re-fitting gladiator sandals on fair feet, still wearing that lovely, gauzy dress in pale blue.

"No, I'm exhausted. But I don't want you to go alone. At night. In a strange place. . ." Sharon told the free spirit, who laughed.

"I'm the child of a hippie. It's my thing. I need sand between my toes. I'll take my pepper spray, don't worry." And with L.D.'s mood that night, I got to tag along.

5

The Hippie's Snow Globe

Let me pause to remind you that our heroine in this story is the large and depressed Sharon Mehlmann. But in the era we met her, as you've gathered by now, Sharon was largely incapable of heroics and also had nothing and no one to rescue. Her teaspoon miracle was still being measured out. Adventures of all sorts happened all around her, though she was often excluded, as we've discovered. One adventure during this time was a story of its own, but I dare not digress to tell it. This is Sharon's story. Her mundane, ordinary story still void of miracles.

I should, therefore, use our time together to focus on Sharon, as Sharon always did. We will begin again as Sharon removed her hearing aids and I whispered her sweet nothings as she dozed off.

Nothing. You are nothing. . .

And yet. How can I teach you about the foolish weaknesses of humankind without the type of adventure you'd be missing if we stayed with Sharon? And is any story complete if not intertwined with another? Do you promise not to tell her if we stray for a time? We must keep her in the cold darkness of nothing while I bring you to an adventure that will cross Sharon's path many times. We will check on her from time to time, that you might be brought to Sharon's same desperation for such an adventure of her own. For now, let's digress.

As Lavender-Dawn Meadow George descended an elevator and crossed a lobby, walked into the night breeze of the Caribbean Sea, and took a path to a white-sanded beach, she was unaware of her station in her own story. As she smiled, removing those sandals and letting the sand mingle with her toes, one might think her liberated, as one entering the home stretch of an already arduous path. But Miss George was about to take the first steps into the place God started her journey as we know it. A journey from which she'd often need rescuing.

She walked along the beach, sandals in hand, hating that the world required that little purse across her shoulder for things like money and contact with others. Letting the back hem of that high-low dress grace the edge of the ocean and dirty in the sand. She was alone with God. Thanking Him for the day and collecting shells in that little satchel. Praying for Sophie and Eric and Sharon. And then, shattering those thoughts, a catcall came from a group of young men as she passed a bar.

"Hey, baby! How'd the universe let *you* be alone tonight? Come over here, let me buy you a drink." The rest of the group whooped and whistled and howled. Oh, to be Sharon sometimes. Mostly deaf when she wants to be. L.D. thought her beautiful, but the best of her was inside, and no guy had gotten close enough to see it. How very, very lucky. L.D. had been inconveniently given a stunningly beautiful outer shell through genetics. Used to such vulgarity, and a wise woman, she ignored the voice.

But it grew closer.

"Hey, I'm *talking* to you." This time, the voice was adamant. Angry, even. Definitely inebriated. And looking for a response, which L.D. granted.

"Yeah, but I ignored you. Because I'm for sure not interested in placating whatever fleshly urge you're—" She turned then. And a tall, muscular, shirtless oaf of a young man, likely a college senior, had bridged the gap between them and was standing three feet from her.

She sized up the spring-breaker. Since L.D. had spent her whole life chasing after Jesus, while her mother had chased after men like this. And since she was not only in tune with the world around her, spiritual and physical, but had also witnessed a few men of the same height and build knock her mother around their studio apartment with ease, L.D. sensed danger. With it, my voice.

You'll never be able to fight him off.

She reached for her purse, hands shaking, seeing in her mind's eye in slow motion the steps to acquire and use her pepper spray. Or maybe she'd just take it out and give him a chance to back off. Maybe she should run.

None of those occurred. His intent was faster than her reflexes. In full view of, and with roared encouragement from the drunken crowd at the bar, the young man reached out and caressed her cheek. Gently, I suppose, except L.D.'s immediate reaction was to slap his hand away.

That made him angry. He took another step into her personal space and outside all comfort.

"Don't touch me again," she said, firmly. As if speaking to a dog.

"You won't say that long, trust me." He reached out again and squeezed her shoulder.

She swatted his hand again. "And you will regret it for all of eternity if you don't leave me alone."

"Baby, I'd gladly go to hell for you," he coerced, reaching then for her waist. When she took a step back to avoid the molestation, she was already anticipating his next move.

He flung forward and grasped the back of her neck with a hand, directing her head to his face. His other hand grabbed the wrist of the arm not carrying sandals, ending the pursuit of pepper spray. Both restraints were painful and terrifying but fight or flight never caused her to flee.

"See here's the thing, though. Hell is a very real and very scary place. If you went, it wouldn't be for *me* per se. It would be because you rejected Christ. But who's counting?" She spoke casually, steadying her voice despite the chilling physical threat, against which she began to struggle.

"See, now you're asking for it," he said, authoritatively to the ever-strong-willed young woman.

"Asking for *what*, Neanderthal?" She dared his eyes, and in looking at his average, obviously unintelligent peepers, he looked between her eyes. His grasp loosened, just a little.

"Whoa, your eyes are—"

But his comment ceased altogether when that great big, drunken college senior fell backward onto the sand with a mighty shove delivered by a figure L.D. hadn't seen coming. L.D.'s protector spoke.

"Hands *off.*"

"What are you gonna do about it?" the Neanderthal accosted, almost standing.

The protector threw himself beachward and shoved his knee into an unfortunate location for the Neanderthal. During his pained groan, and with one quick, silent movement, the protector's fist had contacted the Neanderthal's nose and mouth, and blood emerged directly.

The beast first scrambled, then stood and ran with much drunken difficulty. And, trembling from head to toe, L.D. saw something her eyes could barely comprehend, with a prickle to the back of her neck. Her hero held out his hands when the other man disappeared into the crowd. Puffing his chest, daring anyone else to try something. When assured that no one would come try a similar act, he turned to the shaken, but undefiled woman.

"You okay?" It was a deep voice. Sultry and enticing in any other circumstance. He was handsome, of course. But that raspy, pebbly voice had always been his most striking feature since puberty, when L.D. witnessed the change herself.

She whispered her reply, as it may be complicated to thank this specific male person.

"I'm fine, Sean. Thank you."

He laughed. Mocked her. " 'I'm fine, Sean. Thank you.' ? There is no way you're fine right now, Lavender-Dawn Meadow George. Come here, let me check you over."

"He barely touched me, Sean. I'm fine," she insisted. Seeing caveman blood on Sean's hand and retrieving an all-natural wet wipe from her satchel.

"*Barely* is about three thousand percent too much for my taste." Sean chuckled, wiping his fist and backing up into the light illuminating the beach outside the bar. L.D. followed, letting the

EMT quickly examine her neck and wrist for remnants of the brief assault.

That's when L.D. smelled the liquor on his breath. As her senses calmed with fervent prayer, she looked between the crowd and the ocean at a gorgeously tanned and sparingly dressed young blonde. She was clearly waiting for Sean. And clearly too young to be doing so. L.D. pulled away more fiercely than his gentle examination required after her brush with violence. But he understood, and didn't mention, the discrepancy.

"I'm fine, Sean. I'll let you get back to your bleary-eyed lechery," L.D. whispered, nodding to the object of Sean's wooing.

Sean rolled his eyes and mumbled, his back safely to the young woman standing twenty feet away, "Her profile said she was nineteen. A bit young for my taste. I'm not *Eric* after all. But I try to give everyone a chance. Since I've met her, she's slipped up twice and said she was sixteen. Meaning she is. I'm trying to let her down easy."

"Vigilante Sean, defender of women," L.D. teased. "Also, user of objectifying hookup apps. Need help?"

"I will never forgive you if you attempt to 'help' me right now." Sean knew it was hopeless and was already gritting his teeth in anticipation for her next actions.

L.D. was a Christian girl with good intentions and love for all. But still a sinner. So, she made the best choice she could, considering. She suddenly raised her voice, so the young woman could hear. "Sean Joseph Mehlmann, why on Earth would you consider having *sex* with a sixteen-year-old? She barely has any clothes on and she's clearly drunk. What would your *mother* say? What would Jesus think?"

The young woman spoke up, annoyed and found out. "Your girlfriend is a freak. I'm out."

"She's not my—" Sean tried to object, but the young woman was already walking away at a feverish pace.

L.D. giggled and called after her. "Normally *Jesus* Freak is what I prefer. Because living water doesn't give me a hangover. Wait, where are you going? Sean wants to tell you about living water!"

"That's enough, hippie." A typical Sean thing to say as they watched the young woman depart and he lit up a cigarette.

L.D. called out, "I'll pray for you!"

"Why do you have to do that? People would like Christians a lot more if we weren't so judgy."

"And hypocritical," she added. "Because apparently 'we' still self-identify as a Christian while at a bar trying to find a random girl with which to engage in amorous congress."

"I'm not *you*, Lavender-Dawn Meadow George. When will you stop trying to guilt me into behaving?" Sean begged.

"Exactly right now." L.D. was heartbroken that someone willing to rescue a girl he couldn't stand would drench his soul in so much poison. "Sorry. Contrary to what some believe, I know when my welcome's worn out. I'll go. Thank you for not letting that guy. . ." She cleared her throat, not wanting to consider what would have happened without Sean. "Seriously, thank you."

Sean's jaw tensed as he puffed his cigarette. He spoke coldly. "Glad I was here. I don't think *you* should have been, because generally a woman should avoid being alone on dark beaches in foreign countries, but I'm glad you didn't die or have your pristine wholesomeness ruined."

"Yeah," she whispered, then turned her back. "Bye, Sean."

"Uh, no. I didn't see where your new friend stumbled off to. My family would never forgive me if I didn't get you back to the resort safely after this. I *should* be taking you to a police station." His tone was always so harsh.

"So that you can explain why you *assaulted* someone? Let's avoid that, okay? I really am fine. I've handled worse with less help," She responded, never understanding how he could be so mean. She slipped out her pepper spray, turning and reassuring him, then returned it to her bag.

"Yeah, because that *pepper spray* is what had your back tonight." As if he was tearing her down, once again. He then began rambling about her poor choice to take her walk.

He can't stand you. If not for the respect he has for his sister, he'd gladly watch you get carried off by pirates. I told her as she began to walk away.

But I can never compete, especially if it involves L.D., when God decides to weigh in. Even if all He does is repeat what a mere human said in passing.

"You could learn to listen with your eyes. And your heart." Eric had said it on the plane, but God was saying it now.

L.D. didn't know any better way in the moment, but she wanted more than anything to obey, having heard the clear instruction. So, she put her hands up to her ears, pressing them in until the sound of the waves became a whisper. She turned back to Sean.

He looked confused. Scared even. Frantically asking her questions, she supposed.

"Stop supposing."

She sighed at that instruction. Trying not to notice that his mouth looked like it did whenever insults would roll out, one after the other. Cutting her down for her clothing, her philosophies, her hair, her eyes, her faith in Jesus Christ. A cruel little smirk and mumbling lips.

"No. See him as I do."

So L.D. closed her eyes and prayed, reopening them after remembering that Sean Joseph Mehlmann is a child of God. A straying one; but love covers all sins. His redemption was won, long ago. And when she finally forgave him and granted him at least a clean slate as always, she saw he was done speaking. His eyebrows bent, not with cruelty; but genuine concern that there was something the matter with L.D. And she started to consider, as she saw her in Sean's brown eyes. . .Sharon.

How could someone so cruel not tear apart Sharon, who had always been an easy target for bullies? How could he leave intact Eric, a man who would be easy to ridicule? How had he so joyfully hugged his sister and placed his hands on her expectant belly if he hated all things beautiful? He had a substantial enough college fund, work ethic, and IQ for any profession. Yet he chose to be an EMT and get his hands dirty on the front lines to save lives. *How? Why?*

When he was always so mean to her. There had to be a good reason. And instead of lashing back like always, L.D. finally wanted to dig in and figure out the truth.

"Alright, Lord. I'm listening."

By then, Sean was speaking again. His eyes reading compassion. And finally, he stepped forward and physically pulled her hands off her ears.

"You are freaking me out right now. Are you okay? Is there something wrong with your ears or are you just ignoring me like a child?" His voice was shaking as he gently released her wrists. Confident from her steady gaze that she wasn't going to return them to her ears.

"I'm fine." She cleared her throat, smiling.

"Stop saying you're fine. You're not fine," Sean argued.

"Okay I'm not fine. And I'm terrified about walking back alone. Were you serious about coming with me or were you just offering because it was the chivalrous thing to do and your dad would yell at you if you didn't?" She gave him blatant honesty and he was taken aback.

"It actually wasn't an offer at all. I'm not *letting* you walk back alone. If you feel guilty about that, you could come in for a minute and have a beer, so you don't ruin my night out. I'll buy."

"Don't insult me, Sean. Beer destroys the natural rhythm of the body, and the last time I was in a bar, I was dragging my mother out of it." L.D. instantly regretted the outlash. "But since you mentioned it, let's make it coffee, and let's make it to go. I am not hanging out with this crowd of people."

"What, they aren't good enough for you and Jesus?" he accosted, all the sincerity he could muster.

L.D.'s heart sank. Her countenance with it. "You have me, *and* Jesus, all wrong."

Sean sighed, approaching L.D. and dropping his hands onto her shoulders. Liquor and tainted tobacco on his breath as he assured her purple eyes, "I'm *messing* with you, Lavender-Dawn Meadow George. I think you've got *me* all wrong too."

He was right. For once. She sighed relief. He smiled.

"I'll go grab us some coffee. Stay put? Take out that pepper spray." He backed up, smiling.

"Got it," L.D. said, listening to the night and the waves as she stood on the now empty beach.

Sean had left his warmth at her shoulders. Those big, rough but skilled hands of an EMT. L.D. wondered if maybe the memory of all the people he's saved—all the people he's lost—had somehow seeped into his hands and into his spirit. How could they not?

He's sleazy. A sinner. And he's never been nice to you.

Because someone had to remind her.

"I don't see this working, God," she nearly said aloud. . .not to me, of course.

I agree.

"Lord, show me what You see." She caught sight of Sean appearing from the bar, his hands full of coffee cups.

"They didn't have to-go cups. I had to buy these twenty-dollar souvenir travel mugs. So, you better take care of this thing and root for team St. John for all of eternity."

"Sean! Seriously? I'll pay you back." L.D. reached for her little purse.

"Or you'll forget about my unintentional underage companion." He smirked. Handing her the coffee. "Two raw sugars, right? No milk or creamer because milk is weird," Sean teased.

L.D. took the cup. Did he really remember that? She took to defending the stance. "*Cow* milk is weird. I think cows should drink cow milk, and humans should drink human milk. . .I mean, when they are infants. In ancient times, there was no dietary requirement for cow milk consumption, and—"

"Do you really have to rant when I'm smashed?" Sean cleared his throat.

"Sorry." L.D. winced. "This is a nice cup. Thanks."

"You're welcome. Shall we?" He led them in the direction she came.

"Sixteen is probably legal. You're only twenty-three." She made conversation.

"That's disgusting and dangerous on so many levels." He grimaced, taking a sip.

"And sleeping with an *adult* you barely know is. . ." L.D. was trying to learn. Suddenly curious.

"Way different. There are lines you don't cross," he defended. "I know none of this aligns with *your* standards, but you'd never catch me groping an uninterested woman in any situation, let alone a completely in-over-her-head teenager. The most action I got tonight was a handshake. In my world, I'm a gentleman."

"Your world scares the crap out of me," L.D. admitted.

"Good," Sean said. "Because you don't belong in it."

"Please stop punishing me for ruining your evening, Sean." L.D. shook her head, hating the way he lived his life, and herself for calling him on it. . .again.

"That's not what I meant. I meant you're like pearls before swine. I hate that you had a run-in like that." Sean cleared his throat, and they both fell silent. Not sure what to do when an almost compliment was exchanged between them.

"You know. . ." L.D. started after a time where they listened only to the waves. She concluded the thought with an abrupt head shake.

"What?" He knew the philosophical tone. "What do I not know that you want to tell me?"

"Nothing. You said no ranting." She sighed. "I wasn't going to, but you might have taken it that way anyway."

"Say it. We have like a mile, right? I can handle a not rant." Sean tripped a little.

"Question is, can you handle *walking* a mile?" She giggled.

"Well, the walk and the coffee should get me to a point where I can face my father should I run into him back at the hotel. So, it's required. Just slow down." Sean sipped his coffee. "What were you gonna say?"

"Just that this island is beautiful. Named well, I think. John, from the Bible—St. John as some people call him—is one of my favorites. I love the book of John. If you ask him, he was Jesus's favorite. I'm not Catholic, obviously, but I looked it up when Sophie decided to get married here. And St. John is the patron saint of love and friendship among other things."

"And burn victims, right? There's like a plaque outside the burn ward at the hospital back home that has St. John," Sean asked. Loved conversing with her. Kept it going. "Is he the same guy as John the Baptist?"

"Uh, no." L.D. chuckled. "I thought you knew the Lord, Sean."

"I do. Well. . .I guess I asked Jesus into my heart, or whatever. And I definitely understand that I'm a sinner and need grace and fully accept that Jesus died and rose again, so I don't burn in hell for eternity. But there are a lot of Johns in the Bible, right?"

"You mean you don't know?" L.D. teased, though her spirit tingled with delight at Sean's profession of faith.

"Well, I haven't actually. . .I mean I haven't read the *entire* Bible. I believe it is God's Word, but. . ." he confessed to her.

L.D. responded both softly and sternly. She told him that the Bible is our field guide. That it defines our morality and explains our existence. Its wisdom exceeds the worth of rubies. There is not a more important document. And as she explained it all, Sean listened. *Listened.* He wondered as she spoke if it was fair to the rest of humanity that one woman contain so much outward beauty *and* inward wisdom.

Over an hour and a mile of beach and night passed by, and Sean slowly walked off a fog and shared a civil conversation with Lavender-Dawn Meadow George. The first of its kind. Even I sat back and watched, because it was far too fitting to doubt. That their first true conversation be centered on Jesus, the Bible, and the power of God's grace.

At first, they both feared the other might suddenly turn on them. That the tone would change and the civility scatter. Worse still, they feared the hurts of before might resume tomorrow as if this fulfilling confidence had never occurred. But neither fear was realized. It wasn't long, in fact, before that conversation wound its way from civil, to silly, to genuine, as an intimacy between dear friends might navigate. And it became a doorway to real healing, as topics of immorality and "judginess" were addressed without the usual passionate hurt behind them. It was discovered that all the years had been a misunderstanding.

In fact, Sean aspired to be a husband and father, but didn't think himself worthy to woo the marrying type after all his sinful escapades. Likewise, L.D. didn't judge. She loved all people as they were in that moment. But she knew that with God's help they could do better. Her tendency, to her detriment, was to facilitate that change.

In the normal course of that conversation, L.D. tactfully mentioned the same philosophy she'd proposed to Sharon in their hotel room not long before, and her dilemma regarding Sean. Her new companion considered the philosophy a moment as he stopped in the sand under the light that revealed the path that would return them to their resort. There, they stood conversing.

Sean smiled. And in response to the innocent sincerity sculpted into L.D.'s gentle face, Sean made a choice that he didn't realize would alter his life as he knew it. He felt like he could, at this point. It seemed safe. So, he decided to open up, just a little, just at the right time. "I think you're probably right. Sometimes the best thing about us becomes our downfall in the end. And Sharon's right too. Something in me snaps when I feel like someone is in danger. As evidenced back at that bar."

It was true. Sean was protective. Extremely protective. Even of willing young women he knew were too young. The more he loved someone, the less he cared about the consequences when it came to protecting them. That was Sean. The worst and the best of him. The philosophy held true.

"But that doesn't explain. . ." L.D. took a breath. Not having intended to release those words yet. The others weren't quite formed. She cleared her throat and he waited patiently for her to form the words. "Why are you always so mean to me?"

"I'm protecting you," he said with caution, as to a child asking a simple question.

"Sure doesn't feel like it," she muttered.

"Which *proves* that I'm protecting you," Sean said. "If you realized what I was doing, you wouldn't be as safe. So, I guess *that* method is out the window."

"You should never have to hurt someone just to protect them."

"No offense, Lavender-Dawn Meadow George, but you weren't exactly given the best *Protecting People You Love 101* course. It's a flipping miracle you survived your childhood," Sean answered, tension suddenly rising.

Confused, and a little hurt for the first time in a long time, L.D. didn't respond. She withdrew into silence, watching her day-old wedding party pedicure wiggle and disappear into the sand over and over. Wondering if they could ever have a friendly acquaintance beyond tonight. Wondering if she should just turn and walk to her room.

"Listen."

Without covering her ears this time, L.D. complied. She looked up into Sean's eyes to see that he was seeking hers, though deeply in thought. His previous argument wasn't even complete. How many times had she simply not let him finish talking?

"I'm *protecting* you. The same way you protect that snow globe you keep at my parents' house," he continued. "If the snow globe had feelings, it'd think you abandoned it there because you don't care about it. And that every time you did your little kiss goodbye thing that you were saying, 'Sorry, you're not good enough for me to take you home yet.' It wouldn't have a concept of the home life you had with your drug addict mother and her psychopathic boyfriends. It wouldn't know that it's probably your most valued possession. Or that, for now, it's only safe on that shelf at my parents' house, no matter how painful that is for you. It would just think you were being mean, and you hated it."

"That's a good metaphor for the way my *mom* protected me." L.D. nodded, convicting Sean. "We used to move across the country twice a year when I was little. When she realized I found the miracle that was your family, we didn't move again. And she left me with you all the time while she was off with those boyfriends. It was better that way, and we both understood that. She had less of a chance to corrupt me, and those boyfriends never laid a hand on me like that guy at the bar. I'm thankful for what she did, even if it was technically neglect. What I *don't* understand, Sean, is how my snow globe explains the horrible way *you* treat me. There's nothing you need to protect me from." L.D. was candid. Honest.

Sean answered her, honesty for honesty, "I know you love your mom, and I wasn't trying to insult her. Despite her, you grew up into this—" He hiccuped, but something inside him urged him to continue. "Into this *incredible* woman. God only made *one* person like you, Lavender-Dawn Meadow George. And I spent a lot of my childhood trying to decide whether I wanted to be more *like* you or if I wanted to be *with* you. As an adult, I can see it's probably both. But that what I *don't* want is for *you* to be like *me*. And I know it would corrupt you to be *with* me. Until tonight, you've never been a part of my disgusting world. So, if I keep you away from me, even if I have to be a jerk to do it, I can keep you, you know, *you*."

"What do you mean *with* me?" L.D. was flattered by everything, but asked for the clarification casually, unaware how raw and vulnerable he'd been with that one word.

He laughed first. Looked to the sand. He repeated only that one word, somehow managing to keep his nerves and tears intact. "With."

L.D.'s eyes widened for a split second before she corrected it. She cleared her throat and asked for clarification. "Like, together?"

"Yeah."

"Like a physical thing, or. . .?" she asked further clarification.

"No!" Sean put up his hands defensively to comfort her, then saw her deflate a little. "And yes! You're. . ." He laughed, mussing his hair, grunting at the night sky. "I've never done this before. You'll have to cut me some slack."

"I'm pretty sure there's not much you've never done with a woman, Sean," she teased.

"Except the things I *actually* want to do." He laughed at himself. "The thing is, I don't want to do the things I want to do with anyone but you. But for you, it shouldn't be me. Does that make *any* sense? I know I'm not making sense."

She processed a moment. Formulated a question she knew would change her life. "What do you want to do with me, Sean?"

He first laughed. "Everything." Then cleared his throat. "I know that's crazy. I know it's probably not possible. I feel like an idiot just saying it. But for a long time, I've wanted to be the safe place where you can bring home your snow globe. So, there it is."

L.D. was in distress. Standing with her little purse across her body. The sandals in the crook of her elbow, and a now empty souvenir mug in that hand. Sean's confession filling in all the empty space. She preferred to pack much lighter.

Her free hand went to her brow, and she ran her fingers through from the roots of her hair, finishing at the tips that grazed her backside when she stood. And finally, she found the use of her tongue again.

"This doesn't make sense. A guy who knows what he wants and has it right in front of him doesn't need to sow his wild oats."

"Unless it takes that to *distract* him while what he wants finds what *she* wants so he can finally see her happy," Sean debated further.

"Here's the problem, Sean." She sighed. Tears welling. "You think you have some say over who God does or doesn't appoint for me. You are seriously screwing with the system here by trying to make me hate you."

"The 'system'?" Sean laughed a little. "I thought you were an anti-establishment kind of gal."

"Okay, the plan. God's plan." She tried again.

"What plan?"

"Your parents wanted to *adopt* me when I was thirteen. But when I was *twelve* God told me he was preparing me to be your wife." L.D. accosted with fervor.

"Wait, preparing *you*?" Sean laughed. Stepping back. Processing. "*I'm* the one that needs preparing. *You're* perfect."

"Far from it. I needed to learn to love you the way you are." L.D. shrugged. "I figured it'd be easy. You accepted Christ that year. After that, I spent a few years pretending God didn't say it and just hanging out with S.R. while you went through several awkward pubescent phases. Finally, when my sweet little Sean woke up as a heartthrob, you also started rebelling against God. And then you started teasing me. The past few years, the teasing has turned into cruelty, and here I am, twenty-five and still *saving* myself. But you keep sowing those oats. . .”

“So, wait, you’re telling me we could have had like four kids by now and we’re both still single for no reason?” Sean tried to find the less sincere in the impossibly grave. “Did God bar you from *telling* me? If I knew I could have *you*. . .”

“Dad always advised your sisters and I to wait until we were pursued, and that’s what I’m doing. Still waiting.” With that, L.D. crushed his spirit.

“I don’t know what to do with this. I know I’m not who God wants me to be, and you deserve better than even my best,” Sean said. “And I’ve treated you. . .” He sighed. Nearly releasing the tears.

“And yet He loves you. And died for you. When you chase after Him, He loves you. When you chase tail, He loves you. If you let Him, He’ll transform you in ways you can’t fathom. If you don’t let Him, He still loves you, and can use you to His glory, just as you are.” L.D. sniffled.

Sean cleared his throat of the tears. “How can you know that?”

“Because I’m just a faulty human and that’s how *I* love you. Imagine how much more He’s capable of putting up with.” She wiped a tear. Laughed. Nodded.

“I don’t. . .” Sean sighed. He abruptly began his lifelong commitment to honesty. “I don’t think you’re faulty. You’re the bravest person I know. I caught you witnessing to a guy that was going to *assault* you.”

L.D. snorted laughter.

Sean continued his rant. “And your shampoo smells like Heaven and makes me want to die inside. And the sandals are sexy. And I’m sorry for every time I’ve ever said anything horrible to you.”

She shrugged. Distorted her face with skepticism. “I don’t think you did.”

Sean laughed. "You need a hospital."

"It's true. I finally stopped listening to what you were *saying* tonight, and it was enlightening." She raised an eyebrow and hovered her hand and coffee mug near her ears.

"Oh, when you covered your ears? That has to be one of the quirkiest things you've ever done," Sean confessed.

"Sorry," L.D. explained. "Eric told me recently I should try listening to you like he does. Back at that bar, God convicted me the same way. That was just the only way I could think to do it in a pinch."

"Interesting." Sean nodded. "Is this an exercise you'd recommend?"

"Yeah, I didn't realize how much I was missing by letting you speak." L.D. giggled. Suddenly overwhelmingly comfortable with a person she was scared to be around a couple of hours ago.

"So, I just. . .?" He silenced the ocean with his hands as L.D. nodded, laughing.

That's when he decided that however beautiful her laugh had always been flowing from Sharon's room when they were teenagers or displacing his soul at wedding receptions with dancing and smiles, it took on far more beauty when he watched her body and hair tense and ebb and flow in completely silent joy.

The laughter waned, and Sean took a step toward her, watching her smile coyly. The ocean breeze taking that dress against her legs and his heart to screaming, when he'd have foolishly responded by making fun of all of it yesterday. Sean advanced in this manner, a step at a time, right beyond Lavender-Dawn's realm of comfort, if he'd been anyone else. But her toes were stayed firmly in the sand, and at first when Sean dipped his head, no other senses but his lips perceived hers.

The ocean roared again, along with his soul, as he put a hand on a delicate waist he always presumed would tarnish and shatter at his touch. Before he could rethink it, the kiss swelled with hunger like the crashing waves and the dead of the night. And, though confused and shocked, L.D. let him do it. With the next breath, she kissed him back. Like it was her natural rhythm.

After the kiss, he exhaled, resting his head on her forehead in silence. Searching her eyes in the night.

"Come up to my room with me," he whispered, allowing a hand to run along her spine.

"Are you insane?" she fretted. Thinking about pepper spray suddenly.

"We could talk about all this a little more."

"Sean."

"Or not talk."

"No, Sean! I think you know that." L.D. hoped he did. "Your room is between mine and S.R.'s and your parents'."

"Oh." Cleared his throat. "So not because you're not willing to."

"As much as I'd like to believe I'm capable of telling you no, I'm also willing to do whatever you ask. So please don't ask," she ended in a whisper.

"Sorry. Yes. Leave the snow globe on the shelf for now and kiss it whenever I can. Got it."

"Sean, if you have some weird Spring Break island fever, I'd like to not be a victim of it considering how close I am with your family," L.D. confessed. "A one-night stand doesn't have to include sex, you know. This could hurt us both. You already took my first kiss without asking. And you've hurt me a lot over the years. You can't just—"

Sean sighed in ecstasy. Kissed her again. "Can I have your last kiss, too? Let's get married. If God says you're mine, I'll take your word for it."

"You did not just propose to me." She laughed. "While barely sober. The same night you used an app on your phone to hook up with a teenager."

"See, I knew I wasn't good enough for you!" Sean gritted through angry teeth.

"I told you, I love you as you are! I've loved you however you've *been*. For years. And I love you far too much today for this night to end in your room. Your instructions about who is being prepared for whom need to come from God. I *know* He didn't authorize a sleepover in the meantime," L.D. defended both of their honor.

"I don't remember mentioning sleep." Sean laughed, meaning to be endearing. Lighthearted as before.

"You're disgusting." But she didn't take it that way.

"That's what you're *saying*, but. . ." He kissed her one last time, her natural response excruciating and wonderful.

"Sean, stop it. You're acting like that Neanderthal." She pushed him away and headed to the resort a hundred yards away. "Don't do that again."

"Sure. I'm. . .I'm sorry." Sean sighed. He watched her walk to the resort under the increasing lamp light while I tortured him at the beach.

You'll never be good enough for her. She doesn't even take you seriously. You smoke. You drink. You have some nasty, disgusting habits. It doesn't matter that you've loved her most of your life or that she thinks God made her for you. You've ruined any chance with her. She'll never take you as you are.

"No," he said aloud, agreeing with me. "But I know Someone who might."

To my complete dismay, Sean Joseph Mehlmann hit his knees in the sand on a pitch-dark beach where he kissed the woman of his dreams. And decided to take his next walk with Christ. Allowing Him to begin His work.

6

The Beach's Words

"This is so stupid. I'm not going." Sharon, sitting on the edge of her bed in a blue one-piece bathing suit, was changing her mind.

You look terrible. Just stay inside and watch TV, I told Sharon.

"S.R., please don't make me go alone? What's the point in a beach resort of we don't even go to the beach?" L.D. pleaded, standing at Sharon's feet in a navy and white polka dotted, ruffled, red bowed one-piece that she picked up at the thrift store.

Sharon contemplated while L.D. listened to me and tortured herself.

But what if Sean is at the beach? You'll have to pass by the spot where he kissed you. Can you really do that without letting on to anything? Maybe you should stay in too. The girls on the beach are ten times more appealing to him. He'll probably forget it ever happened.

The taste of it was finally gone after his recent few cigarettes and alcohol had turned her stomach with the kisses. But she could still feel the warmth of his mouth against hers. The wrap of steady arms about her. Unexpected as it was, L.D.'s heart had pounded enough that she was terrified he'd hear it and tease her. When he had asked her to join him in his room, she had been tempted to, knowing he'd fill the hours of the night with those kisses. But that same thought had terrified her. Just like the beach was doing at that moment.

"Can we limit it to an hour?"

"Sure, S.R." L.D. smiled lovingly, and the two women headed down to the beach.

They had a good time at first. L.D. couldn't decide whether she was relieved, worried or just plain disappointed that Sean was nowhere to be found. The women, both slathered in sunscreen, drank fruity little drinks with umbrellas and sat laughing on the beach. L.D. felt like she was fibbing when the two were making fun of where Sean probably was. Probably hungover. Probably entertaining a girl in the room their parents paid for.

Sean saw them laughing. He was out on his balcony smoking. Watching all the beauty. Loving that L.D. got his sister to go to the beach. Loving L.D. in general, actually. But knowing just how far he was from her good graces, let alone her embrace. He shook off the longing and peered back into the open app on his phone.

"That which is born of flesh is flesh, and that which is born of the Spirit is spirit. Do not marvel that I said to you, 'You must be born again.' "

As smoke filled John 3, Sean saw the juxtaposition. A lit cigarette in one hand, a story of rebirth in the other. And everything he wanted so far away he couldn't even hear what they were laughing about. If he needed to be reborn and L.D. was born of the Spirit as a child, how could he ever grow enough for her? He'd *never* get to where she was. At least that's what I told him.

There isn't a more hopeless word than *never*. The impact of eternity is so simple to burden them with. Sean could *never* have L.D. because he'd *never* deserve her. Sharon would *never* look like the size two and four bikini clad bridesmaids. She'd *never* attract a man. L.D. could *never* get that kiss out of her head. And she told Sean to *never* give her another. So hopeless, so easily. All in one word. And yet Sean was thinking about righteousness. L.D. was laughing about bikinis. Sharon was having a good time. On a beach. I guess not even *never* could stop their joy.

But sometimes people do my job for me.

"OMG. Do you see that beached whale?" The voice, of course, of Brielle.

L.D. heard it first and looked around the beach for a literal whale.

The next one laughed. "Is she serious in that suit? You're right. All I can think is 'Baby Beluga.' "

They were talking about Sharon. She sat up from her joyous recline and removed her sun hat. Not knowing what to do but fidget.

Sophie and Eric had told everyone that they'd spend the weekend after the wedding hiding in their room at the resort and begin their honeymoon beach ventures after everyone left St. John. So, they weren't around to protest. Sean could see, but not hear. He didn't know to rescue. Only L.D. was around.

"Belugas are white," was all she could manage. Hating herself for freezing when Sharon needed her most.

"Well thank God she didn't expose us to *that*," another of them said. "Can you imagine?"

Sharon was already halfway back to the resort before L.D. gathered the rest of their things. Sharon barely made it off the elevator before the tears started to flow. The sobs began outside their door, but by the time the other residents recognized the sound, Sharon was inside. Samuel, Lynn, and Sean Mehlmann met only L.D. out in the hall.

"What happened?" Sean had to refrain from commenting on L.D.'s attire before he asked it.

"Sophie's stupid friends just called S.R. a *whale*," L.D. whispered at the end. "That was officially the last time I'll get her to come to the beach with me. They are so *horrible*. She was having such a good time."

Sean wanted to embrace her, but refrained, and instead got out his phone. Lynn was gasping, and Samuel was cracking his knuckles.

"I'm calling Sophie down here. She needs to know about this."

"Sean! Absolutely not. Sophie is on her honeymoon," Mom scolded.

"I don't care, Mom! It's not like Eric hasn't had plenty of time with her." Sean used a recently learned sign at his stomach— *pregnant*—before hitting send on his phone.

While he was trying to convince the newlyweds to come down from their top floor honeymoon suite, L.D. realized she didn't have her room key and started pounding on the door. Sharon only answered with more sobbing. L.D. was stuck in the hall with the awkwardness of arms full of beach gear, in a bathing suit. With the guy that no one knew laid one, or five, on her last night. And his parents. So, she relinquished all the gear, and leaned against the wall, braiding her hair over her shoulder.

"Don't say a word," she said to Sean when he hung up the phone.

"Don't worry, I'm speechless at the moment," Sean said, partially regarding Sharon's situation. But since his back was to his parents, he also winked at L.D. as he looked to his phone again.

Soon after, L.D.'s phone vibrated in the pile somewhere.

"Oh! Maybe she's texting me." But when she retrieved her own phone from a bag, Sharon's was with it. She read the text she had.

"I found a place that has vegan key lime pie and thought of you. Will you go with me tonight? I want to talk to you. Sharon needs you. She goes to bed at nine. I'll meet you at our beach streetlight at 9:30. We'll take a cab together."

Crafty Sean pocketed his phone, looking around and pretending not to have just texted L.D. She was not even able to react aloud with his parents present.

"I'm not going to date you," she responded quickly.

Sean's phone chimed. He smirked at the reply.

"You kids and those phones," Samuel noted as Sean typed another reply.

"The other receptionist has no clue how to do her job. She texts me a lot." L.D. didn't lie. But it was just random information in this instance.

"I was just checking up on my usual partner. He got scheduled with the village idiot and was pretty miffed that I'm out this week." Sean chuckled. Sending his text and pretending to continue typing so L.D.'s text was not connected to his.

"I'm in love with you. We'll be alone at night in paradise. But this is not a date. Stop coming onto me. Seriously though. Just talking. And milk-less pie." L.D. smirked at the text and typed a reply.

"9:30. Don't try to kiss me or I'm gone." After receiving the text, Sean pocketed his phone with no further replies.

By the time Sophie and Eric arrived and L.D. explained the situation with Sharon, Sophie's young friends were taking the perfect moment to step off the elevator with laughter and girlish chatter.

"Is it true?" Sophie asked them.

"Is *what* true?" Brielle asked.

"You made fun of my sister," Sophie said with the same attitude.

"She didn't belong on that beach," another one said.

"Are you kidding me?" Sean began. "Why the heck not?"

"She's disgusting. No one wants to see that." Brielle laughed. Silenced to listen for something. "Aww, is she crying? How sad. Maybe she should lose weight."

Dad was forming a calm, peaceful rebuttal, but hormonal Sophie lost her cool immediately and slapped Brielle across the face.

"She is my big sister, you wench! If you can't handle her being around, you need to stay away from me and my family. I cannot believe I let you all stand next to me at my wedding."

Brielle rubbed her cheek as she walked away. "Between your fat pregnant belly, your retarded husband, and your disgusting sister, you needed something beautiful up there."

"Oh my God, you did not just insult my husband," Sophie began, but Samuel interrupted.

"Hey, Brielle?"

"Yes, sir?" Respect from that mouth? They were all surprised.

"Am I paying for your room?" he asked.

"I believe so." She smiled.

"Not anymore. I think checkout time is in a half hour. I'll go let them know you won't be staying the final night." Dad backed into an open elevator. "None of you are welcome here any longer. You better pack quick and hope there are vacancies elsewhere."

"But Mr. Mehl—" The elevator door closed.

L.D. snorted laughter. Brielle's eyes shot to her.

"You're friggin' gorgeous, you know that? Too bad for your secondhand swimwear and sunbathing with baby whales." Brielle's lip pouted mockingly. "Otherwise you could actually *be* something."

"Quit, Brielle." Sean was torn between defending the woman he loved and saving face.

"Sean, I'm out of a room. Mind sharing for a night? I'll make it worth your while." Brielle took to harlotry.

L.D.'s jealousy suddenly surfaced, and she barely made it through the next few moments without letting on.

Sean only barely faked the gag. "Sorry, Brielle. I have plans tonight. Most of which include 'hell no.' "

The girls disappeared, cruelly sniggering.

"I'm really sorry. I didn't think they'd be so. . ." Sophie sighed. Eric put his arms around her shoulders from behind.

"Nothing a pint won't fix." L.D. knocked on the door again. "S.R.! Let me in so I can check if room service has rocky road!"

"L.D., that's not gonna solve this," Sophie said. "They were making fun of her for being, you know, *big*."

"Seriously?" L.D. laughed in disbelief. "The problem is not with S.R.'s weight, the problem is with *them*. Tell me how you're not being exactly the same way right now."

"Still, you don't want to encourage bad habits just because she's upset." From Lynn, whose love for her first-born child was twice the capacity any of them understood. Except the absent Samuel.

"No offense, Mom. But she needs to know that she is loved just the way she is," L.D. said.

Samuel stepped out of the elevator and handed L.D. a new key, then went into his room. L.D. finished her thought, pointing around the hall.

"You all need to figure that out or she'll never be motivated to do anything. Ever." She slid her key card until the lock shone green and clicked.

"Hey, don't point at me! You know I love Sharon as-is," Sean defended, handing L.D. the pile from the hall.

"Don't get me started on *your* issues, Sean," L.D. lashed.

"Come on, Lavender-Dawn Meadow George, I—"

"And can you quit with the thing with my name? It's not cute!" L.D. landed safely behind a closed door with her best friend.

Sharon sniffled. "I already ordered ice cream. And they even had some frozen grapes, so they are sending some of those up too."

L.D. sat on the bed with Sharon and threw her arms around her.

"I love you so much," L.D. said. "I hate everyone in the world but you right now. Including me."

Sharon smiled a little. "Well *I* love you. But you're right. The rest of the world can just go die."

"Except the room service guy that's bringing the goods," L.D. concluded. And by the time their signature treats arrived, there was some laughter in their tears. And so little doubt in one another that I had to spend the day with Brielle.

7

Stormy's Purpose

"Sean, we'll miss the flight! We have to get through security," Lynn urged. "There are smoking rooms on the other side."

But Sean, after days of loving on only a Bible app in his room, was busy standing in front of an outdoor trash can, a pack of cigarettes in his hand. His last pack. He looked immobile to them, but he was listening.

Cold turkey, are you kidding? There's no way you can do that.

"I don't know if I can, but I know I need to."

L.D. was looking at him. Or trying not to look at him. Or trying to otherwise engage herself. Looking now to Sharon, who I was much more interested in as well.

Yep. You heard her right. She called you a whale. And they all laughed. I told you not to buy the blue suit. You are a big blue whale, Sharon. Not that the color made a difference.

And visibly, she was in tears. Still. After two days of L.D. taking her to markets and Cathedrals and even historical libraries on an island paradise. Nothing had truly helped.

"The joke is on them for not being able to see how beautiful you are, my Rose of Sharon," Samuel said as they approached the ticket counter.

"Yeah, so 'beautiful' I'm worth two plane tickets," Sharon reminded him. "No one is ever going to be okay with who I am, Dad."

"Besides God. And everyone who loves you. And every reasonable person who has ever met you." L.D. sighed.

"You have to put up with me, you're family." Sharon sighed.

"Well *they* are. I *choose* to love you," L.D. commented. "A choice I'd make a million times. We all would."

Which is when Sean joined them in line, looking like he'd just watched his house burn to the ground. L.D. inquired, but only with her eyes, since she had to act normal. And normally, she'd avoid Sean.

"I just tossed my last pack of cigarettes," he mumbled, only to L.D.

"What?! Why?" she said with quiet.

"Well, I'll go through withdrawals on the plane anyway. So, I figure, why not make it count? I have two more days off work, so I'll just use them to feel like absolute guano and quit smoking." Sean laughed. "They say your lungs start to heal immediately. I've always known that, I just didn't care, I guess."

"You're an idiot." L.D. crossed her arms, shaking her head.

"That's probably true, however you just meant it. But I came as I was. Hoping He would fix me. I know I'm a disaster. And all I could read in the Bible was about not being carnally minded and being sober. So, I figure if I want to listen, I need to not have that other stuff in me that makes me feel like everything is great when it isn't. . .what?" he asked of L.D.'s shocked gaze.

"Bible?" she asked.

"In the hotel room. I used to make fun of the fact that they're in every hotel, but this time I was grateful for it," he clarified. Wondering why she was wondering. "Then I downloaded one I liked a little better on my phone. I read a good chunk of the New Testament and found this really good pastor online and I can't get enough. Didn't I tell you that when we had pie?"

"You seemed more concerned about whether smoking is a sin," L.D. recalled. "And other questions. I figured you were still *avoiding* the Bible and just asking me."

"There aren't cigarettes in the Bible. Well. . .like I said I'm not completely done with it yet." Sean sighed. "But you clarified things. Mostly how you felt about smoking, and that matters. *You* matter."

L.D. cleared her throat. Redirected the subject. "But is it safe? You've been smoking for a decade. I told you, God doesn't say specifically that you can't smoke or that you have to risk your life to quit cold turkey."

"I *want* to quit. I feel like from *me*, God does want that." Sean slapped on his charm. "And plus, the girl of my dreams absolutely *hates* smokers, so if I ever want a chance with her. . ."

"Shh! Sean," she whispered. "You said it wasn't a date the other night. We had pie and talked about the Bible."

"And had a good time together." Sean smiled. "Just like our long walk on the beach that *almost* ended well."

"Sean, I'm serious." L.D. rolled her eyes. "You need to stop. It's awkward. Don't quit smoking for me."

"You kissed me back," he whispered, pretending to rub his nose and look like he wasn't even speaking. "Several *incredible* times."

"Sean. . ." L.D.'s heart started to pounding again.

"Am I wrong?" he asked.

"You're not wrong. But I think *that* was." L.D. sighed. "You almost convinced me to do something we'd have regretted for a lifetime."

"I agree. I shouldn't have done or said what I did. Yet another conviction. I'm sorry for the way it went down. But I'm really glad I finally told you." Sean smirked a little. Bent her heart to breaking. "For now, all I want you to do for me, if you're willing, is help me quit smoking. I don't want to enlist the help of my parents and Sharon's having a rough time, but I'm not really a Bible scholar yet, so if you could, like, text me a verse or two to keep me on track? Just if you think about it over the next two days. Because I honestly don't know how I'm gonna handle it."

"Handle what?" Sharon asked. Having only heard those words.

"If they put me next to her on this flight like they did last time. Seriously, someone needs to commit fraud to trade with me if that happens," Sean recovered with suave.

"I'm sorry he is such a jerk, L.D. One of these days I think he'll grow up," Sharon apologized.

"You have so much more hope for him than I do, S.R." L.D. smiled, nodding a little at Sean. Which was the beginning of a secret I told them from the beginning they could never keep.

* * *

"I hate being fat." Sharon sobbed, wounds opening up as L.D. helped her unpack from the trip to busy her hands. "I hate everything about me."

"You're beautiful inside and out. Stop listening to the idiots that tell you otherwise." She sighed, quickly tucking the pink maid of honor dress into Sharon's closet.

"I'm one of those idiots," Sharon said, referring to me, of course. Ouch.

"It's an epidemic. But quit," L.D. demanded of her. "The standard for beauty these days is impossible. You have to decide that you are beautiful the way God made you, not the way the plastic photoshopped Barbies on magazines are."

"But I'm not beautiful. He made me wrong." Sharon sniffled.

"I assure you, He did not." L.D. rolled her eyes, then looked at her phone in response to a text.

"Lavender-Dawn Meadow George, I could use some encouragement not to go buy a thousand cigarettes and smoke them all today."

L.D. thought a moment. Texted him a standard. *"Psalms 46:1. God is our refuge and strength, A very present help in trouble."*

"Sophie and her friends aren't photoshopped," Sharon argued.

"They wear a pound of makeup, barely eat, work out more than is healthy, and I'm pretty sure Brielle's boobs are fake, meaning you already rock the societal standard in that area." L.D. giggled. So did Sharon.

"Well what about you? Do you even *own* makeup?"

"Yes! I wore mascara to the wedding, remember?" she said.

"None of you is fake, and you're perfect."

L.D. sighed. "Oh, if we could all walk around inside out for a day."

"Then you'd still be prettier than me," Sharon confessed.

"And Brielle would resemble a cross between a dragon and a dead mule," L.D. said as she read her next text.

"Thanks, Lavender-Dawn Meadow George. I wonder if 'Not barfing anymore today' is included in God's 'help.' "

"That bad, huh?" she replied.

"Worse, I assure you, Lavender-Dawn Meadow George."

L.D. was annoyed. Concerned. Sharon was confused.

"Who keeps texting you?"

"No one. Actually, someone, I just. . .you know, actually, would you kill me if I had to go take care of something? It's important."

"Would you still leave if I was a positive person who was skinny?" Sharon hated her self-loathing. A vicious cycle. She sighed at tears.

L.D. laughed. "Yeah, except I'd feed you a steak first. I'll come back later, okay?"

Sharon nodded at her compassionate friend as she headed out. She contemplated why she even needed to be around if not even her best friend thought she was as important as something else that she kept a mystery.

• • •

"Just open the door, Sean." L.D. stood outside his apartment listening to the moans.

He barely opened the door before turning and collapsing back onto the couch.

"Yikes." L.D. looked around at the disheveled apartment and closed the door behind her.

"What are you doing here, Lavender-Dawn Meadow George?" he rasped, wincing at the light.

"You feel like crap, and you still have to say my entire name? The whole thing?" L.D. sighed, sitting on the couch near his torso, setting a bag down on the coffee table with a glassy clink. "So, what are your current symptoms?"

"You didn't answer my question, Lavender-Dawn Meadow George," he said with a slight smile.

"Oh, come on!" She sighed. "I'm here because the texting was getting annoying. How can you even see well enough to type my *entire* name? I have some things that might help you."

"Did you rob a pharmacy?" he asked, sitting up.

"Yes, because I've been to a pharmacy in my life," said the hippie. "Oils. I have oils. Can you handle the idea of that?"

"Oils? How is oil going to cure me?"

"Essential oils. Symptoms please. I can't cure you, but I think I can really help."

"My head is exploding, and I barfed all night, so I think I won't be able to kiss you this time." He smirked. "But *that* would totally help."

"Funny." She rolled her eyes, digging through her bag. "You have water nearby?"

"I *do* work in the medical field. We like water. Cures stuff like dehydration from barfing." Sean reached for the bottle on the table.

"Good boy." L.D. mocked, quickly holding a dropper over the mouth of the bottle and letting one drop splash into the bottle. "This makes the water *do* something for your stomach."

L.D. grabbed another amber colored bottle and let one drop fall onto her fingertips. She began gently massaging it into Sean's temples, rendering him gelatinous at her touch.

"This always helped with my mom's migraines," she whispered. "It won't cure the withdrawal process, Sean. But you have to understand that sometimes God calms the storm. And sometimes He calms His child."

He sighed. His body beginning to calm. His spirit aching for her. "This is amazing." He groaned. She giggled and concluded the massage.

"Now cravings." L.D. pulled a tissue from the box on the table. "I made you a blend that if you put a drop on a tissue and inhale it for a couple minutes or however long you'd normally take to smoke a cigarette, it should help curb that particular craving and put more time before the next one. I'm giving these to you neat. It's pure. Full strength. So only a drop, okay?"

Sean complied with her instructions, breathing into a tissue. After a moment, he looked into L.D.'s eyes. Smiled. "Will you marry me?"

She laughed once. "Not today. But I will leave these blends for you. I labeled them and wrote out the instructions. Don't overdo it. You can overdose, just like with all the synthetic, poisonous nonsense you give to people all day."

"You're leaving?" he whined.

"I was with S.R. and I have to go back. But I have an errand to run first. I was hoping you'd come with me, but I understand if you can't." She bit a lip.

"I'd love to, Lavender-Dawn Meadow George. But I'm due for a make out session with my toilet any minute."

"Bring the water and the craving blend and you'll be fine," she urged. "Get dressed. Let's go."

"They say animals love unconditionally, right? I've never actually owned one," L.D. mused. Sean moaned.

"Why am I here, Lavender-Dawn Meadow George?" Sean complained about being at an animal shelter instead of at home in bed.

"You needed to get out of your stuffy, smoky apartment," L.D. said. "I'll find you a diffuser. I have some oils to help with the smell. Your smoky stuff will start to disgust you soon."

"I think these are all excuses to spend time with me," Sean suggested. "And talk about when we can kiss again. Every time I do the thing with the tissue, I think about that kiss. Helps the craving go away faster."

"What about the verses I've been sending you?" L.D. laughed. "Maybe think about one of those."

"Verses are good." Sean closed his eyes. "Lavender-Dawn Meadow George makes my *knees* weak."

"Please stop calling me that? It's creepy."

"You took me on a date. Against my will. To an animal shelter. And you're asking me not to call you by your name. Who is creepy now?" Sean reasoned.

"This isn't a date. This is me being concerned about someone I love. And you're the only other person that loves her like I do." L.D. stated her true motive.

"Sharon? What's wrong with Sharon?" Sean immediately jumped into rescue mode.

"People are so horrible to her and she's just amazing and no one sees it but us, Sean. Even your mom was saying she's too big. I'm scared she'll hurt herself and we'll lose her, and she'll never know how important she is." L.D. poured out her soul at the ailing Sean's feet.

Sean nodded. "So, you want to get her an animal because we can't always be there? Lavender-Dawn Meadow George, we are *always* there for her."

"Stop it, Sean."

"Violet Morning Field Washington?" he suggested.

"Sean!"

"Lavender-Dawn?"

"Better." She smiled. "But no."

"Meadow? We could be on a *middle* name basis."

"That would work, Joseph, except my middle name is the *worst* one."

"Do you like your *last* name?"

"Yes. It's strong and masculine and the farthest thing from my other ridiculous names. But if you call me George, I'll make you bleed," she promised with a smile.

"What about Georgie?" he asked, raising his eyebrows. "I hate 'L.D..' You're too beautiful for a name like that."

"Sure, Sean. Call me Georgie." L.D. rolled her eyes, annoyed.

"You can call me Sean." He shrugged with humor.

"Good. I like your name. It's a variation of the name 'John' which means 'gift from God.' And you know how I love the gospel of John." L.D. winked.

"That was the first book of the Bible I ever read," Sean confessed with a big smile.

"Really?" L.D. was impressed. "You said New Testament, I assumed you'd have started with Matthew."

"I would have. Or I would have Googled the best place to start. But because of our conversation that night prior to the one that we're pretending didn't happen, I started with John. I didn't know where to start, and as it turns out that was a good place for me to get to know Jesus. I cried like a baby through most of it. I also binge-watched a pastor who was teaching through John, and it made even more sense." Sean cleared his throat, smiling a little. Then, as usual, he shied away from sustained sincerity. "So why do we need to get a pet for my sister, Georgie?"

"Because it will love her for who she is and will never call her cruel awful things or even be able to understand the concept of her being overweight. People suck. She can't see how God loves her, and I doubt she'd be willing to read through John like you, so she needs an animal." L.D. was in tears by the end of this. Still aching deeply for her best friend.

Sean smirked at the beauty of her soul. "Will you marry me?"

"Again. . .not today." L.D. wondered if he was even listening.

He nodded, smiling at a couple of puppies playing behind the glass. "I used to know how to sign, you know. ASL? I learned before Sharon got her hearing back and we used to sign. But over time, I don't remember as much anymore. I hate it that I can't talk to Eric. Point being I *did* learn for her. I care about her. She's been my best friend a lot throughout the years."

"I know, Sean. Why do you think I'm asking *you* to do this?"

Sean leaned against that window with dogs behind it. "Sharon works really hard. She's not home a lot. I've called her late in the evening and she's been at work, planning for the next day or whatever. She adores those kids."

"Yeah, but they're not enough, Sean."

"Would you quit whining? All I'm trying to say is we're in the wrong area. Sharon's *clearly* a cat person." Sean stood up and led the way back around the corner.

"So, you'll help me pick one?" L.D. jumped up and down.

"I'm trying really hard, and I can't think of anything I wouldn't do for you. Sharon. I mean Sharon." Sean pretended to have mis-stepped, accepting the shove to his arm.

"Stop!" she insisted.

"Will you go to dinner with me, Georgie?" Sean was sincere again. "No kissing. Just dinner. You and me. And a nice conversation like when we had pie. And maybe some temple massaging."

"I need to think about that," L.D. told him, ever so gently. "I don't mind talking, of course. But S.R.'s having a tough time. The cat isn't meant to replace her best friend or her brother. Sean, if we get involved, she'll be devastated. Can we at least wait for her to be in a better place? Those stupid bridesmaids were so mean."

"Agreed. Sharon first," Sean conceded. "But don't call her S.R. around me."

"Why?" L.D. giggled.

"Same thing. She's too beautiful." Sean shrugged. "Dad named her after a flower. Have you seen a Rose of Sharon? It's the only thing that comes close enough to her beauty. Don't call her S.R. That's *way* off."

"Okay." L.D. smiled, always having found beauty in Sean's love for his sister. "Sharon."

"I'm sorry." Sean winced. "For coming onto you all the time."

"That was super convincing." L.D. shook a sarcastic head.

"I love that I'm finally able to be *friends* with you. And the closer I get to God, the more I want to be. . .more. Crazy, right?" Sean got too close to sincere with that one and immediately sighed. "Let's just pick a cat. For Sharon. I can't stand how sad she is all the time. And you're right. She'd be pissed if we, you know, decided to be an 'us' at this point."

"Just so you know, Sean, it's not crazy, okay? It's just bad timing." L.D. began to wring her hands.

"So, do you like me at least a *little*?" Sean held up a thumb and forefinger an inch apart like a child. Smiling into the question with a squinted eye.

"I'm glad we're being civil. And I told you how I felt."

"I don't mean as a *friend*, Georgie."

"Sean, I kissed you. I had pepper spray. So many options. But I *kissed* you." L.D. sighed, hipping her hands. "To you that's nothing. But I'd never. . ." She smiled at his giddy grin. "Yes. I like you as more than a friend. Are we twelve? Because I feel twelve saying that. Um. . .I like spending time with you? I think you're handsome? How do adults do this?" She snorted laughter at her childhood companion.

He laughed. "I just went for gold and proposed to you after we sucked face, so I do support you if you'd like to go that route."

L.D. sighed quickly. Awkwardly and abruptly changing the subject. "Cat," she demanded. And the two shifted their focus, at least for now.

Sean hobbled into Sharon's apartment with the manifestation of the entire list of even "suggested" things needed for a cat. L.D. followed with the tiny gray treasure in a carrier.

"We have something for you," L.D. allowed. "I didn't want to come back empty handed."

"We? Since when do you and Sean agree on *anything*?"

"I was the second choice. First choice is on her honeymoon," Sean half-lied, setting down the load in Sharon's living room. "And I came to Christ—for real, I mean. He told me not to be so mean to my sister's best friend."

"Came to Christ?" Sharon asked.

Sean kept forgetting in those days that the rest of the universe hadn't been in that hotel room with him when he met his Savior. It was an earth-shaking, life-changing encounter. Almost like a honeymoon, he'd thought then. The long-awaited consummation of a relationship he'd started as a child. But much more powerful. Him saying he "came to Christ" was, to him, like Sophie saying, "I just got married" times a million. But no one reacted to it properly. No one but L.D., who was, fortunately, present.

She explained, "he's 'transformed'. Working on Sean 2.0, if you will. For instance, he hasn't had a cigarette since just before we got on the plane the other day."

"I see. Good job, Sean. So, you started my transition into 'cat lady'? Is that Sharon 2.0?" Sharon asked bitterly, looking at the items they brought.

Sean's eyes got big. He turned them accusingly to L.D.

"Don't look at *me*!" L.D. said. "I was thinking dog. But Sean was worried that with your work schedule it wouldn't get enough attention. Could you *not* though, S.R.? This kitten is sooo sweet. You'll like her. Have someone to come home to."

"L.D., *you're* here half the time when I get home," Sharon reasoned. Pointed at her brother. "He's here the other half."

"My apartment is lonely," L.D. confessed.

"You always have ice cream. For the record, I drive by *every* day, but half the time her car is here so I just go home." Sean's confession. "Why are you two not roomies?"

"We tried that, Sean. We hated it. Especially since I have a studio. Do you have human memories. . .?" L.D. accused, remembering when Sharon moved in with L.D. to share the rent with her during college before either of them made enough money to easily cover it. It lasted six months and almost destroyed their friendship.

While Sean and L.D. pretended to bicker, Sharon was falling in love. She opened the cage and out climbed an apprehensive little gray tabby kitten with black and white stripes and splashes of ivory.

"She's *adorable*," Sharon said.

"They don't like people adopting animals as gifts, so I put her under my name. That way the last names match. They suggested a couple vets, but she's up to date on everything," Sean explained.

"Does she have a name?" Sharon wondered.

"Well the shelter had a name for her. It's in her paperwork. But they said you could choose your own," L.D. suggested.

"Hey, Stormy. It's nice to meet you," Sharon said immediately.

The three friends spent the afternoon setting up cat supplies, not knowing exactly how to use some of them and watching little Stormy play with bits of packaging material and bring Sharon's heart to joy. Well played, "Georgie." Well played.

The Man's Pursuit

The room was bright. A dreamy fog of laughter and linens against the morning. It began innocently; the sun casting beams into ash-brown hair and lavender eyes. But things progressed quickly in intensity and darkness. In the end, she awakened him with a few gentle words.

"I love you, Sean."

He sat up in a start as her words echoed against the jingle of his morning alarm, his heart pounding as before. It was the sort of dream a man hides in his heart. A burden he only shares with his Lord. He rose from bed that morning and ordered himself a shower—cold.

"I'm gonna need your help with this one, God," he whispered as he poured his coffee.

But half the morning, she was the only thing he cared to consider.

"You're not talking my ear off," his partner noted.

"I just don't feel like talking today," he replied.

Just then, a call came over the radio. A transport, they assumed. That had been the flavor that morning. Instead, it was a head-on collision.

"Yes!" his partner exclaimed as Sean threw the parked box into reverse.

The front lines. Little boys envision the glory of battle through a child's eyes. Visions of bayonets and canons fuel the need for professions that put them in the center of the battle. Fighting bad guys and saving lives is no different to them than slaying dragons and rescuing damsels. They grow, become those dragon slayers.

And see how tragic, how very different the reality is. Uriah the Hittite met his end on the front lines after valiantly refusing to go home to his wife. He is in the company of countless men across the ages. Sean nearly joined the ranks when he approached that head-on collision, and a weeping female police officer briefed him.

"It's bad," was all she could manage.

Sean approached to find tragedy. Georgie considered him a hero for having become an EMT and not requiring the glory of a paramedic or a doctor. Sean hadn't ruled it out, but he hadn't yet come to terms with the responsibilities of that profession. Whoever was in his hands as an EMT was a life. Death was never his to proclaim.

I'll spare you. But Sean immediately saw what he'd later note as "injuries incompatible with life." He never had to declare life impossible. He was simply a stabilizer and chauffer for the mortally wounded in this case. And at first, he couldn't focus on the job. The woman was young. Still had color in her cheeks. All he could think of was Georgie. Was she alright? Was she safe? Until his partner called out,

"We have a pulse over here, Mehlmann!"

Instantly, Georgie left his mind. They were able to stabilize another young woman and get her to the hospital. The job required his full attention. And in the end, all he could think about was getting into a hot shower to wash it away. At the end of his shift, Sean got a text.

"Haven't heard from you today. Everything okay?"

Georgie. That's right. The currently unattainable love of his life. He'd managed to not pine for half a shift.

"Everything's fine. Just working."

Thus, the idea I gave him.

You're not capable of mentally behaving. Admit it. Working is easier than dealing with it.

As Sean was clocking out, he looked at the schedule. Normally he'd see gaps and chuckle at the suckers raising families or putting themselves through school that would happily take extra shifts.

Today, he noted his lack of mind-wandering during his shift. His focus on something more important. And subsequently signed up for three extra shifts that week. For now, and until God could convince him otherwise, he needed them.

• • •

Sharon smiled as Stormy purred against her leg while she graded papers. Almost loving the silence. But her front door opened, unannounced, and Sean plopped on the couch next to his sister, moving Stormy to her bed on the other side of the room.

"How's life, Beautiful?" Sean asked.

"Good," Sharon answered. Never able to respond to that nickname without a smile. And now able to breathe much better around her non-smoking baby brother.

"So, better with the cat?" Sean wondered. Ulterior motives that Sharon couldn't pinpoint.

"Yeah. I'm really glad you guys got her. Can't thank you enough." Sharon smiled. "What brings you here tonight?"

"I'm on my way to church. I was early, you were on the way." Sean smiled.

"It's Tuesday. You know that, right? They have church on Tuesdays?"

"Men's study with Dad. I'm sorta like a man, right?"

"You're my baby brother. You'll never be a man." Sharon giggled.

"I'm less than two years younger than you, Sharon." Sean batted his long eyelashes.

"Precisely." She never worried around Sean, even in the most difficult words, that the lisp would be ridiculed.

"I am the youngest, single-est guy in my small group there." Sean shrugged. "Most people my age that aren't married go to the singles group. But Dad says they only do that to meet women."

"Seems like you'd be there, then." Sharon bit a lip, knowing her brother well.

"I'm not in the market. Manhood. I'm in the market for that. I'm not even sure I know what it means."

"Some people say you're not a man until your father dies. Other people say you're a man when you become a father. I'd say that you're pretty far from both, barring any women who simply haven't come forward yet."

Sean smirked, though he still hated the reputation he'd built for himself. Sharon saw it in his eyes. Saw *me* in his eyes.

"I'm kidding, Sean. I know you're trying to change some things in your life, and you should know I'm with you, whatever you're doing. But I'd say since you're not a dad and you have one, that you should ask *him* what it means to be a man. He's a good one, right?" Sharon shrugged.

"And get ridiculed for being an adult and asking how to be a godly man?"

"I don't think he'd ridicule you. I think he'd be happy that you even want to know." Sharon thought twice. Teased. "Why *do* you want to know? You're not trying to impress a girl, are you? In high school this guy pretended to be all Christian and stuff like L.D. to try and date her. Obviously, she didn't *fall* for it but that's a really bad way to get a girl, Sean."

"That's not what this is about, first of all." Sean stood up. Still early, but not willing to continue this conversation. "Second, no one impresses or dates Lavender-Dawn Meadow George. I feel bad that some guy even tried."

After saying goodbye, Sean breathed a sigh of relief against Sharon's door, trying to shut me out.

She's going to find out and she's going to hate you both. And if Sharon hates your precious "Georgie," Georgie will hate you too. You can never have her.

"Saw your car. We can ride together if you like." Dad startled Sean in the dim concrete corridor.

Sean practically yelped. "Dad, you scared the poo out of me."

Dad chuckled. "Sorry. How's my Rose of Sharon?"

"She's good. I'm glad we got her that cat. She seems in higher spirits these days." Sean walked side by side with his father. "Your car or mine?"

"Let's take mine. I assume you'll want to go bug your sister again after the study and your car being here is a good excuse."

Sean smiled. "You know me well."

"You're a good brother. Always have been. Without you and L.D., I don't know what state of mind Sharon would be in." Dad unlocked his car with his remote.

"I'd do pretty much anything for her. I bet G. . .'L.D.' would too." Sean covered the near slip with finesse.

"You know, it takes a good man to think of others before himself. And it seems like that's your thing. The EMT thing. Looking out for Sharon—"

"Wait, you think I'm a good man? Like, not a good *kid*. A good *man*." Sean stopped in his tracks.

Dad smirked. "Sean, you're not a kid. You're twenty-three years old with a full-time job that you love and an apartment, and you enjoy taking care of other people. Know any kids like that?"

"Well no," Sean started. "But I've also called Sharon at two in the morning to come get me from a bar because I was too drunk to drive, and my date didn't work out. Usually they *did* work out. I'm kind of a mess, Dad."

"'But you were washed. But you were sanctified. But you were justified in the name of the Lord Jesus and by the Spirit of our God.' I didn't say you were perfect, son. But by Jesus's blood you are. You were a good man before Christ, but now there's no arguing when God is in the seat of judgment. But you didn't let me get to my point."

"Sorry," Sean said, stepping into the car to cover his near tears.

"As I was saying, you spend a lot of time sacrificing yourself for others. But at some point, a man needs to walk through the door he's held open for everyone else. Even Jesus took bread when it was passed. A man's gotta eat," Dad advised.

"What does that even mean, Dad?"

"It means that if you're letting Sharon hold you back from an area of your life God wants you to venture into, that isn't okay." Samuel nodded, starting his car.

"She's not, Dad."

"So, I'm wrong about there being a girl?" Samuel teased.

"Sharon said the same thing."

"But you, of course, would never tell her that there *is* a girl."

Sean rolled his eyes. "I like girls, Dad."

"This one is different." Dad noticed.

"*I'm* different." Sean shrugged.

"Ah. I see. You're wondering about being a man, because you're after a *woman*. Not a girl. Whole other ball game. I'll keep you in my prayers. Let me know *when* you need my advice." He looked sideways at Sean. "Anyone I know?"

"Possibly. She's a church girl. Woman. . .who goes to our church. She might even be there for a womens study, though she was on the fence about joining one for the summer."

"Why's that?"

"Most women, even Christian women, don't tend to understand her."

"So, not a modern sort of woman?" Dad wondered with an agenda.

"No. In some ways she's very traditional. In others, she's completely countercultural. But never would I use the word 'modern.' "

"Hmm. Traditional and countercultural," The father teased. "Explains the extra shifts you've been taking at work."

"It does?" Sean glanced sideways at his father.

The older man laughed endearingly. "I applaud your effort. Taking your thoughts into captivity is a mature spiritual pursuit. But working too much will drive away *any* woman you're after. I suggest memorizing scripture. That one I just said was 1 Corinthians 6:11. There are times I need reminding that my sin is forgiven."

"I'll keep that in mind. But it's not happening with this woman, Dad. At least not right now. God's timing, I guess." Sean sighed in the mourning of his soul.

"I'm not convinced that's what's stopping you," Samuel surmised.

"We're friends and she's complicated and beautiful. That's what's stopping me." Sean laughed. "So, if it *never* happens with her, which seems likely, it isn't because of Sharon, okay?"

"Well." Dad smiled. "I guess time will tell, right?"

But I told Sean never. And it shook him into silence all the way to church.

Sean and his father breached the doors of the church, and it wasn't twenty seconds before Samuel proclaimed, "Hey! My girl!"

"Hey, Dad!" L.D. accepted the fatherly hug from the gigantic man. She looked to Sean and nodded cordially. "Sean."

"Lavender-Dawn Meadow George." He noted in the same tone, tipping her off that the secret was still a secret.

"You're at church. On a Tuesday."

"Sharon said the same thing. Is that *allowed*?"

"Be nice," Samuel said through gritted teeth.

"Sean 2.0 is working on that." L.D. rescued him. "And I'm supposed to not be so 'judgy' as he says. So sorry. I meant, 'Sean! You're at church! On a Tuesday!' " She'd changed her tone to unrealistic enthusiasm and Sean couldn't help but snicker.

Samuel was completely silent. He didn't need to say anything at all, as fathers go. He simply looked between them. Winked at her. Nodded impressed lips at him. And turned his back, walking away.

It threw them into a quiet panic as they awkwardly parted ways.

Friendship's Dilemma

"It was so bad!" L.D. lamented, head back and eyes shut tight while Sharon laughed hysterically. Others in the coffee shop glanced up a moment from their computers and conversations, smirking at the women's joyful conversation.

"What did you do?" Sharon finally managed.

"I left the stall and I played it totally cool." L.D. snorted. "Yeah right. He was in total shock as I was washing my hands and I just blurted out how the women's restroom was being cleaned and about my green tea binge and how bad I had to pee and how the waiting room was full for an hour and I'd been holding it. It was my boss, S.R. My *boss*. He laughed, and I didn't get fired. But I'm pretty sure I was bright red. And, of course, I made sure to add a completely awkward, 'Good luck!' as I left the bathroom."

"Is this the cute one with the family?" Sharon asked, sipping her latte.

"No, this is the older doctor whose name is on the practice. He *owns* the place."

"You are so much braver than I am," Sharon admitted in laughter. "There's no way I would ever go into a men's restroom, no matter how bad I had to pee."

"There was no one around and I had *just* seen him in his office. I swear he teleported." L.D. sighed. "Smooth as glass, me."

"I had a student last year that tried to sneak into the teacher's area where our restrooms are. But I was standing there the whole time behind her telling her not to." Sharon giggled and snorted. "She couldn't hear me, so she just kept tiptoeing along. It was the cutest thing ever."

L.D. cackled. "That's hilarious. How old was she?"

"Fifth grade, I think? I never had her in my class, so I can't be sure." Sharon shrugged.

"I wonder if she's one of the patients. I give suckers out to the kids as they leave their appointments, and there's this ten-year-old that thinks she's grown and doesn't like to take suckers from me because it's for little kids or whatever. I was pretty proud when I got her to take one the other day by telling her I sometimes sneak them when no one's looking." L.D. giggled.

"Yeah, like you eat processed sugar." Sharon rolled her eyes at the lie.

"I'll have you know that *I* buy the suckers, and you better believe they are all-natural, with no high fructose corn syrup, and void of most allergens." L.D. smirked. "When I have kids, they are *totally* gonna hate me."

"I love that you say '*when.*' " Sharon laughed bitterly.

"I pray that it's in God's will for me, S.R. That's all," L.D. clarified and pointed at her friend with a smile. "Because we have plans, remember?"

Sharon smirked at the hopes and dreams from their "BFF" phase back in tweenhood. She mumbled, "Buy houses on the same street. . ."

"And have husbands that put up with the fact that we are besties forever and our kids will all grow up together and be *best* friends just like we are. And when they are playing at my house, they will have healthy lollipops." L.D. giggled.

"And I'll sneak your poor milk-deprived kids milkshakes." Sharon cackled. The women causing another glance their way in the little coffee shop.

"We're still young, S.R. God has plans for us. Why can't that be in them?" L.D. shrugged.

"I do admire your optimism." Sharon nodded. "But I think best case, I'll be the doting auntie with all the cats."

"Well, I think God is still preparing our future hubbies' hearts for putting up with our rowdiness." She looked at the clock on the wall this Saturday morning, quoting her office's new hours with an eye roll. " 'Now offering Saturday morning appointments. . .in the summer when the kids aren't in school and can come anytime anyway. I better go. I'm late for my slave labor. Say hi to Stormy for me!"

Sharon watched L.D. drive away and took out her planner, readying herself months in advance for a new class of students. She always planned ahead. She liked to know what was coming. That's why it was so frustrating attempting to plan for her future. Of *course,* Sharon wanted to see that childhood dream realized. But she was much more practical than that. She had to plan for a future based on the present. Her. Alone. In this job. In that apartment. With her cat. It wasn't in her makeup to allow that plan to include the "when" of marriage and children like L.D. did.

L.D. was beautiful. A fun, bright light that half the men in the coffee shop had arrived just to see at their usual Saturday morning coffee date. She had a chance for love. A good one. Sharon even suspected L.D. had someone in mind, but she'd probably be scared to tell the downer and the drag that was her best friend. Sharon knew she'd be jealous when it did happen. When. She could count on L.D.'s future but not her own. She tried to let her love for her friend override any jealousy. But it almost seemed like lifelong jealousy was always going to be a part of Sharon's future.

L.D. tried not to think long-term. She was annoyed that she was on her way to work on a day she would normally coax Sharon into going for a walk in the park after coffee instead of Sharon retreating back to her apartment to be miserable and alone. But she'd brought her planner, so L.D. was hoping she'd at least spend a few more minutes in public, albeit shutting out everyone around her. But there was beauty in that too. She did, after all, love Sharon the way she was.

L.D. unlocked the front door of the practice with a sigh. That meant she was the only one there to welcome the three patients already waiting for their Saturday morning appointments. No doctors yet. No medical assistants. She'd have to vamp until they arrived, as usual. It turned out to only be half an hour late that the appointments started. But that meant her day was half an hour longer. Lunch, half an hour later on her half day of work. Still, she remained cheery over the next couple of hours, conversing with patients in both voice and ASL. Content with her life. Because of Sharon, she was the prime candidate to work for the pediatric audiologist. God was so good to give her Sharon.

Suddenly a nurse burst through the side door of the receptionist area.

"Call an ambulance, we have a seizure!"

L.D. picked up the phone. "Who is it? I need to tell them details."

"Trevor. The little guy with—" The nurse began.

"I know Trevor." L.D. laughed, then explained the situation to the operator that picked up.

She knew all the patients. All their ailments. Prayed over them daily. She was their scheduler and greeter in their eyes. But to L.D., she was their guardian. She knew more about their medical histories than they thought, though she was obviously sworn to never let on to it. The nurse told L.D. to let her know when the ambulance arrived, so when she saw it, she was on a walkie communicating with the nurse. When she looked up, she heard a familiar voice that caused her heart to leap.

"I *thought* you worked here. Is Saturday new?"

Sean, in full EMT garb. Naturally, it would be Sean. In the past, she may have found it difficult to be cordial with him. That day, his presence soothed.

"Hey, Sean! Yeah, we just added Saturday hours," she gritted through a fake smile, which caused Sean to laugh. "Trevor is back in Exam Room 16. He's pretty much stabilized, but they told me to go on and let you take him in. It's tricky, I'll take you. Um. . .go through that door, I'll meet you in the hall there." She signed to the one parent in the waiting room, *"I'll be right back."*

L.D. met Sean and his partner in the hall to lead them through the winding corridor, around corners, and through nurses' stations.

"How you been, Georgie?" he asked. "I know we just texted yesterday, but I haven't seen you in a while."

"Yeah, what is with that? I've been fine, but I *miss* you," L.D. teased. Knowing Sean had been working extra shifts and going to church more than ever.

"Trying to continue to transform." Sean smirked. Trying not to let on to the fact that working helped him get his heart in order. "Today's challenge is staying awake. I've been at work since midnight."

"Didn't you get off at six last night after a twelve?" L.D. was concerned.

"Yep. Bauer here needed a partner since his became a dad last night." Sean nodded to his companion who was following them through the halls.

"Wow, here I am complaining about four hours on a Saturday morning." L.D. was convicted.

"Half day, huh? When do you get off?"

"It'll probably be closer to one," L.D. confessed.

"Awesome. Text me? I get off at noon. I had some burning Levitical Law questions that I wanted to ask you. I'll even buy you some food," Sean asked, then saw Exam Room 16.

"Um. . ." L.D. crossed her arms at the awkward situation as "Bauer" smiled knowingly before he entered the exam room. "That sounds eerily like a date. I thought we weren't. . ."

Sean's eyes widened. "No! Not. . .I didn't even consider how that sounded. Just food. And Leviticus. In a public place. Church, if you want. Think about it and text me."

L.D. stayed by the door long enough to watch Sean's spirit come alive at the smile of an epileptic little boy. Sean adored children.

"Hey, Trevor. I'm Sean. How are you feeling?" he asked sweetly as Bauer checked the boy's vitals.

L.D. walked away, trying not to smile over her surprise encounter and the way she hoped to spend the rest of her day. Doubting Sean's word that it wasn't a date. And not sure it mattered.

...

Sean was updating his records when Bauer entered the driver's side door of their ambulance after they'd taken Trevor to the hospital. His heart was abuzz, though he was annoyed with God for the "chance" encounter and the instruction to ask her out. Focus wasn't coming easy.

" 'But you were washed. . .' " Sean whispered to himself.

"What?" Bauer asked.

"Nothing," Sean mumbled.

"So, you gonna tell me who the hottie was back at the audiologist?" Bauer dove in.

He was the kind of guy that went by his last name. A meathead that Sean had partied after work with for years. Sean's wingman in some cases. But never really his friend. Especially not in recent times.

"Georgie is my big sister's best friend and completely off limits, so you can stop *right* there," Sean said, not looking up from his computer. It was instinct for him to protect her.

"Why?" Bauer asked. "You bangin' her?"

Sean looked up. "*Wow*, Bauer." He returned his eyes to his screen. Realizing that he'd used much crasser language when speaking of women before with this same man.

"Oh, the 'suddenly I'm a Christian' doesn't want to *tell* me that he's bangin' his sister's best friend."

"Talk about her that way again. I'm exhausted and haven't seen anyone die yet today." Sean looked to Bauer with a sincere smile through the sarcasm.

"Whoa dude." Bauer put his hands up. "Sorry I asked. I just figured Levitican was some biblical euphemism for something."

"Leviticus." Sean sighed. "And no. It's not a euphemism. It's a book of the Bible that lays out all the reasons why *you're* going to hell."

"I thought we were getting a condo there together. What happened to that?" Bauer joked.

"What happened is there's one reason why I'm *not* going to hell, which is not the party you think it is. It's a literal lake of fire, dude." Sean warned. Not sure why he was throwing pearls of wisdom before this pig.

"And what's that 'one reason'?"

"The blood of Jesus Christ. My Savior. Whom I know about in large part due to Georgie. Neither Jesus nor Georgie should be spoken of in your language. So, shut it." Sean's temper flared.

"You're kind of a jerk now." Bauer said, starting the vehicle and deescalating the situation.

"I'm glad you think so." Sean said it with sarcasm. But meant it with joy.

• • •

The third meeting of its kind occurred at a picnic bench over sandwiches and under the sunshine. Bibles were open and summertime flourishing all around them. They were focused right where they should be. I had to sit back quietly.

"That's good, Sean! That urge you feel to be more like Christ comes from the Holy Spirit. Grace can't be earned. But why would you want to be a slave of sin when you're a bondservant of Jesus? It breaks His heart and doesn't have any benefit to yourself or anyone else except destruction. Because you're golden for eternity with Jesus. But that doesn't mean you can't still waste the one life you're given here on Earth. You should live it to glorify Him," L.D. explained as Sean nodded. "People need to know Jesus. And they often meet Him through the transformed lives of those who do."

"You make everything make so much more sense." He sighed, smiling. "Okay, one more question. It's not Leviticus for once. It's before all that."

"Okay. Hit me." L.D. braced herself for more. Sean asked difficult, mature biblical questions. She enjoyed discipling him, but worried he'd pass her up in the wisdom department sooner than she hoped.

"Why Jacob?" Sean wondered slowly. He explained when she merely tilted her head. "God promised the nation to Abraham. He could have given it to him. A guy with enough faith to sacrifice his own son. But He didn't. Isaac, Abraham's son, was also a solid guy. He only had one wife, and his father and his sons all had a few. But Jacob? He was a cheater. A con man. And when Esau, who I think was way more honorable, got angry over the birthright thing, Jacob ran off. Jacob tested God, then the wife thing with Rachel and Leah? How does a guy not know who he's sleeping with? Jacob just seems like the absolute worst choice if you're going to hand pick a human to father a nation. Lo and behold, Israel gets itself into pickle after pickle, forgetting God countless times no matter what He does to rescue them. So why Jacob?"

"Jacob is Abraham's grandson. He kept His promise to Abraham through Jacob," L.D. inserted as she considered the question.

"Yeah, but the tribes of Israel came from Israel. From Jacob," Sean reminded her.

"I know," L.D. considered it before she nodded. "Sean, I think God chose Jacob *because* he was a disaster. God chooses the weak. That way, if we become anything at all, it is only attributed to God. He chose Jacob because Jacob was the choice that didn't make sense, like so many of God's choices. Because God wants us to know just how well He can transform a mess into a masterpiece that looks like Him."

"Here's hoping," Sean spoke of himself. "I never saw it that way. I love bouncing these things off you."

"Yeah, it's fun." L.D. smirked. "Other than your dad, who I'm pretty sure thinks we're dating, I never get to talk to anyone about the Bible."

Sean sighed. "Georgie, I promise I said nothing to make him think that. I'm not trying to date you. I just like spending time with you."

"Isn't that what dating is, though?" L.D. teased.

"Not in our case." Sean shrugged.

"Right, because if we were to call it 'dating,' we'd be hiding a relationship, which would be deceitful. Whereas with a friendship we're just, you know, not mentioning hanging out with a friend." L.D. gave a little smile.

"Yeah, but that's not why we're not dating." Sean squinted.

"It for sure feels like dating." L.D. called him out, not having planned to do so.

"We text. And on the off chance I'm not working, we get together and eat food and talk about the Bible. How is that dating?" Sean laughed.

"Because, okay, hypothetically. . .?" She began.

"Okay?"

"We were to call it dating. In what way would our current situation change?"

"Well. . ." Sean considered, his heart yearning, considering what he preferred not to consider. "You might let me hold your hand and kiss you and stuff."

"I might. Except without the 'and stuff,' because I know what your version of 'and stuff' is, and that's for marriage, not dating."

"Right, no 'and stuff.' " Sean laughed agreement, then nodded. "And we'd text and hang out and eat food and talk about the Bible. But we're not dating."

"We're not dating or we're not *calling* it dating? Because there's a distinct difference. Like, isn't there a difference?"

"Not in our case," Sean said again.

"What are we in our case?"

"Friends." He sighed, sadly. "Georgie, you know how I feel. But I'm trying to dial things back until God says otherwise. If He never does, I honest to God *love* just being your friend."

"Friends," she considered aloud.

"Is that disappointing?"

"No. I'd say it's a victory." She shrugged. "Not long ago, I was a 'Jesus Freak' to you."

"And now you're a Jesus Freak *with* me. That is *quite* a victory." He laughed, appreciating the transformation. "Now to get you to drink *milk*."

The Dress's Strings

L.D. rummaged through her closet in mid-August, having been handed an invitation to a gala. A patient at work was diagnosed with cancer, and the nurses got together with the child's primary care office and planned a benefit for the family, who didn't have insurance. L.D. got the impression that the evening would be another few hours of work she likely wouldn't get paid for, since they told her she needn't bring a plus one and hoped she could do "a shift" at the door to accept tickets. But she knew the child and the family and would, of course, do it for them.

The problem was, the event next month was strictly black tie, and she would be the first human the wealthy guests would see upon arrival. As she hated to admit every time she realized she fit the awful female stereotype, L.D. had nothing to wear. She didn't keep clothes around for "maybe" and had never attended a gala. She also hated shopping alone.

Don't you wish you'd gone to prom? You're the same size now as you were then. I told her.

"Sharon didn't go, so I didn't go," she rebutted, acknowledging me for the first time in a long time.

Sharon. She could take Sharon shopping. It was a Saturday. She'd seen Sharon that morning and she said she wasn't doing anything the rest of the day because she was resting before school started on Monday. She got out her phone and was about to tap her picture when I intervened.

Yeah, take Sharon. That way you can hear all about how she'd never fit in an evening gown like you because she is too fat. She'd be absolutely no help.

"But she's my best friend."

You need to look good. Your job is on the line. Therefore, you need to hear real opinions from a person who understands fashion. Not passive, "I guess that one is pretty's" from Sharon.

"Right. Better take Sophie."

Sophie? She's pregnant and would live vicariously through your body if you let her help you choose a dress. You'd end up in something Brielle might wear.

"Runnin' out of options. Mom Mehlmann?"

It's Saturday. Lynn is a manager of a grocery store. She has always worked Saturdays. I think you know where this is going.

She sighed. "Not Sean. . ." she said aloud. Her eyes closed contemplatively.

Sean had been a better friend than Sharon in recent months. They'd fellowshipped and had fun together. L.D. could feel the darkness and sadness around Sharon and made sure to be a light for her where she could. But she never realized the depth of that darkness until she then spent time with Sean. Ever silly. Ever sincere and protective. Always open and honest. With a weakness for the female form.

She tapped his picture instead. Calling. Not just texting. Calling meant they were close. Why was she calling?

"Hey, Georgie?" he was startled over her calling too.

"Hey, Sean. Are you working today?"

"For once, no. I'm just holding down my couch and binge-watching Netflix. What's up?" he asked.

"Um. . .I have a favor to ask?"

"What do you need?"

"What do you know about women's fashion? Black tie, to be specific."

"Too much and probably way too little." Sean in a past life had a lot of sinful experience with homecomings and proms and young women in black tie wear. He cringed at who he was. "Why would you be in the market for an evening gown?"

"This gala at work. You seemed like the best person to ask for help."

"Sharon busy?" he wondered.

"No, actually. But I want *your* help, Sean."

His whole body trembled. "I'll get my shoes on and pick you up in five."

"This is a lot of dresses." Sean chuckled, scratching his head in the moderately crowded department store. They both stood back and stared at the first rack after a quick perusal of the thrift store left Sean disgusted by the "prehistoric" fashions.

"Yeah," she whispered. Glad to have him by her side.

"None of these look like organic cotton to me."

"Unfortunately, you're right. I don't think my usual garb would be formal enough, which is why I'm asking for help. So, don't tease," she said, sliding dresses along the rack. She looked up, however, to see that his face was sincere.

"Oh. That's helpful. You're okay wearing synthetic fibers now?"

"Not usually." L.D. shrugged. "But there are always exceptions. I have to be flexible. I can't expect the world to change for my crunchy preferences. It's sweet that you know what they are. Creepy. But sweet."

Sean smiled. "So basically, you need to be able to fit some organic cotton thing under the dress, so the yucky synthetics don't touch your skin."

"Not any less creepy. Synthetic fibers irritate my skin. It's not a weird hippie thing."

"It's totally a weird hippie thing," Sean said through lips that couldn't erase the smile. "Do you have a budget? Color? Length?"

"As cheap as possible, probably something inconspicuous and as long as possible. There was the one at the thrift store."

"The Amish preacher's wife one? No. Long is okay, though, I guess." Sean shook his head. She wasn't one for showing her legs.

He always loved when she did. Though she was a runner and her muscles were toned and lovely, flaunting them wasn't her usual way.

"How about I pick a few, and then you choose between them. That's what I do with Sharon. I usually end up choosing on my own anyway."

"Sounds good."

Sean followed L.D. around the racks as she picked dresses she thought would be suitable in prices she could sort of afford. He stood outside the womens changing room as she put each of them on and shrugged indifferently at all the crystals and rhinestones and satin and lace. She was wrapping herself in dresses designed to enhance beauty. They all fit her well and accented all the right parts of her, to Sean's detriment. But none of them did anything at all to bring out *her* form of beauty.

L.D. sighed, hipping her hands as she emerged with the final dress she'd picked. Something formfitting with even a little cleavage. "If you don't approve of this one, I don't think there's hope for me."

Again, he shrugged indifferently.

"Sean!" she scolded. "I've tried on ten dresses. You didn't like any of them?"

"The dresses are fine. You look hot in all of them. *That* one is *too* hot. Since when do you wear low cut anything?"

"Okay, so hot is now a *bad* thing?"

"For a guy who is trying not to feel things for you, yeah. It's bad. It also isn't you. Can I choose a couple?"

L.D. crossed her arms. Nodded.

It took Sean a moment, but he eventually came to a dress that made him smile. Violet, chiffon, and completely void of embellishments. He handed it to her with a huge smile on his face.

"Sean. . ." She looked it over. "That's completely lifeless and boring. Are you saying I'm lifeless and boring?"

Sean laughed, pushing in into her hands. "It's lifeless and boring because you're not in it."

When she reemerged with an annoyed sigh and hip sway, Sean had to catch his breath. She was stunning. It brought out her eyes and swayed with her gentle curves. Perfection.

"Wow," he said, nodding. "Yes. That one. Wow."

"I like it." She sighed again, gathering her mass of hair atop her head to mimic an updo, and posing, turning side to side in the mirror. "Is it nice enough? I'll be at the door."

"Yes. What's wrong?"

"It costs more than my rent. Granted, my rent is cheap, but a dress shouldn't cost that."

"But it's perfect!"

"Well it can be perfect on the rack." LD pulled at her hair some more. "I can look hot in something else."

"You don't look hot in that." Sean shrugged. "You look *gorgeous* in that. Like don't-even-think-about-it, way-out-of-your-league gorgeous. You *have* to get that dress."

She was flattered. Tempted to blow her rent on it, even. But she knew she couldn't.

"I'll wear it once. It's not worth the price. There were other dresses at the thrift store. We should go back." She sighed.

"Not happening. I've been working a lot." Sean shrugged. "I have these insane paychecks that I have no clue what to do with. So. . ."

"No, Sean." L.D. tried to nip the offer in the bud as she let her wild hair billow back down over the dress, her shoulders, and the entire length of her back.

"Why not?" He tried to ignore the scent and beauty of her hair as it fell.

"Friends who have feelings for one another but aren't dating don't spend hundreds of dollars on clothing for one another," she laid out the dilemma.

"Maybe that's not what we are," Sean said with complete sincerity. "Let me buy the dress. And let me pay for meals when we eat together. And maybe someday we'll combine the dress and an expensive meal and use the forbidden 'D' word."

"That's a lot of strings to attach to one article of clothing," L.D. noted with a nervous smile.

"Maybe someday we'll see what a ring does." Sean spoke sincerely.

"Sean, stop," L.D. insisted, her heart pounding. She began to walk back into the dressing room. "I'll find another dress."

"No." He found his arm had gently reached out and grasped her upper arm, then quickly withdrew it when she turned back to him. "Let me buy the dress. No strings. No marriage proposals. Just a gift between friends. I owe you quite a few birthday and Christmas gifts, so this'll make up for them."

"Maybe you can store it in my closet. I can help you zip it up before we go. Help you. . ." He blinked as she looked down, considering the offer. He recaptured his thoughts with a smile. *" 'Charm is deceitful, and beauty is passing, But a woman who fears the Lord, she shall be praised.' Proverbs 31:30."*

He'd taken his father's advice, you see, and memorized Scripture. He still worked as often as possible, but it wasn't enough. He knew he couldn't keep from thinking of her. From loving her. But with God's help, he could direct his thoughts to her most beautiful characteristics.

She looked up and met his eyes, taking a step back, almost in fear. But only almost. Overwhelmed is more accurate. Warmed to her toes more fitting. "What is *that* look?"

He laughed, glad he couldn't see in the mirror to confirm what he suspected. "Sorry. I just love you and it leaks out into my face sometimes." He cleared his throat. "But friends who are not dating don't say that. Go change out of the dress, that might help. You also need some earrings and shoes and one of those little purse things before I'm done spoiling you. So, we have a lot more shopping to do."

"You sure?" she whispered.

"I won't always have money like this. Later on, we'll have a mortgage and two dozen kids to feed. And chances are *you'll* be in charge of the money because you're far more sensible than I am. Let me do this while I'm still single," he said it like a promise. Whispered. "Go change."

You're in way over your head, dude.

"Yes. Yes, I am."

A thought that Sean took straight to his father's house after dropping off L.D. on Saturday night.

"Dad, I'm in deep," he said, plopping onto the couch next to his father's chair in the living room.

"Same girl?" he asked, not even looking at the son who walked straight into the house without knocking.

"*Woman*, I thought we decided," Sean confirmed. Sighed. "I just spent several hundred dollars on said woman, and I'm not even dating her."

"Hopefully you're smarter than to try to buy her." Samuel flipped the channel, concealing the firm grimace.

"It was a gift," Sean assured. "We're just friends."

"How are you handling *that*?" his father asked, chuckling.

"I'm. . ." Sean whined his laughter. "I'm handling it. I have peace about it. We'll say that."

"Several hundred dollars of peace, apparently." Mr. Mehlmann chuckled.

"You should have seen the dress on her, Dad," Sean tried, flopping his head back onto the couch to his father's laughter.

"A *dress* cost that much?"

"And a bit more for accessories. Don't act like you didn't spend several *thousand* on Sophie's wedding dress." Sean rolled his head to the side, looking at his father and closest male friend. "You're a bad influence on me. This is your fault."

"Sophie looked beautiful, didn't she? Baby in her belly and all." Samuel sighed.

"If it helps, I'm on track to not have a random pregnancy announcement in front of everybody at my wedding. I mean, you know *if. . .*"

Samuel finally advised his son: "God will make it happen if it's meant to happen with this woman. I'll be praying."

"Thanks, I will too. Also pray I practice self-control with my debit card when I go places with her." Sean laughed at himself.

"Will do." Samuel chuckled again. He glanced twice at his son before smirking and throwing his world out of orbit. "Did she decide to do a fall womens study at church?"

"No, she's sitting this one out. She said none of them were in-depth enough, and she wanted a consistent evening to spend with Sha—" Sean's adrenaline tingled at his ears. "Wait, who are we talking about?"

His father took to loud, almost evil laughter.

Sean sighed. Mumbled, "That was a test and I failed."

"Not at all. Unless you honestly expect me to believe there's some *other* young woman you regularly see at church and have enough of a history with for a good friendship to be considered something special," his father mumbled back.

"We really are just friends." Sean sighed. "She was right. She knew you knew it was her. But we're not dating."

"I think there's about one woman in the world for whom I'd buy an expensive ensemble on a random Saturday. She's the mother of my children. But I suppose those children have her eyes, so other expensive dresses do get bought from time to time." Samuel smiled the same smile as Sean.

"Okay, you don't even get to talk about eyes, Dad. Mom's aren't flipping *purple*. How am I supposed to not buy her a dress that makes them go all perfect? I told you I'm in deep." During which Samuel continued the appreciative laughter, while Sean began the plea. "*Please* don't tell Sharon. Or Mom or Sophie or anyone who might possibly tell Sharon. She'd never forgive us."

"I'll respect your privacy. But I thought you were just friends. What's to forgive?" Samuel shrugged.

"We might have made out on the beach on St. John," Sean confessed, to his absolute relief and his father's intrigue. "That was a one-time thing. But I might have mentioned wanting to marry her and being in love with her. You know, a few dozen times."

"Oh."

" 'Oh' is right." Sean sighed.

"How does she feel about all this?" Samuel wondered.

"She's confusing. One minute she's like, 'God wants me to marry you, let's make out.' The next minute she's like, 'Stop proposing to me.' But she answers all my texts. Accepts all my invitations. Sits and talks with me for hours. And when she needed a shopping buddy, she called *me*. I know all that's just friend stuff and just the way she is. Just always there for people and connecting with people. So, I'm trying not to pressure her."

"I knew if you ever took a minute to see her, you'd fall for her," Samuel said.

"I've always seen her. Scared me to death that she found out."

"I think 'scared' is wise when it comes to women."

The Heart's Demise

"No, Zof!" Eric exclaimed to his pregnant wife as she tried to pet Sharon's cat. They were stopping by Sharon's to pick up a gift she bought them. That was commonplace now. This gift was a sound-activated video baby monitor that one of her students' deaf parents recommended.

"Oh, she's safe. She doesn't bite or scratch or anything," Sharon said and signed.

"He doesn't like cats." Sophie put her hand on her pregnant belly in its sixth month. "Especially now."

"Oh. Why?" Sharon asked Eric.

Eric pointed to Sophie, who was finishing up her third year of college studying health and nutrition. Not that it mattered now. She'd have a baby to care for soon.

"Cats carry toxoplasmosis, which you don't usually get unless you're immunocompromised in some way, like pregnancy. And if you get it when you're pregnant and it passes to the baby, it can have devastating effects. . ."

"Oh, is that why he's. . ."

"Yeah, Eric was born with toxoplasmosis and is lucky to have *only* been deaf." Sophie turned so only Sharon could see her. "You can only get it from the feces and only if the cat goes outside a lot. But he's annoyingly particular about every single little thing. I could scream. Actually, I have when he's not looking. Anyway, we better get going. Thanks for this."

Sharon was confused. She had never known Sophie, the newlywed of three months, to ever intentionally speak outside of Eric's hearing, and certainly not negatively. It goes without saying that to abuse someone's disability like that is demeaning at best. Cruel and insensitive. It was odd for Sophie to resort to such behavior when there was no one she loved more than Eric. But the words involved in the infraction were indeed minor, so Sharon's jealous infuriation with Sophie over abusing such a wonderful man were short-lived.

She did, however, wonder if maybe Sophie jinxed her somehow. Because Stormy started meowing at the door for hours not a month later. After a week of begging and pleading with the cat, Sharon finally caved and opened the door, allowing the cat to trot happily away.

The first time, Stormy came back within five minutes. Often, Sharon would have to get up three times a night to appease the will of the cat. But she didn't want to complain, as she would come safely home each time. When she brought it up to her family, they all had a unanimous suggestion that Sharon despised immediately.

"I know it's standard procedure, I just feel bad cutting out my baby's uterus," Sharon whined at a family dinner. But they couldn't complain about the whining. Sharon was the happiest they'd seen her in a long time.

"She'll get knocked up. Look like Sophie over here." From Sean, of course. Sophie all but flipped him off with the look on her plump little face.

"I know, and she tries to get out every time I open the door. She doesn't even greet me anymore. She just wants to go streetwalking." Sharon sighed.

"It's probably time, sweetheart," Samuel said. "She'll probably still want to go out. That's instinct. But at least she won't come back with more of a problem."

"Take Sophie, for instance," Sean tried again. Unusually mean today, with an even more unusual target.

"Dad! Make him stop!" And from pregnancy hormones nine months in the making, Sophie was reduced to a mess of tears.

"Thanks, *Jawn*, she hasn't cried in a whole three hours." Eric narrowed an eye as he spoke.

"Sorry, Sophie. A lot on my mind. I'm just teasing. I love you. You're gorgeous. Pregnancy looks amazing on you and I honestly can't wait to be an uncle," Sean corrected. Sounding much more like himself. Sophie smiled a little.

"Where's L.D. this evening?" Lynn asked Sharon after smiling over her kindhearted son.

But Sean answered, "Work. Her office is doing a benefit. . .and you were asking Sharon. Sorry. I ran into Lavender-Dawn Meadow George at church." He had been texting her under the table at that very moment, in truth.

"Yeah, she has this gala to benefit one of the kids' family. Cancer. No insurance. Anyway, L.D. bought a new dress and got to get all dressed up and stuff, but she's pretty sure since she's the receptionist that they'll probably just make her work anyway." Sharon explained it, signing even, but Eric seemed to be elsewhere.

"Sean, you go to church a lot lately," Eric stated aloud what they'd all been thinking.

"Never enough, honestly. God always has something else He wants to teach me, and I do whatever I can to listen," Sean shared. Winced again at his plight. "I don't expect anyone to understand."

"And there's a girl." Sharon giggled, watching Sean texting.

"Seriously? I thought that was just a rumor." Sophie wondered. Nodding to his phone. "Is that her?"

"Sean, you know how I feel about phones at the table," the mother scolded.

"Sorry. We're just friends, though," Sean said, setting his phone on the butler's pantry behind him.

"What's the name of your 'friend'?" Sophie asked.

Sean froze. Wide-eyed. If he told them, they'd know. That would be a disaster. If he didn't tell them, they'd assume things were happening that were not happening and that might hurt her reputation once they did find out. I quickly rambled that into his head, but God petitioned for truth in his heart at his dad's warm smile.

"Uh. . .she goes by Georgie." Sean cleared his throat. Looking around and snickering at the romance in all the women's eyes. "*Friends*. I'm serious. We text each other about *God*. She's way out of my league."

"Not if you keep up the Jesus stuff," Sophie said with a shrug.

Sean unexpectedly stepped onto a soap box. "Soph, I need you to understand that no matter what happens with Georgie, Jesus Christ is the center of my life. Yes, I'm interested in a woman who feels the same way. But I'm not a Christian for *her*. I'm a Christian for *Christ*. Georgie has been a. . .side effect? Again, there's no easy way to make you understand that."

"I understand," Eric said, to the surprise of all. "Me and Sophie have been fighting for years about what church to go to. We met at my family's church, but she likes your church. We want our son to go to church, so we decided to start going with you."

"He's a blessing, don't get me wrong," Sophie tag-teamed. "But I have a baby bump in my wedding photos forever and ever amen. We want him to know that we did right by him after that. We want him to know God."

Dad chuckled. "Wow. Am I sitting with a bunch of returned prodigals or what? I couldn't be prouder of you guys. Sean coming to Christ. Sophie ready to be a mom. And Sharon—"

"Getting a cat? As a gift?" Sharon huffed.

"I was going to say teaching a younger generation of deaf and hard of hearing children to be successful members of society. But the cat is good too," Dad affirmed.

"Thanks, Dad." She smiled under his loving protection, as always.

"I remember all of my teachers," Eric signed. *"You are very important to them."*

"Thank you," Sharon signed.

"Eric is loaded. I bet all your students will be too," Sean reiterated, only barely realizing it. He stepped on a sore spot he didn't know was there. "Couldn't you afford those um. . ." Sean gestured in a circle to his ears.

"Cochlear implants?" Sophie asked. "He isn't too keen on those."

"God made me deaf. I'm happy deaf," Eric said, smiling.

Sophie looked away from him, clearing her throat. Luckily, at the same moment, Sean's phone vibrated, and he theatrically "sneaked" it back under the table to everyone's amusement.

"When do we *meet* Georgie?" Lynn blurted. "You don't have to be dating her for us to meet, right?"

"Yeah, I could be like, 'Hey, meet my parents even though we are for sure not dating and you're way out of my league.' " Sean chuckled.

"What does that *mean*, Sean?" Sharon asked, though still jealous that her "important" life was not as interesting as Sean's fling.

"She's too good for me." Sean shrugged. "She hasn't had to make the lifestyle changes that I have. She's just always been in love with Jesus. She's even a virgin, if you can believe it."

" 'But you were washed,' " Samuel whispered.

"And it's complicated." Sean laughed. "I'd rather not go into it."

"Does she know how you feel?" Lynn asked.

"Mom." Sean laughed. "Friends."

•••

Later in the evening, after her other two siblings had left for the evening, Sharon sat on the couch, leaning her head on her daddy's shoulder.

"Dad, I just feel like I'm constantly trying to find my way. And I don't remember losing it. Even my self-centered sister and my wayward brother have their lives together and I don't." Pretty much verbatim what I told her. Good listening skills, Sharon.

"And how would you define 'together'?" Dad asked.

"I don't know, happy?"

"Sharon." Dad sighed. "Joy isn't a free gift. But it isn't worked for or earned, either. It has nothing to do with circumstances. Joy is a choice. It is always there as sure as the Holy Spirit, and all we have to do is choose, even in the worst circumstances, to experience it. But you have great circumstances, my Rose of Sharon. You live in a nice apartment. You have a job that you love and a horny cat. . ."

Sharon chuckled. Dad continued, shifting in his chair because of the heartburn.

"You have something to be joyful about. Maybe even more than your brother and sister. Sean is pretty far from figuring things out, but he's choosing to be joyful in the journey. Sophie's life is about to get really tough, really fast. But she's choosing joy. Sure, your circumstances could change. Prince Charming could come along and sweep you off your feet. You never know. But unless you choose joy, you'll be miserable about that too. Does that make sense?"

"Dad, I asked Jesus into my heart when I was a little girl. As soon as L.D. came along and you started taking us to church. But I've never felt His presence like all of you seem to. How do I do that? Is that a choice too?" she asked.

"I would recommend *seeking* His presence if you want to experience it. But Rose of Sharon, when Jesus wants you to see Him, He shows up. It takes more than a little self-doubt to stop the Holy Spirit of God."

Gee thanks, Dad. The older ones seem to know all my secrets.

"Go home and check on that cat. Also, make her an appointment to get her fixed. She'll still love you. I promise."

But Sharon barely got spoiled Stormy's canned food into her dish before her phone rang.

"Hello?"

It was Sophie. "Sharon! Mom is like flipping out. I guess Dad collapsed? The paramedics were able to revive him and he's on his way to the hospital awake, but that's all I could get out of her. Can you meet us there? Mom needs us."

All Sharon could think about on the drive was how beautiful Sophie looked when Dad walked her down that sandy aisle to Eric.

And how if this was as bad as I told her it was, she'd never get to have her father walk her down the aisle. That's *if* she ever got married.

When she arrived, Sean was comforting their frantic mother, and Sophie waddled up to Sharon, crossing her arms.

"Massive heart attack." Sophie sniffled. "He's going through a quadruple bypass. If he makes it through, he'll have to make some serious dietary and lifestyle changes if he wants to see any grandkids grow up. He's in surgery now."

It hit Sharon like a few sandbags, and she was lucky L.D. entered the waiting area at the exact moment Sharon needed to be helped into a chair. L.D. was in a flowing formal gown, with her hair up in some stunning bohemian masterpiece. And she comforted Sharon for a moment before standing to inquire of a random passing doctor, who couldn't tell her anything at all because she wasn't "family."

Something that sent L.D. into a tearful fit down a hallway where she found. . .me.

You'll never have a family. They barely put up with you. You'll never have a chance to ask a doctor anything about any of them.

"L.D.!" Sean called down that hall. Interrupting me. Sort of.

Did you hear what he called you?

"What?" She sniffled, hating the world. "Why did you just call me L.D.?"

"My family knows there's a girl I'm interested in. And at dinner tonight, they asked her name. I didn't want to lie, so I told them her name was Georgie. Which means I can't ever call you that around them. I guess it's your alias now," Sean said in a low voice. "I went home and added a new contact in my phone so that I'm not texting 'Lavender-Dawn Meadow George' or 'The Hippie' anymore. In case they get curious."

L.D. sniffled, a glimpse of a smile appearing. "I text you as 'Joe.' "

Sean smirked, but his concern prevailed. "You're crying. They think Dad could pull through. When we have a heart attack patient that can talk to us in the ambulance like they say Dad did, that's a good sign. Please don't worry, okay?"

She nodded. "It's not just that. I had to work, just like I thought. And they barely let me leave when you called about your dad. Good thing Sharon called too, because they didn't believe me." She looked into Sean's eyes. "My family is not even considered my family. You guys are all I have and technically I'm nothing to you."

"You're the farthest thing from nothing."

"The doctors. My bosses. Nobody believes that."

"Who cares what they believe? We know the truth."

"It matters. *Legally*, it matters."

"I know," he whispered.

"And legally, I'm nothing. Just a friend." She sobbed. "Even to you."

Sean sighed quickly and heavily, his heart breaking for her. "And that's tragic. Georgie, I see people die all the time. None of them woke up that morning thinking it was their time. Dad was just laughing at dinner, and we were talking about the woman I was texting. Now he's open-chested on a table, fighting for his life. Life is so short. We can't wait until we're good enough or until other people are prepared enough. We have to live the life and do the works God has for us without delay."

"What are you saying, Sean?"

"I'm saying that you're beautiful. You look incredible in that dress. And I'm in love with you, and you're usually the only thing I can think about. I'm telling you because I am sick of *not* telling you what I want to tell you just because the 'timing' is off. Time is not guaranteed. So, I am done being your 'friend.' "

"Well what else could we be at this point?"

Eric ran down the hall at that awful, untimely moment. "Sophie is having contractions. And her water broke. I don't know what to do."

L.D. launched into action. "You focus on Sophie, Eric. Sean, you and I will stay with Dad. Mom and Sharon should go with Sophie.

God knows they could use some better news today." They walked back down the hall, so many things left unsaid.

•••

"Crazy day, huh?" Sean commented.

"Go to sleep, Sean." L.D. was trying to nab a wink or two in a waiting room of the hospital. Still in an evening gown. Sean's hoodie covering her.

"Just one more thing," Sean insisted, also trying to get comfortable on a couch next to hers. The arms of the two couches were joined, and the two lay head-to-head conversing.

Sophie was laboring still, but not advanced enough to birth her son. Samuel was stabilized, but not yet ready for visitors. Sharon was in that wing on a couch waiting on word. Sean and L.D. couldn't bring themselves to leave the labor and delivery wing, when at any moment a new life would enter the world. They were in a darkened waiting room seemingly made for the purpose they were giving it.

"Okay, one thing." L.D. tried to keep her eyes open to indulge one of Sean's intense Bible-a-thons she'd enjoyed for the past six months.

"Awesome. So, I read in Psalms somewhere that children are a blessing and finally understood what people mean when they talk about 'a quiver full' of them," Sean began.

"Psalm 127," L.D. mumbled, her eyes drooping.

"Yeah," Sean remembered. "I keep reading that. How precious kids are. Jesus loved children when people wanted to keep them from annoying Him."

"Matthew 19. Verse 14, I think," she mumbled wearily.

Sean went on, "Right. The Bible also talks about how He formed us in the womb."

"Psalm 139," she said, without hesitating.

Sean snickered. "Have I ever told you it's hot when you do that?"

She smiled. "Only every time I do it."

"Yeah, that's probably true."

She sniffled at sleepy sinuses. "Was that your thing?"

"Sorry, almost there." Sean the night owl chuckled. "I know Sophie was on the pill. And I know a ton of Christians that use birth control. Which is their choice, but I don't see from Psalm 127 and Matthew 19 and Psalm 139 that it's what God really wants for us, you know? I've seen people look at big families and say it's irresponsible, but what if that isn't God's heart? I think He wants us to be fruitful. I can't think of a better thing on this planet than being chosen to usher in a new soul to be among the next generation of believers. God loves children, and I think we should too. I know I do. I wouldn't mind having a lot. What I wanted to ask is, am I missing where it says otherwise in the Bible, or. . .?"

"You didn't miss anything." L.D. blinked, smiling at his perspective. Eyes on the chipped corner of a ceiling panel. "There are lots of different opinions on this, and it's not my place to judge the convictions of others. But I agree with *you*. I think any sort of family planning is disturbing and backward if you look at God's view of things. Your sisters, who have both used birth control, always tell me I'm crazy and that I'll probably change my mind when I get married and have twenty kids running around. But I'm honestly not sure how the responsible high ground involves preventing new life. It doesn't seem like God's heart."

"So why do so many Christians plan families instead of letting God do it?"

"You're asking the wrong person, Sean. I'm never putting synthetic hormones in my body or preventing such a beautiful blessing as pregnancy and children in any other way. You might be the only person who has ever seen it like I do. That's comforting," L.D. shared. Another philosophy in her mind. A poisonous stumbling block for Sean. A struggle he could mask no longer.

"Does that mean you'll marry me?" he asked.

L.D. sighed, annoyed. Exhausted. Her heart bending. "Sean, please stop asking me that. How will I know if you ever mean it?"

"I *always* mean it." He let the silence level to sincerity before continuing. "I keep thinking, maybe we aren't not dating because of

Sharon. Maybe dating would just be a weird direction to take our relationship. I want to *marry* you, Georgie. I want you to rub crazy oils on my temples and make me feel better. I want you to live with me and store your weird food in my fridge and feed it to me until it's normal. I want to fight about bills and the nutritional value of milk. And I want us to make two dozen babies together and raise them to know Jesus." Sean cleared his throat. "So, I bought you a ring."

"You did not." She giggled. Reaching back and tapping his shoulder. Enchanted to the point of tears she was glad he couldn't see.

"I did. It's in my car," he confessed, grazing her arm as she withdrew it. "I've meant it every time I asked."

"You asked me on St. John," she conveyed the discrepancy.

"And I meant it on St. John. But I'm glad you didn't say yes because I didn't have a ring then, and I didn't exactly love who I was." Sean laughed. In awe at how God had transformed him.

After a brief silence, not quite long enough for Sean to wonder if L.D. had dozed off, she whispered a confession: "*I* loved who you were."

I'm supposed to plant seeds of doubt. And perhaps if I'd clued them in to what their next twenty-four hours would hold, they'd have doubted even the truth. But I was kind that night and let them sleep. They'd need it.

12

The Secret's Name

L.D. was practically hyperventilating with emotion as Sean opened the door to her apartment, letting her inside. It was 8:00 a.m., and they'd spent the night on firm couches in a hospital waiting room. She paced, letting out phonated, fitful breaths through tears. Sean stood aside nervously. Unsure what to do.

"They didn't mean it how you thought," he murmured, looking around at her home. A minimally furnished and decorated 300 square foot area in which she slept, ate, and cooked, read Scripture and blended oils. An armoire was all that housed her clothes. The only door besides the front door was a tiny bathroom, too small for even a bathtub. The morning light entered through a little window, and the whole thing smelled like her. He had to refocus.

"*Didn't* they?" L.D. shrieked. "Sean, this is the story of my life. How can you not see that?"

"Yeah, mine too. We can let one passenger in the back of the bus with a patient, and only in certain circumstances. Feelings get hurt sometimes. I'm just telling you the medical side of it," Sean explained.

Early in the morning, L.D. had been permitted to check in on still-laboring Sophie. But when she had reached transition labor, the nurses in the room allowed her to keep three guests in the room with her. By then, Samuel was asleep in recovery, so the birth of the baby became the priority. Meaning that the obvious choices were Sophie's husband, mother, and sister. All of whom had looked to the then-present L.D., silently requesting that she exit. She did so with grace, but when "only family" was called in after the birth of the baby as the sun rose, L.D.'s exit took her in a rage to her car. Sean had sped in his own to catch up with her, then coaxed her from her car up to her apartment. Taking her somewhere she could be safe to be angry.

"I don't want the medical side. I'm *never* going to have a family that wants me. I'll always be someone's extra. A stray cat, like you so eloquently put it once," she vented.

"Georgie, that's not fair. I never meant that. Everyone loves having you around. You know that." Sean tried to encourage her, but she continued to pace, still in that gorgeous gown.

" *'Around'*? Is it so much to ask to be a part of something?" she lamented.

"You'll be a part of your floor in a minute if you don't calm down. Um. . .lavender, right? That would work. Where do you keep your oils?"

"Yeah, lavender." L.D. was impressed he remembered. That reality alone calmed her enough to finally sit in a chair. "The cabinet above the sink. And the diffuser is right here."

Sean looked through the oils in her cabinet and brought the amber bottle to the table next to L.D. where she was gesturing to her diffuser. She showed him how to apply the oils, and soon the light scent of lavender was filling the small apartment.

L.D. only had one hand-me-down armchair. She'd thrown away her couch/childhood bed when her mother had been incarcerated. She had two solid metal dining chairs at a tiny bistro table, a set meant for outdoors. There was a twin bed in a corner which could only be accessed from one side. A deliberate choice by the purity-seeking single woman. Sean returned after replacing the oil in the cabinet and sat in a chair he brought from the dining area.

"Feeling any better?" Sean asked.

L.D. nodded. "Thank you, Sean."

As she took a deep breath and allowed God's peace to wash over her, she opened her eyes to see that Sean was already waiting to look into them. She giggled at his lovesickness, and his heart fluttered.

He breathed in deep, and began speaking, to her anticipation. "When are you going to marry me, Georgie?"

"I can't marry you, Sean. Not now." L.D. made it plain, her eyes meeting his again. Glistening this time. She laughed a sob and continued in shrugged tears. "It would destroy Sharon. And maybe she's not family, but I'd never want to hurt her like that."

"She *could* be your family." Sean reached into the inner pocket of his jacket and retrieved a velvet hinged box in classic black. He opened it and gingerly placed it on the table beside L.D. next to her diffuser.

L.D. glanced at the contents, then looked to the floor, responding with a smiled mumble. "It's a feather."

It was as if someone took a rose-gold feather and bent it, forming into a ring, and joined the ends with a single, tiny amethyst.

"Do you like it?" he cooed.

Her rant began directly. "It's not that I don't want to marry you, Sean. Because I do. You *know* I do. The timing is terrible. And I don't mean that in some worldly, abstract way. Because you're right. We don't know how much time we have. But Dad is barely clinging to life and Sophie just had the baby. Can you imagine what a bombshell like 'we've been secretly seeing each other for months and we want to get married' would do? The family doesn't need any more chaos."

That's about the time, I think, when the devious, terrible, insane, wonderful idea entered Sean's spirit.

"So, you're not saying it's a bad time to get married. You're saying it's a bad time for them to *know* about it."

"That is insane," L.D. responded to the silent suggestion. "I'm not doing that to your family."

"*You're* my family. You want to be a part of something? Be a part of me," Sean reiterated. Shrugged. "You called in today, right? I'm off, too. Let's go do something insane."

"*Today?*" she squeaked.

"Yes," he clarified. "It's perfect. Everyone's at the hospital, so no one would know. You can stay at my place tonight and we'll figure out the rest later."

Ah, now we see exactly what he's after. You should have known that the same Sean was still in there. The question is, are you crazy enough to agree to it?

Before she could respond, Sean panicked. "No! Wait. That totally sounded like I'm trying to talk you into bed with me, and I'm not, because. . .Well, the whole 'and stuff' thing is not a mandatory thing right now. We're not even physical at this point. That might be, you know—"

L.D.'s laughter stopped his stammered ranting, and her kindness further disarmed him.

"But don't you want a God-honoring, biblical marriage?"

"Yeah, of course."

"Okay. That means we'd need to figure out how to get us living under one roof, right? So, you were just suggesting a temporary solution. Totally innocent."

"You understood."

L.D. nodded, allowing his relief, then winked, teasing him.

"I feel like you're being nice *now*, but you're later going to tell our children that my marriage proposal sucked."

"Luckily, Sean, you've proposed dozens of times, and some of them were pretty good. Like the one on a beach at midnight. Maybe we'll tell them about that one." L.D. stood up from her chair, making her way to her armoire to finally replace her evening gown with something sensible.

"So. . .are you agreeing to have children with me, then? Thus, finally *accepting* a marriage proposal?"

L.D.'s first thought was a fervent rejection. But with self-control the Spirit had developed well, she was patient for the second thought. For the promised humility. It seeped in like the morning realization that the warm bed must be vacated. At first, rising from bed seems like a ludicrous, impossible notion. But slowly, the responsibilities and potential of the day take over, and what first was refusal becomes action. And feet hit the floor.

"Behold, your husband."

A gift. Wrapped up in a masculine physique and life-saving hands ready to gather her up as the two of them chased after Jesus as one. The gift was sitting across the room, waiting for a response. She tugged at the ribbon.

Casually, she pulled something out of her armoire that Sean recognized. A large, bohemian, crocheted bag she always used for sleepovers with Sharon. She put it on her bed and started packing it.

"I'll have to bring my own toothpaste and shampoo and such so I don't poison myself with yours while we figure out the living situation. And when I'm your wife, I may request that you stop poisoning *yourself*, too. Don't hate me if I fill up a trash bag with everything in your cabinets today. I think you'll quickly learn to appreciate my products."

"Wow." Sean laughed. Eyes startling wildly. "Really? So, like. . . yes?"

"I have some conditions, though."

"Of course, you do." He rolled his eyes, not knowing she saw, and doted. "I don't mind you going through my cabinets, Georgie."

"No, that's not a condition. Can you—?" She walked back to him, then turned and moved her hair over her shoulder, requesting for the gown to be unzipped.

"Uh. . .we're not quite there yet. Please don't tempt me."

"Oh, Sean, you know I have an organic cotton layer under this, modest enough even for your situation. No sneak previews, don't worry."

And she did. Sean unzipped her and watched L.D. slip out of the evening gown. The synthetic fibers she didn't let touch her skin. A modest cotton tank top and knee length skirt, both in off-white, had shielded her. How he adored her quirks.

"So, what are your conditions?"

"Just one, really. I want you to admit that the primary reason you want to marry me today is because you're not sure you have the self-control it takes to wait any longer. None of this 'and stuff isn't mandatory' nonsense. A Godly marriage includes becoming one flesh. So, stop trying to be some martyr or something."

"I'm trying to be a *gentleman* and give you time to be comfortable with it. That's all."

"You're a *man*, Sean. One who has been faithfully waiting for the woman he loves to decide she's going to be his wife. And that woman has faithfully waited over twenty-five years for you to be ready to be her husband. 'And stuff' happens *today,* right after we make this thing legal. Don't argue with me."

By then, Sean had risen and approached her, unaware he was doing so until his arms wrapped around her waist from behind. See, a fog was coming over him. The thoughts and images he wasn't supposed to allow were attacking his very spirit. He knew he should give her an out. A second chance. But he didn't have it in him.

"Please be serious." He laughed at his own desperation, pulling her close and kissing her shoulder.

"See, that wasn't so hard to admit," she teased with snorted laugher.

"Don't make fun of me. This hasn't been easy." He squeezed her.

"For either of us, Sean." She softened her tone, thrilling at the closeness and looking inside her armoire. "Help me decide what to wear to our wedding."

Your wedding. Think about this. Maybe you've been washed, Sean, but you'll never be clean enough for her.

"How about bubble wrap?" Sean began, rightfully earning L.D.'s laugh of confusion. "Or whatever a snow globe wears before completely unstable hands take it off the shelf."

L.D. was disturbed. Heartbroken. "Stop with the snow globe analogy, Sean."

"That's what you are to me." He gazed into a closet that bore all the modest bohemian wardrobe pieces he admired her for.

She turned to him to set him straight. "Well, today I'm marrying you. So, I'm going to promise to always love and respect you exactly as you are no matter how that is, and you are going to promise to love me—"

"As Christ loves the church." He finished for her, stepping away from the embrace.

"Right," she whispered. Enchanted.

"Except I'm human. And I'll mess it up. So, if you have bubble wrap in this closet. . ." He looked to her apartment floor.

"In Ephesians 5, *before* husbands are given the command to love their wives, wives are commanded to *submit* to their husbands in everything. Which means if I'm a snow globe. . ." She drew him in by the hands, placing his arms around her waist, completing the embrace by clasping her hands behind his neck. He laughed at her sudden affinity for physical affection. "I'm okay being *shattered*, as long as I'm with you."

With that, I thought it more effective, though I could have continued my torture, to wait for a more opportune moment to define the depth of "shattered."

• • •

"Fal-*fa*-lel?" Sean asked for the sixth time as they slowly navigated the curves of the hospital parking garage in his car.

"Fa-*la*-fel." She corrected with a laugh. "How did you not know that my favorite Greek place was right across the street from your apartment?"

"So, there's more than one place in town that serves your weird food? It wasn't bad, I have to admit," he complimented as he swung his car into a free parking spot.

"I'm glad I finally got you to try it."

"It's been an adventurous day. Why not, right?" He leaned in, kissing his wife with easy tenderness, then drew back to capture her eyes.

That tone. His deep gritty voice, warmed up just for her, had power over her, as he'd recently learned. Steadfast and stubborn as she was in everything, she wondered if that silky tone could talk her off a cliff and into spurting lava with a word.

She couldn't hide the smile as she crossed her arms and bit at that tender kiss. She cleared her throat. How had she allowed herself to be wooed so? "What is our plan for this hospital thing? We can't exactly arrive together."

"No, because then they'd suspect we randomly got married this morning." Sean smiled at her preposterous fear.

She retained her worries. "I'm just not sure how to keep this extremely huge thing under their radar. I don't feel comfortable lying to them."

As she spoke, Sean was removing his newly bought wedding band and putting it on his key ring.

"Then don't lie. If they feel like they need to ask us point-blank if we're together or whatever, they deserve to hear the point-blank truth. But I doubt they'd ever be that rude, even if they did figure it out somehow. We can continue to act like recovering mortal enemies in front of them. We've been doing this for months, Georgie."

"Sean, *nothing* we did today is anything like what we've been doing for months," L.D. argued.

"Yeah, sitting on the kitchen floor trying to read the names of the chemicals in all my cleaning products was definitely new," Sean quipped. "How could they know about that? Or anything else? They've been here all day at Dad's bedside and holding a brand-new baby. They probably barely missed us."

"I don't know. It just feels like I'm wearing it, Sean. Like an obnoxious neon shirt or something. I can't imagine them not *seeing* it. And if they say something, I feel like I'll disintegrate. Tell me that's reasonable."

"I get it, Georgie," Sean conceded. "How about this? You go meet our nephew. I'll wait here for ten minutes, then go sit with Dad before I come see the baby. That way you'll have time with the baby, and if you want to jet when I get there, you can."

"Is it weird that I feel better about that?" She finally reached for her purse, taking a moment to tease. " 'Our nephew.' You're so cute."

He smiled, teasing her right back. "Get out of my car and go feed that baby fever."

She giggled as she exited, and Sean leaned on his steering wheel to get a better view of her walking to the stairs that would lead her to the hospital. Protecting her until she was out of sight. The white broom skirt and coral top and her hair flowing with her movements.

His thoughts shifted with ease to the way she'd trusted him. Melted at his touch and submitted to his whims as he whispered that powerfully gentle tone between kisses to calm her nerves. The smile that sneaked across half his face completely concealed my approach.

You're disgusting. Does she have any idea how many women you've entertained in that bedroom of yours? How dare you take your bride there? She was perfect. Yesterday, you were bragging about her being a virgin. What did you do, Sean?

He'd burned his old sheets. Rearranged the furniture. But still those voices. Those images echoed. Those rotten apples of women whenever he could that left him hungry. Today he'd procured himself a feast to be expertly prepared whenever he desired. A woman of God. His wife. She deserved to be his first. But Sean supposed he'd forever have the stench of apples on his breath, which I put on his heart.

He realized it all in one long-held breath and exhaled at tears.

"1 Corinthians 6:11."

God requested it. And to Sean's benefit and God's glory, Sean had taken the time to hide it in his heart. Valiantly, he leaned back, clutching his steering wheel, and practically spat in my face.

" 'And such were some of you. But you were washed.' " That deep, smoky voice began. He spoke the rest slowly, through closed eyes and sobs. " 'But you were sanctified. But you were justified in the name of the Lord Jesus and by the Spirit of our God.' Lord, continue to remind me."

• • •

When L.D. arrived in the mother-baby wing, she was permitted into the room with ease. Lynn and Eric were sitting on a bench along the window, the bundled babe in Lynn's arms. Sharon was absent.

"Hey, new mom!" She greeted her unbeknownst sister-in-law.

At her words, the whole room lit up.

"L.D.! You came back!" Sophie emoted. "Oh my gosh! I am so mad! Those stupid nurses said only family could see me downstairs, but when I finally told them you were my sister, they said they couldn't find you. Did you take off?"

"You said I was your sister?" L.D. was beyond flattered.

"Of course. I tell people that all the time. Otherwise I have to explain too much." Sophie said as L.D. washed her hands, trying to keep from crying. "Where did you go?"

"I just headed home. It was a long night." She shrugged. "So, who is this tiny human over here?"

"This is our son, Mel Eric Stiles," Sophie said proudly.

"Mel?" L.D. didn't think it sounded like a full name, but never judged. "That's cute!"

She sat on the bench with Lynn, who handed her the baby with black curls poking out from his blue-striped cap.

Eric shared the stats happily. "Seven pounds, six ounces. Nineteen inches. Ten fingers, ten toes. And he passed his hearing test."

"That's great!" L.D. cooed when little Mel yawned.

Lynn gasped. "That ring is stunning, L.D. Very you. I've never seen it before."

"Isn't it great?" L.D. managed somehow, having forgotten to remove the recently placed ring. "I'm not usually a ring person, but *this* one was a necessity. Where is Sharon?"

"Since when do you call her Sharon?" Sophie laughed.

Since you're failing at this.

"Like I said, long night. Sorry."

"She's been with Dad most of the day. I should be getting back over there in case anything changes," Lynn shared.

"I might pop over there too." L.D. nodded. "Is he allowed to have non-family visitors?"

"You're family, L.D." Sophie rolled her eyes.

"Tell the doctors that. They wouldn't tell me a thing about Dad last night."

"Doctors are dumb. How was the gala, by the way? That dress was really something. Looked pricey," Sophie chatted.

"Uh, it was—"

But at that moment, Sean entered the room. L.D. tried not to react. It hadn't been ten minutes.

"I should have known the hippie would be hogging the boy-child," were his first words. He smiled. "It's okay. I'll wait."

"Uncle Sean!" Sophie and Eric said in unison.

Lynn sighed. "Did you go see Dad?"

"I tried. He was my first stop." Sean rolled his eyes, then washed his hands. "Sharon won't let me take a vigil, and also didn't want me to listen to her reading to him. She did ask me to check on her cat, though. While I'm here, I figured I'd meet my nephew."

"Where have you been all day? I thought you took the day off to be at the hospital with your *family*," Sophie accused.

"I was just. . .you know. . .hanging out at home. Going to lunch. And stuff. . ." Sean said. L.D. glanced out the window, avoiding his eyes, and trying to stay out of the conversation.

Lynn shook her head. "Sean, tell me you weren't with your *girlfriend*?"

"As I told you last night, Mom, Georgie's not my girlfriend."

Clever.

"Obviously. I would have expected that a *girlfriend* supports you enough to come with you to the hospital under these circumstances," Lynn scolded.

"If I'd brought her, you'd have thought it was inappropriate for me to bring my so-called girlfriend 'under these circumstances,' " Sean convicted her.

"He's not wrong, Mom," Sophie confessed. Signing as she spoke, as usual. "And I'd have been mad that he was trying to steal Mel's thunder."

They all laughed, including Lynn as she realized the truth in it. All except L.D., who was enjoying the squeezably cute yawns of Mel until she heard Sean's familiar low, throaty laugh. She looked up and nearly smiled dotingly. Barely held back.

You can't keep it together.

"Jesus, keep me together."

"We've been tossing around Georgie theories all day." Sophie seemed to challenge L.D.'s silent prayer. L.D. marveled that Sean was so unrattled.

"Theories? I've told you what you want to know."

"Yeah, but we haven't *met* her, so there is mystery as to *why*. Mystery lends itself to theories," Sophie chattered. "I think she's a prostitute and you fell in love with her, but you didn't know how to tell Mom how you met, so we haven't met her."

"A *hooker*, Sophie?" Sean turned red, glancing L.D.'s way to check for offense.

"It's just a theory." Sophie shrugged. "Mom thinks you think she's the one and you don't want to scare her off, but that's boring. Eric thinks Georgie is L.D.. Sharon was here when he came up with that insanity and said that made her want to vomit, and she just like, takes you at your word or whatever. So, out of those, Pretty Woman is the juiciest. What's your Georgie theory, L.D.?"

L.D.'s ears burned, and Sean's heart sang as he watched her come alive.

"Who is Georgie, and why am I supposed to have a theory?"

"She wasn't at the dinner last night, Sophie. When Sean told us her name?" Lynn explained. "L.D., Georgie is Sean's new girlfriend."

"Not my girlfriend," he interjected. "They are overanalyzing this. Georgie is a girl I was texting during dinner last night before we all ended up here. A girl. Woman, actually. Who is my friend. Not my girlfriend. Also, not a hooker."

"See, but Sean, whenever you refer to a girl you're sleeping with but not committing to, you generally use the term 'friend.' So. . ." L.D. tried to remove herself from the situation. Seeing it from the outside.

"True. Unfortunately. But Georgie is different. She isn't okay with premarital sex, and neither am I anymore. She's into Jesus and requires the voice of God to tell her when it's okay to commit to a man, because she's only doing it once. Being presented to a guy's family is basically a commitment. Thus, me not bringing her home to Mom. Yet. I'm working on it."

Again, clever. I'll get you soon, Sean. Just wait.

"Okay, I have my theory," L.D. blurted.

"Oh, do tell. Your theories hold up. You totally called that I was preggers at my dress fittings. I didn't know before." Sophie was practically drooling at the gossip.

"Well, unfortunately, Georgie doesn't exist." The woman herself shrugged. "You just described the kind of woman Sean Mehlmann avoids like a cliché. You're not dating her because there's not a 'her.' "

"Ouch," Sean feigned offense. "Dad met her. Nice theory, though, Hippie."

"Convenient that the only person who has met her is literally in a coma," L.D. fought back.

Eric tapped Sophie and began signing for her to translate. She nodded when he completed his thought.

"He wants to know when Dad met her."

"At church. You've probably met her too, Lavender-Dawn Meadow George. Don't you have a cot or something at the church?"

"Funny. What is her last name?" L.D. tortured.

"Um. . ." Sean laughed, seemingly embarrassed, but really just overjoyed beyond control. "Hopefully 'Mehlmann' soon if I have a say in it."

"Oh, I thought you and Georgie were just friends!" Lynn startled.

"Friends waiting on God's approval, Mom. Dad and I have been talking about this for months. I love her. She's torturing me. It's this fun game we play."

"Hooker," Sophie concluded.

Eric chuckled.

"Yeah, the kind that hates the idea of premarital sex. She can't be both, Soph." Sean laughed.

"Yeah, because she's neither." L.D. amused herself, and Sophie ignored.

"True. What about Eric's theory?"

"Sophie, stop this. Leave your brother be," exhausted Lynn tried, and failed.

"I can't keep all your theories straight, Sophie." He crossed his arms and leaned against the sink.

You also can't keep the lies straight. You're going to lose.

Sophie whispered for drama. "Eric thinks Georgie is in the room with us." She flicked her head at L.D.

L.D. giggled. Snorted. "Is she in the room, Sean? Your imaginary woman?"

"Seriously, though. Can you imagine how much of a scandal that would be if it was L.D.? Sharon would *die*. Vomit, like she said. At which point she would die a slow, horrified death. Your theory is morbid, Eric. I don't like it. But it's a plausible reason to keep her from us. Right?"

L.D. was about to lose composure. Almost feeling dizzy and nauseous.

"That is pretty morbid, Eric." Sean managed a smirk. "No offense, Flower Child."

"None taken. You did recently stop calling me a stray cat or a one-woman freak show, so maybe that's proof you're pining for me. I mean. . .it's plausible, like Sophie said." The baby successfully concealed the tremble in L.D.'s arms. And something else. Maybe she was a hippie. But she was also an expert texter and could do it with little help from her eyesight.

"Yeah, but I've been with Georgie all morning, and you've been here. Hogging my nephew," Sean tried. Succeeded.

"I got here forty-two seconds before you did, Sean."

"Oh. You're not helping my case," he goaded.

Sean's unique notification sound for Georgie dinged then. It took him by surprise, but he didn't let it show on his face.

"Is that from. . .?" Sophie grunted disappointment.

"Yeah. . ." Sean read the text with a smile. "She's thanking me for lunch."

"Text her back," Eric insisted with a stoic yet smug look on his face.

"You seriously think. . .? Okay." Sean chuckled, then authored the text carefully as L.D. stashed her phone in the purse beside her. When L.D.'s phone chimed, everyone in the room laughed.

"Here, can you. . ." L.D. handed the baby back to his grandmother as she checked her phone, smirking at the room's anticipation and Sean's surprise. Obviously, he'd only pretended to text her. "It's S.R. I texted on the way in to see if she was here or with Dad, and she finally replied. She asked me to go sit with her."

Sean's eyes widened as L.D. kissed the baby's forehead and stood, taking her leave. "Wait. She asked *you*? She kicked me out a minute ago! Why would she let you stay?"

"I think it's that I have the ability to sit with her in silence instead of jabbering about an impossible, invisible not-girlfriend. But maybe I just smell better?" She said her goodbyes and congratulations to the rest of the family before she passed Sean in the doorway, who could barely contain himself.

"Sharon does prefer 'earthy' scents."

L.D. left the room with faked laughter.

"Sean, I thought we were being kind to L.D.," his mother intended to scold.

"According to Eric, I'm in love with her. Can I hold my nephew, please?"

At which point, Eric winked at his brother-in-law from across the room.

• • •

"Sorry! Eric and I got to talking. He's *so* excited about Mel." It was dark by the time Sean emerged from the hospital to find L.D. leaning against his car in the garage. "So, when are you giving *me* one?"

"I thought I was the one with baby fever." She giggled, accepting Sean's embrace. "What did you think of his name?"

"Mel?" Sean grimaced.

"Oh good." She giggled. Went on to the next topic. "I'm so bad at this secret, Sean. I was wearing my ring and Mom noticed!"

"You did fine. Great, actually. You almost had *me* convinced you don't exist. You just have to relax. It's just our family." Sean shrugged.

"*Our* family? They keep saying that but actually treat me *so* not like that."

"Well when we tell them, they are going to have to get used to you being Lavender-Dawn Meadow Mehlmann. But I really don't think it'll be that hard if we time it right."

"About that awful name you just mentioned. . ."

Something in his soul loosened as he captured her eyes. A new dimension of her had seeped inside him, and he saw what he hadn't not long before. She was trying to mask that she was deeply in thought. He sighed.

"Yeah, I wondered. . ." Sean cleared his throat. "I mean, yeah, the only way to make you hate your name more is to add a name like 'Mehlmann.' "

She doesn't even want your name.

L.D. smiled with remorse. "You're kidding, right? Why wouldn't I take your name?"

"Oh, um. . .hyphenating? Lavender-Dawn Meadow George-Mehlmann."

"Stop talking?" L.D. giggled. "George-Mehlmann? That's like a whole other person."

126

Sean laughed appreciatively. L.D. smirked and finished the thought.

"But I'm a girl, so. . .*Georgie* Mehlmann. Georgie Lavender-Dawn. . .Mehlmann."

Sean practically melted in that chilly parking garage. "You're not serious."

"It's much more professional, and I could finally delete Meadow. I'd keep my first name for the middle because that's what Sharon calls me. Ideally, that'd be my name. But I may have to settle for just replacing Meadow with George."

"Oh, can you not change your first name?"

"I can, but I'd have to jump through like 38 flaming hoops, including a background check, a possible court hearing and publicly announcing my new name in the newspaper. I looked it up when you were gabbing with Eric. Not only would that take more time and effort than our entire engagement and marriage, but I would risk the family finding out because of the newspaper. If Sharon saw that, it would likely land her in the room next to your dad at the hospital. She *voiced* that she'd vomit, Sean. This is bad." L.D. sighed.

Sean was too uplifted to bend to her worries. "Change your name, Georgie. You'll always wish you did. No one reads the paper."

13

Sharon's Goal

"I think I screwed up," Sean whispered in the five minutes he'd found when Georgie forced Sharon and Lynn into a coffee break elsewhere in the hospital. He was listening to the monitors and sitting in a chair, leaning on his arms on his father's bed and holding his father's hand. He sniffled. Spoke through tears. "Dad, I did something. . . *so* crazy, and I need you."

Samuel didn't respond. But he was present in his mind as I convinced him he'd never awaken. He could hear, though not presently understand, the words his son was whispering.

"We made this big decision really fast, and. . .She's all I ever wanted and now I have her." Sean laughed to cover tears. "But I don't know how to be a husband without you helping me."

The women breached the door, and Sean raised his head, feeling a slight squeeze to his hand as he did. The surprise in his face still shone when Lynn came in.

"Did he squeeze?" she asked.

"Yeah." Sean smiled.

"He's been doing that when we talk to him. Doctors think he'll wake up soon."

Sean sighed relief. "Good."

Sharon spent five days total in the hospital by her father's side, only seeing her new nephew when Sophie brought him up to meet his grandpa. Wondering how in the world to find joy in this. Or meaning. Or anything. Then, Dad awakened and ordered her to go take care of her cat, which Georgie and Sean had been presumed to be tag-teaming but were obviously taking care of it together.

The secret was already more than they could contain.

"Will you marry me?" Sean whispered, wrapping his arms around Georgie from behind as she opened a can of cat food. Kissing her neck.

She giggled. "I think you can stop asking that now." She turned and accepted a front hug.

"Maybe someday when I believe we actually did it." Sean smirked, granting her several kisses before allowing her to finish opening the can of cat food. "Did you get a chance to talk to your apartment manager?"

She suddenly beamed a smile. "I did. He let me out of the lease like I thought he would. We might actually get to live together soon, like normal married people."

"That's great!" Sean said through a laugh.

L.D. turned and emptied the can into Stormy's bowl. The overweight cat devoured it immediately. "My goodness, she is fat."

Sean chuckled, distracted. Leaned against the counter and crossed his arms. "When should we move you?"

"No rush. He said I could have until the end of the month. I don't have a whole lot, either. You know that." L.D. shrugged.

"So. . ." Sean pocketed his hands and bent his legs. Beyond excited for the move. An unfortunate work schedule and lack of key situation had landed them sleeping in different apartments the previous night. Both newlyweds had tossed and turned. "What about the snow globe? Does that come home too?"

"How would I explain—?"

The two suddenly heard a key in the door. Their eyes widened.

"I got it," Sean whispered.

"No lies," L.D. reminded in a whisper, putting herself at a more hostile distance from her husband.

The door opened. Sharon's eyebrows scrunched at the sight of them together in her apartment. "Oh."

Sean launched into the explanation. "I know, right? I had to work last night, so she came to look after Stormy for me. Your overachieving friend also came today, when I'd already planned to." Not a lie. Not the truth. "But hey, we both love your cat."

"Did you decide to get her fixed?" L.D. asked.

"Yeah, I probably should." Sharon sighed. "Dad's going home in the next couple days, so you guys are off the hook. Thanks for taking care of her."

The couple left, relieved they didn't have to explain why they arrived and left in one car.

• • •

On the day of the appointment, the veterinarian was taken aback by Stormy's size.

"How much do you feed her?" the vet asked.

"I don't know. . .six cans a day? I feel bad whenever her dish is empty."

"Six?! She could die from being this big for too long. She needs exercise and she needs *two* cans of food a day. Obviously, starting when you pick her up tomorrow. She's too fat. Way too fat."

Sharon went home and moped without her kitty and her daddy. She decided that some lesson planning might be in order and saw that measurements were next on the docket for her new class of second graders. Along with planning materials from her bag, she procured a spoon and a pint of ice cream, glancing at the label before planning to devour the entire thing. Upon the necessity for planning, she rose halfway through the pint and grabbed her measuring cups, setting them out side by side. Taking one empty bowl, and one of dry beans, she began marking different measurements to show how one corresponds to another. After she'd made the marks, Sharon looked at the mark for a half cup. For some reason, it caught her eye as she lifted the last, now melted spoonful of ice cream into her mouth.

She looked at her pint, and suddenly thought of poor, fixed Stormy and how she was "way too fat." She looked at the serving size printed on the side of the ice cream—a half cup. That's where she'd seen that. But when she looked at the mark on the empty bowl, she nearly fainted. That means she'd just eaten four servings. At 200 calories each. That's 800 calories on top of everything else she ate that day.

Some quick internet research, and Sharon discovered a lot about calories. About how much she was eating and not burning. Her astronomical Body Mass Index and what all her weight was doing to even her bone structure. And what a diet similar to her own had done to her dad's arteries.

Sharon smiled and discovered just exactly how to find joy in her circumstances. She was going to lose every last pound of extra weight. I told her she couldn't, but I wasn't loud about it. I wanted to see her try. I could gain power over time in that case.

• • •

"I need to lose a hundred pounds," Sharon told Georgie when she came home to find her petting Stormy and writing in a promptly closed journal three days later in her apartment. Not at all alarmed by her presence. "I just came from the doctor, and he thought that was a good goal. He put me on a really minimal diet where I measure all my food and I have to start burning lots of calories, and—"

"Okay, slow down." Georgie stopped the train on the tracks. "*A hundred*? By when?"

"In six months. Sophie's wedding will give me a good 'before' picture, so I want my 'after' to be near her anniversary." Sharon was determined, Georgie could tell. "Do you still run?"

"I do. But what you're talking is like marathons. And lettuce. Those don't jive. You have to feed your workout. Not just starve all the meat off your bones. Please don't go the Sophie route."

"Yeah, protein. I'm allowed protein and vegetables. No carbs or sugar, except in fruit, and very little dairy," Sharon explained, trying not to lisp.

"Okay. Not sure I can handle the diet restrictions, but I'll for sure run with you," L.D. agreed. "What's the sudden—"

"Dad got so sick so fast. I'm twenty-five, but I'm cutting years off my life by being this big, and no one will date me."

"Sharon, you should know that God loves you just how—" Georgie tried in vain.

"Did you just call me Sharon?" Sharon startled.

Georgie wanted to kick herself. So much to keep sorted all the time. She made a quick recovery. "So, running."

"Yeah, I was thinking the distance between your apartment and my parents' house might be a good start? Next, we can maybe move to between *here* and my parents' house. That's a few more blocks."

"We'd have to make the switch in the next couple days. I'm moving this weekend." She changed the subject, seemingly midbreath. "We can go buy workout gear for you and go for a run. I have a thing in a few hours. But I'm with you now." Georgie nearly gave it away but managed to keep it under wraps one more time. Glad she could wear the workout jacket that covered the hickey on her neck her hair currently concealed.

"Moving?" Sharon asked. "You haven't done that since you were nine. This seems like weird timing. You hadn't even mentioned wanting to move," Sharon noted, understandably so.

"It was a recent decision, and I didn't want to burden you with it," Georgie began, then attempted to conclude the matter with, "You just told me you wanted to lose a hundred pounds in the next six months, and I can't have a simple change like moving out of my dump of an apartment?"

"Sorry. Where are you moving?" Sharon was stuck on the subject, to Georgie's fear.

"Not out of town or anything. Just to a better apartment." Georgie shrugged. She theorized that if the story lined up with the truth, there'd be no lies to tell. "It's that complex where Sean used to live. By that Greek place I love."

Sharon smiled. "He still lives there."

"Oh. Yikes. Let's not tell him, okay? And hope we don't cross paths at the mailbox or something." Georgie laughed the almost lie.

"Your secret is safe with me." Sharon smiled, murdering Georgie inside.

• • •

"Hey, Daddio!" Sean entered his childhood home to visit with his father. First came a compliment. "You're sitting up in a chair, this is good."

"Eating rabbit food." He grumbled about the salad before him on the TV tray.

Lynn, of course, shot him a nasty look of disdain.

"Rabbit food prepared by my lovely bride," Samuel corrected, receiving a kiss.

"Would you like some supper, Sean?" Lynn asked, backing up toward the kitchen.

"No, I'm good. I have other dinner plans. I'm just stopping by."

"In that case, could you look out for him for a few? I'd love to snag a shower since you're here. I won't be long," Lynn requested.

"I'm fine, woman! I don't need a babysitter!" Her husband protested, and her son ignored.

"Yeah, that's cool, Mom." Sean smiled, only checking his watch with a wince after she was out of sight.

"You got somewhere to be?" his father teased.

"Dinner date." Sean shrugged. "I'm taking Georgie to this crazy expensive French place, so she can re-wear the crazy expensive dress I bought her."

"Good for you. I'm told she was stunning in it." Samuel chuckled. "I was otherwise engaged when she came to the hospital from her gala."

Tell him. If he knows, you'll feel better about yourself. I'll go away, I promise.

Sean cleared his throat, silently confirmed the running of his mother's shower through the older pipes of the house before speaking.

"She was still wearing it when I asked her to marry me," he shared, to his father's shock.

"Son. . ." A spoken trail of disappointment. He corrected it to give an air of support. "What did she say?"

Sean smiled a brilliant, childlike grin.

"Dear God, you eloped." Samuel discovered from the shimmer in his son's eyes.

"How could you know that?" Sean's face lit up his amusement. He pawed at his left hand with his right. "I'm not even wearing my ring."

"Your mother mentioned *L.D.* had a new ring on her wedding finger. This is serious, Sean." Samuel's demeanor was much more somber. "You didn't get her in trouble, did you?"

"No!" The young man assured him. Sobering as well. Looking to the ground. "Dad, you had a massive heart attack. And all I could think about was when you told me I eventually had to walk through the door I was holding open. And she's done her fair share of door-holding too. All we did was walk through the door together."

"I can respect that. . ." Samuel said with a question in his voice.

"But?" Sean said with a sigh.

"But how do you expect to sustain a secret marriage in a family like this?" he asked it point-blank.

"Dad—"

"Is it because of Sharon?" Samuel asked.

"Yes." Sean shrugged, telling the truth. "Sharon doesn't need the burden right now."

"Burden?" Samuel confronted him, recovering heart and all. Sean knew it and sat back in his chair. "When Christ demonstrated His love for us, He did so publicly. Even when it required mockery and false accusations. Betrayal. Then death. He knew that being open and honest about who He was and the extent to which He loved us was so much more important. As a godly man, your job is to walk like Jesus walked. And she's your bride. As her husband, you should love her like Christ loves *His* bride. Publicly. Fully. No matter the consequences. I love that young woman as my own child, and she doesn't have a daddy to say it, so I will. A Christ-chasing woman with excellent moral character who has spent her entire life trying not to become what her mother is and instead honor God? She deserves to be paraded. Not hidden. Marriage is cause for joy. But if you don't set this right, it could quickly become a source of shame." Samuel was scolding at that point.

"Dad, I know all that. But—"

"Don't 'but' me. And am I wrong in remembering that your new wife has a strong disdain for family planning?" Samuel scolded.

You're an idiot. Yeah, I'm still here. I lied. Sorry.

"She and I *agree* on that." Sean tried to mask the smile. His father caught him.

"I'm sure it seems romantic now, but just you try to keep a *baby* a secret," Samuel continued the reaming. "Does she have another woman to talk to? A mentor?"

"About what?" Sean laughed, somewhat embarrassed. "*We* talk, Dad. Georgie and me. We're very open with one another. Why would she need to go discuss our marriage with another woman?"

Samuel Mehlmann laughed. Hand at his chest for the pain since the surgery. "Premarital counseling would have done you some good."

Lynn, having kept her promise for a speedy shower, descended the stairs during the most recent revelations, drying her hair.

"I spoke with her," she revealed.

Sean's eyes widened. He gritted his teeth. "Dad, I asked you not to tell Mom!"

"Well, your mom and I are very open with one another," Samuel mocked. Smiled. "But I wasn't aware they'd spoken."

"Yeah, me neither." Sean laughed once. Baffled. "She didn't mention anything."

"We didn't see a reason to worry your little heads over girl things." His mother smirked.

Sean rolled his eyes. "Please tell me you didn't lecture her like you're doing to me."

"I would *never*, sweetheart. I *am* told there's a wedding picture, but it's on *your* phone. I've been promised a copy for my album when you two go public."

Sean could take a hint, and took out his phone, rolling his eyes. He showed his mother the picture they'd taken, and she gasped. Lynn promptly began sniffling as she examined the picture.

"My goodness, it really is her," Lynn commented. "She looked lovely."

"She always looks 'lovely,' what do you mean?" Sean caused his father a smile as he examined the photo as well.

"Is that your couch?" Samuel asked.

"Yeah, we got married there." Sean cleared his throat and explained. "In this state you can self-solemnize. We wanted it to happen that day, and anyone who could officiate same day was pretty expensive, so we just opted to sign it ourselves. Easy peasy, as she said."

"That's barely a wedding at all, Sean," Lynn filed her complaint.

"Mom, *Sophie* had the big white wedding. I'm sure Sharon will too. That's just not what we wanted," Sean argued.

Lynn looked at the photo one more time before she handed Sean his phone. "Even so, please tell me you've done something special to celebrate, even if it's just the two of you?"

"That's tonight." Sean glanced at his phone. "I'm finally getting through all the extra shifts I took, so this is the first full evening we've had together since the day we got married. And we'll go public soon. Georgie and I wanted to start a life together, but Sharon needs to not know about it right now. It would crush her."

By then, Samuel was laughing endearingly. "You really think your sister couldn't accept you two?"

"It's complicated."

"It's crystal clear to me." Samuel shrugged. "You care deeply about your sister's feelings. I respect that. But you are putting those feelings, however delicate, above the feelings of the woman who is flesh of your flesh. That's unacceptable. You need to come out with this."

Sean crossed his arms and nodded in silence, as a much younger, wise young man should do. His father could humble him that way. Make him see the error of his ways without disrespecting him. The deed done, Samuel made a more characteristic promise.

"Until then, you know your secrets are safe with us."

"Thanks, Dad."

. . .

The two women ran the block between Georgie's apartment and the Mehlmann home. Georgie had lived in the studio apartment since childhood, taking over the rent when her mother got arrested. The sidewalk between the two had been trodden well since childhood. Today, Sharon collapsed in tears on her parents' lawn.

"You did it!" Georgie cheered. "I am so proud of you! S.R., you are a friggin' beast!"

"I ran a block and want to die," she lamented from the grass.

At which point, Sean emerged from the front door with his mother.

"What did you do to my sister, Hippie?" Sean accused. Being nicely mean, as agreed.

"She just ran here from my apartment!" Georgie jumped up and down. "Says she wants to lose a hundred pounds in the next six months. I'd say we're well on our way, S.R."

"Your apartment is like. . ." Sean pointed at the building. Impressed. "That's like 200 yards. She ran the whole way?"

"And tomorrow we'll do it twice. Today, we'll just walk back." Georgie shrugged.

"A hundred, Sharon? Is that reasonable?" Dad had joined Mom on the porch. She scolded him for rising and walking.

Nope. Never gonna happen.

"I have to," Sharon said, trying to catch her breath in the lungs beneath her ample breasts.

"I can safely start an exercise routine in a month. I'll join you then. I've got a lot to lose too," Dad said. "I've already started on the healthy eating. We'll do this together, my Rose."

"Thanks, Daddy." Sharon rose slowly from the grass. Hobbling from running on ankles that simply never had.

Sean checked his phone. "I'm proud of you, Sharon. Let me know how I can help. I have to get home and out of this uniform or I'll be late."

"Mens study?" Sharon asked. Georgie pretended to look at a dead flower in the yard.

"No, actually. More like a social gathering. A time of fellowship and bonding. For just two people. Of um, you know, opposite genders." Sean sniffed quickly.

"Oh, a date? Tell me you didn't meet her on an app," Sharon whined, to Georgie's snorted laughter.

Sean laughed his nerves over his wife having to hear what no wife should be reminded of. "It's not that kind of date. I'm going to dinner with *Georgie*. Remember?"

"Oh, the elusive slash invisible perfect Christian girl you somehow wooed?" Georgie, in high spirits and fighting her attraction to Sean in uniform, teased needlessly at an invisible battle.

"That's a complicated issue, Child of the Wind," Sean stated. His charming smile spread across his face.

"I thought you were just friends. When did you start dating her?" Sharon huffed and puffed. Surprised.

"Most importantly, is it time to bring her home to meet us?" His mother asked boldly. His parents teasing him mercilessly. Trying to trap him in front of Sharon.

"Soon, Mom, I just have to work out some logistics." Sean spun his keys, making Georgie think she might die from his near-miss truths and suave. And making Sharon jealous, of course.

"Five bucks says she turns out to be a hoax." Georgie guffawed.

"Do you even *have* five bucks? Don't you people use like nuts and shells for currency?" Sean was walking the line, and he knew it.

"Sean, be nice," his father defended. Astonished they could keep up the guise so well.

"Sorry, Lavender-Dawn Meadow George, I promised I'd be better. Um. . ." Sean realized the line he crossed with the joke he didn't mean. Looked into Georgie's eyes. "Uh. . .thanks for doing this with my sister. Means a lot. But I really am gonna be late. Georgie and I have reservations." Here, he flashed widened eyes at Georgie to warn her of the time.

It was Sharon who reacted. "L.D., what time did you say that thing was? Didn't you have a thing too?"

"Yes, I have to be ready by. . ." Georgie looked at the device on her wrist. "Holy socks! S.R., I have to run. Literally. Sean, would you mind terribly taking your sister home?"

"And have this beauty in my car? You kidding?" Sean winked at his big sister, who snickered. "Yeah, I can do that."

"Bye guys. I'll text you, S.R.," Georgie called as she ran backward, then turned and ran back the way she came.

"Did you know she's moving soon? Her apartment was completely packed up a minute ago," Sharon said to her parents, who were trying not to notice Sean pretending not to watch a long ash-brown ponytail swing side to side.

"Really? Where?" Lynn pretended to wonder.

"She asked me not to say for some reason. But Sean, if you see her at your complex, just know she isn't stalking you." Sharon wasn't great with secrets. "I'm not sure how she can afford it. Your complex is pretty nice."

"Roommate maybe?" Lynn could walk lines as well.

"Maybe. She probably didn't tell me because she thinks I'd be jealous or something." Sharon shrugged. "Let's go, Sean. Don't want you to be late."

Luckily, Sharon was taken to her apartment and not Georgie's. Lucky because otherwise she'd have likely still been there when

Sean showed up freshly showered and heart-poundingly dapper in a three-piece suit to pick her up.

She had barely finished pinning up her hair when he let himself in, stepping around packed boxes. When he arrived in her bathroom, she turned and kissed him. He accepted the kisses, as always, but didn't embrace her. The tension unraveled.

"What?" she defended.

"How could you talk to my mom about personal stuff and not even tell me?"

"Wow. Didn't see the need to coat that one with some tact?" She crossed her arms, wounded.

"I went by the house to see Dad. I didn't know I was walking into an ambush. I hadn't even told him what we did, then in strolls Mom, and she's been 'speaking with' you." Sean made his case.

"I didn't know I needed permission to have a conversation with someone other than you." Georgie's lip quivered.

Sean fell silent. Convicted. "I. . .you don't. I didn't mean that. But you have to see that I deserved to know how big our inner circle had gotten."

"She called *me*." Georgie sighed. "Turns out, she reads the paper and saw my name change ad. I guess Dad told her we'd been talking, and she'd seen my ring, but it was obvious we were married at that point. She just called to check in on me, and I was *relieved* to get to talk to her. This was *yesterday*. I didn't stay over last night because you worked late again, and it didn't seem like I should put that information in a text. I was going to tell you on this date you're trying to ruin."

"Sorry." Sean put a hand up, surrendering. "I'm not trying to ruin the date, this is just—"

"Falling apart?" she interrupted with a sob.

"Yeah. Quicker than I thought. Dad is hounding me, basically saying I'm not loving you properly if I don't out us." Sean nodded. "And he's right."

"Sharon wants to lose a hundred pounds. If we suddenly made this public, it would derail her," she whispered, looking into his eyes.

"I know." He stood firm. "But it isn't my job to not derail Sharon. It's my job to love *you*."

"Right now, that involves keeping this from Sharon." Georgie worried. "Please."

He consented with a nod, smoothing two fingers over one of her feather earrings. He stepped in close to kiss her, but she giggled and moved out of the bathroom away from his kisses to tease him. Putting on shoes to go with her dress.

"What are your plans for us this evening?" she asked.

"I originally made these reservations the day after we bought the dress and was working myself up to asking you to be my girlfriend tonight," Sean admitted. "Or, if we'd made that transition by tonight, I was going to propose to you. I don't think you'd have said yes if we'd just started dating. That would have been a little risky."

Georgie giggled. "So *now* what are your plans since you don't have to pursue me anymore?"

Sean smiled, squinting in remorse at the woman only barely raised at all by an absent single mother. "Dad always taught me *never* to stop pursuing the woman I love."

Georgie smirked, loving Samuel and the son he produced, and relenting with a nod. "You trust his advice as much as I do."

Sean knew where she was going. "Well, I trust God's advice more. So, we'll keep praying and asking Him to guide us through this mess we got ourselves into."

"We got married," she whispered devastated astonishment. "Again, I don't regret that. I'm just waiting for the other shoe to drop on this."

Sean shook his head. "Let's not wait for that. Let's just do tonight, okay? Because I have some pricey reservations. But if we don't go now, we'll be late, and they'll give away our table." He tossed Georgie her purse from the kitchen counter and they exited the apartment hand in hand. "After dinner, we'll go back to my place and cuddle and watch a movie, and then we'll talk for a couple hours during which I'll attempt to seduce you with a fresh batch of frozen grapes and herbal tea. After that. . .the ball's in my wife's court."

Georgie giggled and teased. "Hmm. Well I hope things go your way. I'm rooting for you."

The Lime's Reputation

"Hello?" Sharon's lips stuck together, and her voice was foggy as she answered the phone. She barely heard the response. "Hold on."

She placed hearing aids and glasses and looked at the picture. She was relieved to see a picture she took of Sean at his high school graduation. He looked much more like a man now. More muscle mass and facial hair to alternately shave and ignore. But she kept that old picture of him in her phone. He was only two years her junior. But always her baby brother, to be fortified or revised wherever appropriate.

"Sean, why are you calling so early?"

"Um. . .this is gonna sound. . .you know. I. . .how about nevermind? Forget I called?" He sounded like he was in a panic.

"You woke me up. I'm up now. What's wrong, Sean?" Sharon cleared her throat and blinked her eyes. Rushing to aid the man she knew didn't have a need for it.

"Actually I'm. . .I have reason. Or whatever. To suddenly be, you know, randomly, no real reason. A little concerned about the whereabouts of Lavender-Dawn Meadow George."

"Why do you care where L.D. is this early?"

"I mean I'm not. . .I don't care. Per se. I just. You don't happen to have *seen* her?"

"Sean, it's like five something. Of *course,* I haven't seen her." Sharon grew frustrated. "What is going on?"

"She asked me to help her with something at her new place this morning but isn't answering her phone." Sean suddenly regained his normal suave.

"Oh. I thought she didn't want you to know she moved into your complex."

"Yeah, no. We crossed paths."

"I see. Well she's a heavy sleeper. If you're trying to call her, she probably slept through it." Sharon suddenly heard her cat at the door and rose, nearly forgetting to unplug her cell phone as she walked. "If I do hear from her, I'll let you know."

"Yeah. Thanks."

Sharon almost immediately brushed off the peculiarity of the conversation with Sean and chose to be thankful for once. He'd awakened her in enough time for a walk before work. She let in Stormy, fed her, then dressed in her workout gear and headed out.

She always thought there was enchantment in the autumn air. She walked out of her apartment complex, past rows of older homes. The city was just awakening, but she could smell the light scent of cinnamon and freshly carved pumpkins. The jack-o-lanterns on porches. The leaves crackling past with the breeze. Of course, she didn't walk alone.

Those leaves are like you, Sharon. The tree will survive the winter. But first those leaves have to fall off and die.

"It's a beautiful death," She told me.

Exactly. Everyone thinks your death is one of the more beautiful seasons in life. You just keep slowly dying, to everyone's pleasure. And they'll thrive, like always.

"I'm not going to die. I'm going to get thin."

And then what? You think you'll have a cute little house and children to carve pumpkins with? Someone would need to love you to have all that. Will being thin make someone love you?

"Being thin will make me happier."

And what does happiness solve? I have a better idea.

"I doubt that."

You doubt everything. That's the point of me. But hear me out. You'll never be loved by a man. You'll never have children. So really there's nothing stopping you from the cute little house, right? Why don't you forget about the rest and get a Sharon-sized house? Not so little, but you get my drift. Isolate yourself with walls and commit yourself to a mortgage. You'll never need another commitment.

"Maybe after I meet my weight loss goal."

That's the spirit. I can't wait to go house hunting.

. . .

"Georgie. Seriously. Answer your phone. I'm about to call the police. Where are you? Please don't have left me." He hit the End Call button for the eighteenth time.

She's dead. Lying in a ditch somewhere. The prey of a serial killer for sure. They took her right out of bed, and you missed it. Or she left you. She hates you, pig.

Sean had woken up alone, and all his attempts at contacting his wife failed. Devastated, and worrying himself sick, he tried to steady his emotions with a shave. As he was finishing, he heard the apartment door open.

"Sean, have you left for work? Please don't have left for—" Georgie was finishing the self-directed sentence when Sean exited the bathroom.

"Where. The *hell*. Have you been?" he accosted her. "I was five minutes from calling the police. I called my parents, and even risked blowing our cover by calling Sharon. You scared the crap out of me, Georgie."

"I didn't charge my phone, and it died. I'm sorry."

That's when he looked at her puffy, red, leaking eyes. His tone softened. "Babe, what. . .please tell me what's happening right now. Why are you walking in the door at five in the morning?"

"I left a note." Georgie pointed to the coffee pot.

Sean,

Went to the store. Be back soon.

Georgie

Sean sighed, feeling silly as he pulled her close. "I wasn't thinking about coffee. I didn't make it that far. Next time leave the note near the *bed* somewhere or just wake me up? Speaking of coffee, I should make some. Want a cup?"

"I don't want coffee. I want pie. Vegan key lime pie. Like on St. John? All night long, I didn't sleep. I thought about that stupid pie on that stupid island. I found a recipe, but when I got to the produce section of the store, I realized I really just wanted *limes*. I was up at four in the morning consuming actual limes with sea salt in the parking lot of Walmart because I couldn't wait until I got home."

"Uh. . .okay?" Sean tried. Wondering if he was still asleep.

"You don't understand. I am perfectly in tune with my body. I do not *ever* have cravings," she said, voice trembling.

"It happens to the best of us," Sean teased.

"Don't make fun of me," she insisted. "Twenty-five years, I have this perfect natural rhythm. I marry you, and you sabotage it. Thanks."

"Oh really?" He laughed. "And how did I do that?"

"With your signature! And your sweet-talking and kisses and stuff."

"And stuff?" He smirked, flirting.

"Yeah, specifically the 'and stuff.' " She sighed. Seemingly defeated.

Sean continued his lighthearted tone to soothe her. "So, are you telling me you think you *might* be pregnant or that you've recently confirmed with a test that you *are* pregnant?"

"Which one would you prefer?" She sighed in relief that he understood. But remained tense over the subject matter.

"Well, they'd be the same thing. Because you know your body, and I trust you. But you also know me, or think you do, and you'd probably think I'd want solid medical proof," Sean reasoned with a smile. "So, did you buy a test?"

Georgie reached into her purse and produced a little brown bag. "I already took it."

"Georgie! At *Walmart* like a scared teenager while your frantic husband with baby fever is waiting at home for you?" he scolded, taking the bag from her.

"I left a note." She watched him abandon the medical proof to the kitchen counter, favoring trust.

"In the kitchen. After leaving me in bed."

"I wasn't thinking. I needed limes," she said in monotone.

"You sound like a crazy person right now."

"I *feel* crazy." Her face twisted into tears.

"Good." Sean took her into his arms. "Because when you sleep next to a man who would walk through fire for you and you decide that it's *your* job to go to the store and satisfy pregnancy cravings, *that* is crazy. Ludicrous, Georgie. That's like a known thing. The father goes to the store and gets the limes at three in the morning. You really need to learn these unwritten rules."

Georgie laughed through tears. Whispered, "I just told you we're having a baby. How are you not freaking out?"

"You seem to be handling that side of things. I'd rather be excited. Because *baby*." Sean smirked, leaned in and kissed his bride with tenderness.

You're a poor as dirt EMT, and she's a receptionist. You have a one bedroom apartment and hardly any savings. On top of that, no one but your parents knows you're married or even together. How exactly is a baby a good addition to this situation?

Unfortunately, my words seemed to scatter across his mind as the image of laughing children running around their feet flashed in his heart.

"You taste like limes," he muffled into his wife's hair in their embrace.

"With sea salt. I don't even know how many I ate." Georgie sniffled. His loving reaction having calmed her spirit. "It was wonderful, you should try it."

"I'll pass." Sean laughed, squeezing her tighter.

...

Having only met the woman once, and not since she was sent to prison, Sean was surprised by Georgie's mother's general withdrawal from emotion and life. Crushed by her response to Georgie's kind explanation of her first visit to her midwife and how wonderful a father Sean already was. She showed her mother some pictures through the glass.

"So, you need a man to take care of you now?"

"I love him, Mom. He's a good man," Georgie explained, hiding her deep hurt. "I grew up with Sean, don't you remember?"

"He's not bad-looking, but marriage is for the *weak*."

"Luckily, I'm the first to admit that I'm weak."

"And why would anyone do that?" Her puffy eyes and greasy blonde hair above the orange jumpsuit highlighted her lifelong battle with me.

"Everyone is weak, Mom," Georgie explained cheerfully. "When we admit it, that's when God can do His best work. That's when we're strongest."

"Well having a kid is the dumbest thing I ever done," she cracked like a whip into the air. "And pretty as you turned out, you turned out dumb too."

Sean, fed up, and about to speak, though Georgie had asked him not to, opened his mouth to defend his wife. But she placed her hand atop his and responded by the Spirit.

"Well," Georgie, still a neglected little girl in her heart, cleared her throat against impending tears. "I'm thankful you had me."

The ride home was silent at first. Georgie curled up in the passenger seat, writing in her recently ever-present journal. Finally, Sean worked up the courage to speak.

"Why do you put up with that? Let someone cut you down like that? Seems like an awful lot of effort to visit her every week if that's all you get out of it."

"She's my mother. She gave me life. She didn't have to do that, especially at fourteen," Georgie said out the window.

"*God* gave you life." Sean sighed. "He knows especially well that none of who you are came from that thing behind that glass."

"I know that, Sean. But who am I if I don't even visit my mother in prison?"

"Well. . .I suppose you're not you. And I like you," Sean encouraged.

"I like you too. Thanks for tagging along today." Georgie smiled. Then, from nowhere but a frustrated sigh as she finished writing and put the journal back in her purse, "Am I me if I keep the biggest, most important things in my life from my best friend?"

"I'm praying for God to provide the opportunity and the words for us to tell them everything." Sean avoided the question.

15

Christmas's Miracle

The whole family got behind Sharon's effort. Georgie began running slow half miles with Sharon and Samuel. On up to painful, tearful half miles at a quicker clip. Onto miles that ended in crawling, which progressed to miles that ended in hand slapping and smiles.

After one such mile on Christmas Day, the threesome was met at the porch by the rest of the family, including Eric, Sophie and the baby. And of course, Sean. They were cheering on the runners, and Lynn told them dinner was ready.

"I'm so gross, Mom. I'm not ready to eat." Georgie laughed. Glistening with sweat and working witchcraft in Sean's soul.

"Me too." Sharon shook her head. "Can we go shower at our apartments first?"

"Heavens no!" Lynn said. "If I let you leave, Sean will sneak off with that woman of his before you get back."

"Mom, I told you I wouldn't." Sean rolled his eyes at her wink. "She understands the importance of family on Christmas."

"Well maybe she should *come* for Christmas," his mother huffed.

"She's with her family," Sean rebutted, laughing. His father tried to conceal his snicker.

"I still want to meet her," Sophie said as they all ventured inside. "How long have you been together now?"

"A few months, officially. There were also a few unofficial months." Sean shrugged.

"Yeah, that's a decade in Sean time." Sophie cackled.

"Doesn't exist," Georgie sang as she headed for a bag of clothes she'd brought to change into. She'd just crossed the threshold of the front door and heard her phone ringing. She dashed to her purse and checked it, muttering to herself. "Hmm, I don't know this number. Dang, missed it. Voicemail. Who leaves voicemails anymore?"

She dialed her voicemail as the house bustled cheerily around her. Suddenly, her face read desperate distress and her eyes darted around for the next thirty seconds as she held her phone to her ear. Her next action was to drop her phone in the tile entry in hot pursuit of the downstairs bathroom, where she lost Christmas brunch into the toilet.

"Is she throwing up?" Sophie asked. "Has L.D. *ever* thrown up?"

"No, she says if you don't put things into your body that it could potentially reject, you'll never throw up," Sharon recited.

Everyone worried, and Sean panicked, formulating a cover as he let things play out. Wanting to offer to hold back her hair and administer pregnancy-safe oils, as he usually did to avoid her vomiting, which she hated to do. Never having been faced with this dilemma.

He met his mom's eyes, and they were interrogating him, though her mouth was smiling. His father's face read the same.

"She seemed upset. What was that voicemail?" Sean noted, looking away from his parents.

The rest of the family, not having a simple explanation for the episode, began their investigation.

Sophie picked up the phone, examined it for cracks, then replayed the message. In the same amount of time Georgie had listened, Sophie gave some roar of an exclamation within her hand and her eyes teared up. Almost as though she'd eaten something far too spicy. But she froze there, handing the phone to Sharon, whose reaction was similar.

Sean was next and took the phone as he watched Sophie signing to Eric in tears, and Sharon whispering to her parents. It was a short, professional message.

"Hi, this is Dr. Belton, Assistant to the County Coroner. This number is on file for Amanda George, inmate number PP11615. I've concluded my autopsy and need to know where to send the remains. Please give us a call back within forty-eight hours after notifying the family, at which point the deceased will be in the custody of the state. That's forty-eight business hours, so tomorrow would be fine. Enjoy your holiday."

Sean's first thought, which he portrayed, included an expletive or two. But I'll spare you. His next thought, or thoughtless reflex, rather, included his finger tapping the "Call back" button on the phone. His protective instinct took it from there. Samuel, who had just been told the news, saw Sean's reaction three seconds too late.

"Sean, don't—"

But the person on the other end had already picked up. "Hi. Yeah. Is this the moron that just called this number?. . .No, I assure you, the insult is extremely warranted. Who does it say is on record to be notified about transport of remains?. . .Uh-huh. Except you called Amanda George's *daughter*, who until your asinine message hadn't been notified that her mother had passed. . .Yeah, there are still women who take their husband's name, believe it or not. . .Oh, I *would* allow you to speak with her—on Christmas Day—except she has some underlying conditions that caused her to lose her lunch with that kind of news. I think the cordial thing to do would be to tell me what happened, so I can give my wife a proper death notification, if Amanda is indeed deceased. . .Sean Mehlmann. M-E-H-L. . .Yeah, Georgie Mehlmann is my wife. I'm the second emergency contact. Georgie added me and changed her name a few weeks ago when we were visiting her mother." Sean paced, listening.

As he did, the rest of the family reacted in various silent ways. Samuel watched his son's every move. Sophie was unable to remember the signs to clarify Eric's confused lip-reading. Lynn left to tend to Georgie. And Sharon. Poor Sharon. Less of a presence, but still as much of an emotional wreck, as I'm sure you've gathered by now. Stood stunned. Eyes watering, not from emotion. But because she'd simply forgotten to blink them. And she didn't feel anything at all just yet.

Sean began his half of the conversation again. "I see. And when did this happen?. . .Wow. Thanks. . .Do you need to ask the prison, or can we decide that?. . .Um, just. No. We live two hours from there. Can you send her closer? Just call and let us know. We're not picky, but I know my wife would like to bury her mother. . .Yes, thank you. We would *absolutely* appreciate an official apology. . . Believe me, I understand. . .No, it's your lucky day. I'm a Christian man. You're forgiven already. Thanks for the info. . .Uh-huh. Merry Christmas. Bye."

Sean felt the eyes on him. But his job wasn't done yet. He ignored them and me and everyone in a quick dash to the bathroom, where Lynn was trying to get Georgie to drink some water.

Georgie was crumpled in a sobbing heap across from the toilet, as one might expect. And as none of those who gathered into the little bathroom and hall would expect, Sean sat in front of her, and drew her in. Wrapping arms and legs around her as she leaned in to accept the comfort. No one heard what he whispered. The prayer he used to minister to her.

They watched in awe as Sean finished praying and finally calmed her to a gentle fit of quick sobs. Their whispers were captured inside an embrace for a time, and incomprehensible until he captured her eyes as he wisped her hair aside and whispered a little louder.

"Well, they found her three days ago. She'd been in solitary, and. . .She just decided to end it for whatever reason. She didn't leave a note. Baby, I am *so* sorry."

"And you called them?" Here, she smiled a little.

"God's still working on my temper." He sniffled.

"I didn't even know. And she never—" The sobs began again. Sean kissed her messy hair atop her head as she sobbed into another embrace.

"You said and did all you could for her and more than most would even consider," Sean told her. "And now all you need to do is cry."

"Maternal stress is linked to cognitive issues in babies and children," she panicked with a hiccuped sob.

Sean tried to hold in laughter. "Georgie, if we screw up this kid, I'd rather it be because you cried when you lost your mom, not because you didn't."

To them. The two of them. It was an awkward, devastating, tension-filled ordeal they couldn't avoid, that was sending them into a downward spiral of busted-ness. But to the rest of the family standing nearby, it was like the end of winter. When a man goes outside with a coat on to take the trash out only to realize he can't see his breath. That the trees are budding. There is a tuft of green in the grass. That spark of joy that alights when winter is over, my friend. And spring has arrived. Though for Sharon, it was the opposite. It was the crisp, frosty morning when autumn crystallizes against the cold. And deadens into winter.

For the half hour that followed, Sean and Georgie were in the guest room. He was aiding the headache she'd acquired from crying with a peppermint oil laden cloth at her forehead. And stroking her hair as she fell asleep. The rest of the family sat in silence. Recovering from more than one source of shock.

After a few moments, Sharon considered one aloud. "Can they get in trouble for doing that? The coroner's office?"

"From what I gathered, it was a mistake. They thought they were calling someone at the prison, not her next of kin. Still, if L.D. were the type of person to do such a thing, they could have a lawsuit on their hands," Samuel answered.

"Well," Sharon sighed, acknowledging the other issue—the pachyderm in the corner. "I'm not sure if I know what L.D. is capable of anymore."

"Seriously," Sophie, who had Mel mostly hidden under a nursing wrap at her breast, concurred. "Eric and I have suspected for months that L.D. and Georgie were the same person. But I feel like I live in a different dimension right now. Because they were throwing around words like husband and wife and *kid.*"

Sharon piggybacked, "Knowing Sean, he knocked her up and *had* to marry her."

"And was too embarrassed to tell us about it," Sophie continued. "I can't believe he was stupid enough to bark up *that* tree. Or that she fell for whatever he said to convince her."

"Girls." Their father quieted them. Devastated over their mistakenness. "I'm sure they'll explain everything in their own time. Don't make assumptions."

"Did you know? Sean said you'd met Georgie," Eric asked his father-in-law.

Samuel nodded. Squeezing his wife's shoulder.

Lynn explained, "Sean had been confiding in Dad, who told me. But not even Dad and I knew for sure about a baby."

"I didn't have a clue," Sharon whispered. "I'm trying to think if I was supposed to notice. I see them both all the time. How could I have missed this? They got me Stormy together, and I caught them at my apartment once, but both of those things seemed so innocent. . ."

"Sharon, my Rose, I think they took *extra* care to keep this from you," her father explained. "I know that's a tough thing to hear, and we tried to convince them otherwise, but you should know they kept this private out of love and concern for you."

Tears formed in Sharon's eyes. "L.D. and Sean both tell me everything. How long have they just been lying to me?"

At that moment, the room silenced, because Sean was entering it. He rubbed both callused, life-saving mitts over his bewildered face as he did. He was deep in thought, standing amid staring eyes, and didn't seem to notice they were there until his mother spoke.

"She asleep?"

Sean nodded, thinking out loud. "Finally. I wish she'd had some lavender oil on her, because that always helps her calm down."

"Do you have any at home?" Lynn asked gently.

"Yeah, and we have a diffuser. I should probably move it into our room tonight," he mumbled.

Sharon didn't voice it, but those words, "our room" made her stomach turn. And Sean was speaking a foreign language to him. How did he know what a diffuser was? It was all coming together.

She had moved randomly. Not into Sean's complex. In with *Sean*. Of course.

Sophie spoke one gentle word.

"Sean?"

He reacted. It was hollow and firm, but not unkind. "Soph, we could use a little time to process this before you guys start—"

"No, I get it. I was just gonna say," Sophie poured the compliment straight from her soul. "That was some amazing husbanding you just did."

It took Sean by surprise, especially when the rest of the family nodded in agreement. He squinted, taking a step back. That's when he realized there was no malice in the room. Confusion, for sure. Maybe some hurt feelings. But not a scrap of spite. Still, his reply was said as a question, "Thank you?" He abruptly jumped to his own defense, unnecessarily. "I'm sorry. It happened really fast, and of course we wanted to tell you, but we didn't know *how*, and—"

"Sean." His father stopped him. "Another day."

Sean nodded.

"Here, give me your keys. Eric and I will take your car home so only one of you has to drive later on," Samuel signed. Eric rose, dutifully.

"Yeah, that'd be. . .yeah, take hers. Mine's a stick and she won't insist on driving if she doesn't have her car." Sean first searched the keyring in his pocket mindlessly, then realized he didn't have a key to her car with him. He did stop at that point to remove his wedding band from the keyring and put it on his finger. He headed to Georgie's purse and opened it, removing her keys and handing them to his father.

Sean's mother and sisters watched as Sean was about to close the purse again. He spotted something inside and tilted his head.

It was a freshly wrapped Christmas gift. They'd opened all the gifts together that morning before brunch and before the runners headed out. This one had been omitted. He pulled it out and gently moved the bow to see the tag.

"What's that, Sean?" Sophie asked.

"Uh. . ." Sean shook his head in confusion. He felt and shook the gift as a child might. "Book? It's for Sharon."

"L.D. already gave me a gift," Sharon noted, confused.

"Actually, she gave you *two* and I put my name on one." Sean chuckled. "I didn't know about this one."

Sean came and sat down with the women, casually handing his older sister the gift with her name on it. Still trying to regain control over his faculties.

"This says it's from my sister-in-love." And then Sharon shut down. She put the gift in her purse for another time. The bitterness trickling inside her at last.

Sophie was practically bursting. Sean looked at her with a doting smile only a big brother can properly deliver.

"Sophie. It's a really long story. I can barely even think right now. She had a lot of hope for her mom, despite her being an absolutely horrible human, and her heart is broken. I'm begging God to tell me how to help her through this."

"Yeah, I get it." Sophie physically bit her lip, trying not to smile.

"Okay. . .you can ask me *one* question. "

Sophie squealed. Without much hesitation, and just like a little sister, she used her one question to tease him. "Do you sleep on organic cotton sheets washed in all-natural hippie detergent?"

Sean gave a little chuckle. "The sheets are bamboo. They're amazing."

Sophie was fully satisfied, laughing wildly, and barely able to speak. "You've been indoctrinated. I knew it."

"Uh, no. Not with everything. But she's really not exaggerating when she says she has sensitive skin."

Sophie laughed all the more.

"It's not funny. She gets hives. Tell me how this is different from you learning an entire language and culture for Eric."

"Because I never made fun of ASL or the deaf community. You've been making fun of all things 'hippie' since we were kids."

"Well she forgave me." Temporarily smiling Sean glanced at silently horrified Sharon, who shut down. "That's enough, Sophie."

When Georgie awakened, everyone acted as though no revelations had been made, using Georgie's emotional fragility and the joy of Christmas as the excuse. I used their silence to wrap rifts among and between them, concealing the intentions and the truth from them like that wrapped up gift.

…

Christmas night, Sharon processed. Rather, she attempted not to. But she couldn't keep it out of her mind. The previous evening at church, L.D. had congratulated her. She was three and a half months into the weight loss journey. Sean and L.D. had sat at opposite ends of the row at church. She'd been oblivious to anything but trying to get healthy. Her best friend and brother were actively lying and betraying her.

Just focus on you. That'll keep your mind off them. It's worked for months.

Sharon complied. The now involuntary motor began in her head. Adding up the day's calories. Subtracting the exercise. Listening to me.

You can't make it. This is impossible. You have an old carton of rocky road in the back of the freezer. It will be incredible. Just eat it. You want it. You won't make your goal. You can't make your goal. It doesn't matter. Just eat what you want. You're hungry. Eat.

Over halfway there, and plenty of time until goal day. It didn't matter. Sharon still doubted she would make it. Still craved food constantly. Still hated her siblings and L.D. for being so happy. So skinny. So, satisfied with food and life. And apparently, one another. Her mind stubbornly shifted again at my urging.

Alright. Just do it. Open the gift. You have every right to hate them, no matter what it is.

She grabbed the gift and viciously unwrapped it. When she did, she was a little surprised. Not just a book as Sean expected. It was a journal. One with a glossy cover illustrating the island of St. John. Likely bought at a gift shop there. It wasn't even a new journal, she

158

scoffed. The pages were well loved. Every one of them filled with L.D.'s handwriting. When Sharon opened the front cover, a sheet of paper, folded in half, slipped out.

I doubt you can handle reading that.

Defying me, Sharon quickly opened the note and began reading it.

"*S.R.,*

I started writing in this about nine months ago. I promised myself and God that I'd give it to you when the pages were full. I filled the last one yesterday. It's Christmas Eve, and I'm wrapping the last of the gifts. It's only fitting that I give this to you tomorrow when we spend the day together. The problem is, I lack the fortitude to hand this to you. It'll take a miracle, and I'm praying for one. My whole heart is in these pages. Whether or not that's enough for you to forgive me for what you'll read, I owe this to you.

L.D."

Sharon was already convincing me to let her forgive her best friend. Already touched that some effort was obviously made to earn her favor. I told her they still didn't care about her. Cautiously, curiously, she turned to the first entry of the journal.

"*Dear S.R.,*

Today, Sophie got married. She's pregnant, which I totally called. I'm so happy for them. But that's not why I'm creepily writing you a letter you may never read. I came back from my walk on the beach and wanted to wake you up to tell you something, because I tell you everything, and this something was huge. But I realized I couldn't tell you, which I couldn't bear the thought of. I also couldn't find any paper in our hotel room. So, I went down to the gift shop in the lobby and bought this journal. I wanted to tell you what happened firsthand, even if you never read this.

So here it is. I got my first kiss tonight. It tasted a little like beer and a lot like cigarette smoke. But it was incredible. It happened after a long walk on the beach and him rescuing me like a damsel. I'm not even joking. I thought he hated me, and he's broken my heart so many times. Tonight, he told me he was in love with me, but he'd been horrible to me because he thought I was too good for him.

Somehow it all turned into him kissing me and wanting to get closer to God. You just told me tonight that my faith inspires you. Maybe it will inspire him too. I want to wake you up and tell you this. But I can't. Because my first kiss came from Sean. I don't know how to tell you that I think I'm doing the awful cliché of falling in love. And with your little brother. I love you. Don't hate me if you ever read this.

L.D."

Knowing the beginning, and snippets of the end result she'd learned that Christmas Day, she surmised much more, and could handle nothing else. She tossed the journal in the trash, and the panic attack began, which always resulted in an open freezer. She dug through healthy frozen vegetables and lean meats for the carton of rocky road as I spoke to her.

They are going to have a perfect life with lots of fairy tale love and lots of children. You'll get to be their aunt. But that's all you'll ever be to anyone. That carton is the only thing in your life that never did you wrong.

Sharon stared at that carton, now open on the counter with a spoon. Howling the cries at the love that her two best friends in the world found in one another. Without her, they wouldn't even know each other. And yet, like always, no matter how close she got to it, she was excluded from all happiness. Not even her cat was around. The cat they likely got her during their secret love affair.

It was disgusting. It was outrageous. And worst of all, it was beautiful. Poetic. Just like the halfway-to-thin version of Sharon taking that spoon in her hand.

"Just a teaspoon." She sniffled. Sobbed. "Not a pint. Not a half-cup serving. Just a teaspoon. That's all I want."

She hated her voice. But she spoke it aloud. And then, bitterly shoved a teaspoon of three-month-old, freezer burned ice cream into her mouth only moments before it curdled in her stomach and landed itself directly into her toilet.

"Not even a teaspoon," Sharon lamented. "Not even that."

16

The Couch's Mates

Georgie's first day back at work after Christmas was a day off for Sean. The Friday was a way to ease back into normalcy. He spent an hour that afternoon at Georgie's preferred grocery store scratching his head trying to put together a meal the way she always did. He couldn't heal her. He knew that. But he could, theoretically, cook for her. She needed to eat, but hadn't done much of it recently.

Finally, he acquired the ingredients and spent hours working to do what might take Georgie thirty minutes. When he heard her key in the door, he was already pouring iced herbal tea into glasses.

"Hey Georgie! I made us some. . .of that stuff I can't pronounce. With some chicken." He greeted her as she closed the door behind her.

"Quinoa," Georgie said, hollowed all out as she plopped down at their kitchen table. "You cooked?"

"Yeah. How was your day?" Sean's heart was teetering. Hoping he could cheer her at least a pint.

"Better now." Without warning, and only a gentle nudge from me, she broke down all at once. Crying into her hands. He couldn't get a word out of her for five minutes, then he got all the words.

"Your mom took me to lunch today," she began.

Lunch. You idiot. Why didn't you think of that? You could've encouraged her halfway through the day.

"Oh. How did that go?" he asked gently, plating their meal as he spoke.

"She told me for Sharon's birthday, Dad signed them up for a 5k that's right before their goal day. I think she'll rock it. She was doing well when. . .you know, the last time we talked." Georgie tried to calm herself. She only managed to sob a few more times.

"Baby, she just needs time to process."

Georgie ferociously shook her head. "I've called her dozens of times. I've left her some messages. Texted her. Even freshman year when she thought I cheated on our Algebra final to beat her for the highest grade in the class, she heard me out and we made up the next day. She's never avoided me like this."

It was true. Even New Year's had come and gone. The two women always had a sleepover on New Year's Eve and caffeinated themselves beyond reason, playing board games until the sun rose in the new year. This year, Sharon hadn't even called.

Georgie and Sean had been busy making funeral arrangements, and Georgie was avoiding caffeine due to pregnancy, but a phone call might have been a nice gesture, at least.

"This isn't ninth grade Algebra, Georgie," Sean seemingly had to remind her as he set food and drink before her. "This is my fault. I didn't know what I was giving her when I gave her that gift. I still don't really."

"It was a journal." She rolled her eyes.

"The one you've been writing in since St. John. You've said that."

"It was everything. Practically every day since you kissed me on St. John, I've written something about you and me. Something I would have told her if she knew about us. I didn't want her to have missed out when we finally told her." Georgie sniffled, her face distorting. "According to Mom, she read a page and threw it away. I never imagined she'd react that way."

"Yes, you did," Sean corrected her. "That's why we kept it between us. Let's bless this mess."

Sean took his wife's hand and prayed over the meal, the private interment they'd scheduled for the following morning, and Sharon and Georgie's restored relationship.

"I broke down and told Mom about my mom's burial. She said it was short notice and she wishes we'd told them sooner. But they hardly knew her. She wouldn't even care if they were there," Georgie said bitterly, cutting into a slightly overdone chicken breast. "I asked her not to tell Sharon."

"Why?" Sean wondered.

"You're kidding, right? I don't think our relationship will ever get fixed." Georgie took a bite. Tried to pretend away the bitter tartness of the tough bit of meat in her mouth. But Sean was looking on eagerly for her to comment on the morsel.

"Is it okay?"

"Yeah, it's. . ." Georgie mumbled through the bite, then tried to chase it with quinoa, which was underdone and crunched in her mouth. The forkful of overdressed salad didn't help. Nor did the slightly flavored water Sean was trying to pass off as her signature herbal tea.

Sean sighed. "How bad is it? I really tried. I'm not used to cooking this kind of stuff."

Georgie smiled, which hadn't happened in days. "It's. . ."

"We can just go grab some takeout." Sean deflated.

"It's wonderful, Sean. You cooked for me. I have no complaints." Georgie giggled. The perspective re-seasoned the chicken, completed the quinoa and dressed down the salad. Love, after all, is a choice. Georgie, though she had fewer to share it with, always chose love.

Sean awoke the next morning—a Saturday—and kissed his sleeping wife before he wandered out into his living room. His eyes came into focus across his living room to a pair of worn-out old wingback recliners in maroon. Together with a couch, they were once a complete set. About the time Sean moved out, Sharon was doing the same and Georgie's mother had just been convicted of murder. There were so many life changes that Sean's mother thought it was a good time to get rid of the old furniture, as she did every few years, unaware that the living room set was beloved by so many.

Sharon had been the first to find out, and claimed the couch. She was moving in with L.D. at the time, who asked if she could have the chairs. But Sean had been there, and he wanted the chairs as well.

They ended up each taking one of the chairs, and for years the set was completely separated into three apartments. He had been angry for a time that he didn't have both chairs, thinking the one chair looked odd with his newer coordinating couch. Today he looked, and the set was together again since Georgie's move. Their mutual best friend had the coordinating couch. Sean couldn't get that out of his head. He made his way back to his bedroom, where Georgie was already sitting on the edge of their bed.

"Hey," he grumbled. "We should get ready. Interment's in two hours."

But she didn't respond, except to turn to him with both courage and fear in her eyes. I'd been with her all morning. Dreaming with her. Waking with her. But when Sean sat next to her on the bed and started to read her mood, the words were already making their way to her tongue, despite my efforts.

"I don't want to lose her." Georgie was completely consumed by the prospect. "I've been mourning my mother. But that's more of a relief than anything. The thought of Sharon not being in my life is a hundred times more upsetting. How awful is that?"

"That's not awful at all." Sean shook his head. "I was just thinking the same thing."

•••

Sharon felt the vibration of her phone on the counter as she brushed her teeth that morning. She finished brushing quickly, got a hearing aid in an ear, looked to make sure the caller was not L.D., then answered. Not thinking it through when a recent, grown-up version of a baby brother turned man, showed up as the ID picture.

"Hello?"

"Hey, Beautiful."

In two words, her bitterness was dismantled. He was a powerfully gentle force, rivaled only by the woman who had become his counterpart. How could she have been so selfish to try to ostracize them, even if she felt she deserved some time to process? Did L.D.

deserve to be abandoned? She'd only ever been abandoned. What if they didn't do this to spite her? What if God had plans for them?

Sharon knew He did. And she knew, as Sean spoke, what she needed to do.

•••

"Is this everyone?" The young pastor from the church asked gently.

Sean nodded. He stood hand in hand and shoulder to shoulder with his wife in the January cold. Both of them in black, staring down into the pit beyond the AstroTurf overlay where the box was to be lowered.

No church service. No viewing. No repast. Just a coldly scheduled time to lower the last burden Amanda had left Georgie into the earth. Sean had requested the pastor to comfort his wife and to maybe give some meaning to it all.

But before he began, he pointed behind the young couple.

"They're not with you?" he asked.

Sean started to answer as he looked behind him. Once to check. Twice for the double take. Because approaching across the frozen graveyard were his parents. Eric, Sophie, and Mel. And behind them all, Sharon. They did so in silence, joining the huddle without a word. Sean nodded to the pastor.

"L.D., when Sean called me, he asked me to say a few words. Things like this aren't for the physical form of a person in the box. They're for the person standing in your shoes. So, what I'm going to say is for your benefit alone. And I won't say much. I'm just going to read a passage from Matthew 25.

'Then the King will say to those on His right hand, "Come, you blessed of My father, inherit the kingdom prepared for you from the foundation of the world: for I was hungry and you gave Me food; I was thirsty and you gave Me drink; I was a stranger and you took Me in; I was naked and you clothed Me; I was sick and you visited Me; I was in prison and you came to Me.'

"The righteous will answer, asking when they did such things for the King, whom we know to be our Lord Jesus Christ. And He will say, *'Assuredly, I say to you, inasmuch as you did it to one of the least of these My brethren, you did it to Me.'*

"L.D., or Georgie, as your husband calls you, few people, especially at your tender age, can say that they take no regrets with them from a meeting such as this. Despite your mother's difficulties which became your burdens, you were, and are, a dutiful, faithful daughter, and thus a righteous servant of the King. I ask that all of you continue to serve daily unto Him. Let's pray."

When the short service ended, Georgie chose not to watch her mother's open grave become her final resting place. She squeezed Sean's hand, and the family walked a distance away before regrouping.

Georgie looked around at the familiar faces and let out a sob. "You didn't have to come."

"We gathered that when we didn't get an invitation," Sophie joked, trying not to glance at her brother's firm, loving grasp on Georgie's hand. "But that wasn't going to stop us."

"We're always here for you, L.D.. Losing your mom doesn't mean you don't have family," Lynn said, sweeping some of her daughter-in-law's hair from her face.

Georgie sniffled. Avoiding Sharon's eyes. Even her presence. But, all at once, the flood poured out. "I'm sorry." She sobbed. "I'm sorry. I'm a horrible friend and it sucks that you have to have me as an in-law. And I hate that I was selfish enough to convince Sean to sign the paper that completely ruined everything between us. You don't have to forgive me, because I'm not willing to reverse what happened with him in the past year. But I am sorry for what it did to you, and there isn't a day I don't think about it."

"L.D., let's just—" Samuel tried.

"That's not true," Sharon nearly whispered.

"That's not fair, S.R., I really am sorry," Georgie reiterated.

"No." Sharon crossed her arms and caught them all off guard. "I'm just confused because I thought it was Sean's idea. He asked you to marry him like twenty times. So, he convinced *you*. Not the other way around. And you really were just friends before that, even though you were in love, and he kept proposing to you. You didn't want to date because you didn't want to hide anything from us, but then you got married because *we* hurt your feelings at the hospital and you felt like you didn't have a family. And Sophie, the baby happened *after*. Not long after, but after they got married. He waited for her, if you can believe it."

"How did you know all that?" Georgie's entire countenance changed to confusion.

Sean concurred. "Yeah, *no one* knows that."

"L.D. told me. In the journal. She told me everything. Way more than I ever wanted to know." Sharon laughed. "But I read it, so maybe I *did* want to know."

"I thought you threw it away." Georgie's teary eyes engaged Sharon's.

"I did," Sharon admitted with a sigh. "For like five whole minutes before I got it out of the trash. I've read it several times. It's the best gift I've ever gotten."

"You've been avoiding me for weeks. I needed you," Georgie argued.

"You have Sean." Sharon shrugged, hurt.

"I do. And he's supportive and wonderful." Georgie looked into Sean's eyes. Then back at Sharon. "But I needed *you* too."

"What could I have even done?"

"For one, she was too upset to handle things like cooking. And Mom brought us food a few times. But then *I* tried to cook." Sean winced.

The rest of the family laughed aloud, graveyard and all.

"My condolences." Sophie giggled.

"It wasn't that bad." Georgie accepted Sean's side-embrace.

"Oh heavens. I tried sweetie. I really did. The boy is unteachable," Lynn apologized. "Will you accept some meatloaf as an apology? I can have it on the table for lunch."

"Normally I'd tell you not to go to all that trouble, but your grandbaby says yes to all food at all times. Especially meatloaf."

Georgie patted her belly. Leaving the sting of sadness in the graveyard behind her.

• • •

"Goal day" ended with a father and daughter wearing numbers and holding hands at the finish line of a 5k. A healthy grandpa, and a size eight princess wearing a smile. Everyone else cheering from the sidelines. But Sharon was too busy with her own joy and effort to notice any of them.

The evening after goal day, when the best friends could finally catch each other in passing over a bowl of frozen grapes, Sharon was all smiles.

"Stormy's at her goal weight too," Sharon said, still elated from having lost one hundred and two pounds. "I can't believe I actually did this. I have so much shopping to do."

"I'm pretty sure I can help with that. I need to go shopping too. None of my clothes fit anymore." Georgie looked around. "Where *is* Stormy?"

"Out. It scared me at first, but she goes out some nights and doesn't come back for about three. She usually stays for about a week after that," Sharon shared.

"Sounds like my mother, rest her soul," Georgie muttered.

Sharon cleared her throat. Got quiet.

"I don't like the way that sounds."

"What?"

"Sharon, I've told you I'm sorry," Georgie began to lament.

Sharon giggled. "Sharon?"

"S.R.!" Georgie corrected in a jolt. "I'm not allowed to say 'S.R.' at home. Sorry. I'm the worst."

"It's fine now that I understand." Sharon smiled slightly. "It's heartwarming in a way."

"That we spent nine months constantly worried you'd find out, even when we weren't married?" The best friend ran fingers through her hair.

"That you cared." Sharon shrugged. "At all. I came to realize that's why you kept the secret."

"We were worried you wouldn't make your goal. But you did, and we're so proud of you."

The childhood friends laughed together. Georgie's soul filled with relief that they could still eat frozen grapes together and gossip.

"So, what's next? You lost the weight. What now?"

"I'm buying a house," Sharon said without hesitation. "Something about the size of this apartment, but with a little yard. Maybe I can have a garden. I guess it's my reward to myself."

"Really? S.R., that's great!" Georgie lit up. "When do we go house hunting?"

The Baby's Shower

"That was nice of them, huh?" Georgie said, setting down her purse as they arrived home late on a Friday. Her coworkers had thrown her and Sean a baby shower. The gifts were all monetary and amounted to much.

"Yeah. *Now* will you buy stuff for this kid we're having in three months?" Sean finally acknowledged her hesitance.

"I guess we should." Georgie sighed. Explaining with a strained, humor-filled voice to mask the impending tears. "I've never been around babies. I didn't have that great of a mother. And all the information the midwife gives me is contradictory and confusing. I don't even know what to buy. Maybe I don't know how to be a mom at all. Who knows?"

The tears came. Sean sighed, exhausted from work and a social affair usually reserved for women, at which he knew no one. But she needed him.

"God will equip you to be a mother. Because He's called you to be one," he offered, embracing her.

"Has He?" She sniffled.

"Uh, yeah." Sean extended his arms, then raised an eyebrow and looked down at her belly. She laughed through the tears.

"Will you help me? Can we go shopping together?" Georgie hoped.

"Babe, this isn't evening wear." Sean chuckled. "I'd be useless shopping for baby stuff. I could tag along, and we could try to navigate all this together like we usually do. You know I'm not unwilling. But I have a better idea."

"You do?"

"Golf." Sean chuckled.

"Um. . ."

"Dad, Eric, and I have a tee time tomorrow morning. Mel will be with Eric's parents. Which leaves you, Mom, Sophie, and Sharon with an excuse to go shopping. All your heads together will get us everything we need for the baby," Sean suggested. "It was supposed to be a surprise. But I already asked them. I knew you needed—"

But his wife was already kissing him.

•••

"It was hard, I admit." Georgie sighed. Sipping iced tea at lunch, halfway through the productive shopping day. "I lived there since I was nine. Handing them my keys was an experience, to be sure."

"You have bad memories there," Sharon reminded her.

"Yeah. *Millions* of them." Georgie's lip quivered. "Good or bad, I was walking away from close to two decades of my life."

"To live with your husband," Sharon reminded her. She couldn't understand how Georgie could even want to look back. Complain in the slightest way about anything when she had a husband to go home to.

"I'm not saying it's not a good reason, S.R.. Or that I had a great childhood or that I even *liked* that place. And his apartment—*our* apartment—is nicer and safer and bigger. And when we spent our first couple weeks not spending the night together half the time, it felt *very* strange." Georgie remembered getting choked up over four cracking walls with bad plumbing. "It was just change. A lot of change, all at once."

"You're telling me!" Sharon laughed. "Not long ago, I didn't even know you were *seeing* someone. Now you're married to my *brother*, and I was losing you to him and I didn't even know." Her voice succumbed to tears.

"Losing me? Sharon—S.R.—we're sisters now." Georgie laughed. "You'll never *lose* me. We're just one step closer to our dream. Only in the real version our kids will be cousins."

"I'll see less of you, L.D. Especially since you'll be raising little Seans and L.D.s soon. We'll forever be in different stages of life, and I'll never catch up to you."

Georgie laughed. "You're not *behind*. Stop trying to catch up and just *be*, S.R.. Just *be*. Be who you are, right where God has you, right now. A daughter. A sister. A teacher. An aunt. You are so incredible at those things. Rock *those things*." Georgie was adamant. Begging Sharon to understand the things I never let her.

There's a reason God put Georgie in Sharon's life. She couldn't change her. Couldn't convince her that she was ever going to be enough. But Sharon lived with an ember of hope, always chasing after something she didn't think she'd find. And Georgie was the slow breath that caused that ember to swell.

Sharon nodded, sniffling. Lynn, who had been listening in silence, sighed then.

"I'm still so happy it was you," she said again.

"Me too." Sophie, quiet and withdrawn all day, tried to engage in the difficult conversation. I was torturing her, and they didn't even know. She couldn't conceal this much longer.

"You okay, Soph?" Georgie asked.

"Very," Sophie admitted. "I'm just excited for you."

"I can tell. I don't know how I would have known what to buy this baby without your help. Thank you so much, Sophie."

Sophie tried not to smile too brightly. "I'm happy to help."

"What's going on, sweetheart?" The mother hen began to be concerned as well.

"I don't want to steal Sean and L.D.'s thunder." She bit her lip.

Georgie gasped. "I knew you were looking too hard at the disposable diapers after I decided against them."

"Yeah, we're apparently taking the plunge again," Sophie admitted.

"Already?" Lynn worried.

"It wasn't on purpose, Mom. That doesn't mean we can't be excited," Sophie argued.

"Of course."

"I know. They'll be so close in age. The timing is just awful," Sophie admitted, rolling her eyes.

Georgie snorted laughter. The other women gave inquiring looks. "Your timing is fine, Soph. I had finally finished moving in the night before we found out. That was two weeks after randomly getting married, and we'd only spent about half those nights in the same apartment."

"I can't imagine. Did Sean freak out?" Sophie wondered.

"You kidding? *I* freaked out!" Georgie revealed with laughter. "We've both always wanted a huge family and we were clear going in that we'd never try to prevent it. But I woke up one morning decidedly *not* dating him, and we were married and quite possibly expecting by lunch. I had finally adjusted to that when I started craving limes. But Sean is cool as a cucumber, you know that. I've always envied his peace. He just takes things as they come. Very 'hippie' of him."

"Did he slip something in your drink? How did he convince you to do all this when you weren't even dating?" Sophie asked.

"We didn't *call* it dating. But we'd been talking about how we knew we'd get married."

"So like courting," Sharon inserted.

"Exactly," Georgie realized. "So, it wasn't far-fetched that it happened how it did."

"I only wish you'd let us witness the blessed event, other Mrs. Mehlmann," the mother inserted with a sigh.

Sharon guffawed. "Seriously! That's the part that really bugged me."

"It would have bored you to tears." Georgie raised an eyebrow. "We sat on Sean's couch and signed a document, then we got Greek takeout before we headed to the hospital to check on everybody. Obviously, there was other stuff that morning, like tossing his carcinogen-laden shampoo and window cleaner. But it wasn't exactly a romantic beach in the Virgin Islands."

The other women disagreed. Most notably, Sophie. "L.D., I spent my wedding night vomiting because of unborn Mel's reaction to blackened bass. Greek takeout is way more romantic than that."

"You *could* have had a big, white wedding. Or even a backyard barbeque would have sufficed," Lynn nearly mumbled.

Georgie grinned as she explained. "Can you imagine our wedding, Mom? S.R., you'd have been Sean's female best man, *and* my maid of honor. So where would you have stood? And Sophie, you and Eric would have been helping juggle rings and bouquets the entire ceremony from either side like a circus act. Also, Mom, you and Dad would have given me away. . .to your own son. We decided it was best we didn't put our guests through all that confusion." Georgie set all the women to snickering.

"You'd have asked Dad to walk you down the aisle?" Lynn cooed, a hand over her heart. "He'd have been so honored."

"Of course." Georgie squinted.

"Be sure to tell him that this coming Friday when you all come to dinner." Lynn spread the invitations.

"We're already coming on Sunday for Easter, Mom." Sophie reminded her.

"Yes, but Dad wanted to have supper on Good Friday and take communion with you. Are you turning down free food now?" Lynn teased.

"Yay food!" The purple-eyed pregnant woman high-fived the dark-eyed one, and the two giggled as Sharon looked on.

Food. Your old friend. When will you admit it was never a clean break?

•••

"The reason I wanted to have this meal tonight with all my kids is because God has been revealing something to me that I wanted to share," Samuel began.

174

"Uh-oh." Sean laughed, squeezing his wife's hand atop the table.

"Don't worry son, I'm all lectured out for now, as it pertains to you," Samuel assured his son. Flipping through his Bible, searching for something. "Before I explain, let me read this passage. I'm in Luke 22:14. *'Then He said to them, "With fervent desire I have desired to eat this Passover with you before I suffer; for I say to you, I will no longer eat of it until it is fulfilled in the kingdom of God." Then He took the cup, and gave thanks, and said, "Take this and divide it among yourselves; for I say to you, I will not drink of the fruit of the vine until the kingdom of God comes." And He took the bread, gave thanks and broke it, and gave it to them, saying, "This is My body which is given for you; do this in remembrance of Me." Likewise He also took the cup after supper, saying, "This cup is the new covenant in My blood, which is shed for you. But behold, the hand of My betrayer is with Me on the table. And truly the Son of Man goes as it has been determined, but woe to the man by whom He is betrayed!"' "*

Samuel cleared his throat. "Several months ago, I sat in this very chair with most of you. My new daughter-in-law was absent, and my grandson hadn't arrived. But it was similar. And I had nary a twinge of pain as we ate together. As I awakened from my heart attack, all I could think about was Jesus's last supper. He knew he was going to be betrayed and denied and beaten and killed. He knew His hours were numbered. But he didn't do anything fantastic or noteworthy as far as life experience goes. He broke bread with the people He loved most. And just by obeying God and allowing the betrayal, He accomplished the most important act in the history of everything. As you know, I've never asked that any of you fight your way into history books or do amazing things. Just that you remember that your every breath was bought at a price, but you are loved by the God who paid it, just exactly how you are. So be you. Be humble. And obey your God. Shall we take of the bread?"

After communion and supper as a family, the women and children bonded over photo albums in the dining room. It was an archaic practice, even then. But Lynn loved maintaining her children's photo albums. One for each of them. Presently, they were deciding which of the Mehlmann children Mel resembled. Which was none of them, of course. Eric being black, their son took mainly his dominant genes. So, Sharon and Georgie had taken to making fun of pictures of Sean as a child, which made him laugh with his father and brother-in-law in the living room.

"How's married life, son?" Samuel asked the question he knew his son hated.

"Same as single life. Except now I have a pregnant wife, so everything is a constant roller coaster of her emotions and stuff I did very wrong or very right." Sean chuckled to himself. Eric and Samuel laughed knowingly.

Sharon was listening to the men, which her mother and sisters were ignoring. Jealously wondering if a man would ever speak of her so endearingly, even if he'd meant it otherwise.

"Awww! Baby, come look! Your hair was adorable!" Georgie called into the living room.

"Was?" He pretended to take offense as the men rose and walked into the dining room.

Sean looked at the album of his childhood and placed his hand at the small of Georgie's back, as loving couples do. And as Sharon does, she caught sight of that snow globe on the shelf to avert her eyes. She'd been recently, in Georgie's handwriting, told the significance that I told you. Gazing at it didn't help anyone but me.

"Do you think the baby will have purple eyes?" Sean cooed as he was turning the pages of the years of his life.

Georgie looked up, quickly reaffirming and examining the eyes of Lynn and Samuel, which caused everyone's intrigue.

"Not likely," she said, looking back down at the album. "Mom has lighter eyes, like Sharon and Sophie, but you have Dad's dark eyes. Chances are, you have too many dominant genes for blue or purple to show up. But we can certainly keep popping them out until we have one with my eyes if you like."

Sean snickered when she looked up into his eyes. Nodded. "I like."

"Perhaps you should take it one child at a time?" Lynn suggested, placing a new album on the table from the nearby bookshelf.

"Samuel and I wanted eight. God gave us three. Our three have given us two more thus far, not counting grandchildren."

No one contested Lynn, as they were quietly flattered, and interested in the album she'd just put on the table. The first photo was one of Sophie's pictures from her senior year in high school, taken professionally in their backyard. Right next to it was a bridal portrait, taken on the beach, of course. The pages that followed were photos Lynn had printed from Sophie's wedding. Sophie smirked a little, and looked to Eric, who winked at his bride before flipping through her childhood album at the other end of the table.

After Sophie's photos, she turned to a senior picture of Sean. "I'll have to rethink this one. You two didn't make this easy. Do you have what I asked for, Mrs. Mehlmann?"

Georgie glided across to the living room and retrieved her purse, then pulled out a stack of photos from an envelope. Mostly individuals of the young couple. Save one of the couple holding their marriage license on the couch.

"We were trying to keep a secret, so we didn't take too many pictures, sorry. And really only *that* one was from our wedding day. The rest are from the next few weeks. But I tried." Georgie passed them across the table to Lynn.

Lynn smiled as she placed a goofy one of Sean in his EMT uniform next to his senior photo, where Sophie's section had a wedding portrait. She turned the page and placed the one of them together, then thumbed through the others.

"These are beautiful. Thank you, sweetie. Goodness, this one is stunning," Lynn reacted. "Did you take this one, Sean?"

"Yeah. We printed them for Amanda. Initially. And also made a copy for you when you found out," Sean commented, trying not to react to that photo he'd taken with his phone. A lovely candid of Georgie using a ringed hand to tuck that ashen hair behind an ear.

"We took them to her not long before she. . ." Georgie nodded. Clearing her throat of emotion. "But she didn't want them, so if anyone else wants the other copy—"

Lynn added her copy of the photos to the album, and Georgie put the others on the table. In a millisecond, Sophie and Sharon had divided them, fighting over the one of them together. Samuel chuckled and took it from them, carefully placing it in his wallet.

Lynn sighed as she turned to Georgie's senior photo. Also, a professional taken in the backyard. The sight of it caused Georgie's heart to soar. *She* was included in the album. Included in everything in this home. Lynn began moving her photos and placing new ones with Sean's. "Here's where it gets complicated. I have a section here for you, L.D. Because I wanted photos from *all* my kids' weddings. Except you and Sean combined yours and didn't take *near* enough pictures. Sharon, you'll have to compensate when you get married."

They all chuckled as Lynn turned the page.

There, at the end, was a page with two pictures of Sharon. To Sharon, they were a before and an after. A photo from Sophie's wedding, and a more recent photo after her birthday 5k in workout gear. A classic lack of smile and kind poise about her in both.

"Why am I in the wedding album at *all*?" Sharon asked.

"Because I want them all together." Lynn smirked. "You look so different from your senior picture, so I wanted a recent one, but couldn't decide which one I liked more."

"I was a hundred pounds too heavy in the first one." Sharon laughed.

"You were beautiful in both." Samuel winked an eye.

"Yeah. Exactly *this* beautiful." Sharon sighed. She turned the page of the photo album. Blank, of course, where the others had wedding pictures, however scant. "God just keeps blessing you. Weddings and babies, and I'm happy for you. Mom, I hope you started an album for grandkids too. But don't bother leaving room for me. God apparently has less important plans for my life."

"God has very important plans for your life, Sharon," Samuel encouraged. "But maybe they don't look like your siblings.'"

Just then, Mel began crying in the room where they'd put him down for a nap, but the conversation continued over the fussy baby.

"And you act like we're all sunshine and roses just because we're married. All of life is hard, Sharon." Sophie came out swinging.

"Oh, please," Sharon accused.

"And your life is definitely simpler." Georgie shrugged encouragement.

When Mel's fussing turned into screaming, everyone looked at Sophie. Sophie looked at Eric. Eric was looking at the photo album. Sophie waved her hands a few times, but he was across the table from her. She sighed, frustrated.

"Eric!" she screamed, to no avail. "Eric!" she tried again, hot tears suddenly emerging. She slammed both hands onto the table and Eric looked up, startled when the glasses displaced, and the photo album hopped before him.

"What?" he signed. A sign that in and of itself looks like defensive confusion.

Sophie signed and whispered fervently, "The baby is crying!"

Eric apologized and exited the room. The family stood stunned and silent until Sean accosted Sophie.

"And you couldn't get Mel because. . .?"

"That is *not* your business, Sean." Sophie excused herself to the restroom for a tissue.

After a short silence, Georgie cleared her throat. "As we were saying, Sharon, being single can be less complicated."

Sophie returned quietly, sniffling and wiping tears. Eric came in, bouncing the baby and trying to ask Sophie if she was alright while Sharon began her rant.

"L.D., maybe you're adjusting to being married. But you're married. Someone loves you all the time. My *cat* won't even do that. And Sophie, maybe it's tough being a mom. I get that. But you have a *baby*. *Two* pretty soon, right? How is that not the height of human joy?" Sharon accused. Sophie, red-faced, took a step toward her sister.

"I miscarried," Sophie said. Sniffled into the silence after her mother's gasp. Looked bitterly at her sister. "Sharon, when you're at the height of human joy, it's just farther to fall. You can't lose what you don't have. Be *thankful*, sissy. Oh, to be *you*." Sophie's words were covered by sobs, embraces, and praying hands.

• • •

Earlier in the week, Sharon had taken an ultrasound photo that Sophie had texted the family and blown it up to the size of Mel's baby picture. Hanging it on her wall next to him, Georgie's ultrasound, and all the wedding photos. When she arrived home that Good Friday, the first thing she did was take it off the wall and stare at that beautiful angel that died in the womb.

She began to take the baby from the frame, to use it for something else. But something in her bent and broke. And trust me, I had nothing to do with it. She heard Someone else utter,

"Be thankful."

Sharon went into her school bag, took out a metallic blue marker, and drew a little cross in the corner of the glass, which brought tears to her eyes. She hung that baby right back on the wall next to his brother. Thankful for him. Who he was. For the time he was. And perhaps, for whatever divine reason he was taken so soon.

I must warn you as we return to our heroine, that her story began to darken. If you thought her weight loss journey was her adventure. Her teaspoon miracle. You are gravely mistaken. What happened next didn't seem like an adventure at all. It seemed like she'd never been weaker.

But her purpose had never been greater.

18

The Father's Day

Sharon was the first in the pew, annoyed at the tardiness of the others. She'd had to clean up a hair ball that morning and still managed to get to church on time. Well, her usual fifteen minutes early. And she didn't even like church. She went because she was supposed to. Because her dad thought it was important. So, the others, who adored this place, should have been on time on Easter Sunday.

Sean and Georgie showed up later than was normal for them. Sharon watched as Sean helped miserable Georgie to sit in the row. Kissing her hand, then going to borrow one of the church's Bibles from the back of the room. Sharon rolled her eyes in jealousy of the tenderness.

"You're late," Sharon whispered to her best friend.

"Actually, I just think that Alexandria's Genesis thing is finally kicking in. That's probably why I'm *several months* late." Georgie bit her lip and snorted laughter as she rubbed her belly.

Sharon giggled. "Yeah, I'm sure that's why."

"What are you ladies giggling about?" Sean returned. "And where are Mom and Dad?"

But before the answer, and barely before the lights dimmed for worship service, Sophie and Eric made it into the row of chairs huffing and puffing with a high five.

"How's your heart today, Sophie?" Sharon whispered across the row.

Sophie gave a thumbs up. "I got my husband and son out the door and to church. So today? I can't complain too much."

Sharon got a text from her dad.

"Running Late. Sorry."

She shared the information aloud, but the text tone had prompted her siblings to barely mumble acknowledgment as they all turned off their cell phones and stowed them in various places to worship God.

I'm a wrench, right? Well, metaphorically. A tool that can be used to fix a car. . .or I suppose to kill someone. But I never acknowledged being evil. Or sinless. I'm not good or bad, I just am. And the devil uses me. I can destroy. But I guess my favorite place is here. Self-doubt in a sanctuary during worship? Yeah. I'm here. Watching them deny themselves. Make themselves into the nothing that they are to praise the One who IS. The rest of the world tells them I'm their worst enemy. And I suppose sometimes I am. But I'm also there in the best of worship.

Sharon was uplifted, quite possibly feeling the Holy Spirit as she was taught that death is never forever unless we die in sin. And that though we die to ourselves in Christ, we rise again with Him. Sharon supposed Sophie needed to hear that when tears streamed down her face. They all left the sanctuary with smiles on their faces, standing in the church lobby until they all realized the void all at once.

"Did they not make it?" Georgie asked it first. "To church. . .on *Easter*?"

Sharon took out her phone, and Sophie was already frantically within a voice mail.

"Hospital?" Sharon said aloud. "I got a text from Mom and that's all it says."

Sean turned on his phone, having immediate occasion to answer it. "Why is work calling me? I am legit *off* today." He walked away to take the call.

"Is that voicemail from Mom? What did she say?" Georgie asked Sophie.

"She's just. . .screaming. . ." Sophie conveyed with frantic eyes.

Which is when Sean returned to the group. Seemingly gasping for air. Coughing at tears. Leaning down onto his knees.

"Sean?" Georgie asked, trying to bend and catch his eyes.

He regained some cosmic level of composure not of himself. "That was my boss. They were on the scene of a bad car crash. Took the patients to the ER and once they got the woman with just some minor injuries to calm down, they were able to identify the re. . .the remains of her husband. Guys. . .they were in a crash. Broadsided by an SUV. And Mom is fine. She's at the hospital. But Dad was. . ." Sean lost it and nothing Georgie tried would calm him.

"Sean, I don't understand."

He had paraded her into church. But just then, he shattered her heart by extending his arm against her. Serving to literally push her away.

"Wait." Sophie swayed a little. Tried to sign to include Eric, but it wasn't as clear as normal. "Mom and Dad were in a car accident?"

"But he texted me. They were on their way," Sharon defended.

"But they didn't make it," Sean yelled. "Dad's *dead*, Sharon."

"What does that mean?" Because Sharon didn't understand the plain English words. They wouldn't compute.

"He died on impact." Sean sobbed. "There was nothing they could do, and these are some of our best guys."

Sophie swayed. . .swayed. Lost her footing and caught it once. Finally, Eric barely broke her fall to the floor.

The churchgoers saw the commotion and sprang into action. Retrieving a child from the nursery. Driving three vehicles to the hospital, where Sophie was determined to have simply forgotten to breathe, and Mom was found soaked in tears, clawing at an IV. Hell bent on dying that day until her children surrounded her and enveloped her.

"I left the ham on low in the oven. I think it's probably ruined by now," was the first thing she managed to say.

A churchgoer heard that before heading back to church. And Sharon handed her the keys to her parents' house. Well, just her mother's house now.

...

After they'd coaxed Lynn to sleep with prayer and tranquilizers, Georgie was curled up in a wide windowsill of the waiting room. Sophie asleep across Eric's lap. Their son home with his other grandparents. Sharon staring blankly at a wall. Sean in the cafeteria —another wing of the hospital—head on a table in despair.

"He pushed me away. Did you see that?" Georgie sniffled. "I was right there for him. And he pushed me away."

"He didn't know what he was doing, L.D.. He'd just found out," Sharon said in the tone of voice that matched her posture.

"But Dad is the only Dad I've ever known. I need *him* too." Georgie lamented in tears. "The man who would have walked me down the aisle is gone forever, and my husband won't even let me hold him."

"Who will walk *me* down the aisle, L.D.?" Sharon burst into hopeless tears and Georgie took her friend and sister into her arms.

Sophie's phone rang. Eric gave a look of disgust when she awoke and answered with, "Hey, Brielle." And she walked away.

Georgie sniffled. "I'm sorry to be selfish. This is awful for all of us. But I'm in so much pain for Sean." She sobbed. "On the way to church, all Sean could talk about was how excited he was to go golfing with Dad and our son. Sean's never gonna be okay again, is he? This is so awful."

That night there was still the shock. They couldn't even imagine how to go on without Samuel Mehlmann. They all tried to hold on to some false sense that the tight knit family was all grown and didn't need him like they might have as children. But even that night there was the truth hovering there above them. They knew that their dad was more than that missing piece of a puzzle you must ignore if you want to keep the puzzle. They knew he was more like that fraction of a teaspoon of baking soda missing from a cake. Unleavened. Unsalvageable. Without baking soda, a cake isn't even a cake. So, what was this family without him? Who were they as individuals? He was their strength. Their mediator. Their adviser.

Their accountability to God and their principles. Everything was perfect with him around.

So, they were all pretty convinced that without Samuel, the whole world might just shatter.

Excellent.

19

Grief's Toll

Empty pints of ice cream lay all over Sharon's kitchen and living room where flyers for house prospects had been before. One spoon in each. One day, one pint, one pound at a time. But all she ate was ice cream. No other calories. So, the gain was only visible to her—and to me of course. I told her to let go. It wouldn't matter if she gained it all back. Her father wasn't around to care. And no one else did, anyway.

At the burial, Sean exhaled. He'd been pulling away from everyone. Protecting them from his grief. Holding it all in. And then, after they lowered his father into the ground, leaving him a patriarch, Sean waited until the last non-family member left. He fell into a heap on the wet grass with the wife who had been waiting for the release.

Eric and Sophie and their son held on tight. Sharon and Mom made a striking pair. And Georgie shushed gently as Sean sobbed into his wife's black-covered shoulder at the grave side. Showing emotion, and a lot of it, for the first time since he got the call.

Once coaxed back to his mother's house, Sean switched stages of grief.

"Strong as an ox. He survives a heart attack. A quadruple bypass. He was eating right and running 5k's and a stupid car crash kills him like everything is always just in vain," Sean ranted. Flipped another switch. "Why him? He was a good man. I wasn't always. If I could just take his place. . ."

"Sean, stop that." Georgie sniffled. "You're gonna be a father too. Don't you want to be who he was to you?"

"Of course, Georgie," Sean said, crouching by her side and stopping his pacing. "I just miss him. You know? If it was me, I wouldn't have to miss him."

"But *I'd* miss you." Georgie was still devastated over the nature of his grief. "I miss you *now, Sean*."

"I know," he whispered. They embraced. "I'll be better."

Sophie received a text. After a moment, she tapped Eric.

"Bri wants to take me out for a drink. Would that be alright?"

"A drink?" Eric was surprised. "What about the family? Me and Mel?"

"I just need a breather, Eric." Sophie's tears nearly began again. Eric, though confused, calmed them.

Everyone had someone to be better for. Everyone except for Sharon, she thought bitterly. She looked up in some glimmer of instinct. Everyone except for Sharon. And *Mom.*

Sharon spent long days putting on a face for second graders. Long evenings and weekends helping her mother, only leaving to feed the increasingly wayward Stormy. And long nights bingeing and bawling. Georgie likely would have spent time with Sharon, but she was pregnant and still had to work while dealing with her own grief for a second time within a year, and Sean's grief. Sharon understood. She always "understands." But she was alone. And miserable. I perpetuated it as I could.

Your life means nothing. Just work and help your Mom. That's all you're worth.

When summer hit and there was no job to go to, and only days to help her mother go through her father's belongings and heal, Stormy barely came home for two days a week. And halfway through the summer in her miserable all-alone existence, Sharon cursed God.

Death is so much stronger than I am. It is not a tool I have the power to manipulate. But I'm an opportunist. I need only whisper where there is death. And when I do, the effect is something like a fly that lands on a still lake.

Like when I whispered to Sophie through the ever-useful Brielle, "Well, shouldn't Eric be cheering you up? If he was any kind of husband, you'd be much happier already." And tiny legs on the water disturbed the stillness until all of her agreed in echo.

Sophie was suddenly, though not surprisingly, unhappy. She'd lost her father. A child. But she began to despise and resent her husband and son. To rethink the direction of her life. She began voicing my Brielle-enabled nonsense to her mother and sister.

"If only I hadn't gotten pregnant. I saw an opening for a dietitian at my gym. If only I could have managed to finish school," she huffed.

"You have a son to take care of, Sophie. No one is requiring you to get a job. Eric is a good provider." Lynn meant well, but the argument was misguided.

Sophie stopped talking to them altogether.

Eric showed up at the Mehlmann home one evening Sharon had been about to leave. He had little Mel with him. And poison on his tongue.

"Sharon, will you stay? I'm too upset to use my voice. Can you interpret?"

"Of course, Eric," Sharon signed and said. "Mom, Eric wants to talk to us."

Once they were sitting, Eric jumped right into the deep end signing.

Sharon gasped. Signed. *"Can you repeat that? I think I misunderstood."*

"You understood." But he repeated anyway, his eyes filling with tears.

"What is it, Sharon?" Lynn petitioned.

"I think he's saying Sophie wants a divorce," Sharon said sheepishly.

"What?!" Lynn exclaimed. "That's ridiculous, Eric."

Sharon interpreted.

Eric grunted and shook his head gruffly. Spoke with his hands and Sharon's trembling voice. *"I have been losing her for a long time. Since before we lost the baby. She stopped eating. I know she struggled with an eating disorder before we met, so I knew she could be relapsing. I have tried everything to get her to eat, and I thought she was starting to get better. I found out she has been making herself sick while I slept. I told her she needed help that I could not give her. She told me she has been begging me to give her a divorce for weeks. . .when I wasn't looking."*

"Oh, Eric. . ." Lynn responded to his tears. Eric and Sharon continued.

"She thinks she got married too young. She wants a chance to decide who she is again." Eric was shell-shocked. Blaming himself for everything. *"She is moving in with Brielle and asked me to leave so she could pack. I don't know how to begin to tell my parents. I'm scared I will not be a good father without Sophie's help."*

"You're an *excellent* father!" Lynn interrupted.

Eric shook his head and breathed hard a few times. *"I told her we could talk about this and work things out. I told her I was willing to listen and change whatever I needed to change."* Eric sobbed. *"She said, 'How can you listen? You can't hear me.' "*

"You're joking, right?" Sharon said and signed. More in astonishment that her already miserable life could turn even sourer so quickly. "How could she say that?"

"Because it is true." Eric coughed at tears. *"What if there are gaps I can't fill for her? What if she does need to live her life without me—with someone who is hearing—to be happy?"*

"Eric, that girl loves you. She's just really hurting right now," Lynn said, her own endless fount of tears restarting. "We're all hurting, and we all do it in different ways. I hate that Sophie is doing this. Samuel would have been able to reason with her, but. . ." She stopped.

They allowed the silence, though Eric tended to see more in one uncomfortable silence than any of them could ever hear.

Eric shifted the subject from Samuel. *"Sophie is leaving me. I will not be able to help her with her eating disorder. If you see her, please help her if you can."*

"Of course." Lynn nodded.

Eric turned to Sharon. *"Do you know of any daycares I could put Mel in that would be understanding of my disability?"*

"You are not disabled, first of all. But yes, I know of a few, but the best ones are full, I'm told. I would be happy to go with you and help you find one that is decent. They will be expensive."

"I don't mind expensive. I just want them to take good care of Mel."

"What is he saying, Sharon?" Lynn asked. Feeling disabled herself. Why hadn't she taken the time to learn to sign when Sharon was young the way that Samuel had?

"He's asking if I know of daycares for Mel. A lot of my students have deaf parents and other children who are hearing, so I do know of the best ones," Sharon explained.

"Oh, Eric. Please leave him with me every day," Lynn begged.

Sharon interceded before relaying the plea to foggy-eyed Eric. "Mom, you have a job. You said you might have to get another one to pay the mortgage since Dad is gone."

Lynn tilted her head. "Dad had life insurance. I didn't think he did anymore, but Dad paid off the house for me and then some. Enough to leave some for each of you, even. I already quit my job. Tell Eric I'll watch Mel. He brings me so much joy. I think it would be good for me."

Sharon interpreted. Eric burst into tears. Nodded. Thanked her. And Sharon cursed God again.

...

Georgie sat at the table, across from a non-fat latte with no owner, a matte paper cup of tea between her hands. Looking contemplatively out the window. Ignoring the eyes of every male admirer, despite her obviously pregnant belly. She smiled when she saw Sharon huff and puff in the door of the coffee shop.

Sharon looked twice at the corner of the coffee shop. "Those two guys are staring at you. They're kind of hot, right?"

"No one is as hot as my husband." Georgie sipped her tea with a wink. Sharon sat down smiling her disgust. Georgie looked up with remorse. "Is it true?"

"Yeah." Sharon sniffled. "Sorry I'm late, by the way. Visited Dad today to leave flowers. And ended up venting to him."

"It's alright, S.R." Georgie sighed, understanding. "How could Sophie do that? She has a child. She made a covenant. How can she just walk away?"

"She says Eric wasn't making her happy anymore." Sharon shrugged.

"That isn't Eric's job. Think about it. Unconditional love has nothing to do with how happy someone 'makes you.' Happiness is a decision. Not a circumstance or the state of a relationship," Georgie ranted.

"Dad used to say that all the time," Sharon lamented.

"Yeah. He did." Georgie's harsh tone was offensive until Sharon saw the deeper message.

"What's wrong, L.D.?"

"How did you spend your inheritance? From Dad. Your portion of his life insurance." Georgie grasped her cup more tightly.

"I saved it." The responsible, cautious Sharon shrugged. "I'll eventually use it for a larger down payment on a house if I ever find what I'm looking for. It's proving to be a challenge."

Georgie blinked at the ceiling to cast away the tears with a slowly shaking head. "Sean bought a motorcycle."

"A. . ." Sharon tilted her head, like she often does when she doesn't hear something. Though in this case, she just couldn't fathom it.

"A motorcycle," Georgie repeated, as she often does for the sake of Sharon's ears. "On a whim. Randomly on his lunch break a few days ago."

"Um. . .but you have a baby coming soon." Sharon narrowed her eyes.

"Yeah." Georgie jumped to his defense. "It's not like we needed the money right now for anything else. Sure, a house might have been nice, but we've already rearranged the apartment to get ready for the baby. We all grieve in our own way, and it wasn't a bottle or a pack of cigarettes. So, I let him do it. After a huge fight, of course. I should be glad he called to consult me, I suppose."

"Motorcycles are dangerous." Sharon worried.

"Thus, the fight. Apparently, he'd been studying and practicing on a friend's bike. So, he got the endorsement on his license. He also bought a good leather jacket and a top-of-the-line helmet to make me feel better. And let me say, Sean in leather certainly helps me feel better about lots of things." Georgie masked the fear with a smile, and Sharon giggled.

"So, is there room for you on this motorcycle of his?" Sharon tried to keep her friend's smile alive.

"There is, actually. I rode with him for a few minutes yesterday, but I have precious cargo, and we both agreed I shouldn't make it a habit." Georgie patted her stomach, scared as she was. "It's like he's having a midlife crisis. Except he's in his early twenties."

"Does it bother you that he's younger than you?" Sharon teased.

"He's not *that* much younger." Georgie rolled her eyes. "But he's sort of acting it recently. Scares me, S.R.. What if he goes back to his old ways because he's in so much pain over Dad? I pray for him constantly, but. . ."

"Well that's your first mistake," Sharon snapped. "Don't talk about God around me, okay?"

"Mad at God, huh?" Georgie asked. First Sean, now Sharon.

"Do you blame me?" Sharon said bitterly.

"You can be mad all you want, S.R., but I don't know what you expect Him to do. Should no one *ever* die? Or should you just be immune from having *your* loved ones pass into His arms? Being mad at God for a basic natural occurrence of life doesn't make any sense. I'm sad that he's gone. But being mad at God only proves to keep your best Comforter at a distance."

"It's not a 'natural occurrence of life.' It's death. Don't try to tell me it's not the end of the world, because it was for him. I'm being selfish if I pretend it's not completely horrible that he had to die. It's not *fair*, L.D.!" Sharon's near constant tears began again.

"Not fair for whom?" Georgie laughed a little. "Because your dad is dancing with angels in Heaven. It was a tragedy. But it is not an *end*."

"How do you *know*?" Sharon quoted me verbatim. "How do you know that he's dancing or that there's a Heaven at all? It's a nice thought, L.D. But how can you be so sure?"

"Sharon Ruth, if this horrible, tragic life is all there is, why do we even bother? If we are all going to die anyway, why do we continue to live? To search for purpose? Love hurts us all in the end because it causes more grief than mere death. So why do we love? Why do we perpetuate life if all it does is end? If you understand that God is faithful and Jesus died so we can live forever, everything makes sense." Georgie, through tears, grasped her stomach again. "It makes no sense if this is all there is. S.R.. It hurts us like hell, because that's how life is on Earth. But your dad is *dancing*. You have to believe that, or this grief will *kill* you."

"I'm already dead." Sharon sobbed. She rose and walked away.

There really isn't a point in all this, Sharon. You can never be enough to give this all meaning.

That's what I told her.

But I think that's what Georgie was saying too.

20

Life's Return

Sharon stopped going to church and stopped searching for God's presence, because for all she knew, that was only a myth that died with her father. Sharon walked through the mundane as she prepared for a new school year. She was able to get back on her strict diet, and others praised her for it, but unable to shake the grief that followed her. Clinging like stench, even during times she spent with the various separated branches of her family. No one really spoke about anything important, because they knew it would lead them to talking about Dad in laughter—missing him in tears.

Georgie called Sharon when she was eight months pregnant. "S.R., I want to ask you something. You can say no. But I want you to be in the delivery room with me next month. My midwife allows me to have three people. I'll have Sean there, of course. And Mom. But I feel like the birth of my child isn't going to be complete without you there."

"Yeah. I'll be there."

Sharon was. Her mother also. Sophie and Eric stayed outside the birth center's room, bickering about divorce papers, and for once Sharon wished they were both hearing so that she couldn't understand the silent argument through the room's window.

"I'm done. It's over." Sophie was so angry. So thin. Her once long silky hair was broken and frayed already. Her eyes, sullen and dark. She was living with Brielle. Finishing college. And likely killing herself in the process.

Sharon was devastated. *Why must all life and healing and joy come to an end?*

Georgie labored long and without drugs, as her ways would suggest. And Sharon saw a side of her brother she didn't think could exist at all. She figured she'd be watching him pace and panic like after the funeral. That Mom would have to do everything in her power to calm him, and Georgie would be screaming at him to be more attentive. But in reality, Sean *couldn't* have been more attentive.

Between contractions near the beginning, Sean sat by Georgie's bedside, mumbling light conversation. During contractions, which he learned to simply sense in her eyes, he'd quiet and change his breathing, which Georgie would imitate. Later in the process, when Georgie began to lose her ability to cope with the overwhelming pain and sobbed things like, "I can't do this!" In response to my prodding, it was Sean that looked her sternly in the eyes and said, "Yes you can."

After two hours of pushing, when Georgie finally coerced that nine-pound baby into the world, the midwife smirked a little and called over Sharon and Lynn, who were chosen to announce in unison, "It's a boy!"

And all joy broke loose. The baby with the loud and persistent cry. Sean barely seeing him through the tears, and Georgie finally calming him at her breast. Nothing possible anywhere but joy. Even when the true Sean returned.

"So are we done with the modesty thing, or. . ." He laughed nervously about the mixed company and Georgie's nearly complete exposure to the room. Taking a blanket from the midwife's assistant and covering her.

"What's the matter, babe? Can't handle this new level of hotness?" Georgie teased.

"You just gave me a *son*, Georgie. Like a friggin' beast. No one is as hot as you." Sean winked.

Lynn and Sharon giggled. Lynn spoke up.

"Does my new grandson have a name?"

Sean snickered. "Well, we were gonna go with 'Periwinkle-Midnight' and call him 'Peri,' but—"

Georgie rolled her eyes, smiling. Sean cleared his throat and suddenly got extremely serious. Unable to speak.

Georgie took over the effort. "His middle name will be John, because all this craziness between Sean and I started on St. John and he read John the night he entered into God's sanctification. But what else in the world would his first name be, Mom?" Georgie shrugged. "Except for Samuel."

Sean's face distorted. Lynn began to cry. Then Sharon. Sean lost his battle when Georgie looked at him endearingly.

"I have this weird eye-sweating problem today."

Georgie sighed after the laughter. Staring into her son's eyes. Wonder overtaking her as Sean knelt by her side allowing the same to occur with him.

It was only a pint-sized miracle. Those happen everywhere, all the time. It isn't even a miracle, really. Just science, some might say. Except that life is of God and the wonder in the room was a sign that maybe it isn't just science at all. Maybe nothing is. Maybe life is just measured in miracles. And to Sharon, a woman who had never even experienced a teaspoon, that pint was an overindulgence of joy.

...

"God. . .?" Sharon squeaked into that night with tears on her pillow that I had whispered into existence. "I hated You for taking my dad. But I saw Your beauty in little Sammy's eyes today. Watching Sean become a daddy was really, really special. And I know that You are good and that You mean it all for Your glory. But I am never going to be good enough to be a part of that. I can offer You nothing, God. I'm a glutton. When I'm not eating, I'm thinking about food. I'm jealous of my brother and Georgie and mad at Sophie who had it all and threw it away. I want so badly for all my pain and worthlessness to go away, but I can't make any promises. I guess what I'm asking is. . .despite my weakness, do You love me enough to take me back anyway? I understand if You don't. I was never really a good child to begin with—"

Sharon grunted. Annoyed. Interrupting her prayers, she heard a familiar stretching cat scratching against her apartment door. Begging to be let in. And annoyed, frustrated and hating herself, Sharon rose and lumbered to the door to open it. In walked that proud cat like she hadn't been gone for two weeks. Begging for food, which Sharon provided.

"I don't know where you've been, Stormy. But I know you're probably hungry. Here. Eat up," Sharon said, sadly, and the cat rubbed against her legs as she set her bowl on the ground. Filled with the same canned food to spoil her. Sharon giggled at the affection. "You're welcome, sweetheart. You might be a cat, but you're my baby. And you know you can always come home to me."

For a moment, Sharon longed for an actual baby of her own someday. For that pint of wonder. But in the next moment, Sharon was on her knees in tears of gratitude for the gallon in comparison that she already had.

Stormy was a cat. Sharon, a child of God. His warm welcome home overtook her, despite her weakness, her lack, her rebellion, and sins. His love was greater. Tangibly present, long-suffering, and complete.

21

Sharon's Gift

It went unnoticed for a while. That is, I was quiet about it. Sharon still saw me as a voice of wisdom then. But it happened quickly enough that even a fool would have noticed. Sharon wasn't a fool. So, she caught on.

Most people who come to know the Lord have an experience like Sharon had that night Stormy came home. He reveals His heart to them in the most obvious, unquestionable ways. But some of them are given gifts as well. Okay, so all of them are. I try to talk them out of that, but usually it doesn't work for too long.

Sharon's gift is often viewed as unimportant. She knew that. She didn't fool herself into thinking she could preach in synagogues and convert multitudes for Christ. No, her gift was so subtle. So delicately imperceptible that it took her some digging to find it.

But after that night with Stormy, digging was all she did. She wasn't suddenly a Solomon, though she tried to read the Bible for wisdom every day. She didn't have time to spend hours serving at church, though the prospect seemed rather nice. No, Sharon did her digging on her knees.

"Who am I, God? How can You use me?" she would ask. I think she was frustrated because God wasn't answering prayers. She'd plead. "God, I'm a mess. But please use me for Your glory anyway." She'd cry. "I could really use a dose of Your glory. Otherwise nothing means anything."

God didn't readily answer that, either. At least, she didn't think so. One day, she was reading the gospel of John.

". . .Most assuredly, I say to you, whatever you ask the Father in My name He will give you. Until now you have asked nothing in My name. Ask, and you will receive, that your joy may be full."

By that night when Sharon was peering through her glasses atop her crisply made bed, she had learned a bit about Jesus's name. She had heard this passage before up against prosperity doctrine and how millionaires are made by great faith and grand prayer. But she didn't even need me to doubt that.

See, Sharon knew the character of Christ, and that He taught humility and service and love. She'd heard, falsely, recently that God didn't answer prayers. A lot of that from her own mouth when she was asking for her father back. Surely raising people from the dead was within the character of Christ.

As was comfort. Purpose, even through pain. So, she knew those prayers were likely not lost on God's ears. Especially when a brand-new Samuel Mehlmann had found his way into the world. Sharon knew God answered prayers, but only according to His character and His will.

That's when she realized that when she was asking for a dose of God's glory, He was simply waiting for her to ask the form she'd like it to take.

Sharon always erred on the side of caution. And therefore, what she asked for was merely a fraction of a teaspoon. A grain of baking soda in the cake.

"Lord God, I have a student at school who just lost her baby sister. I know You know that. I know You're with her family, comforting them. But she was such a happy kid before this happened. All I'm asking is that You let her smile." Sharon nearly felt God's smile as she said, "In Jesus' name, Amen."

Sharon nearly forgot about it. But the next day, when transitioning her students from one activity to the next, she felt a tug at the tail of her shirt.

She turned, and that would-be big sister was smiling. That was enough. That would have done it. But Sharon asked the student what she needed.

"Miss Mehlmann, my mom and dad decided to be foster parents. They get to take care of kids who don't have parents. A lady brought two little babies to our house yesterday. Two."

"Wow," Sharon said, trying not to show emotion, but ASL demanded enough to bring it out of her. *"That's wonderful! I am so happy for your family."*

Sharon had asked for the blessing of a smile. God had delivered dancing. That's when she started to be a tad bit, dare I say, brave. She began to pour out her soul before God.

"I hate this dieting, God. It takes up half my time to figure out what not to do. I can't serve You like this. I also can't serve You if I'm so fat I can't even run a block. Help me?"

And no matter what I told her, God would remind her in her spirit, ***"I love you as you are."***

"But I need to be healthy."

"Be healthy. I am with you."

And that would be that.

She didn't always see the fruit of it immediately. Or understand why God did what He did. Some prayers came with answers of silence for a time.

"God, make my sister Sophie well. Help her to at least be a mom again."

But Mel was growing up without his mother around.

Yet sometimes, the prayer was subtle and clear. And God's response came in tidal waves.

"Lord God, please comfort Mom about losing Dad. And please let me see L.D. and Sean more. I miss them so much."

And Sharon would get a texted picture of Mel doing some new and adorable thing from Lynn, who might otherwise be sulking and grieving. Something small. But Sharon could hear the wave coming.

22

God's Provision

"It's insane. During the pregnancy, I had almost no appetite and only ate enough because I knew Sammy needed it, and Sean practically force-fed me. Now I could eat every second of the day and still be hungry. This breastfeeding thing is going to make me fat," Georgie said cheerily, four-month-old Sammy in a sling on her chest as the two friends walked down the aisle of the grocery store. Each woman pushing a cart in the produce section. An errand now the only time the two could find for one another.

"You won't get fat. You might actually get healthy again. You weren't at your best when you were pregnant. Especially having to grieve *two* parents." Sharon was filling half of her cart with fresh fruit and vegetables. The primary staple of her diet. "It's still so weird that you gave birth to my brother's mini-me. Like. . .my *brother*. You married my brother, L.D." Sharon marveled and teased.

"Yeah, and now I have to *feed* him. He eats like a teenage boy, Sharon. Like, this bag of apples?" She held them up before putting them in her cart. "Two days. Gone. Nevermind getting fat, we are going to go broke eating like we do."

Sharon wondered, and therefore asked, her closest friend, "So are you going back to work, or. . ."

"They asked me to come back, but God called me to stay home with my son." Georgie bit her lip. "And his job, as great as he is at it, barely covered *him*. Now we have unemployed me and little Sammy, and we all know how easily I got pregnant last time."

"God will provide, L.D.," Sharon encouraged.

"It's really good to hear you say that. To hear *anyone* say that. Sean has lost so much faith since Dad." Georgie brightened up, not wanting to ruin her outing with Sharon. "And you're so right. God already *did* provide." Shrugged. "Mom asked us to come live with her. I guess *permanently*. She said that nothing would warm her heart more than to watch her grandkids grow up under her roof. She's just so lonely, S.R., and it allows Sean to continue getting paid beans to save lives and I can stay home with Sammy. *And* I know you go see her almost every day, and I hardly get to see you. So, it would mean time with you too. It's an all-around win."

"Except that you have to live with your mother-in-law." Sharon laughed.

"A K A, the only real mom I ever had. I don't even know how to be one. At Sammy's age, my mother would leave me in a swing at her drug dealer's house. Obviously, I'm a different kind of mommy, and I have the Holy Spirit guiding me. But having Mom so close will give Him another tool, you know?" Georgie explained, Sharon nodding. Liking the idea of seeing L.D. more.

The two arrived in the frozen section. Ice cream, to be more specific. And Sharon sighed as she looked at her vice.

"I thought we weren't grief eating anymore, S.R.." Georgie, the dedicated friend.

"I decided. . ." Sharon keeps to herself until she's ready to share an idea all at once. And here, she did. "That I hate being skinny."

"What?" Georgie laughed.

"I like being healthy. Having energy. But with my metabolism and body type, being skinny takes so much effort that it makes me hate myself even more than when I weighed a million pounds." Sharon took out two pints. One of frozen yogurt, the other of her favorite brand of rocky road, checking the labels.

"I guess that makes sense. So, you're just going to. . ." Georgie wasn't sure what Sharon was planning to do.

"Make healthy choices. Keep active. But I want to eat until I am satisfied and not freak out about every medical study or diet trend. I'll probably gain a little weight. But if I'm always worried about being skinny, it doesn't leave room for me to give myself to God.

Honestly, the closer I am to Him, the more self-control I have anyway. And as it turns out, I prefer the texture of frozen yogurt. Who knew? It's like a third as many calories. Hardly any fat," Sharon shared.

"You sound a little like *me* right now. I'm all about finding the natural rhythm of your body. Your body is connected to your spirit, and if your spirit is in tune with God, He won't allow you to harm yourself," Georgie philosophized.

Sharon giggled. "I feel you. But how does Sean feel about all that? He works in the medical field. How does he deal with all your food and lifestyle choices?"

"There is a lot of compromise. For instance, I'm allowed to give Sammy natural remedies and keep him in cloth diapers and bare feet, provided we give him milk when he gets bigger—grass-fed organic, of course. Sean is pretty adamant about it, and I trust him. He's not trying to sabotage me, he just loves his baby, and that's the sexiest thing he's ever done." Georgie bit her lip.

Sharon laughed. "My brother has destroyed you." She smiled. "But seeing you both in love, even if it had to be with each other. . .it makes my spirit happy."

"So, you don't feel. . ." Georgie winced. Saying something for the first time. "I was always worried you'd feel betrayed."

"I did," Sharon admitted. "But only for a little while. I was mostly jealous. You know how I am with that."

"I know. Don't be jealous, just go with the flow. It'll happen in God's time, God's way. That's how it was for us. I met Sean when I was nine and married him at twenty-five. When he told me how he felt on a dark beach when no one was around, all I wanted to do was do things *my* way in *my* time. I loved him then, S.R.. But it wasn't meant to happen then. God made us realize at the appointed time that it was time. Not before that, not after that. We came together because we realized life was fickle because of Dad's heart attack. If we'd waited any longer, Dad would've missed stuff."

"Well, considering I don't get to have Dad to meet my intended, I don't really have much pressure," Sharon said bitterly. A thought that plagued her. "I'm sorry. You're right, L.D.. I'm glad things happened that way for you. I love watching all the joy in your life and the way God stops the world for a love story, you know? I just can't imagine He'd ever do that for me. Not that I'm complaining. I have a great family; I get to spoil my nephews. I have a streetwalking cat waiting at home—maybe—and frozen yogurt in my cart. Life is good."

But at home, when only I was around to encourage her, Sharon had far different prayers in her heart.

"Thank you, gracious Lord for giving Mom more comfort. For answering my prayers about seeing them more. Help Sean to regain his faith in You. Please make Sophie better. Make Eric happy. Watch over my nephews. . .And Lord. . .if it is anywhere in Your will. . .Please let me fall in love. Let someone love me the way Sean loves L.D.."

23

The Father's Sins

"Maybe he had to work late?" Sharon reasoned, carefully wrapping chipped dishes and cheap glassware in paper and placing it with care into boxes.

"I doubt that, S.R.," Georgie said sadly. "It's alright, I'm not worried. I have a pretty good idea where he is."

"Which is. . .?" Sharon watched Georgie wince. Wishing she could attribute it to the baby at her breast in one of those matching chairs that used to grace her childhood home.

"Well, he's drinking again, and I didn't want him to do it *here* anymore. So, he's not doing it here." Georgie cleared her throat. "Can we not talk about that, please?"

"No, we can*not* not talk about that!" Sharon insisted. "Georgie, what's going on with my brother?"

"The anniversary is coming up." Georgie nodded. "You know that. It's doing a number on him. He's not himself."

"Yeah, I planned on celebrating Dad's upgrade with frozen yogurt and grading." S.R. smiled, but her heart sank. "What exactly is Sean doing?"

"Last night, he tried to get me to share a bottle of wine with him for some reason. When I refused, obviously, he polished it off on his own."

"An entire *bottle*? Georgie, he needs *help* if he's drinking that much."

"Try telling *him* that." Georgie finished feeding Sammy and put him over her shoulder. "He's not smoking. . .yet. Knock on wood.

I'm thankful for that. The health risks for Sammy would be something I'd have to fight over."

"Why are you not fighting over the drinking?" Sharon was concerned. About to call Sean and go get him. "Or the fact that you're supposed to move out in three days, and he won't even help you pack?"

"I'm not his personal Holy Spirit. And I can't *make* him want to grow up." Georgie gasped. "Sorry. . .I shouldn't say that about him."

"But he's hurting you, L.D.. This isn't who you married." Sharon came and sat near her friend.

"I married a human. A *wonderful* human and man of God who is a little lost right now." She wiped away a tear just as the front door opened.

"Hey, Babe," he mumbled. Stumbled. "Sorry, I. . ."

"I'm glad you're home but spare me. Are you able to help, Sean?" Georgie put Sammy in a swing and approached Sean to assess the damage.

"Yeah, I brought. . ." He waved his hand at the door several times. Vocabulary escaping him.

Eric entered with a sigh.

"We were celebrating." Sean laughed. "Divorce was final today. But he's here to help pack."

"That's not something you celebrate." Georgie looked to Eric, who steadied himself on the back of the chair she'd just been sitting in. "And neither of you is in any shape to pack. How did you get here?"

"Cab, Georgie. I'm drunk, not stupid." Sean cackled.

"Just go to bed, Sean. You have to work tomorrow." Georgie tried to help him into their room, and he tried to help himself to some kisses. "Stop it, Sean." She turned to Sharon. "Can you get Eric home safe?"

Sharon nodded, tapped Eric, who could barely focus on her. *"Where is Mel?"*

"At your mom's. Can I have a ride there?"

Sharon nodded again. Waved to Georgie, who was fighting off Sean. She drove Eric to her mother's house and led him upstairs to the bed in the room Mel always slept in. He fell asleep immediately while Sharon tapped at his phone.

"Oh, dear. . ." Lynn said. "I suppose I'm glad I planned for Mel to stay the night."

"I hope he doesn't have to work. His alarm clock is at home. This will have to do." Sharon set a vibrating alarm on his phone and on the nightstand.

The women exited the room and closed the door. Immediately, Sharon spoke, sobbing in the upstairs hallway.

"I hate Sophie. How could she do this to him? And Sean is doing the same thing to L.D.. My siblings are *monsters*, Mom. Dad would be heartbroken."

Lynn took her child into her arms. "All we can do is pray. Pray, pray, pray. And keep being the lifeline that L.D. and Eric need. Did you get anything packed?"

"About half the kitchen. I think I'll take off work to help her tomorrow," Sharon promised. "I have a lot of sick days. And Sean is making me sick, so this counts."

"Don't ever stop being you, Sharon," Lynn whispered.

• • •

Georgie turned onto her stomach and sobbed bitterly into her pillow.

"You hate me," Sean whispered from his back. Finally sobering. But not before having requested something he didn't deserve and receiving it.

"I don't hate you," she gritted through tear-distorted teeth. Hoping it was true.

"You're crying," he reasoned. "You hate me."

"I'm under a lot of stress, Sean. And, yes, I'm mad at you. That doesn't mean I *hate* you. I love you, just like always," she muffled into her pillow.

He gritted his teeth, "God, *I* hate me, Georgie. Why the heck don't *you*?"

She turned her head back to him. "I made a promise." Georgie trembled a sigh at the tears. "I'm not God. So, I'm *mad* at you. I am *not* okay with how you're treating me and Sammy. But I *love* you, Sean. As you are. Not *if* you can meet a certain standard. I love you *as you are*. So, you can come home to me as you are. No matter how that is."

"I can be better. I've *been* better. Worlds better. And that's what you deserve." Sean fought tears. "I *love* you, Georgie, and I want to keep my promise. I just don't know how to get back. It's like I'm scrambling through the dark."

"You *can't* get back without Jesus, Sean," she begged. "Please stop trying."

Sammy began fussing in his swing in the other room. Georgie rose.

"I can get him." Sean tried to get up but became dizzy as Georgie threw on a robe.

"Lie down, Sean. I'll grab you some water."

Late in the night, Georgie whispered the tearful prayers: "God, I can't do this by myself. Rescue me. Bring us back."

• • •

"What were you even thinking?" Sean and Eric barreled in the front door of the house while Georgie and Lynn unpacked boxes.

Eric, divorced a month then, was in a state that caused the two women to gasp. A bloodied cut above an eye that was swollen shut. The reduced eyesight and the alcohol in his blood had the man in a disoriented state. Obviously, he didn't even know Sean was asking him questions.

"What do you need to fix this, Sean? Should we go to the hospital?" Georgie asked.

"No, that would be traumatizing for him and I'm concerned there may be someone there that presses charges." Sean sighed. Designated driver for the evening, and sober enough to direct Georgie to his medical bag and begin sanitizing and stitching the moaning patient.

"What happened?" Lynn asked.

"Uh, Eric walked up to this random guy in the bar and clocked him. The guy responded accordingly, as you see. And I dragged Eric out of there before things got worse."

"Who was this guy?" Georgie asked.

"No clue. It's not usually on Eric's radar to be violent, so I would assume he knows him. But maybe not. He's a mess, guys. He was cussing the guy out about Sophie. He's pretty smashed, though. You could barely understand a thing he was saying." Sean sighed as he sewed. "Can he even function with one eye? I'm hoping that swelling goes down."

Eric grabbed Sean's shoulders. "No mo dink."

"No more drinking is a good plan for you, Eric." Sean chuckled.

"You. Jawn. No mo dink," Eric said just before Sean had occasion to lower a passed-out man to his back as he completed the stitching.

"You sure we shouldn't take him to the hospital, Baby? Isn't passing out a sign of a head injury?" Georgie asked.

"Yeah, or enough shots to put down an elephant." Sean chuckled. "He'll be fine."

Georgie lifted Eric's shirt and began rubbing something outside where his liver was located.

Sean sniffed. "Why do I recognize that?"

"I do this when you come home this way," Georgie confessed. "It helps relieve the shock to the liver. The morning might be a little kinder to him."

"Poor boy is in so much pain." Lynn sighed.

Georgie put a rag with some drops from a bottle over his eye.

"What is that? You can't just put your voodoo oil on everything and expect it to work, Georgie," Sean lashed.

"Eric needs to *see*. If this swelling doesn't go down, he's completely disabled. If you want to take a chance with your poison *maybe* working, fine. But I don't," Georgie yelled. Lynn took a few steps back. Wondering if she should gather pillows and blankets for Sean to sleep in the living room.

The two were taught never to let the sun set on their wrath. But when Georgie opened her eyes the following morning, she was immediately hit with a wave of anger and hurt. The two had fallen asleep back-to-back after almost waking the sleeping children with their argument.

Sean sighed next to her. "Georgie, I'm an idiot. I didn't mean it. I'm sorry."

"I forgive you."

"That was fast." Sean smiled.

"As you are," Georgie whispered, and rose from bed. Downstairs in the kitchen, she found Eric. The area around his stitches was swollen, but his eye was open and functioning.

Sean came in and saw the eye. Humbled. " 'I told you so' time?"

"No, but I do have an oil that could work for his stitches there." Georgie winked.

Eric spoke. "I don't want to drink anymore."

"You mentioned that."

"I don't want *you* to drink anymore either."

"You mentioned that too."

"I was interpreting for her." Eric smirked. Looked at Georgie.

Georgie smiled. "You couldn't even see."

"I'm deaf. Not blind."

24

Mel's Voice

"Can I come see you today?" The text read as Sharon was packing up her classroom for the day.

She responded with *"Sure."* Assuming Sean or L.D. were feeling extra cordial and might notify her before showing up at her place.

Something caused her to do a double take. Maybe it was Sophie. Maybe Sophie needed her or wanted to contact someone in the family in some way. So, she checked the name at the top of her screen.

Eric.

Sharon was immediately confused, but just as eager to help out. But she needed more information.

"Is everything okay?" She responded.

"I need an opinion."

"Ok. Do you want me to make dinner for you and Mel?"

"Sure! Thank you."

"What time?"

"Six-thirty? I have to get Mel after work."

"I can get him for you if you want. And I can cook at your house. I'm headed home from work now. Mom has a baby seat for the car, right?"

"Yes, she does."

"Alright, I guess I'll see you when you get home from work."

"You're a saint. Thank you."

Sharon arrived at her mother's house and Georgie, now a resident there, was enthusiastically teaching Mel to play "pat-a-cake" on the living room floor. She always knew the kind of mother Georgie would be, and it didn't even matter that Mel was only her nephew, and only a little. She loved each child as her own whenever they were in her care.

"Hey, S.R.!" Georgie smiled up at her.

"Hey, L.D.. I'd hate to spoil your game, but Eric asked me to get Mel and take him home. I also have to stop at the store and grab something to make them for dinner," Sharon explained, looking for Mel's things.

Lynn walked in from the kitchen.

"Eric invited you to his house?"

"Well, not exactly. But he said he wanted to ask me about something and that's what we arranged." Sharon found a pair of shoes she knew she'd bought Mel and started putting them on his feet.

Georgie looked at Lynn, bit a lip and looked at Sharon.

"What?"

"Wouldn't be a bad fit." Georgie shrugged.

"Oh, are these not the right shoes? Your kid is such a chunk I swear he's about the same size as Mel sometimes." Sharon giggled.

"Not the shoes," Georgie whispered. "Eric."

Sharon's eyes widened. "No! I know they're divorced, but he's my brother-in-law. I've never seen him as more than that. Please don't ever say that again?"

That wasn't entirely true. When Sharon was interpreting for Eric at his church years ago, she couldn't help but be moved by the handsome man her age that sat and stared at her for two hours a week. He was always kind to her, always looking past her size and seeing her heart. But once Sophie came along, all those dreams were recognized as such, and Sharon hadn't considered Eric as a prospect since.

"You're both hearing impaired," Lynn prodded.

"Eric is *deaf.* I'm *hard of hearing.* 'Hearing impaired' is not really something we say anymore. It implies that hearing is the standard and Eric and I are broken. In which case, *you* two are both hearing. Does that make *you* a good match?" Sharon over-exaggerated the silliness of the notion. Offended. Especially since with her hearing aids she was neither deaf nor hard of hearing.

She quickly gathered Mel's things, having watched Eric do it a few times.

"Aunt Sharon is taking you to Dad," she signed.

Mel squealed. Understanding both languages equally, though he could only say a few words in either yet. He put a thumb atop his head with a smile. *"Dad."*

Everyone was signed as "Dad." But Mel understood, and reached up, happily climbing into Sharon's arms.

After getting a few items from the store, Sharon used her spare key to breach Eric's front door. His house was a good-sized three-bedroom ranch, though Sophie always complained it was too small. He'd owned it since completing college. It was more immaculate than her own. Sophie once told her that a messy home was to Eric like a hearing person listening to a chaotic construction zone and an orchestra at the same time. Sharon could relate to that. She hated clutter and messes. It overwhelmed her.

She started on dinner right away.

Eric arrived just as it was done, waking in the door smiling at the smell. *"Smells good, what did you make?"*

"Just some chicken." She smiled.

Eric thanked her and greeted Mel with hugs and kisses.

Don't get any ideas. Preparing dinner for a man that loves his child? I know you want this. But you can't have it. It's never happening for you.

She smiled, averting her eyes to setting the table. Believing me. Whew.

After the meal, where Sharon filled a language barrier between father and son to the point of laughter, Mel fell asleep on the couch beside her. And Eric seemed eager to speak with her.

"Tell me what you need an opinion about." She opened the door to conversation.

He nodded. *"Do you remember what it was like to not hear?"*

Sharon giggled. *"I can only hear well because of hearing aids. I take them out at night. Just like I take my glasses off."*

"What is your hearing loss?"

"Severe for left. Moderately severe for right. I can still hear a lot. Like my cat meowing to get in the door." Sharon rolled her eyes. *"I wish I couldn't hear that."*

Eric laughed. Nodded. *"I think I remember the way my mom says my name. That's how I learned how to say it. Nobody believes me, but my records indicate that I could probably hear for a couple days after birth. Since then, I haven't heard anything. I've never wanted to. I didn't know any different and I didn't need to be able to hear. God made me this way."*

"Have you changed your mind?" Sharon had read it in his face.

Eric nodded. *"Last week, Mel had an ear infection and woke up in the middle of the night. The baby monitor you gave me was unplugged for some reason. I don't know how long he was screaming before I got to him. So, I rushed him to the emergency room because I was worried the ear infection might affect his hearing. Isn't that how you lost yours?"*

Sharon nodded. *"Sort of. The ear infections only occurred because I had some problems with my ears anyway. Mel was just sick. I remember."*

Eric seemed relieved. *"It scared me. I might be all he has. I need to be able to care for him to the best of my ability. So, I think I want to get a cochlear implant. Maybe both. My doctor says I am a candidate."*

"Eric, no!" Sharon said aloud. Returned to ASL. *"Mel loves you and is well taken care of. You don't need to change who you are just because of one bad night."*

Eric nodded. He made the confession. *"Sophie wanted me to hear her and I couldn't."*

Sharon's heart leaped. Then sank. She spoke aloud. "You want to do it for Sophie."

Eric nodded. Signed. *"I'm also buying a big house like what she wanted. I have an offer in."*

"You want her back. . ." Sharon said. Touched. "You're going to try to get her back. That's *so* sweet."

"In my heart, I am still her husband." Eric sobbed. *"And she needs me."*

Sharon smirked. *"My mom and L.D. thought you called me here tonight to try to date me."* She laughed hysterically.

Eric tilted his head. Used his voice. "I love Sophie. But a man wanting to date you should not be funny to you. I admire you very much. I am blessed to know you. You're beautiful."

Sharon nodded. Flattered beyond words. She rolled her eyes and heeded my voice. "Beautiful 'inside'?"

"Inside *and* out." Eric squinted, wondering how she didn't see it. He saw her discomfort and changed the subject. So, do you think I should get the cochlear implants?"

"I think you should be able to live with whatever choice you make. Even if it doesn't work out with Sophie. You should pray about it," Sharon allowed. "I will pray God makes the answer clear to you."

Of all the prayers that Sharon had been praying recently, it was the boldest. Cochlear implants were a small concern in relation to eternity. But Sharon prayed it anyway.

•••

Georgie hummed 'Amazing Grace' contentedly, walking out of the master bedroom upstairs. The one that Lynn had given them, so they didn't feel, however true, like they were living in *her* house. Georgie was braiding soaking wet hair and startled at meeting Lynn in the hall as she closed the door. Muffling the sound of the still running shower.

"Sean home already?" Lynn asked.

"Yeah, he came home a little early." Georgie gestured behind her with her head, as her hands were entangled in her hair. "He wanted to shower before everyone got here for dinner. He delivered a baby in an ambulance today, apparently."

Lynn tried not to notice Georgie's wet hair. Samuel always used to tell her she was too overbearing. Too nosey. Her daughter-in-love need not explain anything about her marriage.

"Everything okay, Mom? Did Sammy wake up from his nap?" Georgie asked, just before Sean hit a ghastly high note while shower-singing Amazing Grace.

Both women snorted laughter.

"No, um. . .I came to get you to ask if you could make some of your tea for dinner. I didn't mean to intrude. I missed him getting home." Lynn was embarrassed.

"It's okay, Mom." Georgie laughed, tying off her braid and hipping her hands, taking to her carefree suave as usual. "This living together thing doesn't have to be awkward, you know."

"I just adore you." Lynn smiled endearingly. "You look happy. I mean. . .I don't mean because. . ."

Georgie snorted laughter again. "Mom, quit. I *am* happy, though. Because *he's* happy. He hasn't had a drink today, so fingers crossed."

"One victory at a time." Lynn nodded.

"Exactly. I'll go um. . .make the tea."

As Georgie did so, she hummed, trying to remember lyrics as she had been with Sean moments ago. In another moment, Sean came into the kitchen singing.

"I really do think 'through many dangers toils and snares' is the third verse, because it ends with 'and grace will lead me home,' which makes sense to lead into the last verse." He analyzed as Lynn came in the kitchen. "Right, Mom? See, Mom will know, Georgie."

"Know what?" She was worried they'd ask her something terrifying.

"The order of the verses for 'Amazing Grace.' We remembered all the words, I think, but not the order of the verses." Georgie looked to Lynn.

Lynn crossed her arms in a lean against the kitchen counter, and Sharon entered and walked through the house just as she was beginning. "Amazing grace, how sweet the sound. . ."

They had all grown up with Lynn's singing. She was the only one of them besides Sophie that could carry a tune in a bucket, and they loved to listen to her sing. She was raised in a creaky old Baptist church and knew all the words to all the verses of all the hymns. Amazing Grace was an easy one. But she dare not simply recite the words. She sang them.

So, Sharon entered the kitchen smiling.

At the end of the first verse, Lynn winked and pointed at Sean. Beginning with " 'Twas grace that taught my heart to fear." And he went ahead and joined in. Everyone fumbling over each line of lyrics until Lynn led them into it.

To Eric, when he arrived, it first looked like just laughter. When he realized it was singing, he smiled. Eric loved singing. Orchestral music often escaped his fancy unless it was deep and rumblingly loud. But singing, he could watch all day. A deaf person caught in a conversation with hearing people can be confusing. There is no auditory guide to bounce him from mouth to mouth to read what is happening. The more people, the more difficult. But when they sing, there is order, life, and beauty to their synchronized lip movements, and in this case, intermittent laughter.

He'd been told, but had no feel for exactly how they knew when to change from word to word and how one could possibly navigate from pitch to pitch. A melody, he was told. The melody guided them. He loved singing—saw spirit deep into the singers, especially in his ex-mother-in-law's kitchen today. He often felt in music what none of them could hear, but never had he heard a melody.

They finished by holding out the last word dramatically and collapsing into laughter as they greeted him. He applauded them first, then watched as they began looking with almost heartbreaking admiration at Mel. Mel, at that point, was in a frustrating phase for Eric. They told him it sounded exactly like it looked. Like complete nonsense. He was "jargoning" constantly, meaning he would babble on meaninglessly to imitate actual speech. He also knew it to be incredibly cute, and first smiled at their reactions to him.

Mel began bouncing, dancing as his lips moved meaninglessly. It took Eric a minute, only until Lynn was crying, to realize what was going on. To confirm, Georgie told him.

"Eric, Mel is singing," She elaborated aloud. "It's beautiful. I've never heard a child his age sing like that. He's almost saying the words too."

Eric dropped to Mel's level and put a hand at his chest to listen, only to receive a giggle. He'd stopped.

Eric's world was silent. But he looked up at Sharon and spoke it.

"I want to hear him sing."

Sharon smiled, though the rest of them were confused.

"Go for it, Eric. Let me know how I can help."

25

Sean's Mistake

"Lord. If it is Your will, please bring Sophie and Eric back together." By then, they had been divorced for three months. Sharon doubted everything, as always, with my help. Everything except God. She knew He could do it. She knew marriage was His will. For Sharon, knowing God *could* was enough to hope He *would*.

But for now, Mel spent his days under the care of Mom and Georgie while Sean worked. Sean was another prayer entirely.

He drove a motorcycle, and sometimes went out to bars at night with Eric. Sharon knew it was breaking L.D.'s heart. She also knew L.D. would never let on. Still Sharon prayed for Sean to remember his priorities.

He was trying. He knew he was putting everything in jeopardy every time he chose anything at all over God and his family. He even had it written on his bathroom mirror.

"Be sober, be vigilant; because your adversary the devil walks about like a roaring lion, seeking whom he may devour." 1 Peter 5:8

But the biblical warning was not enough to turn his heart to Jesus in daily, steadfast worship. Eric was waiting downstairs, and Sean read that verse before checking his button-up shirt and best jeans for perfection.

"Stay home, Sean."

It boomed inside his spirit. But Sean was just so, so stubborn. He mistook that Voice for being silly old me. He kissed his broken-hearted wife goodbye before heading out yet again.

Hours and several drinks later, Sean and Eric were at a nearby club, celebrating his "last night deaf," even though the surgery for the cochlear implants would not yet make him be able to hear, and even when they were to be activated next month, he might not be able to hear anything in a "normal" way. Still, they celebrated. Well, Sean did. Eric was fasting for his procedure.

"I still think we could get you laid tonight. Mom has Mel," Sean suggested. "You don't have to go home alone."

Eric raised an eyebrow at Sean, who suddenly gasped at something he saw across the monstrously loud room.

"Just your luck! There's two girls signing over there in the corner." Sean pointed. "That hot one looks. . .what is she, Asian?"

Eric looked, rolling his eyes. "Filipino."

"How do you know that?" Sean yelled over the music.

"That's Mary. I went to college with her. She was one of Sophie's bridesmaids at our wedding."

"Dude, you already have a foot in the door. Go talk to her!"

"She's married now. With a baby. Happy," Eric yelled. Sensing from the vibrations and Sean's volume that the music was loud.

"And how do you know *that*?"

Eric laughed. "She just signed it."

"Okay, what about the other girl?"

"She didn't come here with her, but they know each other. They are catching up," Eric said.

"And you won't go talk to her because. . .?"

"Because that's Sophie, Sean."

Sean was right not to recognize her. She weighed a sickly eighty-five pounds. She was always a thin, petite little thing, but he'd never seen her so thin or terrible looking. Her ears were prominent against a tight boney face. Her collarbone protruding beneath the midriff revealing halter top. Sophie was a beautiful girl, Sean knew that. And still attractive in some ways today. But he only knew he was looking at her because Eric said so. He could see from across the room that she'd been drinking and looked to see that Eric was in distress.

"She needs help," Sean noted.

Eric nodded. Tilted his head while staring across the room. Confused. Intrigued.

"What?" Sean saw the intense intrigue on Eric's face.

"She's telling Mary about me. She signed. . ." The Eric made a movement with his hands. "That's separated. Not divorced."

"Are the signs similar?" Sean wondered.

Eric laughed. "Sophie knows the sign for divorce. Trust me. But she didn't use it."

Both men suddenly found occasion to sit back against the booth they were occupying. They didn't know then exactly why, but they feared her. They somehow perceived that the changer of their lives was emerging from the restroom.

In the form of the tall, lanky Brielle. She was in a mini-dress that caused both men, married either in heart or in practice, to avert their eyes.

"Look, it's our best friend," Sean said in sarcasm.

Eric rolled his eyes angrily. He knew she was Sophie's greatest source of poison.

"We should go," Eric suggested.

Sean nodded, always happy to avoid the awkward. But when they stood, Brielle and Sophie were headed to the same exit, and the foursome nearly collided.

"Oh look, it's your deaf ex-husband, Sophie." Brielle said it into her hand, finding herself brilliantly amusing that Eric couldn't understand. Eric just shook his head. Deaf. But far from unintelligent.

"Hi, Eric," Sophie allowed sheepishly. She signed. *"I ran into Mary over there. She's doing well."*

"I saw," he told her. Remorse in his eyes.

"How is Mel?" she asked.

"He's doing well. He misses you."

Sophie nodded sadly. "Bye, Eric."

As she attempted to pass him, his heart got the better of him and he grabbed her arm.

"You need help, Sophie. The hospital has a state-of-the-art facility. I could check you in. I'd pay every penny."

"Oh, so that I'd owe you something? Why can't you just leave me alone?" she screamed.

"You don't owe me anything. Ever. I'm just worried about you."

The conversation continued as such. Foggy-brained Sean stepped aside to give them some privacy, and Brielle followed, posing her body and swinging her hair.

"Still married to that cute hippie girl, Sean?" she murmured, looking over the handsome, well-dressed man.

"What kind of a question is that?" He was on guard. Offended.

"One you didn't answer." She took a step closer.

"Yes. I'm married." Sean flashed his left hand in her face. Trying to avert his eyes from the fabric defining her waist and the lack of fabric highlighting her shoulders and bust.

"Seems to me like you're here looking for something 'Georgie' isn't giving you? Am I wrong?"

"She doesn't like me drinking around our son. I'm trying to get some stuff out of my system, Brielle. That's all," Sean shared.

"She seems like a pain." Brielle tried to sound caring as she reached out and smoothed the collar of his shirt. "What time does she expect you home?"

"It isn't like that." Sean's eyelids were heavy. His heart was pounding and his will shifting. He didn't want Brielle near him. But her touch was like witchcraft.

A few years ago, he'd have leaned into her the way she leaned into him. And likely woken up with her in the morning. She made his heart race. Her thick mascara and cheap perfume churned the alcohol like poison against his will. Like a purring lioness with prey in her sight.

"Walk away, Sean."

It was clear, as was the path to the door. Eric was in an argument with Sophie and would welcome the plea to cut the night short. He figured he had two heartbeats to make the decision before she made her case. The obvious decision.

One.

Two.

"I think Eric can handle her. Let me give you a ride," she whispered, her hand at his chest.

• • •

Sophie stumbled into her mother's living room drunk that Friday night when Sharon had been spending the evening with her nephews and best friend and mother. I was with Sophie often, and she tended to try to drink me away. Anyway, all the kids were in bed. Which is what Lynn told her daughter.

"Mel is asleep. I didn't know you were coming. Eric asked me to keep him overnight. You shouldn't drive him, Sophie."

"Relax, I took an Uber," Sophie slurred. "But I'm not here for Mel. I want to see L.D.."

Georgie was in the room and laughed a little at Sophie's stupor.

"Right here." Georgie raised her hand.

"I accidentally ran into Eric and Sean at this place. . .I forget what it's called. It's like five minutes away." Sophie squinted her eyes.

"I doubt that's relevant." Georgie crossed her arms. Wishing Sean was home with her and their baby. But glad Sophie had spotted him, I think.

"You're right. That doesn't matter. I got into it with Eric, so I left in a cab. But Brielle stayed behind because she was otherwise occupied, as usual." Sophie laughed involuntarily. Any emotion caused laughter at the moment.

"With a guy, I assume?" Georgie was annoyed. Swiping a hair out of those purple eyes.

"Yeah. Sean." Sophie squinted again, as if she'd already clarified that. "I think she was taking him back to our place. I came here until she calls me. Eric was trying to break them up, but it didn't seem like that was likely."

Georgie sat in the silence they allowed for her to piece together all her disbelief.

"Sean was. . ."

"Making out with Brielle," Sophie finally clarified. "For now, at least. They were probably headed out soon, though. She was designated driver tonight, don't worry. She wasn't drinking."

Sharon was stunned. Started the fervent prayers inside her. *"God, please don't let him cheat on her."*

I whispered in Georgie's ear. *This is your fault. If he cheats on you, it is your fault. How many times have I told you that you're not even close to the amount of physical attention he needs? I know you try. But you have a baby. That was your choice. A baby. Sammy gets everything now. Did you really think a marriage to Sean could be sustained after that?*

Mom spoke. "L.D., Sophie is drunk. She's probably mistaken."

Georgie laughed once as the front door opened. Eric, completely sober, walked in, looking shell-shocked. He saw Sophie.

"Why are you here? Do you want Mel to see you like this?"

"This is who I am, Eric. When will you figure that out? You need to get over fat little Princess Sophie. She doesn't exist," Sophie said. "And once again, I didn't come to get Mel. I came to tell L.D. where Sean was."

"You didn't." Eric's heart melted and curdled at Sophie's feet, like always. "Zof, no."

"Eric, is it true?" Georgie stood, asking.

"I don't know what she told you." Eric stalled.

"Is Sean on his way to commit adultery?" Georgie squeaked.

"I don't know. He drank a lot. We were about to leave," Eric signed, knowing Lynn couldn't understand that way.

"And he left with Brielle," Georgie clarified. Ignoring excuses.

"No, they didn't leave. I couldn't get Sean to come with me."

"So, he's with her?"

Eric nodded reluctantly. Georgie nodded. "Take me."

"I'll tag along." Sophie decided.

"Do you want me to come, L.D.?" Sharon said sheepishly.

"No." Georgie sniffled. Fighting the tears that were likely my fault. "Stay with Mom and the kids please."

"L.D., maybe it isn't the best idea for you to go," Mom suggested.

"I have to confront this, Mom. I love him too much to let him make a mistake this big. If I can stop him, I need to." Georgie worked feverishly to compose herself as she grabbed her purse, though it was invisible to them.

I tortured her all the way to that bar, because it was my job. But that was nothing compared to what the sight did to her. She didn't even have to enter the bar. They'd found a darkened wall aside the building, and they were wrapped helplessly into one another's arms and mouths.

Mindlessly, Georgie placed a fingertip on her own lips as she exited the car. Feeling him there—the only place he should ever be. Stealing kisses from another's lips, the way he'd stolen her first on a beach. The devastated sigh was unintentional, but it turned his attention immediately to the beautiful woman under the streetlight, peering into the alley.

Georgie's heart was already flooded. Bleeding out. Her ears pulsing.

"Listen."

Georgie didn't want to, but she understood the command. The last time she loathed him and wanted to murder him in her heart, she did something that made her stop. The tears flowed as she slowly raised the heels of her hands and pressed them against her ears. She didn't even hear more than a muffle of them all shouting at one another. She didn't perceive what Brielle paired with her smug expression before she got into her car and drove off. Or hear Sophie's hand connect with the back of Sean's head. Eric's scolding. Or even Sean's first words as he met her eyes and removed her hands from her ears.

But she finally heard him say, "Georgie? Georgie, I. . .I'm sorry okay. Please let me explain." And her ears began to work again. "Babe, I didn't—"

"Didn't *what*?" Georgie said, covering her ears again with the anger brought on by his stumble.

She backed up from him as the tears flowed and he begged and pleaded, following her. She knew she should forgive him. Once again, though never this deeply. And she almost did.

But with the strength of her other senses that occurred while she covered her ears, the straw that destroyed the camel came in as a whiff in her nose.

Alcohol. Lots of it. That was routine now. But in the mix, she caught something else that wasn't routine. Wasn't okay. She simply couldn't forgive him tonight for the cheap perfume that had transferred to him from his brush with adultery.

"Can we go home and talk about this?" he said as she removed her hands from her ears the final time.

"No." She sobbed. "You can't come home. Not tonight. Maybe not ever."

"What?!" Sean's eyes widened. "Georgie. . ."

And all her cool composure melted before all their eyes. "You *reek* of her. Don't come near me."

"Georgie, wait!" Sean called after her as she began to walk the few blocks home.

Georgie turned and took a step toward Sean. Sean was relieved. Until she extended her hand and placed that shining gold feather ring in his hand with angry tears.

"I gave you *everything*. Why wasn't that enough?"

I think the tense of the words hurt him the most. Even Sophie was in tears as Sean called desperately after his wife in the dark. But she just kept walking.

26

Sophie's Heart

Sean walked out of one of the guest rooms in Eric's new house and headed downstairs. He was always going to be Eric's ride to his procedure, but now he started out at Eric's house. He smelled coffee in the air and poured himself a cup in the kitchen. Coffee. A red flag went up.

Eric was fasting. Not even water this morning. Eric was a good candidate for the implants because even though he was an adult, and essentially born deaf, they considered him to be intelligent enough to understand and translate the world around him once he could hear. Following a doctor's orders was not something the responsible Eric would take lightly. Who was drinking coffee?

He didn't. His heart dropped as he carried his cup of coffee into Eric's ample dining room.

"Hey," Sophie said quietly. "Eric is putting his things in the car. He'll be back in in a minute."

"Why are you here?" Sean accused, taking a seat next to his sister.

"Here like, in the dining room? I'm having breakfast, and most likely lunch. . ." Sophie sniffled in reference to her coffee. "Here at Eric's place? Well, I'm a mess and taking him down with me as always, so where else would I be?"

"Sophie, why would you mess with his head like that?" Sean whispered.

Sophie rolled her eyes. "Relax, I stayed in a guest room just like you. He didn't want me to go back home with Bri—"

"Let's *not* finish that name." Sean's eyes closed in desperate pain. Hoping he could blink last night away.

"Good plan. What were you thinking, Sean?" Sophie asked, in tears. "What did L.D. ever do to you?"

"Sophie. . ." Sean was going to get defensive. Accost her. But ended up just letting his eyes fill with tears and waving her off.

"What happened to us, Sean?" Sophie got choked up too. "I'm supposed to be the lady of this enormous house he bought himself. Instead I tossed my marriage in the trash and I haven't even seen my son in *months*."

"I don't know, but we both need to figure this out, Soph," Sean said through tears. "Look at Sharon. How is she so *together*?"

"If only I knew." Sophie shrugged. Looked sternly into her brother's eyes. "Go see Sammy, okay? And you win your wife back, you hear me? There's no fixing me. But I can't watch you do the same thing I did."

"I'll try," Sean promised. "You're sick, Sophie. I really want you to—"

She smiled a little. "Eric says he has an appointment at the hospital. I'm taking the chance. I'm going with you guys and I'm checking myself into rehab."

"Good." Sean sighed. "That's really good, Sophie. We've all been praying for you."

"I know. I'm sorry. . .I've just been. . ." She sobbed.

"You don't have to explain it to *me*." Sean smirked. Grabbed his sister's hand and squeezed. Skin and bones. But he didn't mention it.

Sophie nodded. Worried. "Sean, what kind of a doctor's appointment requires a person to drive you there and a duffle bag with three days' worth of stuff? What's Eric doing?"

"Sophie, no offense, but you divorced him. If he didn't choose to tell you, I can't betray his trust by going behind his back and telling you. He obviously doesn't consider it to be your concern." Sean was gentle, but direct.

Eric appeared at the dining room door. Pointed to his wrist. The siblings nodded. Eric turned his back, clanking around in the kitchen.

"I miss him," she admitted. "I hate myself for what I did. I seriously gave up the name 'Sophie Stiles' to be a Mehlmann again. No offense, but think about it. How stupid does a person have to be?"

"You still love him?" Sean took a sip.

"I *divorced* him. In a cruel, horrible way. I severed all hope of having a life with him. He deserves so much better than that."

"That's not what I asked. Do you *love* him?"

"*Yes*, I love him. Of course, I love him," Sophie said far too loudly to make her brother stop asking. "And I'm *so* glad he's deaf at the moment."

Sean hugged his sister outside the clinic that could restore her mental and physical health, and dropped off Eric in another wing, where they hoped to restore his hearing.

He wondered if there was a wing of this hospital that could save *him*.

Healing's Rain

I barely had to whisper. Everyone in Sean's life was already screaming it.

You're a screw up. You shattered that gorgeous snow globe you had in your hands. Brielle is nothing but a lush and an awful kisser. What kind of person chooses that over Georgie even once?

But far louder and far more convicting was another Voice saying something else.

"I love you, Sean. I forgive you."

I think he needed both voices. The condemnation. The confirmation. To know that he was justified and sanctified by heavenly perfection—so he'd better shape up. For two days, Sean helped his ex-brother-in-law—or maybe just his brother—change the dressings of the incisions behind his ears. On the third day, Sean called his wife.

To his surprise, she answered, and he was elated, even though she answered with:

"Why are you calling me, Sean?"

"I wanted to see how you're doing," he remarked with a lilt of attitude, as was his normal speech pattern.

"I have a baby to care for on my own because my husband cheated on me. And I live with his mother. I've never felt more betrayed. How are *you* doing, Sean?" The same lilt. The same attitude.

Sean resisted the urge to get defensive or make excuses. He didn't deserve to defend himself. He simply sniffled. "The only person worth knowing in the universe chose *me* as her husband, and I blew it. I'm peachy."

"How is Eric?" she changed the subject.

"He's home now. The surgery went perfectly, they said. He should be able to go to work in a few days and start to program his implant in about three weeks."

"Good."

Georgie didn't know what else to say. Sean spoke into her silence.

"How's our son, Georgie? Does he still have the sniffles?"

"No, he was teething. First one poked through last night." Georgie laughed a little.

"What? That's so cool! Does he need anything? I was going to come by and see him after work tomorrow. You and I are a mess, I'm not denying that. But we need to still be the absolute best possible parents for Sammy."

"I agree," she whispered. "I'd never stop you from seeing your son, you know that. We're almost out of bananas, so if you could bring a bunch. . ." She paused before allowing her natural instinct. "Do *you* need anything?"

"You mean other than a time machine?" Sean laughed bitterly. "Why do you care about what I need?"

"Because I'm your wife and it's my job." Georgie shattered his heart. Tore him apart from the hot coals on his scalp to the tingling of his toes. "Lavender—" She began.

"I'm *not* calling you Lavender." Sean laughed.

"Good. That isn't my name. But I mean lavender. The oil. I'll give you some to diffuse. I know you start drinking when work is tough on your spirit or when your anxiety gets going because you aren't smoking. Since I assume you'd still prefer not to rely on either of those things, lavender will help you calm down. That's what I diffuse while we slee—I mean it always helps you sleep." Georgie started to lose her composure. "Just remind me to give it to you when you come see Sammy."

"Yeah, uh. . .thanks."

...

When Sean arrived at the door, his mother was scowling.

"I'm not sure you should be here, son," she said, hipping her hands.

"I told her I was coming, Mom. She said I could," Sean ensured. "To see my son? I brought bananas, too."

Lynn nodded with a smile. "Maybe my kids make terrible spouses. But you certainly have Sophie beat when it comes to parenting."

"It's not a competition," Sean said. "For the record, I screwed up. But I am getting my family back. Also, for the record, Sophie checked into rehab this week. I dropped her off myself."

Lynn rejoiced as Sharon came from upstairs.

"Hey, Beautiful," Sean said, crossing his arms.

"I'm really mad at you, Sean." Sharon led with it. She'd, of course, been praying for days that Sean would come back to being the amazing man he'd become before their father died.

"I'm really mad at me too," Sean admitted. His voice faltering a little.

"What were you thinking? How can you do something like that? I honestly thought you loved L.D.," Sharon whispered after being sure Georgie was still upstairs.

"I *do,* Sharon. And I wasn't thinking. That was the point of being that drunk. To not think. But that's not happening again."

"It doesn't matter. She doesn't want to take you back. You only get to be here because you were with her long enough to procreate," Sharon revealed.

"I don't blame her for feeling that way." Sean nodded. Pulled a chain with her ring on it from under his shirt. "But this'll be here if she changes her mind."

Georgie descended the stairs with Sammy in her arms and an apology. "Sorry, I was feeding him."

"Don't apologize." Sean smiled. His heart leaping at the sight of his smiling son and stunning wife. Why couldn't he have seen all that beauty a few days ago? Georgie handed him his son, and both Sammy and Sean's faces lit up. Sammy had missed his daddy. "Hey, big guy! He crawling yet?"

"You've been away a couple days, Sean. He hasn't mastered all of space and time just yet." Georgie smiled. Frowned when she saw the chain on his neck. "Sean, don't do that, okay?"

"What, hope?" Sean asked. "That's all it is, okay?"

Sean stayed until after dinner, put Sammy to bed for the night, and headed out when Sharon did.

"You're a good dad." Sharon made sure to say as Sean was removing his helmet from the back of his motorcycle.

"Well, I had a good model. I could definitely use his advice tonight." Sean walked over to Sharon's car and leaned on the back of it. She was about to inquire when she saw him sniffling. About to lose it. "How do I fix this?"

"I don't know, Sean. I've never been in a real relationship, remember? From my perspective, people like you have everything they ever wanted and just trample it in the dirt. I've never understood how someone can do that. Do I want to see you back with L.D.? Yeah. But I can also see how she would never want to trust you again. She's the best person alive, Sean. I still don't understand—"

"I'm human. I'm a sinner. I'm grieving. None of that makes it okay or justifies any of it, but I know you want answers and that's all I got." Sean faltered. Coughed.

And Sharon became his reluctant shoulder to cry on. She knew he didn't have another one, so she allowed it. Wrapped her arms around his waist and squeezed tight out in front of their childhood home.

Georgie was inside, peeking out the window. Her heart bending.

You're horrible. Just let him come home. I told her. But she didn't listen.

Every other day for a month, Sean would come see his son. Spending hours with him. Changing every diaper, though he hated the cloth ones Georgie insisted on. Feeding him mushy bananas. Watching him learn to crawl.

Sharon was usually there too. It took her away from grading and praying and time with her cat. But Georgie asked her for the moral support. One night, Georgie asked her to linger a bit after Sean left, when they usually left together. Sharon complied, standing in the doorway of her childhood bedroom where Sammy was sleeping peacefully. That room was closest to the master suite that Georgie now stayed in alone. Mom had given it to them—the memories of Dad too great to bear, and Sean and Georgie's family growing. Mom slept in the guest room on the main level now.

Georgie joined Sharon in the doorway after a visit to her bathroom. Quietly titling her head in a smile like a mother does when admiring her offspring.

"Sorry to keep you waiting. I finally had a chance to urinate." She sighed.

"That's fine. What did you want to talk about without Sean around?" Sharon asked.

"I need to ask you a huge favor." Georgie didn't hesitate to ask. Best friends—sisters—have no need for that.

"Anything, L.D.." Sharon smiled.

"It'll be super easy for you. But it might kill me, so I'm just being selfish," Georgie admitted.

"Um. . .okay? What do you need me to do?"

"I just took a pregnancy test and left it on my bathroom counter. I just need you to read it to me with your wonderful S.R. sugar-coating." Georgie sniffled next.

"You think you're *pregnant*?" Sharon whispered, making sure not to wake her nephew or welcome the ears of her mother. "L.D., Sean moved out like a *month* ago."

"I've been avoiding taking the test for five weeks. I was thinking about how to tell him when I caught him with his tongue down another woman's throat." Georgie met her wet purple eyes with her friend's warm brown ones. Nodded. "I'm 95 percent sure already. All I want to eat is limes."

"So, if you know, why is it so hard to read the test?"

"I'll be a single mom. Already am. But I'll have twice as many people to screw up." Georgie sniffled.

"You are *not* a single mom." Sharon rolled her eyes. "Sean is here every other day. And you have Mom. You have me. Not to mention Sean would come home to you in a matter of minutes if you asked."

"I don't think I *want* him to." Georgie sobbed, whining.

"Then stop complaining." Sharon, angry with her sister-in-law, headed to the master bathroom as instructed.

When she stepped back into the bedroom, Georgie was already there.

Sharon sighed. Whispered, "Positive."

Georgie just nodded at first. Lost her composure. "Will you pray with me, S.R.?"

Sharon did. She prayed for a full five minutes. Poured out her heart like she did at home, since she hadn't had the chance today. After amen, Georgie was smiling and wiping at tears.

"You pray *so* beautifully." She laughed once.

"I lisp."

"You *sing*. I bet God really listens to you." Georgie had always admired her friend. But never so much as now.

"I hope so." Sharon had prayed for restoration of marriages. The health of babies. Renewed joy. Miracles upon miracles.

Georgie sighed. "Lord, give her a man who will know what he has."

Sharon giggled. Laughing at my joke.

Miracles upon miracles.

•••

Two nights later, it was raining. Georgie stood nervously at the window waiting for Sean to arrive. Nervous for the rain. Nervous for the news she had to deliver. When she heard the rumble of his bike outside, she both sighed in relief and hoped for her own death.

Lynn reacted with a gasp at his soaked clothing. Georgie headed upstairs and came back down with a set of dry ones. Many of his clothes were still there, so it wasn't a chore. Sean thanked her lovingly, then went to change as Georgie retrieved her son to see his father.

This time, she asked Sean to linger after Sharon left with an encouraging nod and Sammy was in bed. She pulled him into their bedroom, asking him if he could talk a minute. Noticing her wedding ring still dangling from his neck.

"What's wrong, Georgie?" he asked, sitting on their bed. Deep longing crawling over him. For her touch. But mostly, just to stay.

"I have to tell you something." She sighed. Sitting next to him.

Sean's heart sank. "You want a divorce."

"What? No. That's not. . ."

"But do you, though?"

She was silent a moment, and the next words happened in a whisper. "I don't know how to answer that."

"Do you still love me?"

"If only love alone had the power to fix this." Georgie stood, pacing.

"It actually. . .does. . ." Sean laughed, heartbroken. Meeting her eyes and rising to face her.

"You're right," Georgie realized with a nod. "Love covers a multitude of sins. But this is so complicated."

"Doesn't have to be complicated," he whispered. Touching her hair. His forehead to hers. "It could be. . .*so* easy."

The kiss came as easily as a hello or a goodbye might have a month ago. Nothing new to them. Nothing forbidden. But the tension. The absence. The wait. Kept the kisses coming. Sean whispered again, between kisses. That tone he used in those cases. He'd tell her she was beautiful. How he loved her. Intimate things he'd never say aloud otherwise. Sometimes he'd make her laugh.

Sometimes fall into ease. Georgie was always so easily seduced by his whispers.

"Georgie, we could end this silliness right now. . .I could come home. . .I love you so much. . .I miss you."

But Georgie took a gigantic step back, though longing more than anything for him to put his arms around her. Already seduced.

"What did you whisper to *her*? To Brielle when you were kissing her."

Sean touched the kisses on his lips with a curled finger. Winced in spiritual pain. Ignored my pleading not to speak the truthful memory aloud.

"Oh, stuff like, 'We shouldn't be doing this. This was a mistake. I need to go home to my wife. I never should have come out tonight.'" He sniffled. "And I wasn't whispering. That's something I do with the woman I love."

"What kind of a pathetic sap would I be if I let you stay the night, Sean?" *A pathetic one. You got that right.* "I'm not a one-night stand." She sobbed.

"No, you're my gracious wife."

"I don't have that kind of grace. I'm not who you think I am. You cheated on me. How can I ever let you come home?"

"Just *let* me. I'll stay right now. We don't owe anyone an explanation." Sean paused. Listened to the rain tapping against the window.

"Stop it," Georgie pled desperately. "I'm not ready for that, Sean."

"What would it take to make you ready? Do you not understand that I'm willing to do *anything*?" he begged.

"It would take a miracle," Georgie whispered. "Last I checked, you aren't capable of that."

"Sammy's a miracle and *he* came from me." Sean shrugged. "Well, from God. But he's my son."

Georgie's heart lurched. I intervened.

If you tell him you're pregnant again, this will all be over. You know you can't do this alone. He'll stay. You'll be a family. Give him another chance. He did help create another miracle. All you have to do is tell him.

I'm not always wrong. I get a bad rap. It isn't fair. But where Sharon would listen to me, Georgie assumes I'm lying. And she instead muffled me with pride.

"Get out, Sean."

Sean took his leave, and Georgie took to their bathroom, to stave off vomit. She looked in the mirror, where Sean had written a verse.

"Be sober, be vigilant; because your adversary the devil walks about like a roaring lion, seeking whom he may devour." 1 Peter 5:8

It sickened her. Destroyed her how true it was. And yet, she was headed straight for a lion's jaws with the evil thought she thought as she looked at her face in the mirror. Her hair flowed beautifully across her shoulders, tickling her wrists.

It was her glory, that hair. And it had become Sean's glory. His absolute most favorite thing about her appearance. She couldn't even remember the last trim. She always trimmed her own hair, drawing it up into a ponytail at her brow, and snipping gingerly at the ends.

The scissors were in the drawer. Right there. And she wanted to hurt him. She sobbed as she pulled that hip-length hair up into a ponytail.

"But if a woman has long hair, it is a glory to her; for her hair is given to her for a covering." 1 Corinthians. You like that one.

Thus I warned her not to trust her emotions. But with nearly violent snaps and gentle drifts of sixteen inches of ash-brown hair meeting bathroom tile, she cut it so that it would fall between her shoulder blades. Still quite long for most women. But Georgie Lavender-Dawn Mehlmann was certainly not most women. Instantaneously, she regretted it, and began to grieve yet again. Her hair was given as a covering. She'd never felt more naked.

• • •

Sean rode out into the soaking rain, remembering her kisses. Longing for so much more. He was distracted by the pain. The rain. He'd barely covered his head with the helmet before driving off. Too late, he saw the truck run the light to his left.

And most certainly, that truck didn't see him.

28

Lynn's Suffering

It wasn't enough. That long, loving marriage simply wasn't enough to keep your children in marriages, even with good, godly people. If Samuel were here, they wouldn't be in so much pain. But you certainly could do more. Well. . .could. But likely won't. You've always been the pushover. You are nothing without Samuel. Your existence doesn't even matter a year later.

I tortured Lynn thus each night. Lavender was never enough of a sleep aid for her. So tonight, an hour after listening to a shouting match upstairs, Lynn was awake when her phone rang.

"Hello?" she sniffled.

"Hi, um. . .I'm not sure I have the right number." A stranger's voice.

"You've reached Lynn Mehlmann."

"Yes, a lot of Mehlmanns in this guy's phone. I'm looking for Sean Mehlmann's next of kin. He's wearing a ring, so we assume that'd be a wife. . .Are you his wife?"

"No, this is Sean's mother. His wife is upstairs asleep. Why, what?. . .What happened to my son?" Lynn's heart of a mother began playing out all the worst scenarios. Some of them would prove prophetic.

"He's alive. In surgery now. There was an accident. I think you and his Mrs. better get down to the hospital. What is her name? We'd like to call her. I have a Sophie, a Sharon—"

"She'd be listed as Georgie. But you better let me tell her. They're separated. It's a delicate situation." Delicate. Something like that. "How bad is he?"

"Critical. But I really shouldn't say too much over the phone, ma'am. Except. . .hurry."

Lynn jotted down the information for the hospital, then threw on clothes and bolted up the stairs. Georgie was at the tail end of crying herself to sleep. Lynn would know. She knocked on the bedroom door.

"Go away, Sean," Georgie yelled.

"It's me, sweetie," Lynn cooed. "L.D., Sean's been in an accident. I'll grab Sammy while you get dressed."

Georgie washed her puffy face and dressed her tired body in record time, all while fighting the morning sickness. She was annoyed that Lynn didn't have more information. Annoyed she didn't even mention her hair. But relieved to be the driver so that Lynn could make the phone calls to Sharon, Sophie's clinic, Eric. Brielle never made the list. Georgie somehow found comfort in that. But not in anything else.

If he dies, he'll die thinking you hate him. Not knowing you're carrying his child. Good job.

When Georgie entered the emergency room doors, a nurse met her at the desk. Recognizing her immediately.

"Mrs. Mehlmann? Georgie, is it?"

"Georgie, yes. Tell me what happened," she demanded as her mother-in-law was entering with Sammy.

The nurse sniffled. "You're even more beautiful than the pictures I've seen. I'm sorry. Usually he's the one bringing in the stretcher. I'd never seen him on one. Please excuse my shock. I'm sorry to meet under these circumstances."

Georgie found some strange comfort. "How bad is it?"

"Sean was broadsided by a pickup truck while riding his motorcycle."

"Oh God." Georgie panicked. In tears. "Is he—"

"He's still in surgery. I can't be sure, but I heard them talking about a shattered leg among other things. Which is nothing, Mrs. Mehlmann. Usually 'motorcycle vs. truck' is something only a coroner can treat. From the looks of the thing, his helmet saved his life. At least. . .at least for now." The woman impressed. "If you pray, now is a good time."

Sharon walked in the door just at her appointed moment.

Most people would define a miracle as a divine deliverance. Something wonderful and impossible that happens for the benefit of a person or group of people. It often happens that way. But I say that the greatest miracles are not wonderful at all. They are devastating. Because a miracle is something that ultimately turns eyes to Christ. That can happen with wonderful. But far more often, it happens with devastating.

They all sat in that waiting room. Holding hands through that surgery. Sharon praying her heart out until tears streamed down their faces. Eric. Georgie. Lynn. Mel. Sammy. And whoever was inside Georgie. But it wasn't until they were fatigued and calmed from prayer that she told them.

"I'm pregnant," she said after a low silence with a little laugh. "He might never get to know that. I always tell everyone too late. I tried to tell him."

"But you fought. You're at odds. That's to be expected," Lynn said.

"Expected. But unacceptable," Georgie said. "We were fighting because he wanted to stay the night. That's all he wanted. Instead, I got so mad at him for asking that I pulled a Samson. If I'd let him stay. . ."

"Don't do that, L.D. We can't go back," Sharon said.

"And hair grows, sweetie. You look lovely," Lynn promised. They all agreed.

Suddenly, Mel was trying desperately to get Eric's attention. He finally did. By then everyone was listening.

"What, buddy?" Eric asked.

Mel, just shy of two, pointed at the door to the waiting area and whispered, signed. "Is Mommy?"

Eric frantically put on a beanie he'd been wearing to cover the scars behind his ears. "Yeah, that's Mommy."

Sophie was in scrubs, as was the woman escorting her. The family rose to their feet when they saw her. Partially because they hadn't seen her in a month and hadn't expected to see her tonight. But mostly because she was once again stunningly beautiful. Healthy.

Her escort spoke first. "Hi everyone. I'm Sophie's counselor. We got a call about Sophie's brother and since Sophie is with us voluntarily, she was hoping to come be with everyone."

Tearful Lynn spoke up. "Sophie, we didn't mean to sabotage your treatment."

"It's okay, Mom." She was gentle. "I'd rather deal with this tonight while I have lots of help doing it than miss it all and have to deal with it later on my own. Can someone tell me what happened with Sean?"

They broke the news and prayed again with Sophie present. She held onto Mel for dear life. After the prayer, Sophie seemed uneasy with Eric's kind stare.

"What?" she finally asked.

He waved a hand over his face a certain way.

Sophie smirked through her tears. Not usually flattered by simply being called "beautiful." But this time, she was deeply affected. "Thanks. What's with the hat?"

Just then, a doctor came into the room and Georgie stood up immediately as the doctor approached. It was a position she'd always wanted to be in. To have family close enough that a doctor came out of some back room and addressed her among them. When she arrived in that position, she wanted to be anywhere but there.

"The Mehlmann family?" They nodded. "He pulled through the surgery, but he has a long road ahead of him."

"They never told us the extent of his injuries," Georgie demanded.

The doctor nodded. "His left leg was shattered. Pelvis. A couple vertebrae. He also has a concussion, but that's mild. He seems to have feeling in his legs. And he's young and fit. So, if he wants it, he could very well walk again. But I've seen these injuries go both ways."

Georgie would have taken it like a ten-story building on her chest. But she had the peace of Christ and merely took it in tears.

"When can we see him?"

"He should wake up in the next hour or so, and we want to be sure he's able to do so neurologically. But he'll be in a massive amount of pain, so we'll likely sedate him at that point. Would you like to be there when he wakes up? It could help orient him," the doctor suggested.

"We. . ." Georgie sobbed, reciting my words, "We were fighting just before he got into the accident. We're separated. He won't want to see me."

"Don't listen to her. He needs to see her there if he's going to wake up in pain." Sophie was sure to be heard. But also, sure not to sign.

"Sophie, we should be getting back," the counselor said. "You have a long road ahead too. But if your brother is in the same hospital, we can certainly arrange visits."

"Okay." Sophie sighed. Looked to Eric. Wanted to say something but didn't know what to say. Her face was pained. Remorseful. The few seconds she had to speak were simply not enough.

Eric heard her anyway and acknowledged it with a nod just before Sophie left.

The doctor looked to Georgie. "I'll take you to him. Probably just one of you for now."

"Mom, could you—" Georgie didn't even need to ask. Lynn took Sammy into her arms with a nod.

Georgie had to fight me for every step down a labyrinth of a hall, especially as she approached the room where she didn't even recognize the man in the bed. Road rash on his face. A tube in his mouth. All wrapped in blankets and bandages. Instinctively, she found a hand and held it. When he awakened, panicking, moaning, she was there. His body soothed and calmed as they put the drugs in his body and his eyes caught hers. He squeezed her hand just before falling back to sleep.

•••

Eric walked up to Lynn's house to retrieve Mel but stopped at the porch, turning his head and looking up in confusion.

"That was a bird," Sharon said, laughing. Signing.

"Say that again?" He watched her say it the next time. Connecting the way the word looked. With the sign. With the sound.

"Does it still sound mechanical?"

"Mostly. I think it's getting better," Eric allowed. Shaking his head in laughter. "My voice is loud."

"You get used to it. Remember, it's not that loud to me, just to you." Sharon smiled. She had been there several times during cochlear implant activation for children. Her students' parents often asked for her assistance in gently helping to ease their child into a world of hearing. She supposed that about 90 percent of them burst into tears during the first programming session.

She hadn't expected Eric, a grown man, to have the same reaction, especially to his mother's voice. But he did.

"Thank you again for coming with me to my appointment. I'm sorry about my parents. Sean was supposed to come as a buffer, but—"

"It's not a problem, Eric." Sharon nodded. Having been told today when she helped Eric understand new sounds that Eric had picked the wrong sister to fall in love with. Which was the first time Eric heard laughter.

Eric smiled when he heard something coming from inside the house and opened the door straight away.

Mel was laughing and running around. Lynn and Georgie looked at Eric with anticipation.

Eric laughed.

"Do you hear it?" Sharon said and signed.

"His laughing. . .I don't think it sounds that way. It is mechanical." Eric smiled brightly, even though the others were disappointed. "But his footsteps are clear."

Georgie grabbed her diaper bag and picked up Sammy.

"Where you headed?" Sharon asked.

"Hospital. Sammy didn't get to see Sean yesterday," she answered.

"I didn't think he was awake," Lynn asked, warily.

"He's not. But I'm still going. For Sammy." Georgie sighed. "I'll let you know if there's any change."

She left, and Sharon immediately shook her head. Rolled her eyes, looking at her mom. " 'For Sammy.' "

Eric laughed. Understanding the predicament. Enunciating his words. "I'm glad Mel got to see Zof. . .Zoph-ie. . .S. . .Sophie. . .last night."

Lynn snickered and kissed Eric's cheek. "Me too."

29

Sean's Cheeseburger

Over the next few days, Sean was in and out of consciousness, and never really alert. It was still too soon for me to tell him the damage. Georgie made sure to visit daily. For Sammy's sake, of course. She and I both knew that wasn't the truth. They all knew. But still, they let her visit, because most of them were too busy to do it themselves.

After Sean had been in the hospital about a week, Georgie walked in one morning with Sammy to find her husband sitting up in bed eating a burger. She'd expected to sit and read with Sammy for a couple hours while Sean slept. This looked like she'd be required to have an alert conversation with him.

"You're awake. . ." she said.

Sean looked at her, stunned. Eyes wide open. His countenance was crushed, and he gave a defeated nod. "I deserved that."

Georgie was at first confused, then noticed the object of his disappointment, touching her hair. "I hate it, so the joke's on me."

"I think it's pretty." He shrugged. "Why do you hate it?"

"Because you didn't deserve it." She shrugged back.

"Debatable." He changed the subject. "My concussion is healing. Apparently, the doctor is on his way with a tablet to show me my x-rays."

"Are you sure you want to see those?"

"Yes. I'm an EMT. I've seen worse, however bad it is."

Georgie nodded and sat down. "I can go. I don't have to be here."

"Stay, Georgie. Don't act like you haven't been here every day."

"You've been out of it."

"The nurses talk. I've made quite an impression. I even conned my way into a cheeseburger."

"I see that. But it'll probably make you sick. You haven't had anything solid in a while," Georgie warned.

"How'd you know?" Sean tilted his head and took a bite.

"The nurses talk." Georgie smirked. Setting his heart on fire.

The doctor entered with a tablet, tapping at it as he spoke.

"Hello, Mrs. Mehlmann. How are you today?"

"Fine, thank you," she replied.

"How's little Sammy?"

"He's doing well. Happy to see his daddy awake."

"Old friends, huh?" Sean wondered at the friendly exchange.

"Oh yes, ever since *she* demanded that I show her these x-rays last week." The doctor winked, then turned the tablet around.

Georgie averted her eyes when Sean fought off nausea at his crushed lower half in x-ray form. Pre-surgery, of course.

"Uh. . .wow. . .how many fractures is that?" Sean wondered.

"Seven." The doctor swiped the screen and the image was replaced with another, post-surgery. "Enough to set off alarms at airports for the rest of your life. It took quite a bit of hardware to fix you, Humpty Dumpty."

"Wow." Sean nodded. Taking it in, the fact that so much of him was being held together by metal.

"We don't like to replace joints in people your age. So, we were able to save the knee, though you'll likely be revisiting that a few years down the road. Your hip, however, was unsalvageable considering the repairs we needed to make to your pelvis and femur. It will likely always be bothersome, I'm sorry to say. But with physical therapy, which you'll start this afternoon, you'll learn to cope. You'll need to stick around here for several weeks to get you moving around, and then you'll need to come back on an outpatient basis for several months. But even then, as I've been telling your family, walking without support will not be a guaranteed outcome."

Sean's almost proud smile faded to dust. "Wait. . .I can't *walk*?"

"You're extremely lucky. Someone was looking out for you. No organ damage and very little blood loss, considering. You sustained some minor vertebral damage, but no spinal cord involvement. So fortunately, and I suppose unfortunately, you'll be able to feel everything." The doctor nodded.

"But I'm an EMT. I need a lot more physical abilities than just non-guaranteed walking and good nerve sensation. I have to teach my son to play sports. This accident wasn't even my fault. My light was green," Sean pled. Denial. The first stage.

"You remember that?" Georgie was amazed.

"What, the accident? Yeah. After that is a little fuzzy. But I remember the accident," Sean admitted, touched a scrape across his face. "This is from my visor lifting up against the road when I hit it. And I actually remember the decision at the last second of whether to cover my face or—" Sean's hand immediately and nearly involuntarily curled into his gowned chest, at which point, he panicked. "Where is the chain that I had around my neck? I knew, even in my fight or flight response that it might get left at the scene if I didn't grab it. So, I know it didn't get left."

"Calm down, Mr. Mehlmann. I'm sure it was—"

"Seriously though, where is my stuff? You don't have any clue how important—"

"Sean," Georgie said, pulling a little plastic bag from her purse. "They gave me all your things. I have your wallet and keys. They had to cut all your clothes off, including your leather, sorry. But I have. . ."

Sean cried out in pain as he tried to move his legs over to take the baggie from Georgie. She jumped up, glad Sammy was asleep in his stroller at the moment, helping Sean back to sitting and handing him the bag. Sean took it, unzipping the baggie. He checked Georgie's ring for damage before putting the chain back around his neck. Sighed relief like it was the only medicine he'd need today.

The doctor was observant. Glancing at the ring, then at Georgie's vacant finger. Soaking in the tension before politely excusing himself from the room with a promise to return later when he did his rounds.

Georgie was adjusting his pillows behind him as she asked, "How long are you going to wear that, Sean?"

"Until *you* wear it."

"You're fooling yourself," Georgie said, mindlessly checking the bandages on his face.

"Am I, though?" he asked. "You're *here*, Georgie."

"I told you I'd never keep you from your son," Georgie said.

"He's asleep." Sean gasped in the next breath. "I moved too fast. That night I asked to stay. It was wrong. And I'm sorry. Bad approach."

"*You're* apologizing?" Georgie burst immediately into tears. "Sean, if I'd let you stay, you wouldn't be sitting in a hospital bed wondering if you'd ever walk again. This is *my* fault. That's why I'm here. I owe it to you."

"You wanted to tell me something that night. That's why you took me into the bedroom. What was it?"

"Wow, no brain damage at all, huh? Might have been nice in this case." Georgie sighed bitterly. She was so quickly forced to tell him.

"Nope. Just a mild concussion. I'm glad you made me buy that helmet. If it wasn't important, it's alright. It just seemed important. Like. . .divorce important?"

"I told you that wasn't it, Sean," Georgie huffed. Allowed a short silence where he stared into her and she sat back down on the bench in the room.

He tilted his head with a smirk. "You're pregnant."

She concurred with more peace than she thought she could manage. "How'd you know?"

"I figured it was one of three things. You either wanted me to move out forever, you wanted me to move back in, *or* I wasn't just seeing things when I saw your recipe for vegan key lime pie in the kitchen. Limes again, huh?" He was friendly and cordial. The way she knew Sean to always be.

"Yeah. That was my number one indicator." Georgie sniffled.

"So, we're like. . ." He narrowed an eye. "Eight or nine weeks along? You been sick?"

"Yeah." She nodded. Her heart trembling at "we're." Shattering at the sudden image I provided of Sean kissing Brielle.

"Well I guess I better figure out how to walk so I can be more useful, huh?"

"Sean, don't—"

"If the end of that rant involves you trying to let me off the hook for my kids and their mom, whom I love, you should probably just save it."

Georgie didn't speak for two minutes. Averting her eyes. She rose. "I should go—"

"Bed pan," Sean said quickly.

Georgie got the message, getting a bed pan to Sean's lap before he relinquished that conned cheeseburger into it. Georgie barely held down her natural gastrointestinal response. Which left no room for her to hold back other responses. Rubbing his back. Grabbing water and tissues when he was done. Calling the nurse.

And finally interrupting my own rant in Sean's spirit with, "We'll figure it out, okay. You just get better. Listen to these doctors."

"Did you just say that, Hippie Girl?" he teased, poised for expected vomit.

She giggled. "There isn't an oil for a shattered leg and pelvis, Sean."

"Will you come to PT with me?" he asked.

"I'll see if Mom can watch Sammy," she promised.

30

Kittie's Quest

The knock came at Sean's door just as he was groggily waking up from a nap to a nurse checking his vitals. He was hoping it was his wife, but instead a petite woman about his age with one side of her head shaven and the other side a cascade of pink, walked in. Piercings, tattoos, and a warm smile. A wheelchair in front of her.

"Hey Sean," she said with enthusiasm like an old friend. "Looks like you're my next victim. I'm Kittie."

"Um. . .hi?" He said warily as the nurse taking his vitals smiled and left.

"Physical therapy." She laughed. "Your ticket out of this place starts right now."

"Good." Sean smiled. "Are you supposed to take me to like a gym or something?"

"We have one of those a few levels down, yes. But today our goal is to get you into a wheelchair. From the looks of things and after talking with your doctors, standing and walking are not exactly on the table right now. But getting into a wheelchair is a necessary skill for you to be able to go home."

"I'm not spending my life in a wheelchair." Sean laughed.

"Good attitude. But I don't think you have it in you," Kittie said, spreading hand sanitizer on her hands and approaching the side of the bed with a wheelchair.

"Seriously? Kittie, was it?"

"Yes, sir?"

"Right. I'm in shape. This is not going to take as much as they told you. They don't *know* me," Sean said. "Neither do you."

"Uh-huh." Kittie smiled. "Alright. Let's take you to the gym, then. Get in the wheelchair."

"Uh. . .like. . .right now?"

"Yep. I have half an hour with you. But I should have you running half *marathons* by then with your attitude. Let's get moving."

Kittie took a step back from the wheelchair and hipped her hands.

Sean laughed. "You serious?"

"As a heart attack," Kittie enunciated.

"I see you're trying to prove a point. Obviously, I can't just. . ."

"Like I thought when I walked in. All talk. You're still peeing in a bed pan and you think I'm actually going to take you to the gym?" Kittie smiled. "You're not strong enough, Sean." Don't you love her?

"How did you get this job?" Sean insulted. "You don't *know* me. Don't pretend to."

"You a Christian man, Sean?" Kittie asked, unfazed.

"Yes," Sean answered instinctively. "A bad one."

"Good to hear." Kittie sat in the wheelchair next to him with a smile. "I try to not trust a person who says they are a 'good Christian.' By definition, a Christian has humbled themselves at the cross and confessed their sins, admitting they have fallen short of God's glory. Anyone who thinks or *says* they are better than that or strong enough on their own isn't a very good Christian at all."

"I suppose that makes sense. What I meant was—"

"I know what you meant," Kittie said. "What *I'm* getting at is that you're not strong enough. And that's okay. Because *He* is. And with Christ you are *more* than a conqueror. He raised up from the dead. Walking and getting your wife back after adultery are nothing for *Him* to accomplish."

"That is absolutely none of your business," Sean said, appalled. Astonished. How could she know that?

"Yikes." Kittie wrinkled her nose with a smile. Almost teasing him like Sharon or Sophie might.

"For the record, the adultery did not involve sex or even feelings. No one seems to care about that." Sean was frustrated. Venting it for the first time.

"Likely because wifey only cares about your heart." Kittie shrugged. "Circumstances don't matter. She knows you're *capable* of cheating. That's a scary thing to know."

Suddenly Sean understood. Beginning to wonder how to show Georgie he's a changed man. He realized who he was talking to.

"This is physical therapy how?" He laughed.

"I'm a physical therapist *and* a certified dietitian. I work with your sister too."

"Still not a counselor though," Sean pointed out.

She stared him down with fire in her eyes. "Sean, if you choose to rely on God's strength, there will be a day when you will barely remember laying in this bed, peeing in a bed pan. So, quit worrying about who I am, humble yourself, and let me help you into this wheelchair. Not even Jesus carried His own cross the entire way."

"You're like. . .assigned to me, right? I don't have to work with anyone else?" Sean asked, something in his spirit waking up. Terrified no one else could give him the perspective.

"Yeah, you're stuck with me." Kittie winked. "Sorry." She winced, having barely moved his leg. She looked into Sean's eyes. "This is way out of line. . .but the same strength will also help you be a good husband. Don't give up."

The door opened, and Georgie came in, having caught the last part. "Uh-oh. Giving up already, Sean? Sorry I'm late. I wanted to change Sammy before I left so Mom didn't have a mess to deal with. Turned into a bath."

"Oh, those are the worst!" Kittie said, extending a hand to Georgie. "I'm Kittie. Your husband's torturer."

"I'm Georgie." She smiled brightly. "I'd love to assist you in your efforts."

Kittie smirked. "Excellent. You take his right leg."

. . .

In a week, Sean learned to slowly and painfully pivot his body and legs to the edge of the bed, then use undamaged arms and abs to lower himself into a wheelchair. The last time, Sean was in the wheelchair when Kittie arrived.

"You could've hurt yourself, Sean," she scolded.

"Uh, how bout 'great job, beast!'?"

"That too." She nodded. "Where is wifey?"

"Wifey" came in the room just then, looking green, and only barely acknowledging them before pointing at the bathroom. Her hurling echoing into the room.

"She okay? Should I call someone in?" Kittie panicked.

"She's fine. I did that to her before we separated. She's pregnant."

"Oh. . .how's *that* working out?" Kittie wondered. The two having become fast friends.

"It's *not* right now," Sean admitted. "She just told me last week."

A knock at the door. A timid entry. And Sean's face lit up.

"Hey, beautiful!" Sean said to the new arrival.

Kittie shot him an accusing look. *Still a cheater.* She was thinking.

"Kittie, this is my sister Sharon." Sean was enthusiastic.

"Oh, whew," she allowed. "I've heard so much about you, Sharon."

"Like what?" Sharon said, self-consciously.

"You're a prayer warrior. It's always a pleasure to meet one in person. People like you are the unsung heroes of the body of Christ." Kittie shook her hand.

"Well, I don't know about that." Sharon smiled the flattery.

"Let's hope you're praying for your brother. And the marriage situation." Kittie smiled.

"A lot, yeah."

"I'm in the room." Sean laughed.

"Where is L.D.?" Sharon asked.

"Showing signs of a healthy baby." Sean gestured to the bathroom.

Sharon nodded. "I've prayed for that too."

"Did you like know. . .that she was. . ." Sean voiced his suspicion.

Sharon nodded.

"So, she told you, but not me?" Sean wondered.

"Well she didn't *tell* me. She was too scared to read the test." Sharon shrugged. "So, I did. And apparently, she tried to tell you, but you tried to sleep with her."

"She's my wife, Sharon. I've *succeeded* a lot more times than you want to know. But that's not fair. I wasn't just looking for *that*."

"I know that, Sean. She hates herself for telling you no. Because that's why you rode off in the rain and got in the accident," Sharon revealed.

Sean tilted his head remorsefully. Which turned out to be a good look to have when Georgie came back in the room.

"You alright?" he asked her.

"Fine," she lied. "You ready? Were you in your chair when I came in?"

"Sure was." He smiled with pride.

"And now he needs to get back on the bed," Kittie said.

Sharon took to the bench along the wall, watching Georgie help him back onto his bed. Praying every second.

Kittie left the room and came back with a walker.

"Today we stand."

"You sure? Can I put weight on my leg?"

"No. But we're going to test your pelvis with your right leg. My goal is to get you in crutches in a couple weeks, so we can get you home. Today you'll stand for ten seconds tops," Kittie promised.

Sean screamed the whole ten seconds and Sharon prayed harder. Georgie was devastated at the thought of a beach on St. John.

Walking for a mile. Kissing in the moonlight supported by his strength and his nerve. None of which he had that day.

31

Sophie's Voice

"Hey!" Discouraged Sean looked up to see the rosy cheeks and bright smile of his little sister. "I hear you're doing well."

"Ha!" was Sean's response. He smiled. "Hey, Sophie."

"Don't laugh. I'm serious. They say a pelvic injury alone can take three months until you're even mobile enough to go *home*. And you also have a new hip and a pretty beat up leg. But Kittie is projecting six *weeks* for you to go home. You're doing well, Sean."

Sean laughed. "So, I get to rot in a hospital for six weeks, and then I get to go. . .nowhere. Because I have no home."

"Weren't you staying with Eric?" Sophie sat on the chair nearest Sean in his room. Donning some of her own clothing and a hospital band.

"Yeah, but I need to be on the ground floor. All Eric's bedrooms are upstairs or in the basement. I also won't have a lot of independence for a while, so I'll basically need a caregiver. Eric works sixty hours a week." Sean nodded.

"Five-bedroom house." Sophie smirked. "I don't know what possessed him to buy that thing. The other one was plenty of space, especially for just him and Mel. And in the ranch, you'd have had a perfect ground-floor bedroom."

"You honestly don't know why he bought that house?" Sean was glad to have a distraction from just him and pain.

"Well the other one wasn't in the right district. He already has Mel at the top of the waiting list for the best charter school in town. But he had to move to do it." Sophie cleared her throat.

"Sophie, don't be dumb. He bought a house in the neighborhood where *you've* always wanted to live." Sean shook his head. "When are they releasing you?"

"About a week. I earned all my clothes back, and the clothes before Dad died fit, so they know I'm at a good weight for me. Kittie has me on a reasonable caloric intake. So now they're just making sure I can cope outside the hospital. I'd say they have a lot of faith in me. My counselor didn't even come in the room just now. I was surprised." Sophie laughed.

"Do *you* think you can handle it?" Sean wondered. "I worry about you moving back in with Brielle."

"Your make-out buddy?" Sophie snorted laughter.

Sean threw back his head in disgust. "She is an *awful* kisser."

"Is she really?" Sophie covered her mouth at the juicy scandal.

Sean rolled his eyes. "Yes. But I think the real problem is she wasn't Georgie. Trust me when I say that for her to do what she did took something really dark. There's no way she's not poison for you, Sophie."

"I know." Sophie sighed. "When I get released, a counselor is escorting Sharon and I over there to gather my things. I'm going to stay with Sharon."

"Sharon has a one bedroom apartment. You crashing on the couch?"

"No. We shared a room when we were kids, remember? Before Dad cleared out his office and you got the downstairs bedroom?" Sophie reminisced. "Anyway, I'm staying in her room with her."

"Not to be insensitive. . ." Sean tried to be gentle. "But both of you, technically, struggle with eating disorders."

Sophie laughed. "That's what I told my counselor. But she said Sharon had conquered hers. Sharon would tell you the opposite, of course, because she still struggles with her weight and everything. But quite a few people have told me that Sharon will help me."

Sean asked it boldly. "What about Eric?"

"What about him, Sean?"

"What if he asks you to come home? Would you do it?"

Sophie's eyes welled up. "Sean, the place this conversation is going is. . .I'm in treatment right now. Don't ask me that and screw it up."

"Are you honestly saying you think he doesn't want you anymore?" Sean asked with compassion.

"Would you go home to L.D. if she asked?"

"Without *hesitating*, Sophie," Sean asserted. Coughed at a tear. "But I doubt she'd ask. She caught me with my hands on another woman. I don't blame her. I'm honestly proud of her for kicking me out."

"Exactly, Sean. *I* don't want me. Why would Eric want me?"

"You didn't *cheat,*" Sean encouraged.

"Not. . .technically." Sophie squeezed her eyes shut. "Because we were legally divorced at the time."

Sean gasped at the scandal. "Sophie, you. . ."

"There was a guy at my school. And the whole time Eric and I were separated, he tried to get me to go out with him. So, the night after the divorce was final, I thought, why not? I ended up getting so very drunk and going home with him. Which I think was his intention from the beginning," Sophie whispered. Confiding. "It was so weird being with someone else. I hated it."

"Wow." Sean a few years ago would have been impressed. Godly Sean was heartbroken. "Strait-laced Sophie had a one-night stand?"

"Well, he stalked me for a month after that. I was about to call the cops, but one day he came into class with a shiner and never spoke to me again. Like he was scared of me. He even ended up quitting school." Sophie tousled her hair. "I'm really good at messing guys up."

Sean laughed once. "Now that makes sense."

"What makes sense?" Sophie crossed her arms.

"Nothing. Georgie's pregnant. Did you hear?"

"I did." Sophie smiled. "So after you're all better, can you still—?"

"Can I?"

"You know, help make more babies?"

Sean laughed. "Probably not. I mean yes, physically. But my marriage is in shambles, Sophie. Can we not?"

"Sorry. How is Sammy?"

"Great. You talked to Mel or your baby daddy at all?"

Sophie snorted at the terminology. "No. Have you?"

"They've come by a couple times." Sean remembered Eric loving the depth of Sean's voice. And also, the promise not to tell Sophie he could hear it. "When you get out, Sophie, don't avoid Eric, okay?"

"I won't. Can't. I've been advised to spend time with Mel daily and learn to be a responsible mother. Kids can be quite a cure." Sophie shrugged. "And Eric is super-protective. I doubt he trusts me alone. So, I'll eventually have to see Eric if I want to see Mel."

" 'Have to'? Last I checked, you love him. And it's not a secret how he feels about you."

"Well I haven't told him, so. . ."

" 'So' nothing. Don't avoid him." Sean said. His heart singing out the secret. But she didn't hear.

•••

When Sophie arrived at Sharon's apartment with her things, she noticed some pictures on the wall just to the right of the front door. Four frames. The first was a recent picture of Mel that made a lump form in Sophie's throat. He was *so* beautiful. The second photograph caused that lump to smooth out into a sob. Her name, well, her previous name, was in the corner. "Stiles, Sophie." The date, a time when life made a lot more sense. And a tiny rice-grain sized something inside of a scan of her own uterus. A blue cross drawn in the corner of the glass.

It was the only picture—the only outward proof—of Sophie's second child. That baby was unexpected, but Eric had brought her to a place of desperate anticipation in just one evening after he found out. Sophie had lost that baby. Then she'd lost her father. Given up her husband. She could never regain all that she had lost. But at least. At least there was proof on her sister's wall that she had lost it.

"Oh no. . .I'm sorry if that upsets you." Sharon said, bringing in another of Sophie's bags and seeing her crying in front of the pictures. "I like to keep the most recent pictures I have of all of them. See, I even have an ultrasound from L.D.. I couldn't bring myself to take that one off the wall. But I will if it upsets you."

"No, please leave it." Sophie pawed at her tears. Thinking of how Eric couldn't hear her tears the night they lost the baby, so he'd held her long after they'd stopped. She was sure he knew that. She was also sure that she'd been gifted with the most caring, loving man on the planet. She sighed. Suppressing the losses.

Because Jesus would be more than enough to suffice.

Sophie worked nights at a twenty-four-hour diner and came to spend late mornings and early afternoons with Mel at her mom's house. She had it down to a science. She would leave her mom's to get ready for work an hour after Georgie left for Sean's physical therapy. That way she could avoid Eric completely but still see Sharon for a minute on the days she visited. She would work through the evening, and arrive home at 4 a.m., sneaking in and falling asleep just an hour before Sharon arose to go to her job. Then she would sleep until it was time to go see Mel again.

Make no mistake. I was with Sophie through all of it. But ironically, and to my dismay, Sharon's pessimistic roommate and sister saw far less of her than Georgie did. Even broken, no one could compete with Georgie's light.

"I'm such an awful mother," Sophie would repeat after me.

"Soph, you're here five hours a day. Mom barely even has to take care of Mel anymore," Georgie would remind her.

"But I missed so much," Sophie would repeat.

"You're not missing *this*," Georgie would remind.

Daily, for three weeks or so after Sophie's release, when Sophie would begin to monitor the old reliable clock and work her science and my bidding, Georgie would make the same suggestion.

"He gets here at five. You don't work until six. Spend *ten minutes* with Eric, Sophie. You won't regret it."

"I can't. I haven't signed in months. They say I was starving my brain and I literally *forgot* so much stuff. I'm worried it won't come back to me," Sophie would repeat.

"Don't worry about that, Sophie," Georgie would encourage.

"I don't even know what to say." Sophie would almost consider staying. Every day.

"That doesn't matter. Just *be* here, Sophie. He knows you spend the day here. He hopes you'll be here every day when he comes to get Mel," Georgie would say, readying herself for Sean's PT. Going to support a spouse she wasn't even living with. Hoping Sophie would follow suit.

But every day, Georgie would arrive home just before Eric arrived and Sharon left. And Sophie would be gone, even on her night off.

To Lynn, her home was a trapeze. Grown children coming and going in a daily swing of her front door. She started to see it like Samuel might. Instead of intervening or even commenting on the routine of the swinging door, she watched and waited. She knew it could only be sustained for so long before their arms tired and someone found a use for the safety net.

On Sophie's night off, when the forecast called for rain and Mel arrived with a fever and an ear infection, Lynn smiled and sang her way through the day. Grateful for the answered prayer. Rejoicing at every thunderclap that might send them tumbling.

Despite Georgie's remedies, the barometric pressure had Mel screaming early afternoon as the rain started. Sophie was in tears at her baby's cries, pacing the entire house over and over with him in her arms. It was an hour of such behavior and Sophie's lack of sleep that sent them both to a sniffling crash on the couch.

Georgie stood at the window thinking of Sean, watching rivers form in the streets as I spoke to her.

Wouldn't that be ironic if you tried to drive to the hospital to help him recover from an accident and died in one yourself?

She supposed it wouldn't harm anything to listen to me for once and called Kittie to let her know she couldn't make it that day. Her leave would have certainly signaled Sophie to awaken from her sleep on the couch.

Instead, Lynn placed a blanket on her youngest child.

Sharon was running late, because she'd had to see every student safely onto the late buses. By the time the task was complete, she was soaking wet from rain and headed home instead of to her mother's house. Her arrival would have told Sophie it was time to awaken.

Georgie was playing with her son when the headlights graced the driveway at 5 p.m. She smiled, always loving to see Eric arrive and retrieve his son. She gasped when she looked at the couch and Sophie was stirring.

"What time is it?" Sophie gasped.

"Uh. . .sorry. It's late. You and Mel were sleeping."

"You're still here." Sophie tried to re-orient herself after the long nap.

"I didn't go. The rain is pretty bad," Georgie said. "Sorry to tell you, but. . .look alive. . .quick."

Sophie gasped at the clock. Carefully positioned her still-sleeping son, even in her panic. She flew to the front window to see Eric adjusting his hood as he slowly walked to the door. Odd, because most people would run, but Sophie was glad for the extra time.

"What do I say?" Sophie whispered to her sister-in-law, combing her short hair with her fingers. Rubbing at her eyes. Checking her breath. Smoothing her toddler-tear-laden clothes.

"I'm already praying you have the words." Georgie bit her lip. Feeling as though her skin might actually allow her body to jump from it in excitement. She gave some caution to avoid the awkward. "Probably don't start with 'I love you, please let me come home.' Not out loud."

"I swore off talking behind his back months ago. One of the more psychotic, evil things I did." Sophie smiled. Suddenly at peace. Ignoring all my efforts to remove the safety net beneath her.

"What is he doing?" Sophie asked, still fidgeting as she looked out the window.

Eric was standing in the steady downpour with his head down, a raincoat keeping his head and pocketed hands dry. It was how a grown man might behave in a rainstorm. . .if he'd never heard one before.

Lynn joined her daughter at the window, giggling at Eric.

"He is so precious," she whispered as he finally headed to the door.

"Rub it in, Mom. Thanks." Sophie sighed.

Eric entered, and having seen Sophie's car in the street, waved to her with a friendly smile. She waved back, silently. The sound of the shutting door woke up Mel on the couch, who barely stirred with a whimper.

Eric's eyes were the first to turn to see him. It meant nothing to Sophie until Eric spoke while he removed his sopping wet shoes.

"Is he feeling any better?"

It was still hollow. But the consonants came through clearly and the timbre was slightly different. Sophie tilted her head.

Lynn answered, "He was pretty upset. Sophie took a good nap with him though, so he looks a bit better."

Eric nodded, never having looked at Sophie's mom. "How about the fever?"

"I think it has subsided. But fevers tend to come back in the evenings, so I'd keep an eye out after you get him home," Lynn said. Eric looking up and nodding at the end.

"Yes, ma'am."

It was an ordinary exchange for ordinary, hearing people. But Sophie had loved Eric since she was a teenager. Loving his every mannerism and word. To her, the exchange before her and those in the past were the difference between an apple and an airplane. As Eric placed his boots to the side and turned to unzip his raincoat, Sophie spoke.

"Eric?" Sophie said gently. "Tell me you are completely unaware that I'm speaking right now and that you did *not* get cochlear implants."

Eric froze. His back to Sophie. He wanted to be cute and say, *"I am completely unaware that you are speaking right now, and I did not get cochlear implants."*

But cute does not have a place where beauty has suddenly dripped into the soul. When Eric perceived it and realized where it was coming from, he turned to the sound in disbelief.

Once his brain had learned to sort out the sounds, he would sit for hours with Mel, listening to music that most would gloss over. Beethoven, deaf when he wrote his later works, would have appreciated Eric's tearful appreciation of it being *heard* by a deaf man. Eric fell in love with music all over again. With Mel laughing and crying. With the sound of the rain. With traffic around him and airplanes overhead. The exquisite to the chaotic to the mundane. He loved every sound.

But no sound in the universe compared with what he begged to be repeated as he removed the hood of his coat and took it off.

"Sophie. . .say something else?"

Sophie gasped. Advanced to Eric across the room and examined the devices attached to his head.

"Eric, you *didn't*! Why did you do this? You can *hear* me?" she protested. Scared to touch him. Angry with him. In love with him. "I was really sick and really wrong. I'm so sorry for making you feel like you had to do this. Please tell me you didn't do it for me."

Eric didn't respond except with sudden sobs and embarrassed tears. Waving his hand at her to stop. Signing for her to continue. He couldn't even speak, let alone decide the direction of his heart.

Sophie's eyes widened. "Oh no. . .are you okay? I mean I'm not mad. . ."

"Good." Eric nodded, wiping at his tears.

"You're crying." Sophie was confused. Every time she spoke, Eric would lose his composure. "You're scaring me. What's wrong?"

"Nothing," he finally admitted as Georgie handed him a tissue and took one for herself and for Lynn. "Sophie, your voice. . ."

"Is it weird? I'm sorry. I'll sign, I just don't remember everything like I did," she said.

He sobbed a laugh. "It's *beautiful,* Sophie."

"Oh." She cleared her throat. "You said 'Sophie.' That's not how you say my name."

"As soon as I could hear, I knew I was saying it wrong. I said lots of words the wrong way. I've been practicing," he explained.

"Eric, you. . .you never *ever* said my name wrong." Sophie's tired eyes shimmered with tears. "I liked how you said my name. You don't have to change it back, just. . .You didn't have to change it. *I* had to change, not you. You never did a single thing wrong."

"I was deaf," he squeaked.

"Eric, *everybody's* deaf." Sophie sobbed. Cleared her throat. "Every person has some weakness, because it's a fallen world. But when you let God use that weakness to His glory, that's when you're *strong.* You didn't have to be deaf to be who you are. But it *helped.*"

It took every bit of Eric's vast, God-given emotional strength to keep from pulling his ex-wife close as he nodded, and she worked a tissue against her tears.

"The rain should let up in an hour or so. Would you two like to stay for dinner?" Lynn suggested.

After a dinner conversation and a couple hours on the couch where Sophie and Eric caught up, Eric looked around him.

"The rain stopped. I should get Mel home."

Sophie nodded. Suddenly the silent partner, if they were a partnership, that is.

"So, you work at six tomorrow? At night?" he asked.

"Yeah, six until three in the morning."

"That's a long shift, Sophie!" Eric worried.

"It's not bad. There is a lot of downtime after the dinner rush most nights."

"I thought you were a dietitian now. Certified." Eric was confused.

"Well, no one wants to hire a dietitian that just got out of rehab for an eating disorder, so. . ."

"I think, in time, that will make you an *excellent* dietitian," Eric encouraged. "Be here tomorrow when I come get Mel? Even for a few minutes so I can hear you talk."

She nodded. "Sorry for avoiding you."

Eric laughed. Signed, *"I understand."*

· · ·

After Sophie and Eric left and Lynn and Georgie's gossip having already been expressed in the kitchen, Lynn began crocheting in the living room. Sammy was in bed. The world was oppressively quiet.

Georgie stood in the dining room, staring at a treasure on the shelf. Her snow globe. She used to kiss it whenever she left the house. The sight of it used to give her the warm fuzzies. But after losing Samuel, the gifter, and after Sean went astray, there was only pain within her vision.

Does it even mean anything anymore?

"Yeah," she barely whispered. "I should just put it up in Sammy's room."

So, without thinking, she took the treasure off the shelf. But with a slight smile, she tilted it to watch the glitter fall across the dove and the rainbow as she sometimes did.

That was the fatal mistake.

Before her heartbroken, tired hands understood their failure, she watched as glass, glitter, and water pooled at her bare feet on the hardwood.

The sound, coupled with Georgie's desperate gasp had Lynn in the room in about a second and a half.

"Oh, L.D." When Georgie began to crouch, the mother of three, or four. . .or maybe seven or eight, put out her hands in warning.

"No! Don't move. I don't want you to cut your feet, sweetheart. I'll be right back."

When Lynn returned with towels and a broom, Georgie was a stationary, sobbing mess. Yes. It did still mean something to her.

Lynn picked up the bottom component, undamaged, and removed a shard of glass from its spot in the base. She handed the now snowless, globeless snow globe to her daughter-in-law and proceeded to clean up the mess. Georgie examined the statue, trying to convince herself she was okay.

God Keeps His Promises, it still declared. If only people could do the same.

"It'll never be the same." She repeated my rhetoric.

"Well, sometimes it just can't be, sweetheart." A remark that didn't really involve the snow globe.

"You know, we didn't just sign a piece of paper and call it good, Mom. It wasn't a big white wedding, but the weight of it was the same for us. It was important to us that we dedicate our marriage to God, and promise to—" Her countenance faltered, but she fought through it. "Long drawn-out wedding vows always annoy me. Who can honestly remember all that? So, after we prayed and invited God into our marriage and asked Him to bless it, Sean and I each made one promise to one another. I promised to love him as he is. No matter how he is at any given moment. And he promised to love me as Christ loves the church. To sacrifice himself for me. And. . .we both failed."

"That's to be expected." Lynn finished cleaning up, the Spirit stirring her spirit. "You both married a human."

"I want you to know, I've been praying about it. And he might still be my *favorite* human. But would I be—" Georgie cleared her throat. Trying to regain composure. "Would I be a pushover if I wanted him to come home? Does it make me weak to hope Sean will come back to me and let me take care of him?"

Lynn didn't answer the question. She launched into an anecdote and opened a drawer in the butler's pantry. She pulled something out of it with one hand, then took Georgie's hand with the other, leading her to be seated on the couch as she spoke.

"Samuel got a DUI when the kids were young. We'd gone through some tough times with money and in our marriage. He ended up having to take out a second mortgage to pay a fine and spend about a week in jail. I told the kids he was on a business trip." Lynn toyed with the item she'd gotten from the drawer. "Everyone I knew was telling me he was no good and I should kick him to the curb. It was only a point in a long streak of drinking and basically wishing he'd chosen a different life. The kids annoyed him, and he barely looked at me."

"Samuel like. . .Dad?" Georgie kept her voice low, as if to leave the spirits at rest.

Lynn nodded.

"But he was so wise. So put together. He kept all of *us* together." Georgie marveled.

"He was all of those things. But he lost his way for a time. Just like Sean. But the kids don't even have that part of him in their memory. He couldn't believe how *complete* that redemption was. He never went back. Not because he was scared. But because he was in awe, Georgie, of God's grace." Lynn swiped some tears away. "Grace is always a better teacher."

"Wow," Georgie considered. "So, his stint in jail straightened him up for Jesus, I'm guessing?"

Lynn shook her head. "When he got home from that week, he wanted nothing more than to go out drinking again. That very *night*. But Sharon had brought home a friend. A beautiful girl that he couldn't believe would give Sharon the time of day. He found out this girl was the daughter of a drug addict, didn't have a father around, and when we fed her meatloaf, it was the first time someone had taken the time to cook a real meal for her."

"I love your meatloaf." Georgie sniffled.

"You were a light, L.D.. To Samuel. To Sharon. You've taught Sophie that she can be a good mom. Obviously, you made an impression on Sean as well. You pointed us to Jesus. Not because you can recite the Bible or because you have lovely eyes. But because you were given the worst of life. You have nothing to offer the world according to the hand you were given. So, you just became a reflection of Christ. And suddenly you had *everything* to offer," Lynn continued. "That *inspired* Samuel."

Lynn took the treasure she'd retrieved from the dining room and handed it to Georgie. It was a worn-out vegan leather wallet that she'd spent a pretty penny on a few Christmases ago.

"I think a man's wallet says a lot about him. The things he carries with him everywhere are a good indicator of where his heart is. He certainly didn't die the same man he was when he got that DUI. Open it."

It took two tissues for Georgie to unblur her vision enough to do so. She found about fifty dollars in cash, a driver's license. Debit card. The usual. And a few worn-out, folded-up photographs. A gorgeous one of Lynn, of course. Another of Eric, Sophie, and Mel from a few days after he was born. One of Sharon. A great, big, fat, beautiful one. There were several business card sized papers. With his favorite verses written out. Or prayers. Books he wanted to read. Names and phone numbers of business contacts. Grocery lists in Lynn's handwriting. All stuck in random slots and places all over.

Georgie remembered upon a quick closing of her eyes the way that Samuel would constantly take out his wallet and fumble with it. Adding things. Looking for things. Never making good use of his smart phone. But always commenting that his wallet was "Made of mushrooms," and "Isn't that something?" Georgie laughed through the tears at the treasure before her, putting everything back in, until she came to the final photograph before putting it away, which gave her pause.

The one of her and her love on a couch, holding up a marriage license, that he'd swept off the table the day they filled the wedding album. Everything was so simple then. So easy. Georgie nodded.

"I just. . .I wonder if it's really love at all if I only love him when he's not drinking, and in perfect enough health to work constantly to provide for me and Sammy, and still come home and help out around the house and make love to me every night. Love isn't always easy like that. Christ demonstrated that when we were *sinners*, and He still died. It was *because* we were so weak and sinful that He was able to show His love and be glorified in such a huge way. So, I feel like the less Sean can offer me, the truer it is when I claim to *love* him. Love takes *everything* if it's worth anything, and him coming home is going to be difficult. But I want him home, Mom. Maybe he'll get a chance to love me back, but even if he doesn't, I'm not giving up on him."

"Another example of your *firm* grasp on grace. I don't think you'd be a pushover if you wanted your husband to come home. I think it would be out of character if you *didn't*." Lynn made her offer. "I've already been thinking I want to let him stay in my room down here until he's healed enough for stairs. I'll stay in Sophie's old room. And you two and God can figure out where to take things from there."

"I don't want to take your room again! You already moved out of the master bedroom for us," Georgie begged.

Lynn smiled into purple eyes. "Oh, L.D., don't you understand? I owe you my life. My son's life. My daughters' lives. My entire house would be nothing in return. Let me do what I can to love you."

32

Sean's Home

For six weeks total, Georgie would come and help Sean work to recover enough to be mobile at home. When the cast came off, he could somewhat support his weight with a brace and crutches and started to stand. First with much effort, then with just Georgie's help, then practically on his own with the crutches. Poised like a toddler yet unable to toddle.

And despite my protestation, one day Sean started two hours before Kittie would arrive and managed to be standing in his room when she got there. She laughed when she came in.

"I assume you want to visit the gym today?" Kittie asked.

"I want to *walk* today. Because I want to leave today."

"Alright, once wifey gets here. . ." Kittie said as the door opened to huffing Georgie.

"Sorry, couldn't find anything to wear." She sighed. An odd statement for a woman whose clearance thrift store wardrobe never troubled her mind. Sean looked up to see that suddenly it was visibly apparent that she was expecting. An unmistakable little bump on her belly under the tank top and broom skirt. "I couldn't remember where we'd stashed the maternity clothes when we moved, so. . ."

Sean's eyes widened. He laughed. "Wait, how many weeks are you?"

"Midwife says fourteen or fifteen," she said. "I seriously woke up like this."

"I wish I could wake up as beautiful as you," Sean flirted before both women had to run to catch the collapsing man and put him in a wheelchair.

"Let's get downstairs, Casanova," Kittie said, unlocking the chair.

"Wait." Sean smiled, suddenly reaching out and touching Georgie's stomach. She shied away at first, then allowed him to touch her. He whispered, "Daddy's gonna walk today."

"And if he does, Kittie gets to discharge him." Kittie winked. "You'll have to ride in a car to come see me."

When they arrived downstairs, Georgie helped Sean out of the wheelchair, and she heard a voice.

"Hey, big brother!" Sophie, of course. "And wow, look at you, L.D.! You didn't look like that the other day."

Georgie placed a hand on her belly with a smile. "Yeah."

"Hey, Sophie," Sean said.

"Hey. Sorry, I have no excuse for not coming to see you the past few weeks. Except that I'm pissed you didn't tell me about Eric." Sophie sighed.

"I was sworn to secrecy," Sean confessed.

"That's what he said. . ." Sophie looked burdened. Sad. "I hear you may go home today."

"Yeah or, you know, leave here." Sean's face shone pain. Shifting his weight, both of his arms supported by both of Georgie's.

Georgie smirked. Cleared her throat. "Mom moved out of the downstairs guest room, so you didn't have to try to master stairs right now."

Sean startled. "I'm. . .you want me to come *home*?"

Georgie rolled her eyes. "Don't be stupid Sean. We've already gotten all your stuff from Eric's."

Kittie was ready for Sean to walk. Which he did. With crutches cradling his arms, of course. Five whole steps before he fell right back into Georgie's arms. Stood with her. Glared into her eyes like he needed her to understand.

"Does 'home' mean I get a chance to fix this? Fix us?" Sean begged. "I'm worse off than I was. I'm crippled. But. . ."

Georgie smirked. "As you *are*, Sean. Shame on *me* for forgetting that. We have some rehab to go through with our marriage. But I'm still your wife."

"On paper." Sean nodded.

"Paper gave me your name. That's not what made me your wife," Georgie promised.

Sophie pondered that in her heart and Kittie smiled.

. . .

They functioned like housemates. Well, Sean didn't much function at all really. He was in too much pain to help accomplish anything. He could read to Sammy on his lap, but even the bend required to feed him was excruciating.

You'll never be worth anything again.

For a time, it was easy to convince him of that, especially since his own wife would care for him completely—but only like a patient. She would drive him to his appointments and be Kittie's helping hand once they arrived. But Sean knew that it wasn't much of a marriage at all.

The journey to physical health or even comfort was going to be a long one. He knew that. But that didn't mean he couldn't fix something.

One evening after listening to his wife bathe Sammy and put him to bed, Sean lay awake, waiting for his mother and wife to end their routine evening conversation. He texted his wife.

About twenty times. And deleted every single one. He finally sent one that said, *"Can I borrow you?"*

Something he always said when he needed help desperately but felt bad about asking. Georgie, of course, came running.

"You okay?" she whispered in the crack of the door. "What's the matter?"

"Nothing, I just want to talk," he said.

She sighed heavily. "Sean, I'm exhausted. I was headed to bed."

"Just for a minute. Come here."

Georgie sat next to him, and with much effort, refusing help, he sat up. "I have a question."

"Okay?" She was annoyed. Exhausted.

Sean had already removed it from his neck before her arrival. And held it up in his hand. Her wedding ring.

"I would get on one knee, but. . ." He smirked. "Georgie, will you marry me?"

She crossed her arms. Narrowed her eyes. "We're already married."

"So, put your ring on." He shrugged. "I want to fix us, and I feel like I'm not allowed or something."

Georgie took her ring from him and held it between her fingers. "I said 'as you are.' Then you made a mistake that suddenly fell outside those parameters. I don't know why I couldn't handle—" The tears started. "Sean, I can't do this right now."

"I've been home two weeks. When can we do this?" he asked. "We need to put this behind us because, Georgie, I miss you and I don't want a servant caring for me. I want my wife."

"Were you going to have sex with her?" It slipped out after having been eating away at the tip of her tongue for months.

"Ew. No. She tasted like marijuana and dead rodents and I was literally fighting a battle with her and myself and trying to escape. She was supposed to be giving me a ride home and she kept. . ." Sean sighed. "No. But that doesn't matter. I know I was capable of it."

"Can I trust you not to do it again?" she whispered. "I thought you'd chosen me."

"I got hit by a truck and my first instinct was to make sure your wedding ring was okay. I've chosen you every single day since that night on the beach, Georgie. I'm not going to make excuses for the ten minutes I chose *me* instead. But I do need you to forgive me for it because I don't have enough years to spend regaining the trust I lost. I need grace, okay? Please?"

"I've already forgiven you, Sean. Clean slate," she promised.

Sean cleared his throat. "Did you know you were pregnant that night?"

"Yeah," Georgie allowed through a dry throat. "I was deciding how to tell you I wanted to take a test because you hadn't been acting like the guy who agreed to have two dozen babies with me."

Sean nodded. "I'm. . .I'm sorry that I hurt you, Georgie. I promised myself I wouldn't and—"

"Sean, we have hurdles ahead of us still. It's life in a fallen world. That's guaranteed. So, let's not turn around and revisit things we've already survived. I'm putting my wedding ring on, and we're moving forward," Georgie promised with a quivering lip.

The kiss and the image of that ring on her finger lingered in Sean's soul as he slept. But he drifted into a fitful dream of wrestling with God and woke up moaning in pain. A knock came at his door just before it opened.

"Sean, I think it's about time for your—"

"Mom, shhh. . ." he whispered.

Lynn's eyes widened as they glanced beside him at the sleeping Georgie. "Sorry, I didn't know. . ."

She was embarrassed. What could she have walked in on? So nosey. So overbearing. All she wanted was to get on top of Sean's pain early, before Sammy awoke and Georgie had a hundred things to do. She hadn't even thought Georgie was anywhere but upstairs sleeping.

It took ten whole minutes, but Sean made it to the kitchen on his own with crutches. Lynn pressed her lips together as she handed Sean his first dose of pain relievers. Non-narcotic of course. The addictive personality knew better than to get started on those. He trusted his wife's oils better anyway.

"Sorry for barging in," Lynn finally whispered. "I honestly didn't think she'd be in there."

"It's okay, Mom. It wasn't like that," Sean said as if Lynn should know.

"It doesn't matter how it was." Lynn shook her head. "It *could* have been anything."

"But it wasn't." Sean laughed a little. "We just talked. And she's pregnant and does too much, so she stayed and crashed next to me."

"She's your wife, Sean. It's really not my business," Lynn said.

Suddenly Georgie bolted into the room.

"You okay, Georgie?"

By the time he finished asking, she'd placed his hands on her belly.

"Right here, feel." She smiled. "He wanted to tell his daddy good morning."

Sean gasped at the kick to his hand. "Feisty little guy."

Lynn felt and giggled with joy.

A couple hours after Mel arrived, Sophie walked in the door as usual to find Georgie in the kitchen hiding tears from Sean and Lynn.

"What's wrong?" Sophie was quiet, seeing that Georgie didn't want to be discovered.

Georgie laughed a little. "I think I might have to give Sammy formula." She nearly gasped the backpedal. "Not that—"

"I understand how you feel about breastfeeding, Georgie. I did it for a few months and you're a saint for doing it longer. Are you still breastfeeding?" Sophie wondered.

"Yeah. Pumping mostly, because Sean wanted to feed him. But it isn't going well. Sammy seems to hate the taste and my supply is just—"

"It takes three hundred calories a day on top of your normal intake to feed a growing baby. Five hundred to breastfeed. You can't honestly tell me you are packing eight hundred extra nutrient-rich calories into your diet every day." Sophie shook her head. "Not with the way you run around and take care of Sammy and Sean all day."

"I'm not, I know!" Georgie exclaimed, frustrated. "I just feel like I can't be the mom I planned to be and it's weighing on me. Cow milk. I have to give him cow milk. That kills me."

"Do you want your babies to be strong and healthy or do you want to get your way?" Sophie sighed. "Trust me, I've done my fair share of trying to make sure my needs and desires were met first, and it hasn't worked out."

Georgie nodded, wiped a tear. Sophie's eyes lit up.

"What?" Georgie had seen.

"You're wearing your wedding ring." Sophie marveled, mouth gaping. "How did he get you to do that?"

"He asked." Georgie sniffled. Smiled. "He actually proposed."

"That is *adorable*," Sophie cooed. "See, I knew you two would be alright."

"Well, we have work to do, but I'll never take him for granted again after that accident. Or anyone else." Georgie nodded to Sophie's sudden distress. "How are things with Eric?"

Sophie crossed her arms. "Why did I leave him, L.D.?"

"People do stupid things sometimes. But he's forgiven you. I was asking how things are *now*."

"We went to breakfast together the other morning. I missed out on sleep and got to share a meal with my guys." Sophie smiled. "I know things can't be exactly like before. But I just want to be a family again."

Georgie shrugged. "You're right. They won't be the same. But with how much work you've both put into loving one another, maybe things could be *better*."

• • •

Sophie stayed long enough to see Eric for a precious few minutes every day. Sharon prayed and prayed. Impossible prayers. She watched Sophie come and go. Rarely did she see her awake, but she knew Sophie never slept long.

One day, Sophie arrived at her mother's house on her day off to spend the day with her son, as always. But that day, she came looking fabulous. Her hair perfect. Her makeup done. I hassled her. But she persevered.

Sharon said when she arrived late afternoon, "You look nice."

Sophie smiled. Fretted. "Yeah?"

"Yeah." Sharon laughed. "You know that."

Georgie clarified, having noticed Sophie's million steps up from normal all day. "I think she has something up her sleeve, but she won't say."

"Can't a girl just look nice?" Sophie wondered nervously.

Sean was skeptical. "See, but you *always* look 'nice.' This is like. . .different. Like how Georgie started looking when we were definitely not dating."

Just before 5 p.m., Sophie freshened up her makeup, touched up her hair, and changed into a lovely dress. No one said anything. When Eric breached the door, she was the first thing his eyes caught.

"Wow, Sophie. Do you have a date?" He wondered, heartbroken. "You look *incredible*."

"Eric. . ." she said. "Can I talk to you?"

"You're talking right now. I can hear you, remember?" He sighed. Pointed to his implants.

"Right. . .how easy is it to remove the external part? Just for a minute," Sophie requested.

Eric scrunched his eyes. But his heart was all Sophie's. He reached up and removed them immediately. He smiled as he set them aside on the table in the entryway.

Signed, *"What do you want to talk about?"*

"Excuse my bad signing. I had to relearn."

When Sean and Lynn looked at her, Sharon began whispering the translation.

"I forgive you. You don't need to sign anymore. I have cochlear implants. And we are not together."

Sophie sniffled. Cleared her throat. Stepped back from him. She got brave and looked him in the eyes. Signed, *"I love you, Eric."*

He laughed aloud. *"I love you too. That's all I ever did. You divorced me. Mixed signals."*

"It was a mistake." Sophie sighed.

Eric was bending, but not convinced. *"May I put my implants back?"*

"Not yet." Sophie shook her head. *"When we met, you didn't ever use your voice. I convinced you to try. Do you remember?"*

"Yes. I was able to communicate better sometimes. Thank you."

"You proposed to me with your voice," Sophie reminisced. *"So that I would understand what you meant clearly."*

Eric nodded a smile.

"I want you to understand that I love you the way that God made you. Not because you can hear now. So, I thought this would be much clearer if I signed it." Sophie sighed. Teary-eyed. *"Will you marry me?"*

It took Eric a moment to react. He did so with a blank stare and a step back as the family was gasping at Sharon's translation.

"Repeat that?" Eric thought he misunderstood.

Sophie instead took a box from her coat by the door, opened it, and set it on the table with the implants.

"I pawned our rings for rent a while back. But I was building a savings again and bought these a few days ago. They are not as fancy as the originals. But I promise they will last much longer."

Everyone in the room was crying. Mel ran and embraced his father's legs as Eric's tears began. He still didn't answer.

"Can we please start over and be a family?" Sophie begged. *"Please? I'm so sorry for everything I did. I've been begging God for another chance to show you I'll love you forever."*

Eric sighed, wiping tears. He stepped in and tenderly kissed his wayward bride to the cheers of everyone there. The next few moments were filled with placing rings and cochlear implants. Giggling and embracing and crying.

Eric spoke. "When I read Mel his bedtime stories, he always asks if you can do it. Are you off tonight? You could read to him. And we could talk about things."

Sophie was nodding her head with dramatic fervor.

He shrugged. Turned to Sharon and shook his head for her to not interpret. Signed discreetly. *"Then you should stay the night. I have a few of your clothes in the closet."*

Sophie gasped. "Is that okay?" She returned to signing for discretion. *"We're not married."*

Eric laughed. "'For what God has joined, let not man separate.' You're my wife. The rest is a clerical error."

"One of the things we should discuss is when we'll go to the county clerk and fix this little. . .'clerical error.' "

Eric laughed. "We'll be at the door when they open in the morning."

As the family laughed, Eric signed timidly, *"First, let me buy you dinner. You're dressed for a date. I'm taking you on one."*

Sophie's tearful nod as the little family exited was far more than an accepted date. It was a promise to *dine* with him. And a promise to take care how she listened to *me.*

33

The Mehlmanns' Stairs

"Sean, I'm going up to bathe Sammy. You need anything before I head up? Sean?" Georgie called throughout the house with her son on her hip. Still a "cute" version of pregnant at five months in. She found Sean at the bottom of the stairs looking up.

In therapy, and consequently at home, Sean had been walking on his own. With still a lot of pain, but the balance was improving. His strength building. He didn't even need help showering or getting into bed. It all hurt. Everything hurt. Sean was learning to coexist with the pain. As long as it meant he might someday get the fullness of his life back.

"Oh! Um. . .What. . .are you doing?" Georgie asked of Sean's longing gaze up the stairs.

"Why are there so many stairs?" Sean sighed.

"Well, there are regulations for stair height, so mathematically to get to the second level it'll take that many," Georgie teased in her own way.

Sean chuckled, still wishing his parents had bought a house with a landing at least. "Thanks for that."

Georgie knew Sean sometimes better than Sean knew Sean. He was stubborn. Determined. He'd won her heart and made her want to stay when she had a right to take off running. So, it was obvious what was flowing through his heart.

"So, we're going upstairs? Kittie put you up to this?"

Sean laughed once. "No, I just want to help bathe my son and say his prayers with him. And I want to wake up next to my wife."

"We can do most of that downstairs. I don't mind staying in your room, you know that. There just isn't a tub down here, so. . ."

"And there isn't a lock on the bedroom door down here," Sean implied boldly.

It took Georgie a moment before she cleared her throat. "Oh."

"Sorry. . .that's a lot to ask."

"It's fine, Sean," Georgie interrupted with the awkward reply.

"It was a long shot, I know."

"Tell me the last time that stopped you." Georgie giggled. "Our entire relationship is a long shot. The minute you stop *taking* the shot, that's when I'll worry."

Sean smiled. Somehow flattered.

Georgie put Sammy upstairs behind the baby gate, then helped Sean up the stairs. Lynn sat in her temporary upstairs bedroom listening to his moans and grunts of pain. She finally smiled as she heard the laughter and high fives at the top.

Sean played and splashed in the bath with his son and held pudgy little hands as he prayed with him. Determined to be the father his father was to him. Begging God not to ever let him turn back and forget how many miracles were in the drooping brown eyes of his baby boy.

As soon as they turned from closing the door, Sean's wife met him with a kiss in the hall. He was surprised at the tenderness.

"I thought you didn't want—" he whispered.

"You're still recovering from the last time I told you no," Georgie reasoned, also in a whisper.

Sean laughed. "Just let me sleep next to you. I'm serious."

"Don't argue with me," she whispered.

Sean awoke in the morning with his arms all wrapped up around the sleeping vessel of the most beautiful soul he'd ever come to know. His heart aching at the fact that he ever let her go. Thanking God to have the chance to do right by her again.

•••

"I swear to you, L.D., Stormy is leading a double life." Sharon giggled, passing the potatoes to her gracefully plumping friend. "I can set the clock by when she'll leave and when she'll come crawling back."

"At least she's consistent." Georgie snickered.

"How's your rehab going, Sean?" Sharon wondered. Realizing she'd been talking about herself for too long.

"Pretty well. Technically I'm 'recovered' because I can put weight on it. Now we're into the actual rehab where we can get me restored back to where I can work." Sean smiled. "All I know is, boy or girl, this baby's middle name is Kittie. Because she thinks I could be working before I even meet the new baby."

"That's great, Sean!" Sharon nodded. "I guess I didn't realize there was a difference between recovery and rehabilitation."

Georgie explained, "I like to look at it like the accident took him to a negative number. And the recovery brought him back to zero, where he has basic survival functionality. The rehab is where we try to work to bring him back to the incredible person he was, where he's not even thinking about the basic survival stuff like walking. Kittie thinks he'll always be in some level of pain, so there will be a new standard of normal, but he will still be fully rehabilitated by that standard."

"Like us with losing Dad." Lynn shrugged. "Speaking of which, Sharon. Have you decided to take the leap and buy a house yet? That's a rehabilitation your dad would be proud of."

"I thought about it. But then Sophie was with me, and I felt like if I got a house big enough for her to live with me, I'd have been saying I didn't have hope for their marriage."

"But now that I moved back where I belong, if you buy a house just for you, you're saying you don't have hope for. . .for *your* marriage." Sophie stated her sister's logic knowingly.

"When I decided to buy a house, it was not for the best reason. It was basically me saying I thought God was giving up on that idea. But I don't know what He's doing, and I don't want to make decisions without Him, so I'm just waiting. On Him." Sharon sighed. Wanting a home of her own. Wanting a husband. Children. But wanting more than anything to serve and honor her Lord.

Sophie gave a sideways glance to Sharon. Smirked.

"No, Sophie," Eric said.

"What?" Sharon wondered.

Sophie bit her lip. Eric rolled his eyes. Nodded.

Sophie asked it reluctantly. "Would you ever be willing to go out with someone? You know, someone we thought would maybe be a good match for you?"

"Only God gets to decide who is a good match for me, Sophie." Sharon wanted desperately to shout out approval and date anyone willing to go out with her. She had me prodding her.

Wait on God? That's ridiculous. You'll never find "the guy." Better just to stick with any willing party. You're getting up there in age.

But Sharon remembered the season where she was told to date Eric while he and Sophie were divorced. What a devastating disaster that would have been.

"I absolutely agree, Sharon. But technically you introduced all of us to our spouses. Not for that purpose, but all the same. I was just wondering if I had a chance to return the favor. . .even if you just had coffee with the guy." All of them were stirring with excitement. Sharon, of course, had no concept of how fulfilling it would be for them if she fell in love.

"So, there's an actual guy?" Georgie was intrigued.

"Yeah!" Sophie lit up. "Well, I don't know him that well. But what I learned in twenty minutes was unbelievably revealing."

"It's not the guy that stalked you until Eric clocked him, right?" Sean cackled.

Eric laughed.

"No!" Sophie turned red. "I mean he does show up at my house almost daily. I buy so much online. It's embarrassing. He's the UPS guy."

Everyone laughed.

"Sophie!" Sharon was offended. "I'm not *near* that desperate."

"Just hear me out!" Sophie *was* desperate.

"I have a lot more faith than that." Sharon sighed.

"No, I know. But. . .okay Mel bonked his head on the fireplace, and I was sure he was done for. Mom moment. I've only been home with him full time for a couple months. Thought I'd failed. I got to the car to take him to the ER, but discovered he'd been playing with the interior lights the last time we went somewhere, and my battery was toast. So, I called Eric and by that time I was hysterical and in the twenty minutes it took Eric to get there, the UPS guy showed up. And he waited with me until Eric got there. And I, of course, mentioned that he should go because he still had to complete his deliveries for the day, so he'd be twenty minutes late getting home to his family. He said he was single. And mentioned Jesus about six times. He was sweet and adorable, and I think you'd like him." Sophie finally took a real breath. "That's all."

"Well, I don't feel like I should date."

"Sharon, this is great timing. You don't have to be scared," Sophie encouraged.

"I mean I don't feel like I should date. . .ever," Sharon confessed this with confidence.

"Why not?!" Everyone said in practical unison.

Sharon laughed at their shock. "I don't mean I don't think I should get *married*. I'd love to, even with how difficult I've seen from all of you that marriage can be. But having seen your marriages, I feel like maybe casual dating doesn't really prepare a couple for everything you've been through."

"What do you mean?" Sophie wondered.

"Well, dating is based on spending time together in the best possible *planned* circumstances. So, if you need time or space or whatever, you just take it and the other person understands. But marriage is sort of like jumping into the deep end. You have to do life *together*. All of life. Not just the planned fun stuff. It's unpredictable and messy and people have nasty flaws and damage and dating teaches you that you can just walk away if everything isn't ideal. That doesn't prepare people for marriage—for the kind of unconditional love and grace that God has for us. That's the thing you all had to learn before you could be happily married. And you learned it from life, not dating." Sharon explained, with eloquence, one of the multitude of truths God had hidden in her heart.

"That's fair," Eric said. "But how will you meet someone?"

"That's something I don't actually know," Sharon admitted with a laugh. "But I do know that with a God who loves me and knows me, I don't need to have all the answers. I just need to trust Him the way I trusted He would restore your marriages and your health."

All of them silenced in awe, never having known anyone had any hope for those circumstances. They settled into peace, remembering the character of their God.

Throughout the evening, they all prayed like Sharon. According to God's will, not their own sight. They prayed God would give Sharon a man. The man. In His way. His time. But with her godly wishes attached.

Sharon's attention was on them. On Sophie and Eric, who were outwardly laughing hysterically at some inside joke. Their son delighted by the exchange. On Sean making a face that caused Sammy to belly laugh, and then making the same face at Georgie, who laughed at his silliness.

Sharon was in awe at the answered prayers. The restoration she saw before her. The God that brought it all back, even from legal ends and the brink of death. Lynn watched her smile but didn't need to ask why. She did, however, hope that Sharon was merely at the threshold of zero. And that her life was about to begin.

•••

Sean arose with slight pain from completing the formality of a new application with his previous job. He had just gotten off the phone with the boss eager to take him back. He walked his son across the living room, then tossed him up onto his hip as he reached the stairs.

Georgie was in tears at the bottom. A massive expanse on her abdomen. I was torturing her.

"This baby's never gonna come and I'll be miserable forever." She sobbed. Completely serious.

Sean sighed endearingly. "Two more weeks tops, Babe."

"That's an eternity." She sobbed. "I can't even figure out how to get up the stairs to go to bed so I can toss and turn all night and get up to pee twelve times."

"You can get up the stairs," he promised.

"Can I?" She was skeptical. Sniffling.

"Yeah, I'll prove it," Sean said, setting Sammy down and letting him crawl up the steps before them. He lifted up his pregnant wife and carried her up the stairs with all the strength he didn't have.

They crumbled into a laughing heap at the top of the stairs with their toddler. Georgie saw all restored to her by the only One able as she rubbed oils into Sean's chronically aching hip. Rejoicing for it all. But suddenly feeling a pull to pray. To remember, that so many others would love to have her life, however complicated and painful.

34

Africa's Year

"Our team in Africa is losing a valuable member in about three months. They simply cannot continue as things are if that position is not filled for the next year." The missions pastor was pleading, as he had been for three Sundays.

Sharon averted her eyes, seeing Georgie typing on her phone during announcements three seats over. She rolled her eyes, hoping she wasn't simply taking the time without her children to check her email.

"We have been assured by God that He has already appointed a member of this body of believers to join them overseas, and if that's you, we ask that you please email me, Derek. My email is in the bulletin or on the flyers," the pastor requested. "Remember that a person born deaf in this region of Africa has no means of communicating with the world around them. No support from a school system or government. So, when our interpreter teaches them sign language, it opens up the world for them. It shows Jesus to them. Just because their world is silent, that does not mean it should be empty."

After service, Sharon stood staring at the sign outside the sanctuary.

Sean, having just retrieved the six-month-old Ruthie Katrina Mehlmann, joined her. Whispered, "It's you, isn't it?"

Sharon knew it was. But I'd been reminding her that she'd have to tell her school she needed to take a year off and that her family needed her. She didn't even have a passport. So that's what she repeated to Sean.

"It's a *year*, Sean. You and L.D. could probably have ten babies in that amount of time," Sharon teased the excuse. "They'd forget about me."

Sean cleared his throat. "Well, one more for sure," Continued quickly. "But there's video calling. We won't let the kids forget about Aunt Sharon."

Sharon rolled her eyes. "Is she really knocked up again already?"

He winced. "Let's not make this about me and Georgie. Dad once told me that you can't spend your entire life holding the door open for other people. Eventually you have to walk through to find God's purpose for you."

"Well what if my purpose is 'doorkeeper'?" Sharon brought up a valid point. I commended her for smiling at Psalms 84:10. Because a doorkeeper in the house of God is better than most things outside it. And Sharon certainly viewed most things in life through a doorway at that point.

"Um. . ." Sean tilted his head. Reminded of the same verse. "Never really considered that. But my point is, if God wants you to do this, don't worry about *us*. Obviously, Georgie and I have a different purpose. I know she'd *love* to spend a year in Africa. So would I. But we have to sit this one out. You *don't*, Sharon. They are looking for an ASL *teacher* to reach a deaf community. The job was *made* for you."

"But—" Sharon started.

Georgie had arrived with Sammy. "I already emailed them and outed you with a picture and résumé and everything. You're doing this, Sharon. They've already said they'll contact you."

"How do you have my résumé?" Sharon tried to call the bluff.

"I was sitting next to Eric. The computer guy? He hacked into your phone during service and you had it on your cloud. Sophie and I updated it and—"

"So, this is a *conspiracy*?" Sharon laughed, impressed. "You do know the pastor teaches during that time we all sit in the sanctuary, right?"

"Yeah, I wanted to pay attention. So, complain to Mom who texted all of us and made us do it. We're just honoring our elders, Sharon." Sean smiled. "Especially when she told us that Dad would have *single-handedly* made it happen."

"Yeah." Sharon smiled about her daddy, who never let her settle for only some of her potential. "It's three months from now. I won't be there when you give birth like I was for them."

Georgie shot Sean a death look and rolled her eyes at Sharon.

"Um. . .it's okay. I won't be alone. I'll miss you, of course. But this time someone else needs you more, okay?" Georgie encouraged, then smiled when the same man from the stage placed his hand on Sharon's shoulder.

Sean and his family waved goodbye. Sharon turned.

"Sharon Mehlmann?" the pastor asked.

"Yes sir," Sharon said, shaking his hand.

"Welcome to the team."

•••

Georgie sniffled as she popped the cool, frosted grape into her mouth. Relishing the one afternoon a week Sean forced her to get out of the house and spend some time with her best friend.

"An entire *year* without this?" She squeaked through tears. "Gosh, I'm so hormonal. I'm a mess."

"Stop getting pregnant every three seconds," Sharon teased.

"I wouldn't dare do without loving my man or the little feet running around, you know that." Georgie smiled.

Sharon smiled too. She wouldn't want L.D. to do without all that either.

292

"So, your apartment?"

"I'm moving everything into storage. God wants me to buy a house when I get back, so I won't need the apartment. I've been offered a room at Sophie and Eric's for the gaps."

"Perfect! What about Stormy?"

Sharon sighed almost immediately in tears. "Well, I was hoping since she knows the neighborhood and you guys live just around the corner. . ."

"We'll take her. I'll make sure the kids don't terrorize her too much," Georgie promised.

•••

As a young child, Sharon equated dancing with music. Not in a correlation like most people. They were one and the same. She could feel the beat and see the dancing. After Sharon could hear music, she loved dancing more than most, seeing music in it, even without music.

Therefore, while dancing and worshipping around campfires in the profound African night with drumbeats and untamable joy, Sharon wondered if maybe she was born on the wrong continent. Her students were no longer white middle-class children with abounding opportunity and the awareness of society upon them. They were teenagers, grandmothers, babies, and everything in between. Who had all learned that day to tell someone they loved, "Jesus loves you." Some of them had never communicated at all.

They were watching the music. The dancing. One and the same.

That morning, Sharon had awakened in a new world after a long journey in the days before. Fat. White. Awkward. She'd wondered what possible impact she could have on the Kingdom of God in Africa. By that evening they had her dancing with shameless abandon.

I'd love to tell you more about Sharon's first few months in Africa. Sharon was a creature of self-doubt and being in a new place with a new job, I knew she'd do nothing but doubt her ability to handle the work God had for her to do. However, Sharon never felt more comfortable than in a place where they spoke of her size and awkwardness with jolly and joy. She taught them to speak. To be heard. God's power flowed through her, and she never had a chance to doubt the vessel He was using.

So, for months, I simply wasn't there.

• • •

"It's been two weeks. I don't think she's coming back this time. What if she got lost or hit by a car?" Georgie stood at the back door in late summer. Listening to crickets and looking into the darkness for the fat gray cat.

"We'll call the girl that lives at Sharon's old place in the morning and see if she's turned up there again. It's only half a mile away. If Stormy did get lost, she'd probably go there where toddlers don't pull tails," Sean suggested.

"What would I tell Sharon if something happened to her cat?"

"Don't borrow trouble, baby." Sean kissed his wife's hand and brought her inside.

The next morning, Georgie contacted Mina, the woman who lived in Sharon's old apartment. She was kind and understanding but hadn't seen the cat. She said she'd call if she saw her. Georgie wasn't optimistic.

Sophie entered the house midmorning with Mel and set him loose in the house. She announced her reasoning immediately. "He's making me crazy."

Georgie giggled, nodding. "Sammy needed a break from just his sister, so no complaints here."

Sophie sat in the living room with Georgie, who had swollen feet up on a coffee table, sucking a kale lime smoothie through a straw.

"Any sign of kitty?" Sophie asked.

"Nope. I'm drowning my sorrows as we speak." Georgie slurped the end of her smoothie, but after one unsuccessful attempt at sitting up, Sophie had to take the glass from her.

"You're such a natural at this. I was *so* miserable when I was pregnant with Mel," Sophie remembered.

"Oh, I'm miserable." Georgie laughed. "But it's not so bad. The last one was harder. Maybe they'll get easier each time."

"How many times do you think you'll do this?" Sophie wondered.

"Well if I continue to get pregnant with one baby when the previous child is five or six months old until menopause at say, fifty. . ." Georgie bit her lip. "It'll be about twenty total."

"And you're planning to raise them all in *this* house?" Sophie was astounded.

"That's the plan for now." Georgie nodded. "Mom does better with us around and always tells me she hopes we never leave. Might get a tad crowded after a few more kids, but God will provide."

Sophie sighed. "You know I never—" She cleared her throat. "I never went on any kind of birth control after Eric and I remarried. So technically we've been 'trying' to get pregnant for. . .what's it been? A little over a year?"

"Oh. . .I'm sorry. I didn't mean to—"

"God's time," Sophie said abruptly. "And we have Mel. I'm thankful for all that I have. I don't want you to think I'm not."

Georgie nodded with compassion. Smiled. "So, um. . .if you don't mind me asking, what anniversary do you and Eric celebrate?"

Sophie giggled. Nodded. "Both. And the day we met. The day we went on our first date. First time we made love. The day we found out we were having Mel. The day he proposed. The day *I* proposed. Rehab and cochlear implant anniversaries. Sundays. Thursdays." Both women giggled. Sophie smiled. "I *adore* that man. He's put up with more than most. I celebrate every day I get to be with him. God is so good, you know?"

"All the time." Georgie smiled. Then her phone rang. "Hello?"

"Hi. . .Georgie? This is Mina. Is the cat gray with a green collar?" She asked.

"Yes!" Georgie said.

"Oh good! She's here."

"Oh, thank God!" Georgie sighed relief. "I'll have my husband come by and get her when he gets off work, is that okay?"

"Yeah, that's great! I'm just glad she's safe."

For two months, Stormy continued to disappear for weeks, then return to her old home. Sean collected Stormy from Mina every couple of weeks until Mina finally offered to just keep her for the year, having grown fond of her during the brief visits. After receiving permission from Sharon over video call, Georgie found that she rested easier with Stormy in the care of a stranger than with her. Mina commented that she hoped she could take the kind of care of Stormy that Sharon had. That's when Georgie knew that Stormy didn't actually need anyone. She appeared to be well taken care of but functioned as a stray.

It was no wonder why that's what Sean used to call her.

...

Lynn needed to take her blood pressure medication that she kept in the kitchen, but she was waiting for her daughter-in-law's giggles and her son's rumbled whispers to make their way upstairs. It annoyed her at first, but then she smiled, always feeling like she could be much more like Samuel. She leaned against the kitchen door out of sight.

"You're so ridiculous," she heard Georgie whisper.

"I'm serious. The tree is big enough," Sean whispered. The sensual-sounding whispers simply his charm, not his intentions.

"Do you think you could build it with your leg?" Georgie whispered back, the same gentle speech.

"No, I was planning to use my hands," Sean teased.

More giggling from them both.

"You don't remember Dad talking about a tree house when we were kids?" he asked.

"I do. But the tree was smaller then."

"Yeah, that's why he said he wanted to build it for. . .for grandkids." Sean cleared his throat of tears.

"If Dad knew how much you still cry over him, Sean. . ." his Georgie whispered.

"I know," he whispered. "Can I build the kids a tree house?"

"Your choice. And yes, Sammy and Mel would *love* it. Ruthie too, eventually. I'm scared it'll be dangerous, but—"

"Shhh." Sean shifted the conversation. "Let's not worry about danger. Like three pregnancies in less than three years. You thought *that* was okay."

Georgie laughed accusingly. "I didn't think that was okay all by myself, Mr. Mehlmann."

"You think this one's a boy or a girl?" he asked.

Lynn took the opportunity to enter the kitchen to find the couple wrapped up together in a lean against the kitchen counter. Sean leaning, Georgie with her back against him. Both of them cradling a gigantic mass at Georgie's stomach. They didn't even budge from the intimacy upon her arrival. She loved that about them.

"Boy, I'd say," Lynn commented. "I figured you'd cave the other day when the ultrasound tech asked if you wanted to know. I do love finding out the day they are born, though."

Georgie nodded a smile that morphed into a frown.

"What's the matter, L.D.?" Lynn wondered.

"She'll be back in just a few months." Sean knew just the matter at heart.

"Yeah, but she won't be there to announce what the baby is. I didn't think I'd miss her so much." Georgie sighed. "But she's been gone so *long*."

"We can video call in the delivery room," Lynn reminded, tossing back medication and swallowing it.

"There's no guarantee she'll be available when the baby comes." Georgie smiled. "Besides, she's having the time of her life and I'd never want her to feel guilty about that for a second."

"Because you're amazing," Sean growled, kissing his wife.

Lynn cleared her throat. "You two have a room upstairs."

"The *kids* are upstairs, finally asleep." Sean sighed.

"And you're down here talking about things you want to do for *them*." Lynn giggled.

"You're such a *dad*, Sean," Georgie teased.

Sean laughed once. Squeezed his wife. "You used to say that to Dad."

"Well I didn't have one of my own, so it was a compliment," Georgie confessed.

"I know. And every time you said it, even when we were kids, I wished you'd eventually say it to me," Sean confessed, smoothing her hair. "I always wanted you to think I was as good a dad as *him*."

"Why did it matter what *I* thought?" Georgie giggled.

"Because I hoped you'd be my kids' *mom*." Sean chuckled, confused. "Duh."

"Even if I ended up being like *my* mom?" Georgie was hormonal. Teary-eyed.

"There was no chance of that happening."

"How do you figure?"

Sean nodded to his own mom. "You spent too much time with *her*."

It didn't matter to Sean whether a person needed to hear a compliment or whether it might annoy them. Sean overpaid his compliments. Over loved the people in his life and had already made them all forget he'd ever gone astray.

Lynn took that moment to kiss her baby boy on the forehead, her daughter-in-law on the cheek, and little Jacob somewhere near his hip, I think. I was born anew in him a few days later, as with all of them. Children always strive to please their parents and have a sense that they never can. I'm that sense.

But Lynn knew that if Samuel could see his son now, he'd think that was a fight that Sean had long over-won.

• • •

I caught up with Sharon about halfway through her time in Africa. She had just interpreted a church service in a remote church and the attendees were headed home. The associate pastor who had taught at the service was named Ryan. A blond, good-looking thirty-two-year-old that was usually assigned to the "bush" churches. The two would travel together with the translator and make small talk. Ryan patiently waiting for Sharon's interpretations and the translator's words every few sentences. After today's service and months of practically ignoring her, Ryan approached her before their ride back to the main camp was ready.

"So, what's it like being at an advantage over everyone?" he asked.

"How do you mean?" Sharon wondered.

"You can hear. They can't. You can speak to them and understand them. I can't. Without you, they wouldn't have the foggiest what I'm saying. You're at an advantage," Ryan explained.

"I guess I don't see it that way." Sharon smiled. Thinking this was the same small talk as always.

"It's like Christ. Without Him as an intermediary, we would not have access to the Father. He's our interpreter in a sense," the pastor explained.

"I suppose that analogy makes some sense. Except that God could have reached every one of these people *without* me. Because of the Holy Spirit, who isn't inhibited by language barriers or other 'disadvantages.' " Sharon was somewhat offended. She was once deaf, and life was silent. But she was never clueless.

"Fair enough," the pastor said. Then he did something that nearly gave Sharon a start. He gave her the same sort of smile she might see Sean or Eric pair with some sly innuendo addressed to their wives.

Ryan was flirting with her.

Hmmm, let's see how you screw up. . .I mean "handle" this one.

Sharon, as Sharon goes, handled it frustratingly well, even in all her big fat awkwardness.

"God, I have no idea what to do right now. Help, please?"

Ryan chuckled. "You sign beautifully, Sharon. You hear and sign my testimony all the time. But I haven't had a chance to hear your story. Maybe this evening at the fire, I'll get a chance."

"I'd love to give you that chance." Sharon smiled.

He was a pastor. He'd been a widower since the age of nineteen when he lost both his first child and his wife in childbirth. A testimony for Christ's healing that had always resonated with Sharon as she signed it. And one that spoke to the people in Africa when God had called Ryan, as so many men have the same story.

The conditions were ideal. No dating or real chances for immorality since they were members of a larger team from their church. He was attractive. Experienced in life. She'd pleaded with God to be allowed to fall in love with a man under similar circumstances. Sharon couldn't help but wonder. . .Alright, so I definitely helped her not wonder.

It's never happening. Of all the women on the team, you are certainly the least desirable.

By the time Ryan found Sharon around a smiling, dancing bonfire that evening, she was completely sure that his intentions before were strictly professional and she shouldn't even hope for anything more.

"What's your story, Sharon?" Ryan asked straight away.

"What, like, the whole thing?" Sharon asked, trying to conceal her lisp.

"Sure!" Ryan laughed.

He listened with the patience of a pastor to Sharon's testimony. She talked about losing her father and the pain and destruction it brought to her beloved family. She spoke as a Christian, only pointing out the things that she felt would glorify God. She didn't mention the struggle with her weight. Her battle with jealousy. But she did talk a lot about prayer and redemption. After a time, Ryan spoke up.

"Wow. You're an incredible gal," he commented. "My condolences about your father."

"Thank you." She nodded.

"What's with the earpieces?"

Sharon had forgotten to mention. "Oh! Hearing aids. I was born mostly deaf, so I started signing before I could speak. They came out with a hearing aid that worked when I was about five. That's why I lisp. Re-teaching yourself the sounds is pretty tough. Anyway, I can't hear most of what you do without them. A lot of the way I function is like a deaf person still. I have a deaf brother-in-law and we really understand one another."

"Wow. So. . .Eric you said? Is deaf?"

"Yes. He has cochlear implants now, but he was completely deaf for twenty-eight years or so. I'm told that the first time he heard my sister talk, he couldn't handle himself. They were divorced at the time, and he'd spent a lot of time pretending he didn't still love her. He was busted that day." Sharon remembered hearing the story she'd missed.

"You seem to really love your family," Ryan noted.

"Yeah, I do," Sharon replied without hesitation. "I missed the birth of my latest nephew a couple months ago. I had to meet him over video call. Usually I'm in the delivery room."

"I'm sure they miss you. I bet you don't even know the impact you have on them."

There was a moment of silence between them watching a two-left-footed member of their team dance for Jesus with passion that no one would laugh about or question. Then Ryan asked something pastor-like that made Sharon question everything.

"So, what's your greatest strength?"

Sharon didn't know how to begin to answer that. But she remembered an old and dusty conversation. "My friend. The one that married my brother? She says that our greatest weakness and our greatest strength are usually the same thing."

"That's an interesting theory," noted the handsome pastor.

"Since then I've discovered that it's biblical," Sharon said with resolve. "It seems like the thing we value the least in ourselves and consider *weakness* is the place that allows God to show His glory. Take it a step further, and the worst of our lives can turn around and become the best parts of us. Just think how many people you've shown God's love by talking about what happened with your wife."

"Well said. 'His strength is made perfect in weakness.' " Ryan agreed.

"So, if you want to know my greatest strength, I have to start with weakness." Sharon laughed once. "Because I honestly can't see it as strength."

"Okay?" Ryan laughed.

"I hate everything about myself." Sharon nodded. "I'm fat. I lisp. I'm undesirable to men. No matter what I try to do, I can't change the way I feel. It's like I have a physical other voice in my head keeping me down like a tyrant."

Tyrant? Harsh, Sharon. Harsh.

"Sure, I can sign well. But that's just something I learned. Not something God granted to me as a gift. So, if you want to know my greatest strength, you'll have to find it in my weakness." Sharon smiled.

"Well God can transform and redeem anything to His glory. Just because a drug addict comes to Christ, that doesn't mean addiction is a strength. Losing weight and speech therapy and finding a man who can look within to see how beautiful you are, are all attainable things. What if God's just not *done* with you?" Ryan said. "For instance, I think you're an incredible woman. Because I looked within like God does. To be honest, the woman I thought you were six months ago, and the woman you are in your spirit are such different things. I was hoping we could get to know one another a little better."

Sharon at one point in naivety would have seen the gesture as a compliment and just allow herself to be flattered. She did, once. It ended in an STD.

Sharon cleared her throat. Smiled. Prayed *"God. Please give me the words if what is in my heart is Yours to say."*

She spoke. "I don't think God is ever done with any of us. Even on our last day, we may seem like a work in progress by the standards of the world, so that journey is not ours to judge. Before my dad died, he and I lost a total of two hundred and twenty-five pounds between us." Sharon took a moment to laugh.

"Wow," Ryan chuckled. Astonished that at one point she was even bigger. Crediting God for partially curing her gluttony. "I. . .I didn't know. Um. . .congrats. That takes a lot of dedication."

"Thanks, but I gained about half of it back. By the standards of man, I was beautiful. *Desirable.* And when I was thin, that's when I was the farthest from the Lord. I was worshipping dieting and exercise. Making sacrifices to be *desirable*, instead of making a choice to serve God. My weakness wasn't my weight. Because I was born deaf, and He's doing amazing things here because of that weakness. My brother tells me I'm beautiful. Not just because of what's inside my heart, Pastor Ryan. Because he thinks I'm physically *beautiful.* God made me just the way I am. Inside and *outside.* I don't know how to be *confident* in who I am or how I look. Even though I'm healthier and happier now than I've ever been, I still hate being fat and lisping and being single. But I know that God can use me today, just how I am." Sharon stood, smiling and excusing herself. "Changing any of that when God has me where He wants me. . .*that* might throw a rock His plans."

I tormented her for months. When she was doing God's work, she couldn't be touched. But alone at night when she could have been enjoying a marriage-bound romance with a pastor? I took advantage of the opportunity.

How could you throw that away? He said he could tolerate the way you look. He might even encourage you to lose the weight again. And a pastor? That's totally your thing. You'd never have to worry about straying from God by spending time in the wrong kind of company.

And so on, and so forth. Then, when the church sent a team for a couple weeks in the summer, Pastor Ryan fell head over heels for the coordinator of the Vacation Bible School program for the children. A lovely, infectiously cheery woman in her mid-twenties. Sharon dreaded my time with her the evening after she saw them giggling and mingling their spirits for a lifetime. Something she'd seen in her siblings.

But what I had hoped would make Sharon cry and hate herself, God flooded with peace that had no logical explanation. She slept like a baby that night, then woke up and befriended the young woman.

Just after Christmas, Sharon packed up her things and awaited a bus for herself and a couple other temporary members that were bound for the States.

"So, you're headed home?" Ryan inquired. Speaking to her for the first time in several months.

"Yes. Bittersweet," Sharon lisped unabashedly.

"I'll be sad to see you go," he said.

"I'll miss it here." Sharon nodded to the new ring on Ryan's finger after a month-long sabbatical in the States. "And I wish you the best of luck in your new life."

"Thank you, Sharon." Ryan nodded. "You'll always be in my prayers."

Sharon was starting to think that Africa had been her miracle. One day there would have changed the very structure of her soul forever. Like a doorkeeper in the house of God. Removing want and replacing it with a sense that this life is just a temporary glimmer. But Sharon spent a year there, setting her sights on eternity.

She still desired to fall in love. But not nearly as much as she panted for the purposes of God. A true doorkeeper. For the rest of her life, if God willed it.

They told her Africa is like that. That she'd have to re-assimilate once she went back to the States. She was thankful, therefore, when the arms of her mother had met her at baggage claim. And she barely noticed the banner and balloons, because at her mother's door she was greeted by tiny people that are never done justice over the internet.

Georgie pulled Sharon into a wet, tearful embrace.

"Don't ever do that again, okay?" She sniffled.

Sharon giggled. Perhaps she was needed here after all. "I'll do my best."

35

Doubt's Influence

I didn't expect it. Everything outside was telling Sharon she needed to love herself. First, when she slid up to a weight that was comfortable and healthy for her, but still not the societal expectation, they told her to love herself. When she bought a cute little house in the same neighborhood as her apartment, but with only one bedroom, they said she should love herself. When Georgie and Sean welcomed child after child after child into the world, they told her to wait. And to love herself.

Sophie would fret, even though Eric got an enormous promotion and Sophie decorated that already enormous house accordingly. She'd fret for years because she couldn't get pregnant while pregnancy became Georgie's natural rhythm. Then Sophie was silenced with a set of twins.

Sharon had every right to be jealous of them all. But they figured that when she was instead the world's most content aunt, that she was simply learning to love herself. Her life of living alone at age thirty with a cat. So, you'd think that she and I would have become enemies. Because you can't both doubt and love yourself. It doesn't work that way, right?

I didn't expect it when instead of accepting herself, Sharon chose to accept. . .*me*. And it made her the best person she'd ever learn to be.

Sharon woke up on her thirty-first birthday, then went for a nice easy run, returning to a hearty breakfast. She passed all her smiling nieces and nephews on the entryway wall of her house, kissing her fingertips and touching them to each picture. Sammy, Ruthie, Jacob, and Gracie Mehlmann. Mel, Lynn, and Joy Stiles.

She stood on the bathroom scale.

You're fat.

"Still fat." She sighed at the number.

That's probably why you're still single. Not even a loser would want you.

"I don't need a loser guy. I'm the lover of a King." She smiled.

You have a point. Well what about a non-loser? Someone your dad would have approved of.

"My dad approved of *me*. So do Eric and Sean and my mom and sisters. And I'm fat."

Yeah, maybe. They'd never say otherwise, at least. But you'll never be happy with you. You hated you when that number was much lower. You'll always wish you were married with children.

"That's a thorn in my side forever."

Forever. I'm here to stay.

"But His grace is sufficient."

You are weak. His grace is NECESSARY. You sort of suck without it.

"I'm weak. But His strength is made perfect in weakness."

Good for His strength. You're still fat. And alone.

"If I had my perfect life, I might forget how powerful He is to sustain me. So, I need to rejoice in my weaknesses. When I'm in Christ, I'm connected to all the power in the universe. And if my weakness makes me close to Christ, then I'm the strongest when I'm weak."

2 Corinthians 12, right? Like. . .do you even know? I don't think you quoted that properly.

"That was probably botched. . .I should go look that up."

You need your Bible to clarify the way you talk to yourself alone in your bathroom?

"Yeah. I do."

Besties. We were besties. She never really told me to leave her alone. Mostly agreed with me. And yet all I did was beat her down. Make her small. But whenever she was convinced of how small she was, she saw how big God is. We had a partnership, really.

Then Stormy, the cat that had welcomed her home from Africa by purring for a week straight and not leaving again until Sharon was settled in her new house, left and didn't come back. And we had a problem.

"How long has she been gone?" Georgie asked. Put up a finger for her friend. "Ruthie, don't even think about it! Jacob! Grandma's roses are not for eating."

Sharon smiled, catching little Ruthie midair in her constant jumping between the coffee table and the couch and following Georgie to the front yard to correct the next child.

"Sorry, S.R. I just have to—"

"Don't apologize for doing your job." Sharon held Ruthie upside down. Listening to her giggle uncontrollably. "And I'll keep doing mine."

"Aunt Sharon is silly," Sammy declared.

"My life is a circus. A really messy, chaotic circus where nobody wants to buy a ticket because then they would need therapy," Georgie said. And then laughed. Loving every second. Sharon would buy thirty tickets. She righted Ruthie, kissed her on the cheek, and watched her giggle away. "When did you last see Stormy, S.R.?"

"Two months." Sharon sighed. "Even when she was lost and kept going back to the apartment, she was never gone that long. I really think she's gone this time. I actually heard some screeching tires the last night I saw her, and I swore I saw her lying there on the street. But then I ran out and she wasn't there, so I knew I was just worried. But maybe not. Because she hasn't been back."

"Oh, S.R.. I am so sorry. I hope she turns up. I'd never forgive myself if the atonement cat broke your heart." Georgie poked out a lip and hugged her friend. "If it helps, I might be pregnant."

"Gracie is five months old!" Sharon pleaded.

"She weaned early, and not breastfeeding exclusively leads to the next Mehlmann kid. Every single time, so far. This isn't news, Sharon. Thank God Jacob breastfed for a year, so my body could heal." Georgie sighed. Whispered, "Don't tell Sean, it's not a sure thing yet."

Mom came out into the yard just as Sean pulled into the driveway.

"Hey, Baby!" Georgie called as he exited his car.

Before Sean got to her, he had children hanging off his limbs, and pretended, dramatically, to be in a swamp, attacked by alligators. He reached Georgie and kissed her tenderly as he rubbed at the pain in his hip. "Hey." He stepped away with inquisitive eyebrows as he backed up, half playing with the children.

"What?" Georgie asked of the look.

"Was it positive?" he mumbled discreetly.

"What are you talking about?"

"I saw you grab a pregnancy test at the store last night even though you tried to hide it, and now you have that look on your face like you have something to tell me. You can't hide stuff from me," Sean explained. "And Sharon is keeping a secret, and Mom is pretending not to know what's going on so that she can secretly find out if we are going to go ahead and do the addition to the house. So, are you knocked up, or what?"

"It was a weird test. But yes, I took one, and I'm craving limes, like always." Georgie hipped her hands and rolled her eyes. "I know Gracie is young, and we're still paying off hospital bills. This had to have happened the *day* she weaned, baby. I'm *so* sorry."

Sean smiled, looking a little melancholy, but not upset. He kissed his wife's forehead before sitting on the grass and letting his children crawl all over him.

"I'm not sorry, Georgie. Two dozen, remember? Until then, I will be grateful for every second with each one." Sean savored kisses on each child's head. Over and over as they played.

Georgie gasped a little. "It happened again."

Sean nodded a little. "Car accident. He was three."

"Oh. Baby, I could not do your job." Georgie teared up.

"I'm sorry, Sean." Sharon sighed. "Do you need anything else, L.D.? I really should get home. I have some planning to do."

"Nope. Thanks for your help, as always." Georgie waved goodbye, joining the pile of family on the grass.

"No problem. Congrats on number five." Sharon didn't let them see her sniffle as she walked to her car.

When she arrived home, she gasped at the gray cat curled up on her doorstep, taking her inside and feeding her as always.

"Stormy, you lost your collar!" she scolded. Also noticing a healed scratch on her side. Kissing her repeatedly. In the morning, Sharon bought Stormy a new collar. A purple reflective one with a bell. Just because she was so glad to have her home, even if she was just a cat and not a fifth. . .or first. . .or *possible* child.

Sharon wanted children. She wanted to be thin. She wanted to be loved by a man. But mostly, she just wanted Jesus. She found her joy when she denied herself in favor of Him. As she often whispered, a quote from the book of John:

" 'He must increase, but I must decrease.' "

36.

Stormy's Collar

"Promise not to be gone for two months this time?" she asked Stormy at the door, then sighed and opened it, watching her kitty walk away after only a week at home.

That afternoon, Sharon returned from placing flowers on her father's grave and sighed in relief when Stormy was on her doorstep. While placing her bowl in front of her, Sharon noticed something strange on her collar. Paper? A piece of paper carefully rolled inside the ring attaching her new bell.

At first, Sharon thought it strange that Stormy managed to get such a neat piece of trash stuck in her collar. Then she unrolled it.

"I am the worst human being on the planet. I have joked for a while that my cat is two-timing me. But the new collar gave her away, and then it occurred to me that I'm the mistress. Please accept my apology. She was injured by a car a couple months ago, and I kept her in until she healed. Now all I can think about is crying little kids because they thought their family kitty was dead. She came right up to my door several years ago, so I figured she was a stray. I just kept feeding her and she would stay a few days or sometimes weeks at a time. I didn't know she was so loved. I'm sure she'll find you. Whoever you are. Please keep her in so she doesn't wander back to me. And tell her I said goodbye.

~Angel"

Sharon was in shock. Looked at her cat. Laughed. "You unfaithful little spawn!"

She got Georgie on the phone, who laughed accordingly.

"For *years*?" Georgie asked.

"Apparently. No wonder she was so mad when I was in Africa. We tried to take her from her 'mistress.' What do I do? I mean, she's this 'Angel's' cat, too. She probably loves her as much as I do." Sharon reasoned.

"Yeah! Send a note back and tell her you'll share custody. This is hilarious, S.R.. Two-timing kitty. Sean will get a kick out of that." Georgie said. "Keep me in the loop on this one."

Sharon penned the note and waited for Stormy to get the urge to leave in four days. She was sure to attach the note securely.

"My family is in stiches over this. She is indeed mine; she came from a shelter as a kitten. But we wouldn't dare keep the unfaithful kitty from her mistress. She's too precious not to share custody. If you can, when she decides to come back, just let me know if you've doubled up on any of her shots, so I can get her checked out. I'll continue her vet care and you can continue to care for her when she finds you. By the way, thank you for taking such good care of her.

~Sharon"

Five days this time, and Stormy came trotting up the steps to Sharon's apartment. Another note attached.

"Our kitty is as vaccinated as they come. After about a month of her visits, I went ahead and got her shots to make sure she didn't bring anything 'home.' I kept her a couple extra days this time, so I could go to the vet and remove her records. They thought this was funny, as well, and also cleared her health-wise. Thankfully, they think we gave her extra shots in safe intervals, but I'll leave that in your hands from now on. One question: what is her name? I've called her 'Rain' all these years. Like rain clouds because she's gray? It was raining, and she was drenched when I met her, poor thing. Thanks for letting her stay in my life. You have no idea how much that means.

~Angel"

Sean and Georgie showed up randomly on a Saturday afternoon when Sharon was cleaning and Stormy was happily bathing herself on the couch. The visits happened frequently, as Sharon's house was only two blocks from her mother.

"Hey guys!" Sharon looked around their feet. "Where are the kids?"

"We are on a date." Georgie hipped her hands and batted her eyes.

"Mom heard us arguing about something last night and thought we could use some alone time." Sean closed the door behind them. "It was an argument about the baby's *name*, but she doesn't need to know that."

"So, you came here?" Sharon asked. "On a date."

"We had lunch. Went for a walk and decided on some names. We weren't ready to go home yet and thought we'd stop by," Georgie said. "How is your two-timing kitty?"

Sharon moved the magnet on the fridge. "The last note from Angel is here. I had just told Angel Stormy's name, and she said she'd start calling her Stormy, as well. But honestly, I like the name Rain. I didn't tell her that, though. Stormy is technically *my* cat."

"Rain is a nice name." Sean tilted his head at Georgie as he took the note from Sharon.

"I'm sure my mother thought Lavender-Dawn Meadow George was a 'nice name' too. Our children get good strong biblical names they will love for a lifetime, Sean. Nothing less." Georgie insisted as Sean read the note.

Sean chuckled and winked at his wife. Then took a moment to analyze the note. Smiled. "Sharon. . .?"

"Yes?"

"Have you *met* Angel?"

"No. I don't even know where she lives. Possibly the old apartment complex because that's where I lived when you got Stormy." Sharon shrugged. "I didn't give her any personal info. I know Mom was all worried about that."

"That's not *my* chief concern." Sean chuckled and handed the note to his wife. "Sharon, Angel is a *guy*."

Sharon rolled her eyes. "A guy who takes in a stray cat and sneaks her ice cream? And is named Angel? That sounds like *me*, not a guy. The first note said 'mistress.' "

"He's a guy. . ." Georgie winced, giving back the note. "Look at the handwriting."

"You can't tell from handwriting," Sharon defended.

"I used to be a receptionist for doctors. You can tell." Georgie grabbed the first note from the fridge as she thought about it. "Angel is a common name. I mean. . .with Latinos. Your cat's mistress is a Latino guy. Look! The first thing he said was a slightly sexual reference. 'My cat is two-timing me?'. Male."

"You do that all the time." Sharon rolled her eyes.

"Not in notes to strangers," Georgie defended. "This is kind of hot, S.R. You share custody of a cat with some Latino guy, probably within a mile radius. He's your kitty-daddy. That's almost a boyfriend."

"How is that hot? She's my sister. No," Sean said, tacking the notes back up on the fridge.

"Maybe show Eric sometime. He's good at reading between the lines. Or you could just ask in the next note," Georgie whispered. "Five bucks says Angel is a guy."

Sharon bit her lip as she slid the note into the collar.

"My family decided to take it upon themselves to profile Stormy's mistress. Since I think they are incorrect and there is money involved in this bet (I don't gamble, I swear!), I'll tell you my personal opinion of who you are.

Female. African American. Age 40–45.

I have zero bigotry or bias toward anyone, trust me, so I honestly don't care. But I'm just trying to prove my best friend and brother wrong, you understand? Let me know if I won five bucks.

~Sharon"

The reply was on Sharon's mat when she returned home from work three days later. As was becoming custom, she read a note while Stormy munched on her can of food, wondering why there was a five-dollar bill attached to it as well.

"Sharon,

The funniest part about your last note is that I don't often use my first name—Robin—because to me it sounds more like a girl's name than Angel does. But don't worry, this happens all the time with a name like mine. Your profile made me laugh for two days straight. As awesome as being a forty-something black lady might be. . .I'm not.

Here's my correction: Male. Polynesian/Mexican/Caucasian (long story). Age 33.5.

I included the amount that information just cost you. You can buy Stormy her spoiled kitty canned food. I always wondered why she turns her nose up at my dry kibble. And while we're at this:

Female. White. Age 75–80.

I'm probably wrong, because I can't imagine a little old lady making bets with her friends and family. But you do have a "classic" sort of way with words and handwriting. Don't be offended. I was raised mostly by a single dad who couldn't afford normal childcare. After school, I had to go to a lady's house named Sharon. So naturally that's who I imagined the first time I saw your name. She was one of the sweetest people I've ever known.

~Angel (begged my dad to let me go by Angelo, but he refused)"

Sharon giggled. Her life changing suddenly. She's been exchanging cat mail with a strange man, when she thought she'd been safe within her own perception of Angel. It might be dangerous, and she knew she should probably stop. But with some insistence of her gut, Sharon attached a note when Stormy went out again—worried she was sharing too much. But somehow feeling comfortable with the person on the other end of Stormy's collar.

"Angel,

I am so sorry! I hope I didn't hurt your machismo. I certainly understand being weird about your name.

My best friend/sister-in-law (my brother married my best friend. . .long story), the one I gave that five-dollar bill? Her name was once Lavender-Dawn Meadow. I'm not even joking. She changed it when she married my brother. We've called her L.D.

since we were kids. She can't stand her name, and all of their children have painfully normal names.

I'm Sharon Ruth, so I have the name of an older woman no matter what. I feel bad for my niece (Ruthie) who is named after me. My dad, who passed away suddenly a few years ago, named me after the Rose of Sharon. A flower mentioned in the Bible. I hated my name until the day he died. And then I just wanted him to call me his 'Rose of Sharon' just one more time. My name means everything to me now. But despite my name:

I'm white. . .ish (technically of Hebrew and German descent). Female (obviously). I turned thirty-one recently.

Robin Angel is a very nice name. But I'm a little curious about the "long story" associated with the Polynesian/Mexican/Caucasian description.

~Sharon Ruth"

"So, did Angel just stop writing?" Georgie asked one day while Sharon was helping her at the house.

"Huh?" Sharon pretended not to hear. A perk of the hard of hearing. Georgie knew better, but Sharon needed the extra time to come up with an explanation.

"Has Stormy not been home? You haven't mentioned those letters ever since you lost that bet," Georgie teased.

"Well, it got weird after that. And there isn't much more info to exchange about Stormy." Sharon shrugged.

She wasn't lying. Because this was certainly weird to her. Having a friend, other than Georgie, confide in her and love Stormy as much as her. But she didn't want to be accountable to Georgie. She'd make fun if she knew Sharon was continuing to speak to a strange man she'd never met. It might scare her mother. And Sean got protective at every mention of "Angel."

Still, Sharon peacefully awaited the next arrival of her two-timing cat.

37

The Letter's Intent

"I assure you, my 'machismo' is undamaged. Though, the only times I can recall there being a chip taken out of my machismo were because of women. First, my wife left me for her boss. With my unborn son—who turned out to not be my son—but that was ten years ago. More recently, I was crushing on this girl, but before I worked up the courage to talk to her, she moved away. She was too pretty for me anyway. But Jesus has restored my machismo since then.

So. . .the long story: My mom was Polynesian, and I was born in Hawaii. She died of cancer when I was five, and Dad couldn't handle being around her family, so I was raised on the mainland. It's really weird, because I was twenty-three when I suffered through that divorce I mentioned. And just five when my mom died. But I barely even think about my ex-wife anymore, whereas losing Mom still hurts. Which is why you have my deepest condolences for your dad. For lack of better words: That sucks.

What's with your brother marrying your best friend? Like. . . awkward. That's all I can say. How did that go down?

~Angel"

Sharon giggled as she wrote her reply, but when there was a knock at the door, she had to hide the notes in the box of them she kept on the kitchen counter. Sean entered before she was finished.

"Sharon! Please tell me you are not still talking to that guy?" Sean demanded.

"Can I live my own life, please?" Sharon asked. "I let you live yours, even though it involves regularly impregnating my best friend."

"So, you have nothing to worry about!" Sean laughed. "You knew and loved my wife before I ever got involved with her. No worries. But Sharon, I don't trust a guy who talks to a girl using a cat's collar. A cat he stole. Do you see the difference? Dad isn't around to say this stuff. You know he'd say the same thing if he were alive."

Sharon sighed. "Did you need something Sean, or are you just here to criticize me?"

"Jake left his. . ." Sean started.

"Oh, right," Sharon said, handing her brother a lovey. Rarely could they visit with four children and take everything with them when they left.

"Thanks." Sean backed out the door. "You be careful, Beautiful. Tell me if you need me to fight somebody."

"I will." Sharon took out her note and a pint of frozen yogurt to finish them both.

"Angel,

My brother dating my best friend was awkward at first, I admit. They only told the family after they'd been married for months and she was pregnant.

After I found out, I slowly started to realize how much they care about me. They tried not to be in love for six months, and then got married without ever dating. Not only was that one of the more romantic things I'd seen, but they didn't tell me because they were worried I'd be jealous of it. I was going through a rough time in my life back then, watching my little sister get married and have a baby. It's all I've ever wanted and learning that God might have a different plan for me has never been easy. They knew it wouldn't be easy when I found out. They got me Stormy during that time and having her around has been wonderful. Especially when we lost Dad not long after we found out about their marriage.

Now I'm completely in love with Jesus Christ, the Lord and love of my life, and I have eight nieces and nephews to love on (counting the current one cooking in L.D.). I have a job that I love, and half of a cat. I'm good.

Please allow me to express my condolences as well. I was all grown up and on my own before I lost my dad, and I'll probably never be over it. Losing your mom as a child is awful. My mom is alive, and my brother lives with her, so she's swimming in grandkids. God knew she needed that—she really loved my dad. Is your dad still living?

~Sharon"

Over the course of a few months, Sharon learned that Angel was single, looking to God for all he needed. Just like Sharon. And with my help, he learned that she is overweight, though not like she used to be. And that she had a slight lisp that her second graders didn't notice only because they were deaf. Sharon learned that Angel was probably overweight too but kept active because of his job. His dad was alive in a nursing home with early onset Alzheimer's. Angel worked long hours but still managed to see his father every day.

After a while, Sharon started to see Angel as a diary. Because no human could be that perfect. I tried to tell her that if he met her, he'd want nothing to do with her. Or at the very kindest, think she was "beautiful on the inside." But she didn't listen. She just kept pouring her heart out onto pieces of paper, and into the eventual empty medicine bottle Angel attached to Stormy's collar. Instead of receiving a stone wall of indifference like she received from most people most of her life when she finally chose to share, Sharon received Angel's heart back in equal or greater measure.

Romantic, right? But Sharon didn't even see it that way. If Angel had been that woman she thought he was, she swore she'd have done the same thing. And I suppose she could have. See, Sharon and Angel never breached any "romantic" topic. But that doesn't mean Sharon wasn't in love with Angel's soul, however intangible.

They would talk about family. Jesus and church. Encourage one another through past heartaches and pray one another through present circumstances. Stormy seemed to understand. She began leaving Sharon after just twenty-four hours but returning twenty-four hours later. Not unfaithful at all. Just a reliable, beloved messenger.

It all changed with the reply to Sharon's question: "What do you do for a living?"

"Angel" told her he was a delivery driver. UPS. And Sharon knew.

You're so stupid. How embarrassing.

Sophie was creative. Manipulative when she allowed it, but she always meant well. She must have decided that Sharon needed some sort of fantasy love in her life. And forgotten that she'd tried to set Sharon up with her UPS guy years ago. The profession was a slip-up that couldn't be ignored.

How cruel of Eric to have even confirmed the handwriting for her. Maybe he didn't know. But with the transparency of their marriage relationship in recent years, how could he not? Sharon was convinced after just a few moments that they were all in on it. A ruse too clever for one mind to accomplish.

She forced Stormy out the door with a reply that didn't even include a signature.

"You almost had me convinced."

She was ragingly, tearfully upset when she arrived at the family dinner that very evening and tossed the box of letters on the kitchen island Sophie was standing next to.

"Why would you do this to me?" she screamed.

Sophie's eyes were wide. She looked around at the stunned family. "Sharon. . .I. . .what?"

"I'm not stupid. And I'm not desperate. You didn't have to embarrass me like this." She sobbed.

"Sharon, you need to calm down." Sean put a hand on Sharon's back. She swatted it away.

"It was all of you. I know it," Sharon huffed.

Sophie carefully set down the child she'd been holding and opened the box that overflowed with letters immediately. She began reading one.

They all gasped. Georgie, plump now with child, snapped her gaze to Sharon.

"How long have you been writing this guy?"

"There's no guy, L.D.." Sharon crossed her arms. "You guys made him up. I don't know how to forgive you for this."

Sophie began sighing and swooning reading a letter. Lynn gasped at the one in her hand. Sean coughed at his.

"Sharon, this is not safe. You told him the school where you work and everything. . ."

"Not like it matters. It's you. All that personal information that I'd never tell anyone was all just. . .so who writes them? It has to be either you or Eric, Sean," Sharon accused.

"What makes you think we did this. . .or *would* do this, Sharon?" Lynn asked.

Sharon showed them the latest letter, where "Angel" claimed to be a delivery driver. "Sophie tried to set me up with her UPS driver a few years ago, remember?"

"Sharon, I backed off when you told me to. I understood your thing about dating after God convicted me that you probably had it right. God did that by my UPS driver suddenly changing. Apparently, he switched routes according to the guy after him. But I've had like four since then. I haven't forgotten about that one, I won't lie. Something about him stuck with me. But I'd never do this to you, Sissy. This guy likes you. He trusts you. This box of letters is extremely romantic."

"You're lying," Sharon argued, wiping tears with a tissue.

Sophie read another letter. Smiled. "Sharon. . .you're not gonna believe this. . ."

"What?"

"What if my old UPS driver and your kitty-daddy are the same guy?"

"That's impossible and there's not even a way you'd know that. This is mean. I forgive you, okay? You don't need to keep lying."

"I'm not lying!" Sophie pointed to the letter. "My old UPS driver was this enormous guy. I couldn't tell what race he was, but if he had told me he was this, it would have made sense. And Sharon, the name on his uniform was 'Rob.' The natural assumption would be Robert, but he says his first name is Robin, and that makes sense too. Sharon, this guy is seriously legit. I met him. I tried to set you up with him."

"That only proves you wrote these letters, Sophie."

"No, it proves you should listen to your sister. Because what if you were supposed to go out with this guy and God had to do this to get you to listen?" Sophie smiled.

Georgie giggled. "Sophie, when you tried to set them up, they'd already been sharing a cat for years."

Eric chuckled. "Sharon, you need to let Angel out of the friend zone."

Sharon's eyes widened. "I haven't even met him, why would I be anything but his friend? Even to say we're friends would be—"

"Seriously tragic." Sophie gasped. Reading her letter. "He says: 'I look forward to seeing Stormy every other day. I always have, but now I know when she comes that she'll be carrying a piece of you. I am astonished we have never met. I know we haven't because if we had, I'd have surely recognized the beauty of your soul without you uttering a word.' "

Georgie piggybacked, " 'You don't have to ask me to pray for you. It has been my pleasure to pray for you these past few months.' "

" 'I bought some stationery in your favorite color. I hope it makes you smile.' " Lynn put a hand over her heart.

Sean laughed. " 'My favorite gospel is John. He gives more than an account of the life of Christ. He gives value and truth to it that can bring a sinner to his knees. I know. I've been there.' "

"That's why I thought you were in on it," Sharon admitted to her brother. "John is your favorite."

"I can see that." Sean nodded. "But I didn't, Sharon. None of us would do this to you, let alone conspire and *all* of us do it."

"This seems like a real person," Eric conferred.

"We can look into it if you want. Look for divorce records. His father is at a nursing home. We could call them. There are ways to check into this guy," Lynn suggested.

"Isn't that rude?" Sharon asked.

Lynn glanced at Sophie. "When my seventeen-year-old daughter brought home a wealthy twenty-three-year-old, do you honestly think Dad and I didn't confirm every bit of who he claimed to be?"

Sophie opened wide a shocked mouth and laughed through it. Eric chuckled as well.

"It was mostly your father!" Lynn diverted some of the blame. "But now I don't have Dad, so. . .let's all do this together? Because even though we didn't do this, that doesn't mean Angel is who he says he is. First of all, what have you told him?"

"A lot. Everything." Sharon sighed in self-hatred. "He's told me a lot too, as you can see."

"Which could all be a lie." Sean shook his head.

"I don't know, Sean," Eric considered. "He doesn't know Sharon any more than she knows him. Even if he is interested in her, they were just passing notes to begin with. Why would he need to lie? And if he wanted to lie, why would he talk about his shortcomings?"

"Well it would be just like my life for this great guy to be made up in someone's head to torment me for no reason." Sharon sighed. Sniffled.

The silence was oppressive.

"What does your spirit say, S.R.?" her best friend asked.

Sharon shrugged. "That he's as real and sincere as when I get a text from one of you."

"And do you have any feelings for him?" Lynn asked.

Sean laughed bitterly. "Seriously?"

"I don't know. That's a really hard question," Sharon admitted. Ready for honesty. "Yes. Whoever wrote those notes is someone that I feel connected to very deeply. This person has glorified God and never puffed himself up like he would if he wasn't sincere. But I suppose he could just be a really good con artist. In which case he'd be pretty disappointed to only get me out of the deal."

"Only you?" Sean laughed. Teased. "Just you, huh? One of the best people alive. That's all."

Eric had been looking at his phone, and finally lifted it to the device at his ear. Tapped some numbers periodically like he was being walked through a menu.

Sophie spoke during that time. "I say go for it, Sharon. Keep your guard up. But if anyone deserves for this guy to be real and exactly who he says he is, it's you."

Eric startled them, not speaking to them. "Yes, I was just wondering about a driver named Rob or Robin Sanchez? He went above the call of duty a few years ago for my wife and I'd like to thank him, but his route changed. . .Yes, I'll hold." Eric smiled and winked at Sharon. "No, I understand. I don't need contact info, but if you could just tell me how I could connect with him. . .And that's your main office? Thank you."

Eric hung up from the phone call Sophie had watched with doting eyes. In disbelief still that he could have them.

"He does still work there. I'll try to go leave him a message on my lunch tomorrow," Eric promised.

"I'll do divorce records," Sean said, warily, tapping at his phone.

Sophie rolled her eyes in disgust. "Yeah, unfortunately those are public record forever."

"Marriage records too." Sean winked at his little sister.

"I'll call the nursing home," Sophie offered, smiling at Eric.

"I have a diaper to change." Georgie sniffed.

"I'll serve dinner," Lynn said. "Let's take this to the dining room."

In half an hour, Sharon's family had proven, fact by fact, the existence of Robin Angel Sanchez as she knew him. Her heart panicked.

"I wrote him a nasty note," Sharon admitted. "Because I thought he was you guys."

"He'll forgive you. If not, he's not worth it." Georgie winked.

38.

The Man's Hope

It was a week before Sharon saw Stormy again. She hated herself.

You scared him off. Admit it.

But Stormy returned with a legal-size envelope rolled up and taped to the collar securely.

The first page was handwritten and read,

"Sharon,

At first when I received your most recent note, I thought I'd offended you in some way. But when I got a note from your brother-in-law, I realized I simply needed to make you feel at peace with me, as I am. I'm also delighted to have met some of your family in the past. Sophie seemed to be a dedicated mother, and I could barely believe what you've told me about her past. God is so gracious, isn't He? It was a joy to speak with her that day.

By now, I assume you've done your own background check. But just in case, I've included as much proof as I could that I could never lie to a sweet spirit such as yourself. I hope you'll continue to write. I hope this doesn't put you off. I live for your letters, Sharon. My life has never been so full as now.

~Robin (masquerading as 'Rob' at work) Angel (still a guy) Sanchez"

Sharon burst into hysterical laughter as she got it all opened up, then thumbed through the same records they had dug up, and more. Including a copy of a note from Eric. A résumé. Church bulletins. Some elements, such as his current address and phone number, were redacted, with silly little notes explaining that he didn't want her to think he was being too forward. And finally, something that made Sharon's heart leap.

She unrolled the photo paper slowly. Heart pounding. The tears changed their tune.

It was a professional photograph, taken at a studio and dated two days ago. He'd had pictures taken for her.

In my eyes, he was average. Just a big guy you'd smile at in an elevator or pass on the street going the opposite direction. But to Sharon. . .oh, Sharon's beautiful soul.

Black shoulder length hair. Well-dressed. Kind eyes. He was perfect.

He's too handsome for you.

So, though Sharon sent an apology note explaining her doubt and thanking him for the records. And though she hung his photo in a frame on the wall with the family. Though she proved her existence with a copy of her birth certificate. She did not return the courtesy of a photograph.

Truthfully, she didn't know which photo she'd include anyway. Her "before" at Sophie's wedding? Her "after" around Sean's? Her "post-after"? A recent photo-shoot her mother arranged a few months ago. Sharon could trick him. Show him the thin version of herself. She could scare him off with the fat slob she thought she once was. Her face would never be as soft and feminine as Sophie's. Her weight would never be as a model's. She didn't want him to have to go through that disappointment. So, she sent the letter alone. Being sure to tell him he was handsome. And that, of course, she would continue to write.

They wrote. Until they moved beyond the faceless diary and addressed one another as old friends. Until Sharon sent a photo of the newborn Adam Mehlmann in the arms of his parents at the hospital. Until Stormy's messages were as much a part of her life as her family and friends.

As with most relationships, however far into the "friend zone" a man is, a good man will dig his way out with little trouble if he wants to.

And yet Sharon was taken by surprise when it happened.

Stormy's medicine bottle contained just a tiny sliver of paper where the two had been stuffing pages. A tiny sliver in fond handwriting that read:

"To: 'The rose of Sharon, And the lily of the valleys.' Song of Solomon 2:1

May I have your phone number?"

Sharon gently reached into the medicine bottle and removed a flower that unfolded in her hand. A Rose of Sharon.

And though she cried in flattery and joy, Sharon was filled with all my poison. And responded with.

"'...Do not stir up nor awaken love Until it pleases.' Song of Solomon 8:4

May I have some time to pray about that?"

Sharon considered it with the first note but confirmed her need to consult God and family when the next note read.

"Take all the time you need. I promise to only text until you allow otherwise. I'd just like a more direct line to you. But please don't stop writing in the meantime.

Yours, Angel"

Sharon brought some of the correspondence with her for the next family dinner after days of prayer. Adam was two months old at the time. Before speaking, she placed the note about the Rose of Sharon on the table.

They all read it with various gasps and coos.

"He put a flower in, but that's at home between two books so I can preserve it," Sharon explained.

"For the grandkids you have with Angel?" Georgie giggled.

"I'm terrified," Sharon admitted. "Song of Solomon means he's serious."

"You've been writing almost a year, Sharon. Is it okay to have coffee with the guy *now*?" Sophie begged.

"I have that picture of him, but he's never even *seen* me." Sharon sighed. "He'll run the minute he does."

Lynn rolled her eyes. "Sharon, why can't you see that you're a *lovely* girl?"

"Spoken like a true mother. Thanks. But I'm not even a girl, Mom. I'm almost thirty-two years old," Sharon argued. "Fat. Hard of hearing. I have a lisp. . ."

"Sharon, I fell for a guy that didn't hear my voice *at all* during our first attempt at marriage. And sometimes I make him take off the external implants because I loved him *deaf*," Sophie said, to the laughter of all. "This guy knows all the things you see as flaws. He probably already loves you. I think you can trust him with your phone number."

"I agree," Sean, the protective skeptic said. "It's a miracle that Stormy hasn't lost a letter yet. You could lose all chance of meeting him if you lose that cat. It's a good idea to give him a more direct line, like he said."

Coming from Sean, Sharon agreed immediately.

The time between sending the note in the collar and her phone chiming was roughly seven-and-a-half minutes. All she'd written was ten digits. Some parentheses. A dash. But apparently, he'd gotten the message. Her anxiety flared. She didn't recognize the number on her phone, of course. But at one sight of the text, her worries were soothed.

"This is Angel. Is this Sharon?"

"Yes, this is Sharon. You must live close. I only sent Stormy out a few minutes ago."

He replied.

"Wow, really? Sorry, I probably seem desperate. I only texted so fast because I figured there was lag time and didn't want you to think I blew you off."

Sharon panicked.

"It's been a week since you asked for my number. I hope you didn't think I was blowing you off."

"No, I just assumed you'd skipped town with my cat and I'd need to call a lawyer for custody. Kidding," He joked.

"I wanted to make sure I wanted to pursue this. I spoke with my family." She was serious. Taking a photo of his photo and inputting his info into her phone.

"*So, I assume you do?*" Angel asked.

"*I'm scared. But I think God is leading me in that direction.*"

"*Good. We'll take it slow, okay? I won't even call you.*"

"*Are we giving up on sending messages through Stormy?*"

"*We don't have to.*"

Sharon sighed in relief. "*Good. I think that would make me sad.*"

The next day, Sharon was waiting to go retrieve her students from the lunchroom when a text came in.

"*I'm on lunch and thought about you. How's your day going?*"

Sharon had been thinking about Angel as well. "*Pretty well. What are you eating for lunch? I'm having salad.*"

"*Low on groceries. It's a fast food day for me. Bacon cheeseburger.*"

"*Sounds like Sean. The first thing he asked for after his accident was a cheeseburger.*"

"*He sounds like a stand-up guy. Salad gets you through a day?*"

"*Back when I lost the weight, I learned to love salad. Anything else makes me sleepy in the afternoon and I have to take one more run in a week.*"

"*I burn a lot of calories at work, so a salad would just make me hangry.*"

One afternoon, Angel sent a text when he knew Sharon to be arriving home.

"*You won't believe what happened this morning.*"

"*What happened?*" She took the bait.

"*Do you remember me telling you I crushed on a girl a few years ago, but she moved away before I could talk to her?*"

"*I think I remember that. You said she was too pretty.*"

"*She ran by my house this morning. I guess she didn't move after all.*"

Sharon was crushed. She was just about to end, abruptly, the greatest adventure of her life. And I told her in so many words.

You were never going to be what he wanted.

She breathed through the sudden tears and shaking limbs and tried to take it with grace.

"Is she still too pretty for you?"

"Yes."

"I think you should talk to her."

"Why would I do that?"

"Because you're braver than you think you are."

"I finally believe that because of you."

"Thanks." Sharon sobbed. Barely read the next text.

"Which is why I'm not going to talk to her. I'm sticking with you."

"No, Angel! She's prettier than me. I keep telling you I'm not pretty." She sobbed now for a different emotion. The next text didn't come in for five minutes.

"You said your brother-in-law cried when he heard your sister's voice. But he already loved her, had married her, and had a baby with her. Hearing her voice was just icing on the cake."

"So?"

"So, I don't have to see you to know you're beautiful."

She'd been chosen. Sight unseen. I was almost losing my foothold.

Similar conversations occurred daily. The mundane. The sappy. I'll spare you both. Because one evening, Sharon received her usual text when Angel got home from work.

"Okay, I'm just going to ask. Can I call you?"

"Uh. . .now?"

"My phone is in my hand. You're probably finishing up your froyo. Yeah, now. Unless you need about a year to be okay with it. . . ☺"

Sharon giggled at herself and the fact that Angel knew her so well. She sighed and authored the text with caution.

"Sure."

Sharon's phone rang. *Angel Sanchez.* Her heart seized. Could she speak to him? What would he sound like? She couldn't let him think the worst now. So, she took a breath. Cleared her throat. And answered.

"Hello?" A quiet, timid introduction.

"Hey!" An enthusiastic tenor voice. "I wasn't sure you'd answer." But still masculine. A heartwarming rasp.

"I um. . .almost didn't." She laughed.

"Well, I'm glad you reconsidered." He chuckled. "If you don't have time right now, I understand. I'll call back later."

That voice. So soothing. So sincere.

"No, it's fine. I already finished grading my papers."

He sighed. She panicked. What did she do wrong? She froze in silence. He explained.

"Sharon, your little lisp is like the cutest thing ever." He guffawed like an enchanted teenager.

"Uh. . .thanks?"

He laughed. "Sorry. I'm glad to finally hear your voice."

"Yours too," Sharon admitted. "Is there a reason you wanted to call, or. . ."

"Well it's the next step in my master plan to get to meet you," Angel admitted with humor.

Sharon giggled. "My brother thinks it's weird you hadn't asked yet. Even for a picture."

"I *would* love a picture, but any way I thought to ask might have seemed like I was trying to screen your looks for being acceptable to me or something." Angel sighed. "Which I don't need to do, obviously. The version of you in my head based on your descriptions and now your voice is all I need."

"Need for what?" She wondered.

"To think about you? I don't know. It might be good to be able to recognize you in a lineup." Angel laughed. Sharon laughed. Angel sighed. "You have a *great* laugh, Sharon."

One crisp morning, practical Sharon slipped her phone in the pocket of her athletic leggings and set out on her tri-weekly run. About half a block from her house, she got annoyed, and then suddenly overjoyed when her phone rang. It was Angel's personalized ringtone.

Midstride, huffing and puffing, she came to a stop and then paced on the sidewalk as she answered the phone.

"Hey," she managed between breaths. "It's early, you okay?"

Angel didn't answer with words immediately. He made a sound. A sort of laugh combined with a cry. A sound one might hear in a movie theater when a big twist occurs. It was a subtle sound of surprise. An 'aha.' Sharon was about to ask Angel what it meant until he recovered in less than a moment.

I bet he was just coughing.

"Yeah, everything's great. You're breathing hard."

"I'm just finishing up my run."

"Sorry, I. . .I just had a couple random questions that kept me up all night."

"Okay?" Sharon finished her run as a brisk walk, listening to Angel talk.

"Yeah, so you. . .you went to Africa? For a year."

"Best year of my life," Sharon remembered.

"I bet!" Angel was cheerful. Encouraging. But he wasn't interested in hearing more about Africa just then. "And before that, you lived. . ."

"I lived in the same apartment from the time I was about twenty-two. Then I went to Africa for a year, then bought my house. I stayed with my sister for a couple months while I house-hunted. Haven't I told you that before?"

"Just clarifying. . .Stormy during that time. . ." Angel was interrogating. Like a detective or a trial lawyer. Sharon didn't know why, but she honored him with answers.

"She was at my mom's with everyone until she got confused and kept going back to my old apartment after she'd spend time with you. Are you. . .is something wrong?"

"And you run. Like, three times a week. Early morning. But only for the past few years."

"Yeah, before that I was extremely overweight. Now I'm still not skinny, but I'm healthy."

"And you lost all the weight when you lived in the apartment."

"And gained half of it back." Sharon sighed, walking in her front door.

He thinks you're lying to him about something.

She spoke into a silence she knew to be occupied by his thoughts. "Angel, I've been truthful with you this whole time. I feel like I can be open with you. If there's a discrepancy. . ."

"No! No, nothing like that. I just, uh. . .Hmmm. Wow. We both have to get ready for work. I'm so sorry to interrupt your run. Thanks for letting me pick your brain. I just had this weird. . .thing. . .don't worry about it. Can I call you tonight?"

"Please do." Sharon forgave the odd hiccup of a phone call, taking Angel at his word.

The phone calls accelerated the relationship. In just a week of nightly conversations, the two were moving ahead in their hearts. As always, Angel made the first move.

"Sharon, I want to meet you," he said at random after they'd been talking about politics. Agreeing on nearly everything.

"You know that scares me, right?"

"So, it should make no difference then, that I'd love to hold you in my arms while we talked like this."

"You know how I feel about dating, Angel."

And he did. He knew how she felt about just about everything.

"I feel the same. But I also want to *meet* you."

You're disgusting. Bad idea.

"Angel, I can't."

"Sorry, yeah. I don't ever want to pressure you."

"I know. And thank you." She sniffled. She'd found him. He was perfect. She just couldn't bring herself to let anything happen.

"So, if. . .if I can't meet you. And you don't like dating. How can I ever marry you?"

Sharon's heart locked up. No one had ever used that word. Those words. In the context of Sharon as a bride. Angel must have sensed her silence. He laughed. Got brave.

"What I mean is, I get you not wanting to date. Just tell me what the alternative is. Because this ends two ways. We stop talking and I dream about you for the rest of my life. Or we tell our grandkids about how sometimes God uses a cat to introduce people."

Sharon giggled. "I get to pray about that, right?"

"Of course," Angel promised.

The silence stagnated until Sharon winced, glad he couldn't see.

"I heard once. . ." She sighed. "I heard that in Bible times a man betrothed to a woman would build her a house. And when he was done, day or night, he would come get her and marry her and he would parade her through the streets, and they would feast and celebrate their marriage for a week. And she had to have an oil lamp burning 24/7 to signify that she was ready for him. I always thought that was so beautiful, because that image is also used in the Bible to describe us as a church being ready for Christ at all times."

"Wow. Society has really dumbed things down over the years." Angel chuckled.

"They have. A romantic like me basically had no chance of a story like Jane Austen would write about. Where they would write to one another and grow fond, even in absence. Letter writing is a lost art, and I'm really glad Stormy still brings me your letters. You've just given me so much hope, Angel."

"Why do I feel like I'm being dumped?" He sighed.

"No! I can't dump you, we aren't dating. I meant the opposite, Angel. I enjoy what we have, and I know it should lead somewhere. I'm just terrified. What if you're just a really patient serial killer?"

Angel laughed. "Well, I'm not. I'm a guy who is deeply in love with your soul. So, I'll pray long and hard that God works this all out. Not only for our benefit. But an end that leads to His glory."

Sharon was in awe. "You have a beautiful soul too, Angel. You are aptly named."

"As are you, my Rose of Sharon."

Her father used to call her that. No one but him, and only Dad when he was up for an eye roll. Yet when Sharon heard it come from a mouth she'd never seen animated, she knew then that all of this was God's doing. That maybe Dad was whispering in His ear. He would have gotten a kick out of all of this.

"Oh Lord. Work this miracle according to Your will."

39

The Miracle's Time

Sharon had not yet removed her shoes at her mother's house for a Sunday afternoon dinner when she sighed at her ringing phone.

Georgie squealed. "Is that him?"

Sharon checked her phone. Nodded. She answered under the careful watch of her family.

"Hey, Angel," she said with uneasy calm. "I'm actually at my mom's right now, can you call a little later?"

"Sorry, um. . .was Stormy there when you left? I sent her your way a few minutes ago. I only ask because I was headed out and I heard some thunder, so I wanted to make sure she was okay," he raced through the thoughts quickly.

"No, she was—" Sharon heard the thunder as well. "Oh, no. I hope she's alright."

"If you want, I can just turn around and—" Angel started.

"No, I'm pretty close. I'll go let her in. Thanks for letting me know," Sharon said.

The two said goodbye, then Sharon looked to her family. "I need to go check on Stormy. I'll be back in like 10 minutes. I am so sorry."

"It's fine, Sharon. She's your baby. We'll wait for you." Sophie smiled.

Sharon drove off quickly and the family began moving about to get ready for the meal. The doorbell rang.

Everyone looked at everyone else. Sean's brain clicked first. He answered the door, knowing who'd be behind it.

336

When the door opened, Sean looked up. He had to. The man was tall. Moderately wide. And identical to the photo Sharon had on the wall of her house.

"Uh. . .Angel?" Sean asked.

The whole family gathered in the entry until Lynn gave them all a look that caused them to take a seat.

"You must be Sean," the man said in a warm tenor voice.

"Okay, did you just lie to my sister on the phone to get her to go away?" Sean asked.

"No, I really did let the cat out. She'll probably be on Sharon's doorstep, but she's hungry. So that buys me like two minutes, so she can feed her. I don't have long." Angel seemed determined in something.

"Long for. . ." Sean accused.

"She mentioned a family dinner. So, I knew I could catch you all in one place. I just need like five minutes," Angel begged.

Sophie broke away and appeared. "It's you!"

"Hi." Angel smiled. "Yeah, it's me."

"Won't you come in?" Lynn said, placing hands on her children's backs for them to sit.

They all stared him down as Lynn directed him to a chair.

"I'm sorry to come unannounced. It usually isn't my style. But I realized I didn't have any of your phone numbers. Could have gotten Sophie's from my work records, but that's against the rules, so I was out of luck. I went on the county assessor site, which is public, to find your address, Mrs. Mehlmann. I figured you wouldn't fault me for that considering recent searches of public records by individuals in this room." He chuckled.

Sean laughed a little. "So what's up? I thought you wanted to meet Sharon. Why did you call her away?"

"She's wary of me. Understandably. I figured if I could talk to the people she loves face-to-face that she might be a little more comfortable. So, I'm Angel," he said, nervously. "You probably know far too much about me. But you probably don't know that I'm highly interested in Sharon."

"Duh," Georgie teased. "What does 'highly interested' mean. Like. . .specifically."

Angel smirked. "Uh. . .in. . .love with? Really odd to say, she won't even send me a picture of her, so I know that's weird."

Georgie squealed as Lynn left the room. Angel smiled at her. "L.D., right? Or Georgie." He looked around the room. "Most of these kids are yours. I know them all by name. Sharon talks about them constantly. I feel like I know all of you."

Lynn handed Angel a photo album. Sophie protested. "Mom, no! She would not be okay with that."

"Exactly. This poor boy will never get to see our beautiful Sharon if we don't intervene," Lynn insisted. "Go on, Angel. Those are pictures of Sharon ranging from birth to recently when I had pictures taken. She hates having her picture taken, but—"

Angel was already smiling at the first page. Sharon as a baby. A child. On up to an overweight teen, an obese adult. A thin adult. And finally, a reluctant portrait with Sharon's classic rueful smile. Angels' smile, however, was first of some smug self-satisfaction. And then an odd sort of nervous laugh.

"Everything okay?" Georgie ventured.

"I knew it," he whispered to himself, then looked up at everyone. "You're sure this is Sharon?"

Their hearts sank. How could they explain this to her? He was upset by what he saw.

"That's our Sharon." Lynn sighed. "I know she's—"

"No! She's beautiful. Perfect, in fact," he said. "Here's the thing. My back fence is the wall of an apartment complex not far from here. Behind the wall, there are parking spaces. I think they are assigned to the people living in the apartments. And, uh. For several years, there was this girl who parked her car right behind my fence. And a couple weeks ago, it finally clicked. . ." Angel flipped back a decade in Lynn's album and pointed to a very fat, very insecure photo of Sharon. "That this is her."

"You're kidding." Georgie couldn't force her face to make an expression. "Sharon told me you'd crushed on this girl in an apartment—"

"It was way more than that, which I didn't tell Sharon. I didn't find that appropriate. But. . ." Angel laughed, almost maniacally. He began speaking quickly, which they knew from Sharon to be his usual way. "Everyone in my life knew about 'Apartment Girl.' It was totally pathetic. My divorce was relatively fresh, but the first time I saw her, the Holy Spirit says, 'Keep an eye on her.' "

"Yeah, I bet." Sean didn't like where this was going.

Angel shrugged, confessing. "It's not like it was difficult. But when God tells you to keep an eye on this curvy piece of perfection, you do it. And I kind of. . .I fell in love. Didn't know her name or the first thing about her, but there's just something about the way she carries herself that's stunning. I watched her lose the 'curvy' for a while, which was. . ." He turned to the skinnier photos. "Still beautiful, but I like the curves. I can't lie. I was happy when they started to come back." He looked to glaring Sean and Eric. "Sorry. All those years I kept telling myself I needed to just walk up to her and ask her to dinner. But God kept telling me not to. Told me to wait. Then she moved, which I told Sharon about. And I was *devastated* until I started writing Sharon. God gave me peace. He told me that I could either pine for a beautiful girl I'd never met, or I could have Sharon."

"Have?" Sean interrupted with haste.

Angel laughed. Not afraid of Sean. He appreciated him with a convicting raise of an eyebrow. "It was the Holy Spirit's terminology, Sean. Not mine. He said have. And between Sharon, sight unseen, and an impossible dream girl? Easy choice. To solidify that choice, or just to torture me, Apartment Girl started running by my house every other day. Also told Sharon about this, by the way. And here I am thinking I'm being faithful to Sharon by not looking at this beautiful girl jogging by my house. Then it occurs to me that Apartment Girl and Sharon have the same timeline. Sharon lost weight when Apartment Girl did. Gained it back when she did. Moved when she did. And Sharon runs three times a week. One morning when I knew she'd run by, I called her. I *watched* her answer her phone. Sharon. . .*is* Apartment Girl. Your photos just confirmed that for me."

"Wow." Sophie marveled. "And you were sharing a cat with her."

"For almost the entire time. Yes. And my first thought is, who needs to be punished for convincing Sharon she's not gorgeous? Please tell me it was no one in this room."

"Yeah, that'd be pretty much just Sharon telling Sharon that at this point," L.D. clarified with a laugh.

Can't punish me for doing my job.

"Well, maybe I can convince her otherwise. Because she's *beautiful*."

"I know, right?" Sean insisted. "She thinks I call her that to make her feel good about herself, but—"

"But someone as beautiful as her couldn't possibly be wrapped in something *not* beautiful. It's like physics or something."

Lynn and Sophie and Georgie were all in tears they were trying to hide. Angel drove the message deeper, releasing a couple dimples no one would know he had. Looking back at the album. "So anyway, who do I talk to about getting this girl in a white dress?"

"Excuse me?" Lynn asked. "You've never *met* her."

"I know her better than all of you combined. We talk on the phone like two hours a night now. Tell me how not having held her hand matters," Angel wondered. "I don't need physical contact to love her. That should be a comfort to all of you."

"But shouldn't you. . .I mean, you can't just *marry* her, Angel." Sophie laughed once.

"I'll ask her permission." Angel rolled his eyes, teasing. "But first I want yours. I know Sharon was quite the daddy's girl, so if Mr. Mehlmann were still gracing us with his presence, this would likely be a private meeting with him. But I figured the rest of you *together* would suffice."

"That makes sense, but Angel. . .man. . .*marriage*?" Sean squeaked. "Marriage is a big deal."

"I just want to be willing to make a commitment to her before she ever has to see me casually. I don't ever want her to doubt that she's worth the ultimate commitment when I've never so much as touched her. To her, that would mean the world. I have faith that God wants me with her. Isn't that what faith is? Believing without seeing?"

"That's faith." Georgie smirked. "This is insanity."

"Says the girl who up and married her best friend's brother just because he got a stray hair one day," Angel teased, winking at her. "You'd never even been on a date."

Sean, of course, stepped in and defended both his wife and sister. "Not *officially*, but this is more than a relationship status discrepancy like we had. What are you gonna do? Just propose?" Sean asked.

"I'm going to ask for her address. And when I feel like the time is right, I'm going to show up and parade her through the streets and marry her as soon as I can." Angel shrugged with complete sincerity. "In ancient times, that's how it was done. So, I'll just ask all of you to make sure she keeps her lamp lit. If all of that is alright with you, of course."

As the silence crystalized, everyone looked to Sharon's protector. To her baby brother, who everyone only knew now as the trusted patriarch. While they watched Sean consider the wildest question he'd ever been asked, I spoke with Angel.

I told you this was a bad idea. What sane family would allow you to take someone like Sharon off their hands? Let alone in such a risky manner? This is the first time they've met you. Sharon is precious to them. They don't trust you. You're about to get kicked out of this house. This was too bold. You know you're not bold, Angel. You're a gigantic teddy bear. Your love for Sharon may not be enough here.

"Um. . ." Sean cleared his throat. There was resolve in his eyes, like he had information they didn't. I don't know for sure. I wasn't allowed into his heart just then. "Angel. Some guy in high school broke Sharon's heart, and I—"

"Spent the night in jail." Angel sighed. "I know. But this isn't that, Sean."

"I know, Angel. I was just gonna say. . .when that thing in high school happened, I promised God I'd never let another guy do that. That was a stupid promise, and God has given me grace for making it. Because the truth is, you will break her heart more than anyone else possibly could. If things go well, and you guys have kids, *they* will break her heart. You will die to yourself every day if you love her at all. That's what a husband does. He loves his wife like Christ loves His church. Well, Christ died. I know you're human, and you'll mess it up, but. . ."

Angel's eyes were glistening, but he smiled. "I like the sound of this 'but.' "

"Yeah, but." Sean chuckled. "Sharon already has Jesus to love her perfectly. If you're telling me you want to *try* to love her that well, then yeah. I want her to be loved like that."

"So, I can. . .I can ask her to marry me?" Angel was sniffling.

"Yeah, but seriously dude, if you hurt or abuse her in any possible way, you will hear from me." Sean felt a kick from his wife. "In the most godly, nonviolent possible way that I can possibly accomplish. . .if someone hurts my sister."

"Good." Angel stood and faced Sean with an outstretched hand, "Hopefully I'll hear from you in other situations as well."

Sean shook his hand. "Count on it."

Angel's phone rang and he quickly answered. "Hey, Sharon."

"Hey! Stormy is safe. Just thought you'd want to know. I'm headed back to my mom's now."

"Oh good. Thank you! Drive safe, okay?" He smiled, winking at the enthralled Georgie.

"Will do," she promised.

Angel hung up. "I have to jet. Thanks for talking."

"You should stay, Angel. You could meet her face-to-face right now," Lynn pleaded.

"I wouldn't dare bombard her like that." Angel smiled. "But thank you."

"How did you know she'd call and warn you she was coming back?" Sean asked in wonder.

"Like I said, I know my girl." Angel smiled. Then quickly left, and drove off just as Sharon was pulling in.

She came in, startled by the shell-shocked look on all their faces.

"What happened?" She worried. "Everything okay?"

"Uh. . .nothing?" Georgie tried. "Stormy okay?"

"Yeah, she's fine," Sharon supplied, still agitated as she removed her shoes and jacket.

As Sharon walked into the living room, she passed behind the chair Angel had just been sitting in. And stopped mid stride before backing up two steps.

They watched her close her eyes and take in a deep, confused breath. Then look around, sniffing at the air, spinning in circles. Sharon looked at Sean, the closest male to her.

"Do you have a new cologne or spray or deodorant or something?" she asked.

"No, why?" Sean wondered. Deeply amused.

"I smell. . ." Sharon sighed. "I'm going crazy."

"What do you smell?" Sophie asked, almost flirtatiously.

"Just how Stormy smells when she comes home. And how the letters smell. It's usually really faint, but when you're hard of hearing, you learn to use your other senses," Sharon explained. "I was just with her. Maybe I smell it on me, but it's pretty strong. . . do you smell it? It's probably just me. . ."

"Wow," Georgie whispered. Falling in love with her best friend's love story.

Sharon looked at the table next to that chair to find a photo album.

"Why do you have this out, Mom?" she wondered.

Sharon got a text from Angel.

"I like your family."

She gasped. Couldn't form words. "He. . ."

Georgie nodded fervently, weeping with joy.

"A girl's nose doesn't lie, Sharon." Lynn giggled.

"You. . .you met him? I was gone ten minutes!" Sharon was in disbelief. "How did he know where you live?"

"He lured you away," Sophie said. "And stalked you. Charming."

"Oh please, Sophie. It was not like that," Georgie corrected.

Sharon's eyes widened as she shook the photo album in her hands. "Mom, you did *not* show him this!"

"She did," Sean supplied. "But apparently he's been lusting after you for a decade and had no idea it was you. Says you run past his house every other day."

Sharon rolled her eyes. Clarifying. "No, that's some girl that he thinks is too pretty for him. I honestly think he was in love with her, but he doesn't tell me that. He calls her 'Apartment Girl.' "

"PS We have to talk about your version of 'pretty,' Apartment Girl."

Sharon gasped. "Is this a joke?"

"He says he's known for weeks and didn't tell you," Eric added.

"He's *so* sweet, Sharon. Dad would have loved him. I'm not even joking," Sophie said.

"Why didn't he stay?" Sharon sighed, looking around.

"He didn't want to freak you out." Sean nodded. "And you would have freaked, so he seems to know you pretty well. Also *claims* to know you pretty well."

"So why did he come if he didn't want to meet me?" Sharon huffed.

"Something about keeping your lamp lit?" Sophie said. "You sure about this guy, Sharon?"

Sharon shrugged. Nodded with smile-less poise.

40

The Messenger's Fate

"Rise up, my love, my fair one, and come away." Song of Solomon 2:10

Sharon's heart leaped at the note on Stormy's collar. She unrolled the rest of it with haste.

My Love,

May I have your address? Before you jot it down because you trust me, understand that at some random time, I will show up and take your hand and ask you to marry me. Your brother said I could, I promise. I love you, Sharon. Let's take this up about two thousand notches.

Your Love

Sharon took a breath. Or ten. I tortured her. She dialed Angel's number.

"Okay, even if Stormy runs at cheetah pace, there's no way you live more than a hundred yards away. I *just* sent her out." The joy in Angel's voice took Sharon from cold skepticism to molten acceptance in a mere few seconds.

"I bet we're on the same block," Sharon said timidly. "You must live somewhere on my new running route if you didn't see me before."

"I live right by Vineyard Cedar 'Luxury' apartments where you used to live. Always thought that was odd. Like, is there some random cedar in a vineyard somewhere?" Angel joked.

Sharon's heart seized. But she continued the banter. "I just never understood 'luxury.' My brother had an apartment a couple of miles

345

away and it was far less rent and just as nice. He always made fun of me for that until he moved in with Mom."

Angel laughed. Cleared his throat. Spoke tenuously. "So, um. . .can I have a street name?"

"Angel! I barely got the note. Give me a minute to decide?" She sighed.

"Of course. If I wanted to force myself on you, I'd just walk outside when you run by in the morning instead of hiding behind my curtain. I love you, I want this to be your choice."

Sharon laughed. She paused. Nodded. "I'll send my address with Stormy when she wants to go out again. And I'll be ready for you to show up."

Angel sighed his victory. "I'll be counting the seconds."

Sharon never much liked irony. Or poetry. And when she arrived home from work the next day to see Georgie and Sean crouching in the street outside her house with a few other people, the children in their minivan in her driveway, Sharon knew exactly why.

Sean saw her approaching and stopped her.

"We wanted to surprise you, so we came over and put the note you wrote in the thing and let her out. . .but she just bolted into the street and got clipped by a car. Idiot didn't even stop. We think a couple of her legs are broken."

But Sharon got to her cat before he finished speaking. Stormy was breathing and crying out in pain, much more wrong than just a couple broken legs. As if knowing she was about to lose her only companion was not enough, she could see her note was still in the little bottle. Angel had never. And would never receive it.

"Ohh. . .Stormy." Sharon teared up, not knowing where or how to pet her. And a couple bystanders offered to put her out of her misery. An anthem Sharon felt like had been her entire existence all her life. She shot back bitterly. "Just go back inside. If you don't want to watch her suffer, don't."

"Oh no. . ." One man had just arrived and said with some kind of deep compassion.

Sharon was shaking and didn't quite know how to answer anymore idiocy. She was on the pavement trying to decide even how to lift Stormy with the least amount of pain.

"She probably isn't gonna make it, Man," Sean mumbled, not looking up. "I'd leave if I were you."

"I can't. This is my fault," the man said.

Sharon's eyes immediately shot up to meet his voice. She stood. Stepping back a couple feet.

He was in a tank top and cut off sweats, revealing one completely tattooed arm and pillow soft bulk and muscles and shoulder length hair. Georgie gasped quietly, having just looked at him. Sean was in shock.

Sharon experienced a strange emotional phenomenon. Like when Georgie first looked at Sammy. She knew his soul already and seeing him in person was just a formality of an introduction.

"Angel?" She sniffled, wiping a tear from her cheek.

Angel exhaled like he was at the finish line of a marathon, and took a step back, blinking his eyes. Likely not having breathed in a few moments.

"Hey, Sharon," he winced. "This is not how I saw this going."

Sharon rolled her eyes with a smile. Then the tears came for Stormy.

Almost as instinct, Angel bridged the gap between them and captured her tears into his embrace, shushing her. "We'll figure this out together, okay?"

Sharon sighed. Releasing years of tension and pain and aloneness inside his warmth, despite tragic circumstances. "Always hold me, Angel."

"You got it." He squeezed her tighter, winking at Georgie once.

Sean was uncomfortable, but none of that mattered when Stormy cried out, and both of her owners fell to a crouch, knowing wonder was secondary at the moment.

"Let me get her bed from my house. You want to hold her while I drive to the vet?" Angel began to act. He stood again, walking off toward the edge of the asphalt, opposite her house on the narrow street.

"Sure, but, my house is just right here," Sharon said, pointing to her front door.

Angel chuckled once. *"Seriously?* Because. . ." He pointed to his house. Directly across the street and two doors down from hers.

"You're kidding me!" Georgie exclaimed.

Angel tried not to smile. Shook his head back into reality. "Okay, Sharon. I'll be right back. Just do the thing with her ears and she might feel a little better."

"Okay." Sharon nodded, stroking at Stormy's ears for thirty seconds until Angel returned with her bed.

With enormous arms but with gentleness like a butterfly's wing, Angel placed the ailing cat on the bed after putting the bed in Sharon's arms.

"We can take my car. It's still running right there." Sharon gestured with her head.

"Okay, I'd be an idiot to allow that." Sean laughed nervously.

Angel gently opened the bottle on Stormy's collar and read the note with a smirk. A smirk that it took Sharon .2 seconds to fall in love with.

"Sean, eventually you have to stop trying to control your thirty-two-year-old sister's life." Angel chuckled. Georgie giggled. Angel looked at Sharon. "You gave me your address."

Sharon nodded, coyly.

Angel whispered one single laugh. Like he was melting somewhere deep. Barely righted himself. "Let's go take care of our baby."

41

The Story's End

"It was awful, Mom!" Georgie sobbed with Lynn.

"I was surprised she even made it to the vet," Sean confessed. "Sharon said he put her down immediately."

"Oh no!" Mom gasped. "Where is she? Why didn't you stay with her? She's probably devastated, she shouldn't be alone."

"Because Georgie wouldn't let me follow them with all the kids in the van." Sean stated the truth.

"Them?" Mom wondered.

"She wasn't alone, Mom," Georgie assured.

"You mean Angel?" Lynn worried.

"Yeah. He's still with her. I slipped her my pepper spray, don't worry."

• • •

"It really sucks that this is how we met." Angel sighed, getting Sharon comfortable on her couch with Stormy's favorite toy after leaving the vet.

"But I think it would be a lot worse if we hadn't." Sharon sniffled. "I'm pathetic. If I was alone, I'd probably be mourning this cat like a child."

"You're not pathetic," he said, smiling. "I loved the thing too."

They stared into one another's eyes, coming out of it after a few moments in laughter. She voiced it. "I can't believe you're really here."

"Me neither. I'm not about to complain, though," Angel said. "I feel like a bad person, because when I saw Stormy laying there in the road, I was more disappointed that I wouldn't get your address. Then, obviously, it hit me that unfaithful kitty was hurt and that was worse."

Sharon thought on that for a moment, then snickered. "I feel like I have nothing and everything to say to you. I have no clue where to start, Angel."

"I bought a suit to come meet you in. And a ring. This is all botched." Angel nodded. "But can I take you to dinner?"

"I don't want dinner. I just want froyo," Sharon admitted.

Angel chuckled and went to her freezer, then began searching the kitchen drawers.

"What my woman wants, my woman gets." Angel laughed.

Which basically melted Sharon completely. What finished it off was when Angel returned to the couch with one pint of frozen yogurt.

And two spoons.

I may have lied in the beginning. Sometimes I have to when it comes to God moving, you understand. But I suppose I have to come clean now. You and I both know, that wasn't a teaspoon miracle or even two. Maybe for someone it would have been.

But for Sharon, it was a whole overflowing gallon.

...

I was there for all of it. When Angel confessed his love face-to-face that evening. When he proposed that week, as he'd promised. When the wedding came and went, and four children came to stay.

Filling, to overflowing, the albums their grandmother maintained for them all.

Two of the children were adopted from Africa. One from Mexico. And after years of unrealized hopes, there came a surprise of a little girl they called "Meadow Rain Sanchez."

"Are you *kidding* me?" Georgie had responded in the delivery room. "No. Appreciate the gesture. But no."

"You can't just delete a part of who you are, L.D.. I was always upset that you did that, so I'm bringing it back," Sharon explained boldly.

"Okay, but 'Meadow Rain'? Not even Dawn or something?" Georgie protested.

"A lot of who you are is because you hated your beautiful name." Sharon rolled her eyes.

"Yeah, you too. Your point?" Georgie hipped her hands about her ever-pregnant belly.

"I *love* who you are. All of it."

Sharon never trusted that she was worthy of any of it. Always considered herself a failure and inadequate. Of course, Angel didn't see it that way, and neither did the children. Or anyone else in Sharon's life. They all adored her. She was, in fact, the kindest, gentlest woman I've ever been a part of.

But I am a thorn in Sharon's side. Her infirmity forever. She is weak. And God has not the occasion to change her.

She seeks Him every moment. Needs Him every hour. Knows that He is capable of anything, even through her. Her breath and lifeblood first flow through the cross, and her children see it. Her husband admires it. Sharon is a beacon to all around her, and she'll probably never understand why, nor will those around her ever attain what she has.

They make the mistake of trying to both eradicate self-doubt and live in faith. But don't you see? It is not until you have humbled yourself that you can see God for the mighty Redeemer He is.

As it is written in 2 Corinthians 12:9-10:

"And He said to me, 'My grace is sufficient for you, for My strength is made perfect in weakness.' Therefore, most gladly I will rather boast in my infirmities, that the power of Christ may rest upon me. Therefore, I take pleasure in infirmities, in reproaches, in needs, in persecutions, in distresses, for Christ's sake.

For when I am weak, then I am strong."

Acknowledgments

Disclaimer (Updated 2026): A traumatic moment or season can change a person, even causing them to be broken and remade. God is faithful to teach us a new song, but we cannot carry many of the old tunes with us. This book was written "before" one of those moments, and these acknowledgments reflect that version of me. However, in reverence for the way that God uses our *whole* journey to shape us, and because even reading them to modify them is simply too painful for me today, I left them intact.

…

I'll be brief, but please don't close this book before you allow me to thank the people who made it possible.

Jesus, His Father, and the Helper: Thanks for dying on the cross for me and accomplishing beautiful things in my life when I have nothing to contribute but weakness.

RJ: Thanks for letting me be your imperfect bride and your partner in serving our King. And stuff…

Caleb: Thanks for the cover art. Don't stop taking pictures. Don't stop loving Jesus. You're awesome. I don't even mind that you're a cat person.

Levi and Chloe: Yes, you're awesome, too.

Melanie: Thanks for the red ink and encouragement, as always.

My parents: Thanks for giving me life and teaching me about Jesus. Flaws are irrelevant after that.

Deziree: Thanks for reading the rough version of this. I'll miss you, friend.

Kathleen: Thanks for always calling me first. I won't tell.

Tiffany and Lesley: I wrote this for you, and I'm betting you know why. I love watching God use you exactly where you are today. You are not always in my life, but you are always in my prayers.

Coda, Dinah, and Sky (RIP): "My" kitties. Often the bane of this dog person's existence. Often the soft purr that God uses to get me through the day. Seriously, though, stop complaining about your cushy life at four in the morning. It's not cool. But thanks anyway.

Anyone who gave this book a chance: Thanks for reading. I hope it was a blessing. You, my friend, are a blessing to me.

Finally, Self-Doubt: Thanks for torturing me and tearing me apart until I was nothing. For when I am weak, well… I think you know that by now.

Other Works by
Rebekah Tyne McKamie

To My Beloved Richie (2017)
He destroyed her. A lifetime later, he's still destroying her. No reasonable person would blame her for hating him.
So why would God ask her to forgive him?

The Snow Fence: a novel (2015)
Seth has a gift, an inspiring relationship with God, the company of friends, and a fence he's completing one painstaking section at a time. As his dog Willow can attest - that is all a man really needs.

Please Note: This book was written and published before Mrs. McKamie obtained the education and experience of a professional book editor. It has since been refined, but to keep the integrity of the story intact, no major sentence structure or developmental changes were made. Please do not consider this work to be indicative of her current writing and editing abilities, but rather a "snapshot" of what they were. Keep writing. Keep growing. But don't be scared to see how far you've come.

Contact the Author

Website: https://www.rebekahtynemckamie.com

Instagram: @rebekahspelledlikethebible

Facebook: https://www.facebook.com/rebekahtyne

Photo by Caleb McKamie

www.ingramcontent.com/pod-product-compliance
Lightning Source LLC
Chambersburg PA
CBHW050857130726
47900CB00013B/162